BROKEN VOWS

KIERA
FALLON

BROKEN
VOWS

SIMON &
SCHUSTER

London · New York · Amsterdam/Antwerp · Sydney/Melbourne · Toronto · New Delhi

First published in Great Britain by Simon & Schuster UK Ltd, 2026

1 3 5 7 9 10 8 6 4 2

Simon & Schuster UK Ltd, 7th Floor,
199 Bishopsgate, London EC2M 3TY

Simon & Schuster Australia, Sydney
Simon & Schuster India, New Delhi

www.simonandschuster.co.uk
www.simonandschuster.com.au
www.simonandschuster.co.in

The authorised representative in the EEA is Simon & Schuster Netherlands BV, Herculesplein 96, 3584 AA Utrecht, Netherlands. info@simonandschuster.nl

A CIP catalogue record for this book is available from the British Library

Paperback ISBN: 978-1-3985-5777-2
eBook ISBN: 978-1-3985-5778-9
Audio ISBN: 978-1-3985-5779-6

Typeset in the UK by M Rules

Printed and Bound in the UK using 100% Renewable Electricity
at CPI Group (UK) Ltd

FSC www.fsc.org
MIX
Paper | Supporting responsible forestry
FSC® C013604

To all the strong women who refuse to
back down, but might bend over . . .
for the right person.

1

Lexie

The golden magenta morning sunlight splinters through my blinds and I blink against the light. *Ugh.* It's too bright. I place the pillow cradled in my arms over my eyes, then nestle under the warm covers.

Wait! Why is it bright? I bolt up in bed so quickly my head rushes with a nauseating whoosh and grab my cell phone—my *dead* cell phone—to check the time. "No. No, no, no . . ." My heartbeat thunders in my chest. This can't be happening. Please for the love of Christ, tell me this didn't happen.

It's January in New York City. I'm due at work at eight a.m., my subway ride is forty-five minutes long and, ever since fall ended, I've been getting up in what feels like the deadass of night, to arrive at work on time. I tear myself from the bed, scamper across my studio apartment to look at the stove and *shit.* It's true. My worst fear. The stove clock flashes 6:32 a.m. An hour after I should have gotten up.

"Oh God, oh God . . ." I dash to plug my cell into a different outlet, add the landlord to my internal hit list because he *promised* these outlets were fixed, and race into the shower.

I hate this apartment I moved into a few months ago, with its shoddy electrical work, barely functioning stove, and outlets that trip more often than a drunk sorority girl in heels. But it's all I can afford and an hour closer to work than my other apartment. But why, for the love of God, did this have to happen *today*? The day that my traditionally cool, calm, and collected manager, Sydney, owner of a boutique wedding-planning agency, has been frantically obsessing over for weeks. In my past life, I clearly shattered one too many mirrors, burned someone at the stake or forgot to toss salt over my shoulder because I swear bad luck trails me like a toxic fog.

The shower is the quickest of my life and I forgo beachy waves for putting my hair in what I hope looks like a sharp, professional ponytail and not what it actually is—that I overslept like an amateur for what might be the most important client meeting we've ever had.

I stuff my heels into my backpack and shove on my sneakers to run the four blocks to the subway station. Even though I'm bracing against the bitter wind and blinking fat snowflakes from my eyelashes, by the time I sit down, I'm fanning my sweaty face and double checking that I brought extra deodorant. I flip my phone to selfie mode to finish my makeup and confirm that I'm at least somewhat presentable for this mystery couple.

My white shirt is clean and crisp and makes my red hair

pop. More than one person has complimented the way white brings out my green eyes and dusting of freckles. This shirt is the best one in my small business-wear arsenal, and the one that says, "I am *more* than an assistant planner." Which is true. Five years after clawing and begging to get hired—which is not easy to do in this city with limited education and zero resources—I've busted my ass to prove my worth at *Shades of White*. I'm ready for Sydney to stop looking at me like the inexperienced assistant coordinator she hired and start seeing me as a lead. And today, if all goes well, I'll solidify the next step in my career. You know, if I weren't stumbling into the office forty-five minutes late.

Breathe.

As the train rumbles on the tracks, I tap my thumbs against the phone to text my co-worker Justin.

> Lexie: Alarm didn't go off. On my way. Please cover for me.
>
> Justin: Already did. I told Sydney you weren't feeling good and went to the main lobby bathroom.
>
> Lexie: I seriously love you.
>
> Justin: Brace yourself. She just color-coded the folders on my desk. FFS.

Lexie: Jesus, her anal retentiveness is sky high lately.

Justin: Truth.

By the time I reach the building lobby, I'm a certifiable sweaty catastrophe. I shrug off my jacket, swap my sneakers for heels, and shoot Justin a message that I'm heading up.

Ding. I tiptoe out the elevator doors, peek around the corner through the glass wall, past the tall pale oak reception desk with our *Shades of White* logo written in script and thank the wedding planner gods that Sydney added a twelve-tiered-cake-sized flower bouquet in the center that partially blocks the hall view. I grit my teeth at our twin receptionists, Amanda and Megan, who both give me knowing nods.

My heart is racing so fast that I'm convinced it's going to jump from my chest and splatter on the floor as I pivot, duck behind some office greenery, dart across our bastardly, unforgiving open-plan floor, and practically swan-dive into my chair. True to his word—did I mention I love this guy?—Justin winks at me from the other side of the room as he wraps Sydney in conversation.

Justin oozes charm without even trying. Perfectly coifed blond hair. Bright baby blues. A great ass—although I swear I only observe from afar. He's even achieved the impossible by coaxing a smile out of Sydney, who's been one big ball of stress lately.

Still trying to catch my breath, I open my laptop and start

reading through emails when Sydney's signature heavy heel clacking against the hardwood floors grabs my attention. Her black glasses slip down her nose as she frowns and storms my way. *Crap. Here it comes.* "You look like shit. Please don't tell me you have the flu."

And good morning to you, Sunshine.

I grab a notebook and fan my face. "Nope, no flu." No, I just woke up, plowed through a group of businessmen running down the street, slipped on snow on the sidewalk, stubbed my toe on a garbage can and probably caught tetanus while barefoot in our lobby. But I'm great. "I'll be fine. I must've eaten something bad last night."

"Good, because we have no room for errors, Lexie. None." She purses her ruby red lips, and swipes a hand down her glass-like, straightened-within-an-inch-of-its-life, blonde hair. "Because this new project is going to be *incredible*."

A squeal squeaks through her slim, pale throat and she gives me a pat on the hand.

"You should run back to the bathroom and fix all this, though," she says, her clunky gold bracelets jangling as she waves at my face. "We don't want these clients to walk away before they even sit down."

She gives me a sly grin and a squeeze on my shoulder. I swear if anyone else said this, they'd get an elbow to the jaw. But Sydney gets a lifetime pass.

Sydney came into my life at a time when everything was falling to pieces. After getting unexpectedly expelled from my university in Boston, I was lost, depressed, and desperate for a fresh start. Restarting my life wasn't going to be easy, but I refused to give up. My mom and I needed—*deserved*—a better life. So, I hustled my way into a catering gig that needed immediate help. And that's how I met Sydney.

She was the wedding coordinator at an event I was working. A consummate professional while I, on the other hand, was a walking disaster. My day had already gotten off to a bad start after trekking out of city limits for the wedding. But during the reception, a groomsman got handsy with me. I'd panicked, stumbled, and crashed into another waiter carrying a tray of champagne flutes. My manager's face turned a shade of red I didn't know existed, and right as he opened his mouth to surely fire me, Sydney swept in like a knight in shining designer shoes. With a few smooth words, my manager let me off the hook. She patted my arm, gave me an encouraging smile, and told me to get back out there.

Later that night, she handed me her business card, said she had an eye for talent, had noticed my knack for putting people at ease—champagne-fiasco aside—and insisted I visit her office the following Monday. I stood there, beaming, and fumbled a shocked "thank you." When she'd left, I looked down and read: *Sydney Thompson, owner of Shades of White, a wedding planning business.*

That following Monday, in a half-priced clearance business suit two sizes too big, I was ushered into a room filled with people just like me—nervous, overdressed, and clearly more qualified. That's when it hit me: this wasn't just a meeting. Sydney had invited me to *interview*. My gut sank. I wasn't special as I'd naively thought. My name being called was the only thing that stopped me from bolting. Even though my knees shook, I pulled my shoulders back and walked into her office.

She sat there, calm and unreadable, as I stumbled through her questions. By the end of the interview, the only thing I knew was that I was painfully unqualified.

But later that day, one phone call changed my life forever with two words: You're hired. And I've spent five years desperate to prove she made the right decision.

In the bathroom, I swipe my pinky across my cheekbone to catch a few rogue mascara flakes and add a dot of concealer under my eyes to mask the seven years' worth of sleepless nights since the incident that changed my life in Boston. I need to look presentable and professional, and nothing screams poised and prepared like purple halos.

When I step back into the office, Justin's standing at my desk, holding two coffees. "Not only are you cute, but you can read minds. Do you ever get tired of being a superhero?" I say, practically ripping the mug from his grip and guzzling some much-needed caffeine. "What a shitastic morning. I miss my old apartment where the outlets didn't randomly fizzle out. I swear my place is a walking fire hazard. What did I miss?"

He sits at the desk adjoining mine and takes a sip. "Not much, but Sydney is driving full speed ahead on the struggle bus today."

"I don't think people say that phrase anymore," I say. "The algorithm sucked you into some suburban mom bullshit."

"Whatever." Justin flips open his laptop. "It's weird, though, right? We all signed the NDA, but she still won't give us any details. This couple must be huge."

He's not wrong. The buzz of heightened energy crackles in the air. The office is normally lively, but today something's different. From the hushed rumblings of co-workers scooting from desk to desk taking bets if the clients are celebrities or politicians, to Sydney's abnormal skittishness, there's an extra charge. Something big is about to happen, and we all know it.

As I take a seat, I cringe at Sydney. She's spritzing the plants with a lemongrass-scented synthetic spray, and feverishly wiping them with a cloth. *Yikes.* Is she trying to kill our office greenery? I open my mouth, but Justin shakes his head at me, probably knowing I'm about to say something dumb. I promptly anchor my lip between my teeth. My mouth has gotten me into trouble before and now is not the time to point out that dousing plants with cleaning products might not be her brightest idea. Clearly whoever this mystery client is, they're big enough to make her dust imaginary specks from every surface. But if she comes over here with a lint brush and a can of hair spray, she's getting tackled.

A flutter of nerves moves through my stomach. Although I was raised by a single, hard-working mom who worked double shifts as a hotel housekeeper to feed and house us, I'm not impervious to being around big names. When I was twenty-one, I worked as a hostess at a high-end restaurant and once a month or so brushed shoulders with a celebrity. My former manager used to say I had to strike a perfect balance between subservient and confident. People who ate at these types of restaurants wanted to *feel* us taking care of them, without us *telling* them.

I learned how to smile, charm, and seduce. The three main tools in my arsenal.

Seduction doesn't always mean sex. People love to feel wanted. Desired. *Special.* Male, female, it doesn't matter.

So maybe this is a celebrity who hired out our small firm to handle the nuptials. And maybe it's just some anonymous rich businessperson. Either way, I'll do whatever it takes for them to fall in love with me. Nothing will stop me from cinching this promotion.

At least, this is what I keep repeating to myself because I'm way more nervous than I want to be. I place a hand on my stomach and tell it to calm the hell down.

"Lexie! Justin! Hurry, up," Sydney yells and waves at us from across the room. "They're coming!"

I bolt up from my chair as Sydney props open our glass doors, and we all face the elevator. Justin stands next to her, and I'm positioned the way she likes me, a few steps behind—the dutiful assistant wedding planner, ready to take notes, smile, and kiss whatever ass needs kissing. I run a flat palm down the snug pencil skirt that's hugging my curves and take a breath. Okay, fine. I'll admit it. It's more than just nervousness, I'm *so* curious to meet this mystery couple. My smile spreads as the numbers on the elevator counter rise.

Ping. The elevator door opens, and a slow thud starts in my chest. *Wow.* Standing in front of me is one of the most beautiful women I've ever seen. It's impossible not to compare myself. She's such a perfect feminine specimen, she might as well have been created by AI. Sharp, high cheekbones. Shiny Caribbean-blue eyes. Dark chocolate-brown hair. Her tiny waist is the same size as my left boob. She holds an effortless, glowing beauty and looks like boarding schools and generational wealth.

My eyes drop to her hand that must be folding under the weight of a ten-carat diamond, with her fingers clasped around another hand. My gaze travels up until it settles on a face. In a flash, everything changes. Like I bumped into an electrical fence, I stumble back and freeze. The blood drains from my cheeks as I take in those eyes, that no matter how much over the years I tried to drink, fuck, cry, or scream away the memory, I'll never forget.

Standing in gray slacks and a sharp navy button-down with tattoos peeking out from precisely single-rolled cuffed sleeves, is Theodore Astor.

The man who ruined my life.

2

Lexie

The high-pitch ringing in my ears spreads to my head and nausea travels to my stomach. This can't be happening. Justin's smile fades as his gaze sweeps mine. Sydney says something to me, her smile pained and unmoving, but the ringing is too loud and disorientating and I can't make out the words.

I'm not here, in the office. I'm back *there*. In Boston. Seven years ago.

I'm going to be sick.

"*Lexie.*" The snap in Sydney's tone pulls me into reality and I blink through the red spots invading my vision.

"Ah." I clear my throat, and take a tentative step forward. "Yes."

Sydney flashes me a concerned look but doesn't drop her smile. "This is Lexie," she says, waving her hand towards me like I'm a prize at the fair, "an assistant coordinator who'll be helping us plan your very special day."

My breath locks as I wait for the reaction of the man who destroyed everything. Will he drop to his knees and beg for forgiveness? Hide in shame? Storm out, cheeks flaming, without looking me in the eye like a cowardly piece of shit?

"Welcome to Shades of White." My voice is unnaturally high. I flinch against the sound and wait for his smile to change when he realizes who I am.

One moment passes, then two. And . . . *nothing.* Literally nothing but a politely generic smile.

"Lexie?" Theodore asks, and I brace myself for the flicker of recognition to cross his perfectly groomed, five-o'clock-shadowed face as he places me and the different name I go by. "Is that short for Alexandra?"

Is he actually serious right now? How can he not know who I am? There's not even a flash of acknowledgement in those deep bourbon-brown eyes. Not a nervous hand through his inky black hair. Not a twitch in the twenty pounds of sheer muscle he's put on that towering frame since the last time I saw him. *Nothing.*

As a naïve young student, I spent a year daydreaming that somehow in a sea of other girls, Theodore Astor would notice me. How his gaze would linger, sharpen, settle. How I'd pretend not to feel it at first, resisting his charm while he bided his time. In those fantasies, he was intoxicatingly relentless. He'd corner me in his father's office—my mentor—lowering his voice as if the walls themselves were listening. He'd murmur all the things he *wouldn't* do if I kept ignoring him, his words brushing my ear—both a threat and promise. His breath would warm my skin as he traced the line of my neck, a hand would slide slowly up my leg, always stopping just short of where I wanted it most.

That was before he ruined my life.

And he doesn't even remember me.

"Nope, short for Lexie." I shake his hand, hard, fighting the urge to dig my nails into his skin. "Nice to meet you, Mr. . . ." *Two can play this game, asshole.*

"This is Doctor Astor," Sydney chimes in as his grip firms against mine before he drops it.

Doctor? Don't people have to take an oath to be a doctor? They're meant to be compassionate and caring—not so cold and calculating that demons themselves run in fear.

"But please, just call me Theo," he says, holding the type of confidence that comes from wealth, looks, and a mother who never told him no. His grin drips with sex and honey, carrying the power to dissolve the thong from any straight woman within a ten-mile radius. For a while, that smile held my dreams before it haunted my nightmares. And yet, there's a sensation that this smile is the pocket of sunshine hiding the ominous, shadowy clouds of an approaching storm.

He adds, "Unless you're needing me to look at some festering wound, or read your chart, then Dr. Astor it is. Otherwise, Theo is perfectly fine."

He actually thinks he's funny, does he?

Theo wraps a protective arm around the woman next to him. "And this is my fiancée, Annabelle Barlowe."

Before my mouth drops to the floor, I suck in my cheeks.

Barlowe? As in one of the renowned billionaire families, as close to royalty as you can get in America—*that* Barlowe? Jesus Christ. No wonder we had to sign an NDA.

"Very nice to meet you all," Annabelle says with a dazzling, warm smile, and moves to shake my hand first, then Justin's, then Sydney's. I wonder if she has any idea of the devil she's about to marry.

"We're so honored to have you as a client. Oh, wow, what a beautiful ring," Sydney interjects as Annabelle finishes shaking her hand.

"Thank you! It took us a while to find the perfect one," Annabelle says.

I slide only the quickest glance to Theo. "Oh, a proposal without the ring?" The question is innocent enough on the surface, but I know it's probing and silently beg Sydney and Justin not to read anything into it. I clear my throat. "I love that, actually. Imagine spending the rest of your life with something you hated."

"Right?" Annabelle tucks a strand of dark hair behind her ear. "Theo's a bit of a control freak."

"I'm right here," he interrupts.

"You know what I mean." She playfully rolls her eyes. "He likes everything to be perfect and didn't want to ruin the moment with something I wouldn't like."

"Well, it's gorgeous. A local jeweler?"

"No," Theo says. "We went to Boston for this piece."

The hair on my neck stands. "The city must hold a special place for you both."

"Yes, it does," Theo says, his gaze unwavering. "Have you been to Boston?"

Asshole. As if he doesn't know. The mention of Boston takes me back to a time when I still had hope for the future, when his father would tell me to keep working hard and used words like *potential* and *gifted*, and I believed him.

I wonder if he had any idea his son would strip it all away from me.

"Yes, I have," I say, trying to remain professional despite my growing anger.

"They have a tremendous independent jewelry scene." His voice carries a lightness that makes me want to rip my ears off. "Next time you're visiting, you should check it out. I'll give you the names of a few places."

"Thank you," I say, but I really want to punch him in the face. I live in a shit studio apartment in the Bronx that I can barely afford, survive on take-out and cheap wine, and whatever funds I have left at the end of the month go straight to my mom so she can take a day off from her back-breaking work. He must know we come from completely different worlds.

"Why don't we go to the conference room," Sydney says. "Lexie, could you grab some refreshments?"

"Of course." I force a smile, because I'm an assistant wedding planner, not an assistant, as Sydney often forgets. But this time I don't mind if it means escaping Theo. Once I round the corner and step into the breakroom, I push out a shaky breath. *He can't hurt me. He can't hurt me.*

The knife rattles in my trembling hands and visions of me thrusting it deep into something other than this cucumber invades me. How does he not remember me after what he did?

I'm adding a few sprigs of mint along with the cucumber into the crystal water pitcher when Justin tears into the room. "Are you okay?"

No, I'm not fucking okay. I've waited five years for a promotion, and even though I'm grateful I got this job in the first place, that gratitude only extends so far. This wedding was supposed to be my big break. After a year of pushing for a raise and being told the timing wasn't right, I knew the moment I heard about this mysterious new client, and the budget we'd be working with, that this was finally my shot at the raise and title I deserve. Instead, Theo shows up like some evil phoenix, rising from the ashes just to torch my dreams the second things start going right.

"Lexie, hello!" Justin waves in front of my face to grab my attention again before retrieving grapes from the refrigerator. "What's up with you?"

God, I love Justin. He always shows up for me without me even having to ask. Growing up an only child, I always wondered what it would be like to have an older brother, and Justin is as close as I'll get. But I'm not ready to tell him about Boston. "Nothing." I avoid his eyes and add cookies to the tray. "I just know I'm going to bust my ass for this wedding and Sydney will probably still deny my promotion."

"Do you actually think she'd do that?" he asks, snipping the grapes from the vine. "I mean, Sydney's Sydney, but you've been due for a long time, and this wedding's the ticket, right?"

I shrug.

Theo can't hurt me. I repeat this over and over, but deep down, I know he absolutely can. He *did*. A man like Theodore Astor will never change. He salivates off destruction and the bodies he leaves in his wake.

"I think I should ask Sydney for you and me to swap," I say. "You can assist on this one, and I'll take over your current project. What do you think?"

"Are you kidding? Working on a Barlowe wedding is a freaking dream." He wipes his hands on a towel and reaches for a bag of pistachios. "But are you sure? You might be giving up a golden opportunity."

He's right. But I'm also saving myself from future manslaughter charges and prison time, so it's a win-win. "I'm absolutely sure. I don't think I'm a good match for them."

Justin starts filling up a bowl with the nuts. "That groom, though, right?" he says, wiggling his brows. "Pretty sure if you looked up the western definition of tall, dark, and handsome, it'd have his picture."

A short puff of air comes through my nose. The devil is not sexy. He's nauseating. "Yeah, well, he seems like a total dick." I keep my voice low even though the conference room holding Theo and Annabelle is across the office.

His eyes scrunch. "The groom? Are you serious? He seemed pretty cool."

"I've met guys like him before. I *know* guys like him. A

bullshit level of charm, the type of guy that thinks his looks and money excuse bad behavior, is not *cool*." I death-grip the stirrer for the water pitcher. "I can't believe people are impressed by him."

Justin stops picking at the nuts and gives me a hard stare. "You are channeling a hell of a lot of hatred on a man you've just met. I mean, I love talking shit as much as the next person, but you don't even know this guy."

If Justin only knew. I've had years obsessing over the man who stole everything from me. For seven years, he's occupied my mind more than what's considered healthy or sane. "There's just something about him I don't trust." I hesitate, then remind myself that Justin's safe. "And I don't know if I buy their relationship."

His mouth drops. "*Lexie.* What the hell?"

I don't care that I sound unhinged. My heartbeat has not slowed since I laid eyes on Theo, and the fact that I'm not jumping on a desk and screaming at him is a miracle. "Someone who seems too good to be true, always is," I say. "There's something off about those two. I smell it in the air."

The ping of a cell phone in the hall stops my words and Justin's eyebrows rise. *Shit.* I close my mouth and add the final touches to the tray, while he returns to his desk.

Breathe. No matter how much I want to tell his fiancée that he's a piece of shit and she should run away, no matter how much I'm owed for what he did to me, nothing good can happen with me fulfilling a revenge plan.

I need this job. I need this promotion. I need my fucking life back.

So, I'm going to do nothing but sit, smile, and obey. Just like I did all those years ago.

And I feel as sick about it now as I did then.

3

Lexie

My heels click against the hardwood floors but don't drown out Sydney's laugh. I exhale short, quick breaths. God, I want to rip off Theo's perfectly chiseled face. But, not only would this give Sydney fuel to deny my promotion, *again*, I'd be out of a job.

So, I'm going to suck it up, be professional, and after the meeting, tell Sydney that Justin is going to assist on the account.

All I need to do is get through the next hour.

The tray trembles in my hands and I squeeze the sides tight as I step inside the conference room. Sydney, Annabelle, and Theo are gathered around the round table. Theo's leaning towards a pink-cheeked, ultra-wide smiling Sydney. In less than twenty minutes after meeting, he's charmed Sydney into falling for his act.

And honestly, I don't know how Annabelle stands for this behavior. *Gross.*

"Promise me if you go there, you'll try the caviar arancini. It's the best in the city," Theo says as he scribbles on the back of his card, and hands it to Sydney. "When you call this number, just give them my name and they'll get you in."

"I cannot believe you're friends with the head chef," Sydney says, holding the card against her chest like he just handed her a priceless heirloom. "Lexie, remember last year when we tried to make a reservation at *Basil and Sage*?"

I set down the tray and focus on filling up the water glasses. "I do, yes." I force a smile. "They were booked up for a year, right?"

"Yes! Well, thanks to Theo, we won't have to wait anymore," Sydney says with the same amount of glee as if he said they named their newborn after her.

I curb the urge to roll my eyes and instead offer Theo a small nod before sitting next to Sydney and looking directly at the notepad she discreetly passed my way.

"It's the least I can do since you'll be stuck with me and Anna for the foreseeable future."

"Hey." Annabelle elbows Theo with a smirk. "I apologize in advance for him. At this rate, you'll be asking for more than just money once you realize what you've signed up for with us."

"Perhaps chocolate on demand should be part of the terms," Sydney chimes in.

"Excellent idea. And maybe wine for good measure." Annabelle glances at me. "Lexie, do you drink wine?"

Warmth spreads through me at Annabelle's casual attempt

to lighten the mood and include me in the conversation. "Probably more than I should admit."

"I knew I liked you." She lifts a brow. "White or red?"

"Whatever's available. But I'm currently in my Malbec phase."

"A woman after my own heart!" she says. "The next time we visit I'll bring a bottle from my collection. I forget the name, but it's from the Uco Valley in Argentina. You'll love it. Actually, I'll bring two, just in case." She winks at me as if we share some kind of secret in-joke.

It makes me wonder what someone as beautiful and sweet as Annabelle sees in a man like Theo. She's a *freaking* Barlowe—she could have anyone in the world. And yet, she chose the devil himself.

"So, you started your company eleven years ago, is that right?" Theo says to Sydney as he reaches for a glass of the mint and cucumber water.

"Yes, that's right," she says. "You did your homework, huh?"

"I did. You come highly recommended, and now that I'm here, I can see why. You run a tight ship, your staff seem to genuinely like you—which is not always the case—and we couldn't be more relieved that our wedding is in safe hands."

Could Sydney get any redder? Please tell me she's not falling for this crap. I might be expected to act professional, but that doesn't stop my pen from biting into the page. *Just sit still and smile, Lexie. It'll be over soon.*

"Thank you. We're thrilled to have you as a client." Sydney flips open her own notebook and taps the pen against the page. "The first thing we need to do is talk about dates. When are you thinking of getting married?"

"July 15th," Theo says so quickly, so firmly, that my head quirks.

A hushed, weighty silence fills the room.

Sydney's smile drops. "July 15th? That's only six months away." When his stern glance doesn't falter, she swallows. "Okay, erm, that doesn't give us a lot of time. If you want to get married in the city, we'll probably need to look at a minimum of twelve months out."

Theo's jaw is taunt. "It will happen on July 15th."

A scoff leaves my mouth. I cough to cover it up, but not before Sydney shoots me a death glare. The air in the room constricts. Every panicked emotion spreading on Sydney's face is happening on my insides. Planning a wedding of this magnitude, in New York City, in six months is nearly impossible.

Annabelle is quiet at his side. Clearly, for whatever reason, this date is significant.

Like a true professional, Sydney's smile returns. "Have you considered a destination wedding?"

I'm sure with the Barlowes' money they could rent their own private island, which might be necessary, considering this wedding will probably attract every member of high society.

"Anna and I have spoken a little on this, but we haven't decided yet whether to have the wedding abroad or in the city," Theo says.

Sydney clears her throat. "Well, we could take a look at the contract, chat about expedited fees and things, but it'll be a tight squeeze," she says, masking the panic she must be feeling. "Don't worry, it's our job to walk you through your options. Let's start with the guestlist, which will help narrow down venues and locations . . ."

Sydney's voice fades into background noise as she launches into her rehearsed routine. I check my watch, then check it again, irritation prickling beneath my skin as I wait for an opening—any excuse—to leave.

"Lexie, right?" Theo's voice cuts cleanly through the room. Through me.

Sydney stops mid-sentence. The sudden quiet feels deliberate, as if he's engineered it.

I straighten slowly, hyper-aware of his attention. My nails dig into the soft flesh of my thigh, grounding myself, keeping my legs from betraying me.

"What would you recommend?" he asks, eyes fixed on mine.

Why the hell is he asking me? I glance at Sydney who's giving me a tight, unreadable expression. "Oh, um, Dr. Astor—"

"Please. What did I say about calling me by my last name," he says, pulling that same bullshit disarming chuckle as earlier.

And there it is again. Nothing behind his dark eyes that indicates anything except him clarifying his name. *Goddammit.* Maybe he doesn't remember me.

I wasn't prepared for Theo to actively seek my advice. After spending years trying to forget him, the very last thing I want to do is give him the time of day. I swallow hard and resist the urge to scratch at my neck. "I, ah—"

"As I was saying," Sydney cuts in smoothly, *thank God*, "our company is dedicated to finding you the perfect venue. But first, we should establish what matters most to you, so we can identify a location that truly reflects your needs."

Theo turns his attention to Sydney. "The most important thing to me is that Annabelle's happy."

I hate that there's actual sincerity in his tone.

"And that Bruno Mars is available to perform," he throws in. "Think you can pull that one off?"

"Not sure he's in our contacts, but I'll see what I can do." Sydney relaxes at his joke.

Theo reaches for a handful of nuts and rolls them in his palm. "Teamwork makes the dream work, right?"

Annabelle groans, saving me the trouble of doing it.

A long moment passes and Theo looks back at me. "So, what do you say?"

I'm momentarily confused before remembering the conversation. "For a performer? I have no idea." Sydney's stare burns through me and I quickly follow up with, "So much talent out there, huh?" I reach for my water and pray for the floors to crack open and suck me out of this space.

Theo pins me with a hard, very unamused stare, before his expression softens. "No . . . what are your thoughts about a destination or city wedding?"

I don't know his game plan here, but I'll bet my life that it's not to hear what I think on whether Annabelle should walk down a sandy beach aisle, or one inside St. Michael's Cathedral. "Depends on what you like. There are advantages to both."

I focus all my energy on taking fake notes when the room goes silent. When I peek up, Sydney is unblinking, Annabelle is giving me a sympathetic smile, and Theo leans back in his chair, crossing his arms, clearly not letting this go.

"Would you care to share the pros?" His smile doesn't camouflage the darkness in his tone and something hot flickers in my gut. "If you don't mind, of course."

My eyes narrow before I politely reply with, "Oh, of course. Sure. A wedding in six months' time limits your options in the city. But if you go abroad, it opens the entire world. Do you want all of your friends and family to attend? Then, logistically, a destination wedding might be a little tricky. How many guests will you have? Outdoor or indoor? There are lots of things to consider."

I'd like to think I sound direct and professional, but I think I probably sound more like a blubbery fool. I hold my breath and peek at Sydney. When she nods, I exhale.

"All great points," Sydney says, sliding a binder towards them. "Let me give you this brochure that highlights some of the amazing partnerships we have with resorts abroad that will cater for a wedding like yours." As Sydney talks them through the options, I discreetly watch Theo and Annabelle, searching for any sign that this is all a farce. Instead, there's an easy intimacy between them—comfort, affection—which is absurd, because Theodore Astor is the furthest thing from affectionate.

"We really need to think this through, Theo. I mean, with our parents . . ." Annabelle trails off.

Theo's lips tug into a grin. "I don't think anyone in this room wants to hear about the family drama."

I would. Knowing Theo's life isn't as perfect as it looks might actually make this whole situation bearable.

Sydney pushes her dark frames back up her nose and clears her throat. "Why don't we regroup on the venue once you've had a chance to discuss? We'll also need a rough guest-count estimate. From there, we can move on to the more decorative elements, like reviewing designs, themes, the type of celebration—traditional, formal, rustic. I imagine your families would appreciate something a bit more elegant. Perhaps a black-tie event?"

"I'll take any excuse to see my lady dressed up."

I mutter under my breath sarcastically, "Does he ever stop?"

Theo casually plucks a grape from the tray and brings it to his mouth, only to ask, "Did you have something to say, Lexie?"

Shit. There's no way he heard me. And yet the gleam in his eyes tells me he knows something. That this is deliberate. Another move in whatever game he's playing.

The moment this meeting ends, he'll probably drop the company and pin it on my incompetence.

"No." Too much awkward silence passes and I pray the sweat beads brewing below the skin at my temple stay put.

Sydney tries to get the conversation back on track when Theo cuts in. "You're awfully quiet, Lexie. If you're uncomfortable sharing your ideas since you're just an assistant, please let me know and I'll keep referring to your boss."

Just an assistant. Heat floods my cheeks. God, I seriously—seriously—hate this man. Of course, he says it in a way so that no one else would catch the insult wrapped in fake kindness.

But I do.

The urge to stay silent loses out to something sharper.

"I'd be happy to offer ideas where needed," I say evenly. "But my professional advice would be this: regardless of your family's expectations—or anyone else's—you should choose what feels right for you. Not for them." A long pause follows, and I grind my feet into the floor to keep from wiggling in my seat.

"Well, that's great to hear," Theo says. "People like us live in the spotlight and it's easy to forget it's okay to be our own people."

Annabelle reaches for a cookie. "With my parents being, well, who they are, there's going to be a lot of eyes on this event."

My ears perk at the heavy-hearted tone.

"Yes, there will be. And we're ready to handle this," Sydney says, firmly. "Lexie is an incredible assistant, and we have a full staff ready to cater to your needs."

Annabelle looks at Theo. The silence builds as whatever secret language they share passes between them. He gives Annabelle an almost microscopic nod, then turns to me. "And you're available to take this on with such short notice? Full commitment, no distractions."

"Of course," I lie. The second they leave, I'm marching my ass into Sydney's office and demanding Justin switches with me. "I live to serve."

"I have no doubt." Theo strums his fingers on the table, then slides the chair back. "Would you two excuse us for a moment."

"Of course," Sydney says, and watches them step into the hall. The second the door closes, I brace myself for her wrath.

"This feels promising," she whispers. "But six months is tight. We need all hands on deck. Overtime, weekends, everything. But we got this, Lexie. This is *huge*."

This is not lost on me. The opportunity for the company, for Sydney, for the team is incredible. But I absolutely will not be part of it. I can't. I've been around Theo for less than an hour, and my skin is itchy, my throat is dry, and if I have to do this for six months, I'm pretty sure my entire physiological system will crash.

I wish I were joking.

A few moments later, the door creaks open and Annabelle and Theo walk back in. "Anna and I chatted and we've decided on a change of plans," Theo says, as they take their seats. "Sydney. Thank you so much for your time. But Anna and I would like Lexie to be our lead wedding planner."

4

Lexie

What? No chance in hell did I hear that right. Theo wants me as lead? No . . . no this doesn't make any sense. A two-million-dollar budget and Theodore Astor is handing it to me on a silver platter? I've done nothing to show them that I'm capable of leading a wedding. I've been waiting for a chance like this, the break I need to show I have what it takes to rise in my career and hoped this big new client would push me up the corporate ladder.

But not *him*.

The silence is so thick in the room that I'm sure everyone can hear my unsteady, galloping heartbeat.

"Oh, wow," Sydney says, breaking the unbearable tension. "Lexie is a talented member of our team, but she's an *assistant* wedding planner." This is the only time in my life I've been grateful for her subtle reminder of my position. They're going to listen to her, right? They have to. I absolutely cannot plan Theo's wedding. "For an event this high profile, I'd feel more comfortable with me as the lead."

"The decision is final." Theo's voice is filled with the conviction of a man who doesn't get told no. He smiles through the words and his eyes twinkle with the Astor family charisma. But the energy in the room shifts, like the way pressure builds when gray clouds roll in midday and overpower the sun.

"I agree with Sydney," I say, maybe a little too quickly, because, seriously, I can't do this. "I'm an assistant at the agency, not a lead. I'm still learning. I'd hate to be the cause of something . . . negative . . . happening with your special day."

"Nonsense," Theo says.

I stare at the sweet, beautiful Annabelle. *Say something!* Where's the typical bridezilla who'd throw a fit about a junior staff member planning her wedding? Why is she just sitting there with nothing but an encouraging smile?

Theo leans forward on his elbows and pins me with a gaze. "I can already tell you're the right person for the job. Sydney, there's no problem here, is there." A definite statement, and not a question, and *seriously, what is happening*?

My eyes snap to Sydney, whose ego is no doubt taking a hit. "No, of course not. Lexie's incredibly gifted," she says with a flex in her jaw. "And I'm happy to assist in anything you may need."

There's absolutely no way on God's green earth that I can spend the next six months with Theo, planning his wedding. *His wedding!* I can't even stomach being around him for an hour, and I'll be responsible for the most important day of his life? This can't be happening. I didn't wake up late today. I didn't stumble into my office and face the man who stole everything from me. I didn't just hear that he wants to work directly with me. I'm in bed, cozied under my million blankets, waiting for the alarm to go off.

"Really, I'm flattered, but Sydney should lead this. She's the best at the firm." I'm not even blowing smoke up Sydney's ass. When I say Sydney literally lives and breathes this job, I'm not exaggerating.

"And I don't doubt your talents. But I've always preferred working with someone who sees things the way we do."

What?

"It's nothing personal," Annabelle adds at once, apologetic.

She smiles—but it doesn't reach her eyes. The expression appears like a reflex, practiced and precise, as if she's smoothing the moment before it can wrinkle. Her fingers curl lightly into the fabric of her skirt, then still.

And suddenly I see it.

Not affection. Not ease.

Compliance.

The kind of smile you wear when disagreement isn't an option.

The buttons on my shirt dig into my skin. My blouse feels like a tight-laced corset compressing my insides. There's no air. I need to get out of here, into a bigger, safer space, far away from Theo and this whole situation.

"Thank you so much for everything, Sydney," he says. "I'm sure you understand."

There's a finality in his tone that makes my belly tighten.

"Lexie, are we good here?" he asks.

Sydney's glare is nearly as invasive as Theo's—if that's even possible—and she's absolutely screaming at me with her eyes to suck it the fuck up.

"Yes, of course," I lie, feeling like a poisonous vapor is inching towards me, and I'm verging on suffocation. "Thank you so much for the opportunity."

"I'm so excited!" Annabelle breaks the awkwardness. "Okay, what are the next steps?"

My face is blazing so hot right now, it no doubt matches my hair. "Before leaving, you'll sign the official contract. I'll email you my cell number, high-level instructions, and build a task schedule. Do you prefer I email daily, bi-weekly . . ." I continue to rattle off the usual onboarding information, having sat in many of Sydney's meetings over the years, while making the firm decision that the moment they leave, I'm demanding Sydney assigns Justin as lead.

Theo checks his watch. "We need to head out." We all stand and Theo reaches to shake my hand. When his skin meets mine, the burn that travels through me makes me want to douse my arm in ice-cold holy water and expel the evil that's penetrating my flesh. "It was wonderful meeting you, Lexie."

Meeting me. Like it's the first time. Like he didn't decimate everything good in my world and alter the trajectory of my life.

Sydney pushes herself from the table. "I'll walk you two out," she says. "Lexie, could you meet me in my office?"

Normally, Sydney would ask me to escort the clients out, but she's clearly using this moment to reinforce who's in charge. This time, I'll happily let it go to avoid spending another second in Theo's stifling company.

The moment they step outside the door, I plant my sweaty palms against the conference table and exhale rattled breaths. Of all the event planning agencies in the city, why did Theo have to choose this one?

In slow counts of four, I breathe in and out, and flicker back to the last time I saw him, to the way his dimples deepened with his evil sinister smile when he pulled the rug from under my feet. I hate myself for the crush I carried on him for a year. For lusting, chasing after him like a child trying to capture their shadow, when he didn't even notice me until he ruined my life. Me, the sad girl from Queens who held her breath when he walked into his father's office, who couldn't focus on her studies as he moved through the world like it already belonged to him. Me, who latched on to every single word he spoke like the syllables themselves were precious relics.

When Theo visited his father's office, I wanted him to notice me and tried to prove I was worth his attention—smart enough, interesting enough. If I asked the right questions, maybe he'd see me. Instead, he'd leave as soon as I started talking, like I wasn't even worth his time.

And yet, I kept chasing.

During every shift I worked at the campus coffee shop, I'd take espresso orders and scan the line of students, praying for Theo to come in, imprisoning my hopes inside his dirty chai tea order. I'd take the miniscule seconds of our interaction, no more than the scraps he gave everyone else, and balloon them in my mind. I'd fantasize that he went home and thought about me the way I thought about him.

Pathetic, that girl. I want to shake my nineteen-year-old self.

My head pounds and I dig my thumbs into my temples. I storm down to Sydney's office and she enters a moment later.

"You good?" she asks as she slides into her leather chair. "You didn't look great in there. Do you need to go home? Maybe you are actually coming down with something."

A small piece of me wants to open up and tell Sydney everything that happened in Boston, but I can't. I thought I'd buried the shame but clearly didn't. "I can't be the lead on this account."

She pulls her ruby-red lips into a flat line and exhales through her nose. "Listen. I know this isn't ideal. Did I think the meeting would go this way? Of course not. But they've asked for you and it's the biggest client we've ever had. But, you won't be alone. I'll be here to support you the entire way. You can lean on me for absolutely anything." She inches forward. "You've got this, Lexie. I believe in you."

As warm as those words are, I shake my head. "You don't understand. I just . . ." *Shit.* How do I not come off incompetent and inexperienced, while still rejecting this job? "I can't."

"You can." She straightens. "And you will."

The words are sharp, and I'm sure as neutral as I'm trying to keep my face, it's betraying me. I'm about to pull out my employee trump card—the right to refuse service for a client—when she drums her fingers against the desk. "These are not the type of people we can turn down. If they asked you to be the entertainment, we'd get you some singing lessons and put your ass on stage. These are the *Barlowes.* Something like this can make or break a business. You understand this, right? There is no saying no."

Her deep blue eyes narrow and my gut sinks. She's not letting me out of this.

But I *can't.*

A moment passes, then another, when she takes a sharp breath. "If you complete this wedding the way I know you can, you'll get the raise we've been talking about."

My heartbeat kicks up. I'm thrilled, of course, but if I'm going to be forced to work with Theo for the next six months, a standard salary bump alone won't cut it. "They requested me as *lead.*"

"Well, sure, on this one project."

"If you're trusting me to lead the biggest-budget and highest-profile wedding in our company's history, you have to trust me to do this for others." *Stay strong, stay strong. Do not fold.*

"But, I'd have to work with the investors for approval, run some numbers, review staff assignments . . ."

I love Sydney. I really do. But right now, she's full of shit, and today I have no fucks left. "I have no interest in being a temporary lead. If I'm lead on this one, then I'm lead on all. Or keep me as an assistant."

I may sound confident right now, but my knees are quivering so bad they feel like they're going to spasm. No matter, though, I'll sit here all day until she decides. Her hands are tied, and even though I wish she would've promoted me on her own, I'll take this almost any way I can.

The longest moment of my life happens as she looks at me, at the ceiling, and then back at me. "*Deal*. You take charge of this wedding and you'll be an official lead at the company."

And now my heart has certifiably grown wings and is flying outside of my body. Yes, my ego wants the title. But my *livelihood*, my mother's livelihood, wants the money. This promotion comes with a thirty percent salary increase. Thirty. Percent. This money will pay for my mom's rent, allow her to go part-time, help heal her body and mind from years of hard labor and the disrespect she encounters while catering to the elite.

And all I have to do is sell my soul to the devil for six months.

"Thank you," I say, ignoring the tightening in my gut.

She slides her frames back up her nose. "First order of business. Can you please clean up the conference room while I send this contract to legal?"

Not exactly lead duties, but I'm not pushing my luck. I make my way down the hall. Just six months. I can do this.

I'll focus on the end goal, treat Theo like any other client, and swallow the last bit of my pride that he doesn't remember me.

Binders, mood boards, snacks and files are scattered across the table. I gather a few books and start shelving when I hear the door click open. "Hey, I'm heading on a coffee run," Justin says, poking his head in the door. "You want your mocha?"

"Only if they'll put vodka in it." I reach for the cardstock and stuff it into a folder. "No, I'm good, thanks. Honestly, I just need some time to myself."

"Gotcha," he says. "So leave the door open and tell everyone to come ask you a ton of questions about the power couple. On it."

I hurl a pen at the door, but he slips out and shuts it before it connects. I grab a few folders and crouch to file them away in the cabinet when the door opens again. "Jesus Christ, dude, do you ever listen? What part of I need quiet time is hard to understand?"

"Is this how you speak to all your clients?"

I glance up and suck in a sharp breath.

Theo.

He steps into the office and stares directly at me with an intensity that makes the hairs at the back of my neck stand upright.

"Sorry," I say, nearly tripping over my own feet as I stand. *What the hell is he doing here?* "I—uh—I thought you were someone else."

"No need to apologize," he says, speaking slow and intentional. Voices drift past the open doorway as a few coworkers chat in the hall. Theo's gaze flicks toward the sound, then back to me. "You don't have to look so scared, I don't bite."

At his remark, I straighten, refusing to give him the satisfaction. "Can I help you with something?"

"I think it's important we get to know each other better."

What? I grip the folder against my chest. "Ah, yes, sure."

He leans against the wall and shoves his hands in his pocket. "I just wanted to say how thrilled Anna and I are that you're leading the account. I know it's a quick turnaround, but I have complete faith that you'll make the day perfect."

Why do I feel like there's more to his words than he's letting on? I force a smile, my knuckles whitening around the folder. "I'm looking forward to helping you prepare for your special day. You really make a beautiful couple."

"Do you actually mean that?"

The sudden darkness in his expression throws me. "Of course."

A smile cracks through his stony exterior, but it isn't warm.

"Is that so?" he asks.

"Yes."

"Truthfully?"

What the actual fuck? He wants to talk about honesty—when he's the one pretending he doesn't know me?

"I. Don't. Lie." My trembling fingers lose their grip on

the folder and invitation samples, card stock, and business cards scatter. *Great.*

In a few long strides, he's bent at my side, helping to gather the items. He grips a few invitations and when I look up to thank him, fire burns in his dark eyes.

"*Lexie.*" Five letters whispered right at my ear with so much venom my stomach knots. He's close. *Too* close. His stormy cedar scent reaches my nose, the heat from his body radiates off him like a furnace. "That's not what you were saying earlier," he murmurs. "When you decided you didn't trust me—or my relationship with my fiancée."

Shit, shit, shit. He heard my conversation with Justin. And depending on how much he overheard, there's no way to back track. Hot blood rushes to my neck.

"I'd love to know *exactly* what you mean by something's 'off' about me and Anna," he says through a tight jaw, using the excuse of helping me to disguise his real intentions.

Dizzying heat courses through me. I blink through the spots, but it's no use. *Someone please save me.* "I . . . don't know what you mean."

"Oh, Lexie. I thought you just said you don't lie." He rises with me. God, he's so tall. He towers over me by at least six inches, his shirt pulls taunt against his broad, tight chest, his neck veins thicken as he narrows his eyes. "I was in the hall and heard everything."

Goddammit. Why did I not keep my mouth shut? "I'm really sorry," is all I can push from my dry mouth because what else am I supposed to say? But I still stand by those words. Someone like Theo is probably the definition of a psychopath. He can't care for Annabelle, at least not in the authentic way she deserves, and there *is* something off.

He closes the distance in a single step, my ass brushing the wall. The room narrows, compressing until it feels like there's only him and nowhere left for me to go.

His tapered eyes have turned even darker, from bourbon brown to a midnight sky, and I shrink. "Who the fuck do you think you are?"

His voice drops, low enough to send a sliver of fear through me. My knees wobble, threatening to give, and I grind my heel into the floor to steady myself. "That was . . . an unfair conclusion," I manage, hating how small my voice sounds. "To draw after just meeting you." *After knowing exactly what kind of man you are for years.* "I'm—" My breath stutters. "I promise it won't happen again."

His jaw flexes at my words and he goes even more rigid. I press my body further into the wall and Theo notices, because he suddenly starts inching closer. I can't run. I can't hide. Oxygen traps in my lungs.

"There is nothing, and I mean *nothing* that will ruin our day, do you understand? Someone like you will not break us apart." His gaze flashes down at me and I want to gouge his eyes. Someone like *me*?

A moment passes, then two. Each second more excruciating than the last. My heart pounds so heavy in my chest that if he doesn't step back soon, I'll pass out. I want to scream that he shattered my world, and if his wedding day is ruined, it's just a taste of the payback he deserves. "Why . . ." My chin verges on trembling. I bite the inside of my cheek until it relaxes. "Why did you ask me to be your planner? Why not leave the second you heard me say those things?"

He plants his palms on the wall beside my head, caging me in beneath the breadth of his body, and I hate that he smells so good. I rise onto my toes, a useless attempt to make myself taller—bigger, stronger—anything but what I feel right now. It fails. He's so close now that the air between us hums, a crackle of static jumping between our chests.

"Because no one gets the better of me, least of all someone like you. As they say, keep your friends close," he murmurs, his face now only inches apart from mine. His eyes flick to my lips before moving up, locking onto my eyes with a piercing intensity. "But your enemies closer." His voice is a low, icy drawl that sends a sickening wave of goosebumps crawling over my skin. As if he realizes our proximity, he pulls himself back and his tone sharpens, each word cutting like a blade. "Let me be crystal fucking clear. I don't trust you. Not even a little. Right now, you are a threat. Believe me, you do not want to find out what I'll do to neutralize a threat. If you even think of hurting Anna, of hurting this wedding, of fracturing what we're building, I promise you'll regret it. And I *always* keep my promises."

My throat tightens as I force down a hard swallow. Inside me, there's a relentless tug-of-war, a chaotic triangle pulling me in three directions at once. One side wants to kill him.

Another urges me to play it cool—be friendly, obedient, treat him like any other client. But then there's the third side, the one itching to break free, the one that wants to fuck with him.

He moves away from me, adjusts his cuffs with a sharp tug, and smooths his expression into something almost pleasant. "Now, I'm going to head back out there, grab my fiancée and tell your boss how excited we are to be working together." His gaze sears into mine. "And you're going to do nothing but be a fucking gem."

Gem. My whole body goes still.

Oh my God. Does this mean he remembers me after all?

Back then, after everything fell apart, I disappeared. I had to. I needed distance—from the person I'd been, from the name everyone knew. So, I buried *Gemma* and started using my middle name instead. Lexie. Maybe it was naïve, maybe dramatic—I was only twenty at the time—but I couldn't risk anyone Googling my name and uncovering what happened in Boston.

Still, a flicker of vindication curls through me. No matter how indifferent he acted when he first arrived, this has to mean he remembers me. *Right?* Could someone who ruined a life really forget the person they destroyed? Maybe to him, I was just a passing amusement or a sadistic distraction. To me, he's the villain who stole my future.

Revenge is a sweet, dirty intoxicating little bitch. One that has been coursing through my veins for close to a decade. Flickers of memory surface—every dead-end job, my mother's deteriorating health—fueling the fire burning in my chest.

I lower myself from my tiptoes and cower under his invasive stare, purposefully, giving him the illusion of control.

"Absolutely," I say, blinking up at him through my heavy eyelashes, wondering if my green eyes that an ex referred to as "hypnotic" will have the same effect on Theo. "I'll be whatever you need."

A moment passes where he studies my face and sizes me up. I swear I can see behind those dark eyelashes and know exactly what he's thinking. He doesn't trust me. And for right now, that's okay.

I raise my chin, straighten away from the wall, and school my features into casual politeness. "I'm looking forward to working with you and your beautiful bride-to-be." For all the power he holds, that his family holds, I can't be scared. I refuse. I'm no longer a quiet, shy, nineteen-year-old terrified of her own shadow. I'm an adult woman, presented with the opportunity to turn the tides. Theo's already taken everything. There's nothing else left to lose.

Theodore James Astor may have thought he buried me all those years ago. But I assure you, he hasn't. The time has finally come.

Starting today, I become judge, jury, and executioner.

Game on, motherfucker.

5

Theo

Gemma.

Seven years later, and not a goddamn thing has changed. The feigned innocence. That sinful mouth. The predatory smile she disguises under playful grins. The way she moves. *Fuck*, the way she moves. She's a master at masking her identity. No one would know the vixen that lies underneath those innocent, beautiful, spring-green eyes.

How dare she whisper *I'm looking forward to working with you and your beautiful bride-to-be* as she tugged in that juicy bottom lip? She gets off on teasing and luring, on breaking people. She knows exactly what she's doing. She knew it back then, and she knows it now. Gemma Welch may now be Lexie Welch, but that's the *only* thing that's changed.

I repeat Lexie's name over and over in my head, so I don't slip up and give myself away. Lexie was always good at toying with people and I saw how it gnawed at her that I didn't recognize who she was. I fucking loved it. She hasn't earned the right to know the depth of the marks she'd left me with all these years, how she hooked beneath my skin like barbed wire, ripping me open from the inside out.

I thought I'd done a good job of pushing her from my mind. From my soul. After everything that went down in Boston, I moved on. I graduated early, top of my class. Finished residency with the highest evaluations possible. Became the youngest attending physician in my clinic's history. I was *good*.

So fucking good.

But then, six months ago I ran into her again by chance, on a random Sunday in an unfamiliar neighborhood. She was sitting by the window of a coffee shop with her long, lush red hair piled on top of her head, reading a book, and sipping on a drink. The sunlight beaming through the window haloed her like an angel and time stopped. Suddenly everything I'd once buried came rushing back. I thought I was hallucinating. I'd stared for so long, taking in the slope of that pale neck, the plush mouth, the way her eyes showed every emotion of whatever she was reading.

I've been unsteady ever since.

But I'm no longer the man I was back in Boston. All the pressure, the eyes, the family legacy weighing on my shoulders, has lifted. She has *no* idea what I'm capable of now.

I push my chair up to my desk and try to focus on reading lab results, but she's distracting me again, just like she did back then. I wanted to know *everything* about her. Her thoughts, her secrets, her mouth, the way she moved, how she tasted. I wanted to know her dreams, her hates, what scared her, what made her laugh. I could read everyone, but I couldn't read her. I couldn't even get close enough to read her. She was an impenetrable vault, and I was desperate to break in.

It comes in waves. Chronic pain is like that. Good days and bad days, like I tell patients before I hand them off to the surgeon. The bad days will overpower you to a point where you can't breathe. The good days, when it's dulled and muted, you can breathe, you can function, but you still feel it festering beneath the surface. Even on those days, it's never forgotten. Lexie is always there. She's always *been* there.

As I give up the lab results review and instead open an email from the medical director, I flash back to the first day Lexie and I met. Maybe it was the naturally bright red hair that struck me or that familiar doe-eyed expression of a first year out of their comfort zone. I didn't notice a lot of first years. They were young, immature, and uninteresting. I was a senior then, elbow-deep into applying for medical schools and fighting the societal pressure of being the son of the great Dr. George K. Astor. My father and I had just engaged in one of our frequent screaming matches, and I'd stormed out of his office, determined for the millionth time in my life to never speak to him again.

I was still burning with anger when a voice sounded behind me in the quad. "Excuse me!" I turned, irritated, probably growling, to find a girl holding out ear buds in her palm. "You dropped these back there," she'd said, tossing her thumb behind her shoulder.

I don't think I even bothered to look at her properly at first. I mumbled a half-assed thank you and turned to head towards my next class, when she stepped in front of me, blocking my way, and asked for directions to the library. I remember specifically thinking, *can she not fucking see I'm in a hurry?* I almost told her to check the goddamn campus app for a directory but decided not to be a complete dick and barked out something about taking a left at the science center and if she reached the freshman dorms she'd gone too far.

And then she placed her hand on my arm. The bravery of it caught me off guard, sparking a reluctant curiosity. I took my time studying her as she met my gaze with those innocent eyes, and I was certain she'd see the darkness in my soul. Then she asked, "Are you okay?"

I couldn't remember the last time someone had checked in on me. Who genuinely wanted to know if I was okay. My family sure as fuck didn't care. I was the only child, a prop to be used when they needed me and otherwise ordered to shut up and be grateful for "everything we do for you."

I couldn't answer. The way her simple question left me feeling raw and vulnerable was so terrifying that I stormed off. But the image of the sweet gap-tooth smile and pale cheeks flushed with nervous pink wouldn't leave me.

Lexie *saw* me. She didn't know who I was, nor what sat in my trust fund account nor the expectations that came with my father and family name. She just saw *me*. Her momentary touch and those piercing green eyes haunted me until the vision of her shifted from me feeling exposed to putting me at ease in a way nothing else ever had—and it felt so damn good.

For a month, I looked for her, yearning, to the depths of my being, for that mental reprieve she provided. I walked through the quad any chance I could. I went to the library that she'd asked directions for, I spent my breaks roaming campus, craving that green-eyed dopamine hit. A few weeks passed and I started to play off my initial reaction, convincing myself that I'd overreacted. I was just exhausted from taking the max course load, weighed down by the pressure of being George Astor's son. Something just set me off me that day.

But then, I finally saw her again and the spark from that first encounter sharpened into something lethal—a fire-pointed arrow that pierced me down to the bone. Everything else fell away. The pressure. The noise. Watching her across the library ignited a need I couldn't escape. Lexie became both my distraction and my purpose—the high that carried me through the day.

I memorized her class schedule, her study habits, her work shifts at the campus coffee shop. When I couldn't see her in person, I studied the photos I'd taken in secret, a substitute when I needed the fix. And sure, I could've talked to her, maybe even asked her out, but things were complicated with Annabelle, my father, our parents, and my studies. And Lexie became something else entirely. A gift. A perfect doll-faced genie held behind this fragile glass wall. Untouchable, but magic, *my* fucking magic—and no one else's. I knew one day I'd be able to touch her. I'd get close enough to that skin, to taste it, to smell it. But until then, I needed her in the box.

After spending the holidays without her, I happened to be walking one of the university corridors when I heard it—that golden-laced giggle, which I recognized instantly. I'd heard it a hundred times, wanted it to belong to me alone.

But it was for *him*.

When I stepped through the office door, the fogged plexiglass announcing, "Dr. George K. Astor, Dean of Social and Behavioral Sciences," Lexie glanced up, shock transforming her face before she nodded in greeting and looked away, like she'd been caught doing something she shouldn't. She was *my* release, *my* drug, *my* angel. And there she was, doting on my father.

And my God, he saw her. The same pale cheeks, pouty lips, and soulful innocence that captivated me also captivated him. The moment my father introduced her as one of his *brightest* and *most promising* students, I knew. My father is a narcissistic piece of shit and no one impresses him.

Over the semester, I made a point of stopping by his office regularly. I watched the attention Lexie gave my father—attention she never once spared for me—and I couldn't understand it. Why she'd offer that gift to *him*. He didn't deserve it and I couldn't stand watching her give it to someone who already had everything.

I needed to put an end to this torture. So, I asked her out.

She said yes.

And she didn't fucking come.

No one stands me up. Ever. I paced outside the auditorium for an hour, convincing myself that maybe I gave her the wrong time, the wrong day, or even the wrong fucking address. *Something.*

But she didn't just stand me up. She showed up at the same goddamn place on my father's arm. It felt deliberate, like she'd played me, led me on because she knew exactly how much power she held. When she looked up at him with those soft, trusting eyes, I was ready to murder.

Because I would've given her the world.

But she wanted him.

Even in my humiliation, I couldn't let her go. She had no idea what she was walking into by choosing my father. I told myself I wasn't being selfish—that she needed protecting, that only I could keep her safe. Keep her *mine.* Because I needed her. Not him.

I'm an Astor, for Christ's sake. We don't beg. We don't lose control. And yet she reduced me to something desperate, something I barely recognized.

Now I'm done being that boy. I'm going in with eyes wide open. I know what she's capable of, and I refuse to let her affect me again. I have plans much, much bigger than her. So, I'll keep her close until I'm done.

And if she fucks with me again, only God can save her.

6

Theo

My phone pings with a notification and my jaw immediately flexes at the name. The very last thing I want to do on my lunch break is sit in my office and have anything to do with my family. Against my better logic, I swipe open the message.

The article shouldn't surprise me, and yet it creates the same heated coil in my gut as any other article my mother forwards. At this point, I don't know why I even bother. The stethoscope slung around my neck feels like a noose. I toss it onto my desk and close the office door, drowning out the staff and patient sounds from the clinic floor.

I sit back on the squeaky black leather chair and read the message. "You should at least make a feeble attempt to see him." No greetings, no concerns for my well-being, no nothing but that one singular line, which mirrors everything about my upbringing—direct, cold, laced with guilt.

Oh, Mother. I'm sure she knows about my father. The Astor family lineage—brilliant, connected, wealthy. And masters of delusion and denial. My mother may be the daughter of a shipping tycoon and the one with the money, but she'll never leave him. Appearances will always matter more than truth. Sweeping dirty secrets under the rug is an Astor family pastime.

And yet, as a glutton for punishment, I tap open the article.

"Dr. George K. Astor, Dean of the prestigious St. Benedicts University in Boston, *New York Times* bestselling author, and credited for his groundbreaking studies on neurodiversity and corporate leadership, will be signing books and taking audience questions at Columbia University . . ."

The words blur. Everything blurs. Since seeing Lexie last week in the flesh, smelling that vanilla on her skin, reveling in the way her freckles faded over the years and how her thick red hair begged to be wound and fisted in my grip, I'm pushed into a different reality. I need to fucking focus.

I tap off the article. I already know what it will say. The public adores this version of my father. The charming, gifted scholar, who can seduce a room of students and professionals alike in a single hour.

They don't want to know about the father who, when I was a child, was only present in my life when I was useful to him—when my behavior could be observed, corrected, or folded into his research.

They wouldn't want to hear that he demanded obedience and that the alternative was something far worse. Children expect yelling, anger, noise when they're in the wrong. What they don't expect is to be treated as though they no longer exist. When I was ten, he went an entire month without speaking to me after I said I didn't want to attend a conference with him, as if refusing to perform had rendered me obsolete.

They'd be appalled to learn that the doctor celebrated as a beloved family man was the same person who perfected cruelty behind closed doors. I was never a child, but a subject.

I thought he only did the fucked-up mind games on me. But as I grew older, I realized I wasn't the only one.

I've waited years to expose the truth. Building a case against my father, uncovering the rot beneath the world-renowned scholar and the lives he's destroyed, has cost me time, money and more energy than I care to measure.

The need to burn his reputation to the ground, to show the world who he really is behind the cloak of degrees, bestselling books, and my mother's powerful lineage, has consumed me. And finally, I'm close.

There's too much riding on this for any kind of distraction. And yet, ever since I saw Lexie six months ago in that coffee shop window, my focus has been fractured.

Lexie *cannot* jeopardize my mission.

She's one of the smartest people I've ever met. Where I had the kind of education money buys, hers came from the street and a sharp instinct for learning. When I overheard her talking shit about me and Anna at her work, it was a reminder—I can't let that happen again. I've worked too hard to quietly expose my father's atrocities, and I refuse to let Lexie—the woman who chose him over me—blow up everything I have planned.

The call I've been anticipating comes in. "This better be good news."

I don't hold back the fury in my voice and I can almost hear my assistant Michael's heavy sigh through the receiver. Having been on our family's payroll since before I was born, I quickly learned Michael is a man who can do anything. Things that need to be swept under rugs, he sweeps. Evidence of wrongdoings, buried. Whispers and gossip, stamped out with blackmail and threats of retaliation. Michael is the man that gets shit done, no matter what it is.

So, that's why, right now, I don't understand how hard it is to get me one goddamn studio apartment.

"It's fifty/fifty," Michael says. I immediately grit my molars. I'm a doctor. Fifty/fifty is unacceptable. Fifty/fifty means an equal chance of living or dying. That's bullshit. And if those odds aren't at one hundred by the end of the week, someone will pay.

"A west-facing one bedroom opened up—"

"*East* facing." I exhale fire through my nose. "It *has* to be east facing."

A long pause follows. "The west facing has better views, more space, is available immediately—"

"This is non-negotiable." I push myself from the chair and pace my small office. What the hell does Michael not understand? He needs to make this happen and right the fuck now. My neck is hot. I hook my finger in my collar and tug.

It's been three months of apartment hunting, and my patience is running thin. The need to be close to Lexie again after so many years apart was eating me alive and, no matter how hard I tried to ignore it, I couldn't rest until I did something. So, I settled on getting a place close to her. But then the engagement happened—the perfect excuse to be in her presence one last time before I get married. I told myself I'll get my fix and finally get her out of my head for good. With so much standing in my way, I realize how badly I need this one space to help quiet my spinning thoughts—especially after hiring Lexie as our wedding coordinator last week.

I have the means, I have Michael, and patience has never been my virtue. I get what I want, when I fucking want, and I despise being told no. But I'm desperate.

And I'm never fucking desperate.

"Listen to me. I don't care what you have to do. Find dirt on the landlord. Grab the west facing one and bribe one of the renters in the east-facing apartments to switch. Threaten a tenant. Do you understand me? This gets taken care of this weekend."

"You're going to be married this summer," Michael says. "I don't understand why—"

"It's done. This weekend. Understood?" My grip is so tight on the phone that I might crush it. I hang up before he has the chance to push out an exasperated sigh and give me his version of a fatherly scolding. Michael has never let me down. He *will* get this done. He has no choice. *I* have no choice.

A knock on the door snaps my attention. I drag my hands down my cheeks and exhale. *Fuck*. "Come on in!"

The door cracks open and Erica, the bubbliest of the RNs in my unit, pops in. "Hey Dr. Astor, do you have a second?"

Right now, no.

I need to figure out what the hell I'm going to do if I don't actually get that studio, and how to stop feeling like a jagged razor blade is slicing my cells. "For my favorite nurse?" I say with a smile. "Always."

Erica's mouth twists and she gives me a pointed look. "You know nurses are worse than a church circle when it comes to gossip, right? So, you may want to stop telling *everyone* they're your favorite. You might start some street fights if you aren't careful."

I laugh because Erica doesn't deserve to be on the receiving end of my bad mood.

I rest my palm on the desk and lean forward, trying to focus on her and not my raging pulse that still hasn't calmed down. "My money's on you in a street fight. You can take them."

That gets the expected grin. I always know how people will react around me. I anticipate, I read, I study them. I learn what makes them happy, what makes them tick. I know exactly what to do to make the nurses adore me, my family fear me, and the women around me soften.

Most women. Until Lexie.

Erica pushes open the door and a dozen or so of the nursing staff trickle into the office behind her singing Happy Birthday.

"Completely unfair, Erica. Next time I talk shit you have to warn me people can hear me." I chuckle as the team serenades me, and the head nurse walks toward me with a candle-laden cake. "You guys, this is too much. Really. Thank you. Is this chocolate? You all know the way to my heart, that's for sure."

"You've officially left your twenties behind, Dr. Astor," another nurse says as she cuts into the cake and slides pieces onto paper plates. "How does it feel to be thirty? Wiser than yesterday?"

"Hmm. Wiser might be a stretch. How about more tired?" This is not a lie. My sleepless nights are getting worse, and last night I clocked maybe four hours. I hit the gym twice, running and sweating and pumping until I nearly broke, and nothing alleviated the burn. The time stretching from where I am to where I need to be is so fucking long and tight it's going to snap.

I take a bite of the terrible cake and choke down the artificial coloring in the frosting. "Delicious. Thank you so much everyone," I say, looking each one of them in the eye even though my mind is trapped on Lexie. "You all really know how to spoil me."

The nurses gather around, asking about Annabelle and my "surprise" engagement that just hit the news last week. I'm like a boxer in the ring dodging prodding questions about how I proposed, how I even met Annabelle—a *Barlowe*—if we'll have kids right away and what my parents think. I maintain a smile and keep my answers short and polite.

No one here wants to hear the unglamourous side of this proposal. A year in the making. Lots of emotional torment. Anna and I devising a plan. More lawyers than Depp's defense team ironing out prenup details. The conversation with her parents and the brisk phone call to mine letting them know what would most likely be covered on *Page Six* and possibly in the *New York Times* depending on the slowness of the news day.

People want to hear about the fantasy, indulge in the make-believe that feeds their inner romantic. So, yeah. I smile, I nod, I talk about how exciting it is. And I leave out everything else.

"I bet your parents are thrilled," Erica says as she cuts into her cake with the side of her fork.

"You have no idea." Thrilled is certainly one way to put it.

My mother will enjoy having a new daughter-in-law to parade in front of her friends. As for my father, he may be pleased that he's gotten his way—but only because he has no idea what's coming for him.

After I push my cake around enough on the plate to make it look like I ate more than I did while calculating the extra reps I'll do tonight to offset this monstrosity, I order—*playfully, of course*—the staff back to work.

Once the door closes, my chest tightens. I grab my phone, knowing that I wouldn't see a message from Michael pop up in the last twenty minutes, but checking anyway. The thud in my chest turns loud and angry, and I feel thick blood pumping through my veins.

I will do everything I can to stop Lexie from ruining my plans.

Including getting as close to her as possible.

7

Lexie

The kink in my neck is raging at an eight out of ten. I crack it, roll my shoulders, dig into it with my thumb until it cramps, and nothing releases the tension.

"You know, I've heard there's a fantastic cure for those little stress neck aches you've been getting." Justin bounces his eyebrows like the juvenile he is and flops down in his chair. As long as he doesn't start thrusting his hips—which typically throws me into a fit of giggles—I'll be good. I groan, prop my elbows on my desk, and rub my temples. "Oh shit, you actually aren't great. What's up?"

What's up is that I have to push aside my seething rage toward Theo and actually do my job. These past two weeks since he stormed back into my world, a low thud has pounded in my skull. When high-profile people want to plan a wedding—in the city, in six months—the pressure is tremendous. It's not like I can just bump someone off the

Four Seasons roster even if it's for an Astor or Barlowe. The venue is the most difficult piece to land during the wedding planning, and right now we're working with very limited options.

And I *hate* admitting this, but overseeing this wedding is stressing me out. I'm plagued with nightmares that I'm lost while driving to a venue or that I forgot to book catering and jolt upright in bed with my heart racing. I've always taken direction from Sydney: I review things she's already reviewed, I follow up emails she's already sent. And now, it's all on me. I have to prove that I deserve this spot, work with a man I hate, and plan a billionaire daughter's wedding.

"I'm good," I say, tugging on my sleeves, ignoring my constricted breath. "It's just a lot of pressure."

Justin nods. "Yeah, it is. I told the hubby who we were planning for—"

"*Justin.* That's under NDA."

"Dylan doesn't count." Justin shrugs and opens his laptop. "You want to come out with us tonight for Happy Hour? We're going to hit up the martini lounge after he gets off work. We can try and find you a new sexy man."

I grin at the "sexy man" comment. A few months ago, I joined Justin and his beautiful-as-him husband, Dylan, for drinks. A guy with sandy blonde hair, trimmed beard, and sharp suit slid in next to us, shook our hands like we were constituents during his mayoral run and made me laugh. He had a great ass, found out later that night a nice dick, and we seemed to click.

Sort of.

I usually rely on fourth-of-July-level sparks, but this was more of a backyard-barbeque-sparkler type of spark. But my gut hasn't always batted a hundred with men. By the end of the month, I pulled my classic line of being too busy at work for a relationship and stopped returning calls.

Something needs to break my funk, but, tonight, I need more than a double dirty martini with Justin. "Raincheck. I need some serious solo time tonight."

"If you change your mind, just shoot me a text."

I nod and pull up my spreadsheet checklist—the wedding planner's bible. A client once mentioned that being a wedding planner sounded like so much fun. That all day you get to sample cake, look at beautiful venues, and help pick out flowers. I almost laughed. Sure, these existed, but really, it's a highly skilled project manager, business negotiator, relationship builder, therapist role. And one with a whisper network as tight as the mafia. You piss off one person in this industry and you have no idea how quickly doors will slam in your face.

But normally, yes, I do like my job. Is this where I wanted to be? Absolutely not. Am I still grateful that I landed here? Definitely.

I scan the emails that came in overnight. All typical items that I'd cover as an assistant: vendor invoices, a salon booking confirmation for one of Sydney's bridal parties, a pitch from a new bakery. But now I have budget reports, forwarded design proposals, questions about city liquor permits if we have an off-site venue—and my blood pressure starts rising. This opportunity is everything I've wanted. But Jesus Christ, it's *a lot*.

I don't even register these, however, because I'm too distracted by the one tucked a few rows below from Theo. Sent almost forty-eight hours ago.

For some jobs, two days is not a big deal. But unless I'm at a wedding, or with a client, I pride myself on responding to all client emails within an hour. I want them to feel like they're my top priority.

And the rush filling me from not responding to Theo builds in delicious layers. Each hour I don't respond and make him wait, each hour I picture him pacing and wondering if I've forgotten about him, feeds me. I know I should respond. Instead, I email the bakery and confirm we'll be happy to accept a sample and quick meet-and-greet.

As if I've conjured the devil himself, my cell rings with Theo's name on the screen. I toy with the idea of denying the call, but then remember I need this job and in doing so, I must be professional. I swipe to answer, but the line disconnects.

I go back to answering emails and setting up the expense spreadsheet, checking my phone every few seconds to see if Theo has called me back. My laptop pings fifteen minutes later—a message from Megan, the receptionist, asking me to come to the lobby.

As I stand, my eyes snag on my phone. I hesitate, then swipe it off my desk and bring it with me. Why did I let my emotions get the better of me? Something seriously might have happened. I unlock my phone and start drafting a message to Theo, then lose patience and call him instead—only to hear a faint ringtone in the distance. *Weird.* When I round the corner, my whole body freezes, my fingers tightening around the phone at my ear. I should know by now there are no such things as coincidences. Not when it comes to Theodore Astor. Because he's standing right in front of me, phone in hand, with Annabelle by his side.

What are they doing here? Please, *please* don't tell me I forgot an appointment. That would just be my luck—trying to prove I deserve a promotion and miss a meeting with the highest-budget client our firm has ever had. Or worse, they're here because I failed Client Etiquette 101 when they needed me.

"Hi there," I smile, probably way too brightly, as I mentally scan my calendar and pray I don't break out in a cold sweat.

"Hey, Lexie!" Annabelle says, as she dangles a designer bag in her hands. "Hope it's okay to just drop by like this without an appointment." *Oh, thank holy Christ.* "Theo said his phone was acting up and couldn't get through to you, and since we were shopping in the area, we could just stop by."

He did, huh? A hint of a smirk tugging at his lips beneath his groomed scruff indicates something else.

I want to dig my heels in his foot with enough force to break a bone. He has not earned the right to stand here totally impassive. And God, I hate that he looks good. Today, jeans and a casual dark long sleeve that's obviously cut to accentuate those rippling biceps. He's gorgeous in anything and he knows it. I *hate* that he knows it.

I don't trust him. He's clearly orchestrated this. Probably to throw me off my game. And it's working. Though Theo's easy smile masks something darker—he's wearing the same look as last time they were here: no recognition of me, no acknowledgement of the damage he left behind, no memory of cornering me in that conference room. He smiles like I'm a stranger.

By the time I'm done with him, he'll never forget me again.

"Yes of course," I say, matching his casual smile, hiding the knots in my stomach. He wants to knock me off alignment, and I refuse to give him the satisfaction. "I was just composing an email to the two of you, so this is perfect. Why don't we head back to the conference room. Please follow me."

Without waiting for a response, I turn and exhale my constricted breath.

I lead them past my desk where I grab my laptop and then head down the hall. We pass Sydney's open office door, and before we reach the conference room, her signature Chanel N°5 fills the air before I actually see her. She silently appears, snapped into existence by the hint of a Barlowe in her presence.

"Annabelle and Theo, so nice to see you," she says, stepping in front of me, which is just fine as I need to catch my breath. "I'm surprised Lexie didn't tell me you had an appointment, otherwise I would've greeted you in the lobby."

"We didn't have an appointment," Annabelle says. "We just decided to drop by."

I don't like the look Theo gives me. I can't quite read it. Smug maybe? There's a flicker of intent behind it, like a predator deciding whether to pounce or retreat. "And I'm so glad you did," I say. *Puke.* "You are always welcome here."

The corner of Theo's lips lift and I brace myself. "I'm happy to hear that," he says. "I find that when someone is hard to reach by phone or email, it's more effective to speak face to face."

Shit. Hives are for sure going to break out over my body. My impulsiveness is going to be the death of me. The very last thing I need is for my boss to think I'm incompetent.

"I apologize for the inconvenience," Sydney adds, giving me a discreet death stare before pasting on a warm smile for them.

Annabelle jumps in, playfully tapping Theo on the forearm. "Pay no attention to Theo. He's a doctor and assumes everything is life and death, even when it's not." She gives me a quick side wink. "He's being overly dramatic because he skipped his morning coffee. What he failed to mention is that we didn't give Lexie much notice before showing up unannounced."

God, *I* could marry this woman—if she weren't so blinded by her love for Theo. Why she decides to save me, beyond simply being a good person, I don't know. Sydney softens at Annabelle's reassurance, but Theo goes rigid.

"You're too kind," I direct at Annabelle before turning to Theo. "It's great to have someone who keeps you grounded."

"She does her best," he says with a grin, but his gaze drilling into me shows anything but amusement.

I hold his gaze, refusing to back down or give him the satisfaction of thinking he's won this round.

Sydney rests a firm hand on my shoulder. "Lexie will be available to answer all questions *anytime* you need her. If you're having issues reaching her, then please don't hesitate to contact me."

Well, fuck.

"We're a team and can always step in for each other," Sydney adds. "And it's actually good timing that you're here. I have some good news. We received the contract back from the photographer you wanted. Their team was thrilled to work with you and your family and adjusted their schedule to accommodate."

I breathe a sigh of relief. When she offered to take over that part for me, I almost hugged her.

"Lexie, did you manage to hear back from the videographer?"

All color drains from my face. *Oh shit, oh shit, oh shit.* No, I never heard back from the videographer because I completely forgot to contact them. I was supposed to do that the first day, but I was so distracted it slipped my mind. I think I'm going to throw up. How did I miss this in my project plan? I'm now panicking that I may have missed out on other things.

"Lexie?" Sydney's jaw stretches. "What did the videographer say?"

I open my mouth to either lie or drag out some lame, half-hearted excuse, when Theo says, "Actually, we told Lexie to hold off on contacting anyone right now because we have a family friend who's trying to make it work in their schedule."

What? We never had this conversation. He *knows* we didn't. I glance at him, but his eyes are focused on Sydney.

"Wonderful. Glad to hear it. Please let us know as soon as possible if they can't make it." Sydney smiles. "I won't keep you any longer. Let me know if you need anything."

"Of course." I turn back to face the couple, my head swirling. *Please don't sweat.* "Why don't we head to the conference room?"

After I escort them there, I run back to grab my notebook and pen, whisper to Justin that the couple is here and pause at the mirror for a quick hair and make-up check. Outside the room, I stop and shake out my twitchy arms.

I'm in control now. Not him. There's nothing he can do to hurt me, but there's a ton I can do to hurt him. I exhale three short breaths, lift my chin, and enter the room.

8

Lexie

As I approach the conference room, I catch Annabelle leaning in to whisper something to Theo as they wait for me. He laughs in response and she practically glows at his reaction. There's evidently an ease between them—the kind of comfort that comes from years of knowing someone—but I can't shake the feeling that something's missing. I work with couples every day, and my instincts are rarely wrong. Perhaps it's because he's a psychopath and she has yet to uncover this fact.

"So," I say, heading in and taking the seat across from them, "what brings you into the office today?"

Annabelle glances at Theo first before answering. "We've been thinking more about what you advised—especially the headcount. If our parents had their way, it would be half the city by now. They've been planning for this since we were in high school."

High school? Why wait fifteen or so years to get engaged? I hate that my curiosity piques. "Oh, so you're childhood sweethearts?"

"More or less," Theo says, reaching for a water bottle in the middle of the table.

"Let's just say it's been a . . . bumpy ride," Annabelle mutters with a wink.

"Anna!" Theo says, shaking his head as if thoroughly amused—though I don't believe it for a second. "We swore we were going to keep that between us."

How does he do this? How does he pretend that he's this kind, normal, functioning member of society, and how does she not see behind the bullshit veil?

"Oops, *sorry*. But we're together now, and that's all that matters." She throws her arms around his neck and gives him a loud kiss on his cheek. When she pulls back, she looks at me. "What about you, Lexie? Are you married?"

I blush. "Oh. Um, nope."

"A special someone, perhaps?" she asks. Clients rarely ask personal questions and it catches me off guard. With the exception of Justin, I usually keep my professional and personal life separate. Still, Annabelle waits expectantly. When I glance at Theo, he's so still he looks like he's not breathing. *Interesting.* Is he curious, too? "No special someone."

"Those days as a single woman were so much fun," she says, then adds quickly, "No offense, Theo. But there's nothing like that first spark—when you meet someone and everything feels exciting and tingly. But I do *not* miss the whole getting-to-know-you phase." She makes a face. "It's just . . . gah."

"I think 'gah' is the perfect way to describe it." Throughout the exchange, Theo remains eerily quiet. I don't want to engage with him any more than necessary, but his silence puts me on edge.

"Okay, let's be honest. If you were getting married, you'd do a destination wedding, wouldn't you?" Annabelle says. "All these people staring at us all day . . . it's pretty nerve-wracking."

I smile at her exaggerated, gritted expression. At her sincerity, I decide to offer her a truthful reply. "Some people love that," I say. "Others find the whole idea terrifying." I pause. "If I was planning my wedding, I'd keep it small. Intimate. I've always imagined somewhere like Lake Welch. My parents took me there all the time when I was a kid—I used to think it was named after us." I chuckle and explain my last name is Welch. "It's my favorite place on earth. My safe place. When I get married, I picture just me, my fiancé and the lake as our witness."

My insides turn warm remembering how my dad would hold my hand in one palm and a plastic bucket in the other as we hunted the beach for perfect skipping rocks. When we were there, the world quieted. Even as I grew older, the lake was my sanctuary. The one place where I could fully breathe.

I hate that I just inadvertently gave Theo some personal insights, but his face is stone-cold, totally unreadable. I clear my throat. "But this is about your day, not mine. Since you're here, why don't we look at a few invitation samples." I scoot back from the table to grab a binder off the bookshelf and feel the heat of eyes on me. Today I wore my fitted khaki pencil skirt that Justin once told me that, even as a gay man, he couldn't help but appreciate the way it hugged my ass.

The eyes boring into my backside probably don't belong to Annabelle. I ignore the tiny flutters making their way through me and instead accept that I now have more evidence that Theo's disgusting.

When I return to the table, Annabelle slides over to the left and pats the seat in between her and Theo. "Here you go," she says. "That way we can all look together."

Jesus Christ. Every second I'm with her, she dispels all my preconceived notions of a billionaire. I'd assumed she'd be like the *Devil Wears Prada* Miranda Priestly character walking around with a faux American-British accent, dripping with high-end jewelry, luxurious cashmere, and sharp tailored suits. But not Annabelle. Besides her Hermès bag and massive diamond ring, I'd have no idea she came from money.

Which begs me, once again, to wonder how the hell she wound up with someone like Theo.

As I flip through the invitation binder, Theo moves close enough that I'm hyperaware of him at my shoulder. It feels like a jolt—every nerve lighting up at once. I don't like being so close that I can see the tight ridges in his forearms flex under the dark tattoos when he turns the page. It's distracting, and I cannot be distracted.

"This is pretty." Annabelle rubs her hands over a gold-embossed invitation.

Theo leans in and my breath stops. "But would your mother approve of *our* invitation for *our* wedding."

"Ugh, you're right," Annabelle sighs in defeat and Theo returns to flipping the pages. The air feels charged, like the first frost of the season, carrying a bite. The longer we sit, the more convinced I am that Annabelle doesn't want to be here. She's looking at the pages but not *really* seeing. She's not a giddy bride, and this goes beyond being easy going. Does he make all the decisions? I bet he does. I bet he's the type of man that doesn't let her see her friends, that chooses her outfits, that checks her texts and controls all the finances.

As we continue looking through the options, I feel a knee pressing mine. *His* knee. It's nothing more than a graze and maybe he notices, maybe he doesn't, but my traitorous thigh hums with electricity.

I move my leg away.

"What do you think?" I ask Annabelle. "Anything jumping out at you?"

The engagement ring flashes under the ceiling lights. "Honestly, I don't know." She dips her head at me. "Between us two, though, Theo's *way* pickier than me, so we should probably just let him choose."

"You do know that I'm literally sitting right here and can hear everything you say, right?" A glint of light flashes in his stormy eyes, reminding me a little bit of his dad.

I still keep up to date on Dr. George Astor, the mentor I

so heavily admired. He's currently on a book tour which will probably win all the same awards as his first nine books. And I can't help but think that should be me. Right now, I should be several years into my practice, established enough to turn down clientele, and finishing up drafting my first book. I wasn't meant to do this—explaining the difference between tri-fold or gatefold invitations, discussing minimalist versus traditional design, giving the pros and cons of metallic foil stamping and wax seals.

No. I should be making triple what I do now, supporting my mom so she can retire, and have letters behind my name.

Theo has letters behind his name. Of course he does. People like him are handed everything, and yet they still take, take, take. The only thing that releases the twist in my belly of how our paths turned out is thinking of how hard, and how quickly, I'll take him down.

"Why don't you two keep looking, and I'll grab another book from my desk," I say, needing air that isn't saturated with his aura.

"Actually, Lexie, would you mind showing me the restroom?" Theo asks, rising.

Dammit. It's as if he has this sixth sense of my need to escape him. It would appear rude if I refuse . . . "Of course."

I head for the door, but he reaches it first and pulls it open. *Whatever.* The chivalrous gesture isn't for me—it's for Annabelle. I know exactly what kind of man he is.

Down the hall, he silently follows. Maybe I'm reading into it, but it feels a step too close, too comfortable, too familiar.

The moment I turn the corner, Justin rounds the same corner and gives me his cheesy double thumb guns salute while clicking his tongue. "What's up, Buttercup?" his face drops when Theo comes into view. "Oh sorry, I didn't realize you were with a client."

"All good, just showing Theo here to the restroom before I grab a few more things."

"I can take you," Justin offers.

"It's fine. Lexie was already leading the way," Theo's sharp tone sounds behind me.

Justin and I share a quick, knowing glance—high-profile client, deep pockets, must tolerate all his eccentric whims. We keep our mouths shut. Justin continues down the hall, pausing only to give my shoulder an apologetic squeeze, and I continue counting the seconds until Theo leaves.

I usher Theo past our lobby to the shared, public bathroom on the building floor. The halls are quiet, the dentist and CPA office on our floor closed. When we reach the bathroom, Theo doesn't move. Instead, he crosses his arms and burns his gaze into mine. "He a friend of yours?"

The tone makes me wince.

When I remain silent—because fuck him, I don't owe him anything—he glances behind his muscular shoulder at the empty hall and narrows his eyes. "I *asked* if he was a friend."

"Justin?" Theo has not earned the right to know who may or may not be my friend. Why does he care? Is this the part he warned me about, keeping me close because he doesn't trust me? I let a long moment pass before I respond.

"We're all really close here at *Shades of White*," I say, repeating the words printed somewhere on our website. His silence turns lethal, filling the space between us, and I can feel his frustration building. A vein stands down his neck—thick, flushed—as if he's drawing everything in the room toward him, including me. The reaction it provokes is embarrassingly potent. At this rate, I'll be reciting the whole damn 'About Us' page. "Sydney cultivates a sense of community and family among us planners so we can provide the best service."

For the quickest of seconds, a whisper I nearly miss, Theo's heated gaze drops to my mouth and then my tits, then sweeps back to my eyes. "You didn't answer my question."

I hate that this look—a brief, scorched flash that might even be subconscious—tightens something low and traitorous inside me. I hate that it still elicits the same response as when I was younger—a rush of intoxicating dark energy, a heat-laced fear combined with a craving so urgent that it'd wake me up in the middle of the night, forcing me to rub myself to relieve the pressure.

As much as my whole being hates him, as much as I want to bring him to his knees, my body betrays me. But only for a second.

"Your boss said you'd answer all my questions, anytime." His gaze deepens, sharpens, threatens.

I do not like fucking threats.

"Perhaps I should let her know that I'm not receiving prompt responses."

Oh, this is too good. He's salty about his emails being ignored, and I love it.

"Go ahead," I say. Even though I'm skating on extremely thin ice, the thrill of not backing down sends a sharp rush through me. "If you want to run to my boss and tell her I won't give you insights into who I spend my free time with, be my guest." I straighten my spine and meet his gaze. "Somehow, though, you don't strike me as that kind of man. But I've been known to misjudge people before." *Like you, when I held that stupid crush.* "So, tell me, Theo. Are you the type to let other people do your dirty work, or can you handle a little challenge all on your own?"

The faintest look of amusement appears on his face. He swipes his tongue across his lower lip, leaving a soft glisten of moisture behind that I hate myself for following. "You certainly are feisty, aren't you?"

"You have no fucking idea." He hasn't even *begun* to see feisty. I hold his gaze a few more moments, making sure that he knows he didn't win this round, and instead I'm offering up information of my own free will. "But yes, to answer your question, Justin and I are friends."

I don't know what has taken over me. Sure, I've grown a backbone over the years, but it's like a steel rod has been implanted into my spine. In Boston, no one protected me. This man destroyed me, and I couldn't do anything to stop him. I'll never let him do that again.

"My guess is that you're used to the world revolving around you, getting what you want, when you want," I say, lifting my chin. "I'll plan your wedding, and I'll be phenomenal at my job. Other than that, I don't owe you a fucking thing, including details about my private life."

The faint grin is instantly replaced by his jaw muscle flexing. He inches closer.

This time, I don't step back.

"Nothing takes priority over our wedding. Not your friends, not a fucking boyfriend, not other clients, nothing." Oh, why are those words a thin whip licking at my skin? Sharp, biting at the flesh, but oh so yummy. He's off-guard. He's upset. He's rattled.

And it's *glorious*.

"Don't think I've forgotten what you said to your *friend*. Don't think I can't read you like a fucking manual," he seethes. "I know women like you. The innocent smiles, the sweet eyes, switching to an angelic voice when it suits you. You think you're smooth, calculating even, but you're not. I see everything."

His voice is hard, lethal, and it should terrify me. It should make me want to run and hide and seek shelter in anything but his firm arms and dark scent. But it doesn't. I'm drawn. In the most fucked-up way, I'm captivated by the rage.

But I also want to laugh. An uncontrollable smile lifts at the corner of my mouth because I'm getting to him. Two weeks in, and he's already shaken.

"Tell me, Theo," I say, arching a brow. I don't break my gaze, I don't back down, I don't even flinch. This time, I take one step towards him, and he freezes. Then another step. And now I'm so close that my breasts brush up against his rock-hard torso, but I refuse to retreat. My heart pounds as I lean forward. "Is this supposed to scare me?"

I want to eat the anger that flushes his face.

"You say you know women like me?" My voice is calm, steady, in control. "But I know men like you. The type of men that carry a delusion that everyone should fear them. Your grandiose self-perception because of money and privilege and being coddled your entire life makes you think if you snap, people should bend a knee for you." I pin him with an unbreaking, sharp gaze. "You should know right now, I will *never* fucking bend for you."

A darkness that I've never seen flashes on his face. He puts his mouth to my ear, his warm breath feathering across my skin. "Do not play with fire, little girl."

The hot, raw words vibrate against my ear and my heartbeat thuds in the column of my throat. "Or what?"

His hands slide to my waist, and he tugs. Hard. "Bad, *bad* things will happen if you do."

The fear is intoxicating. *I* caused this. *I'm* making Theo sweat. The man who ignored me for a year, can't ignore me for two minutes now. I open my mouth to challenge, to push, to pour accelerant on that fire, but the creak of a door sounds, and Theo takes a wide step back.

"Well, hello you two." Sydney's voice cuts through the thick air. "I need to run an errand but wanted to check if you needed anything. Theo, is Lexie answering all your questions?"

In a snap, the red in his neck disappears. "She sure is," he says in the chipper tone of someone discussing good weather, not someone who just experienced this wrenching charge. "She's giving me all the information I need to know."

God, he's a lunatic.

Once she leaves, and he turns towards the bathroom, I race back to the conference room, desperate for some distance between Theo and me. After I slide into the chair in front of Annabelle, I glance at the invitation binder resting between her hands. "Did you find something you like?"

"So many and none at all," she says with a short chuckle, though the faint hint of defeat in her tone doesn't go unnoticed. "Honestly, we should just let Theo pick."

"We meet a lot of women who wouldn't dare let their partner plan the wedding. You definitely have a lot of trust in him, huh?" I keep my voice bright, trying to lighten the mood but also using this chance to get to know them better as a couple. What is it about Theo that has Annabelle under his spell, blinding her to the fact that he's the devil in disguise?

Her gaze flickers to the floor, the corner of her lip drops, her throat rolls with a pebble swallow. *And there it is.*

At the university, I planned on getting a psychology degree. I loved the study of human interactions and micro-expressions. And had I not done a few of those intro courses, I wonder if I would've noticed these subtle fluctuations.

But I do, absolutely, notice a chink in her otherwise perfect armor. A crack in the façade she's so carefully maintaining, revealing just a glimpse of something deeper—something she's trying desperately to keep hidden.

"Of course I do," she says, softly, twisting her engagement ring. "He's going to be my husband after all."

This should be the happiest time for a bride—dreaming up all the exciting plans for marrying the love of their life. So why do the words coming out of Annabelle's mouth sound dull and lifeless?

"And we couldn't be more thrilled that you've chosen *Shades of White* to help plan your special day. If you don't mind me saying, you two make such a beautiful couple. I can't wait to see the look in Theo's eyes when he sees you walking down the aisle." I try to remember all the times I've watched Sydney handle moments like this, but in my eagerness to learn more about Theo and Annabelle's relationship, I might have pushed too hard. Annabelle doesn't respond or soften at my words like I'd hoped—if anything, she seems more withdrawn. Crap. "I'm sorry if I overstepped or misread the situation. I just wanted to reassure you that it's completely normal to feel nervous or unsure about wedding planning. But that's why I'm here, to help you through it, step by step. And you'll have Theo right by your side. I mean, he's contractually bound to be there, after all." I laugh to avoid any more awkwardness.

Her gaze flicks to the floor ever so quickly but there it is again. I catch it in her forced grin, in the way her eyes go distant, in the way she's nervously twisting that ring. Then, as if on cue, she snaps her head up and smiles brightly. "He is, isn't he?! I'm so lucky we get to spend the rest of our lives together." Her voice is cheerful, and she lights up when talking about Theo. But the way she chews on her bottom lip and hesitates before speaking next betrays her ease. "It's one thing to talk about the wedding, but actually making decisions makes it feel so real. I think I've been getting in my head. Ignore me—I'm probably just dealing with some irrational cold feet, which I hear is pretty common for brides, right?"

Her question makes me pause. In my experience at *Shades of White*, cold feet can surface at different points in the planning process, but I've never seen it happen this early. It might be cold feet—or it might be something more. The difference is, I know Theo. Or at least, I knew him back then. And this leopard never changes its spots. Maybe Annabelle's instincts are screaming at her to run, but she's been with Theo for a long time and it's hard to break free.

Maybe I can help her save herself.

"People talk a lot about cold feet. But I think it's important to listen to your gut when something genuinely feels off. That can often be a sign," I say as gently as I can. "Nerves, excitement, even anxiety are normal. But hesitation this early on can sometimes point to something deeper—and it's worth taking the time to understand *why*."

The room is silent as a long moment passes. I wish I could better understand the thoughts behind those eyes.

She runs her palm across the top of the invitation binder. "Have you ever had cold feet?"

Her voice is hesitant, and she's looking at the cover, not

me. I've never had the urge to hug a client like I do now. I want to comfort her, tell her to run, tell her she's too good for him. "I don't think I've ever had a relationship even serious enough to warrant cold feet."

It's the truth, and it's all I can offer.

She flips open the binder and scans the page. "I sure hope you find someone special," she says, tucking a long piece of dark hair behind her ear. "He'd be winning the jackpot with you."

My heart pinches. This woman is way too good for someone like Theo. She clearly fell like so many others into his charming façade and has no idea what lies underneath that pretty-boy smile. Is he after her money? Do they have a solid prenup? I wish I could scream to her that Theo's a liar. That he's dark and evil, and just because she hasn't seen it yet, she will. But you can't just come out and say something like that. I'd get fired from the account, fired from my job, and she wouldn't leave him anyway.

The door opens and both Annabelle and I glance up.

"Hey, you ready to go?" Theo says to Annabelle as he tucks his phone into his pocket. "I've got that physicians meeting tonight I've got to get to."

She pushes herself back from the table. "Yep." She slings her bag over her shoulder. "I promise we'll get back to you by the end of the week with a rough headcount. Anything else we need to do before then?"

I close the binder, deliberately avoiding Theo's gaze. "Please make sure to discuss alternate options—and consider a destination wedding more seriously if our top city venues don't pan out." They won't. If a venue is still available at this point, there's a reason. "We'll need a decision on the invitations by Valentine's Day. Beyond that, I'll send over some high-level themes and color schemes." I offer a polite smile. "And of course, call anytime. I'm here for whatever you need."

I'm here for Annabelle. *Not* Theo.

Annabelle reaches over and gives me a hug. This is not uncommon in our business, but something in me shifts and turns urgent. She's warm, kind, and clearly clueless about the man she's about to marry. She doesn't see the real Theo—the serpent disguised as a seraph. I've thought about nothing else for nearly two weeks, but now it's confirmed.

I don't want to hurt Annabelle, but I will absolutely go through with my plan to take down Theo and expose him for who he really is. And after I do, and the pain subsides, she'll thank me.

And Theo will be ruined.

9

Lexie

The frayed edges of the flannel blanket have been there since I was a kid. On nights my mom couldn't afford a babysitter, I'd trace its worn edges while watching cartoons, eating dry cereal, and waiting for her to come home. Over the years, it became a lifeline for me—wrapped around me as a frightened kid, a lonely teenager and during late-night study sessions. It was even draped over my lap when I opened the letter offering me a full-ride scholarship to St. Benedicts University in Boston.

But when I went to college, I left it behind at my mom's. The moment I stepped onto campus, I wanted, *needed*, a new life with nothing tying me to the past—including my beloved blanket. It felt like my history was somehow imbedded into the fabric, that each thread carried a restraint that taunted me with the threat of failing and returning to the life I was desperate to escape. As I tug the blanket over my mom's chest now, I feel those same tattered threads and wonder if somehow, deep down, I knew back then I'd land in the place I am now.

"It's freezing in here. I think you should turn up the heat," I say, and step over to the thermostat. *Ugh.* It's freaking January, not even fifty degrees outside, and my mom has the heat turned off.

"Ah, nothing that a warm cup of tea won't fix," she says, waving me away, but not pulling the blanket off her chest. "You hungry, honey? I can make us a couple of ham sandwiches."

I shake my head. I'm actually famished, but I refuse to eat my mom's food, knowing she works way harder than me to get those groceries. And—not that I'd ever tell her this—but I ate one too many (*a thousand too many*) of those sandwiches growing up, and now the sight of ham on wheat makes me want to vomit.

The local news plays on the small TV in the background as I grab the fresh bottle of scent-free lotion I brought over today and sit next to my mom on the faded green couch. The broken springs dig into my back as I shift into a spot. "Give me your hands."

"You're always fussing," she says, her wrinkles deepening around her tired eyes as she smiles and holds her hands out.

My mother has the hands of a ninety-year old woman. They carry this cracked, reddish-gray tint from thirty-plus years of handling cleaning supplies and bleached towels. She only started wearing latex gloves in the last decade or so, which seems to irritate her almost as much as the chemicals. I pump a few droplets into my hand and start massaging.

It wasn't supposed to be like this. When I got my scholarship, I knew that our lives would change. If I worked hard, which I was absolutely prepared to do, I could graduate in a little over three years. I'd take the max amount of credits, work in the school coffee shop, study my ass off, and when I was done, I'd get my mom out of this place. I'd make enough money to finally upgrade her to a one-bedroom, maybe even something with a view. I'd get a job, work through my masters, then a PsyD, and eventually she'd reduce her work hours. And once my practice took off, she'd be able to retire altogether.

All of our dreams, the hard work, the sweat, would finally, *finally*, be worth it.

I thought the scholarship of my dreams was the break I needed. But I was wrong. Sophomore year, I landed the break of a lifetime when my dormmate dropped out of school in the middle of the semester leaving vacant her student aideship with the revered, highly sought-after mentor, Dr. George K. Astor. Someone whose books were not only textbooks at our college, but required reading across multiple Fortune 500 leadership teams. And he chose me to fill the open position. *Me.* A scholarship kid from Queens, with nothing but a truckload of ambition.

I'll never forget the way he smiled at me, how the crinkling around his eyes fanned to the gray at his temples, how he'd pull off his glasses and look at me, so thoughtfully, seeing me when I'd been invisible for so many years. He even took time from his insanely packed schedule to read one of my papers and invite me to visit after hours for one-on-one tutoring sessions when campus was quiet.

But the real privilege came on a Friday evening when Dr. Astor invited me at the last minute to be his guest at a university fundraising event. He promised to introduce me to some people and help me start building my future. I couldn't believe that he'd chosen me out of all his students. For the first time since starting school, I began to believe I could really make it in this field.

I was momentarily conflicted, though, because I was supposed to meet Theo at the same event for a date. An actual, real date. A few days earlier, at the coffee shop, he and I had a run-in. I'd accidentally knocked into him while cleaning up some tables and dropped a half-filled latte on the floor. I thought he'd do his typical staring at me with disgust, make a hurtful remark, and walk off as if I was unworthy of his time. But, he surprised me. He'd stayed. He even helped me clean up. For the first time, we had a real conversation.

Having his undivided attention, I was on cloud nine. I mean, Theo Astor was paying me attention. Me! He asked about my classes, I mentioned how hard it was to land an internship as a sophomore, he laughed when I told him I was in the middle of St. Ben's infamously hellish Chem 101 monotone lecture, which required ingesting a bucket of caffeine to sit through without falling asleep. After a while, I loosened up.

We didn't chat long, and he'd left as soon as we'd finished cleaning. An hour later, I got a text from an unknown number asking if I was free the following Friday.

I let them know they had the wrong number, only to get an immediate response: "I'll give you exactly one guess who this is. Actually, I'm too impatient. It's Theo. I've got something that might solve your internship problems, but you'll have to meet me next Friday. One-time offer. My kindness doesn't extend far." It wasn't exactly the most romantic way to ask me out, but *holy shit*, Theo had been thinking of me!

But when Dr. Astor asked me to go to the event with him, I couldn't turn down the opportunity. In my trembling excitement for my date with Theo, I forgot my phone in the dorm, but asked Dr. Astor to text Theo, to let him know I couldn't make it because I'd accepted his invite.

Theo never spoke to me again.

I tried to shake off my disappointment and forget Theodore Astor even existed. Until he forced his way back into my life and sabotaged everything the following week.

And now . . . I'm planning his wedding. What sort of fucked-up underworld am I living in? I should have said no. I should have known from one look at Theo last week, in his designer clothes and perfect haircut and smug face, that he was going to be trouble. Our firm is just like a bar—we can refuse service for any reason. But I need that promotion. My mother's future depends on it.

I sold my soul. I pray to Christ it was worth it.

As I switch to massaging my mom's left hand, I push away

any other thoughts of what happened back in Boston and focus on what's going to happen these next six months. It's been three days since Theo cornered me in the hall, and I cannot shake what happened. I still feel the heat of his chest against mine, the way my body singed with fear, the sharp masculine cedar and salt scent filling my nose. I cannot understand why, if he truly doesn't remember me, he wants me to be his lead planner. Yes, he overheard my conversation with Justin. But is that enough of a reason? Keeping me close because he doesn't trust me?

Although I've never been in his position, coming from a wealthy, powerful family and marrying into an even wealthier and more powerful one. Maybe this is just what happens with the billionaire boys' club—you're surrounded by distrustful people you need to keep close.

"Drink your tea before it gets cold," Mom says, nudging at the mug.

I take a few sips, but it's not needed. My insides are on fire. I thought that I'd buried this rage. Did anger simmer beneath the surface over the years? Yes. But I was like a hibernating bear. The fury dulled. Muted, even.

At least I thought.

But when Theo stepped into my office, the cave opened. Everything in me burst out and the monster I've been suppressing wants out.

"So, I need to tell you something . . ." Mom starts, and I immediately freeze. "Hey, that wasn't an invitation to stop," she says, bumping my arm. I resume rubbing her hands and hold my breath. "Now, I'm gonna tell you, but you can't freak out, okay? You promise me right now, otherwise I'm keeping my lips zipped."

"I promise," I say, but it's a lie. The only time my mother has ever said "I need to tell you something" was when I was ten years old and she told me my father died.

She looks at the lotion bottle, not at me. "I've been having some dizzy spells and last week they had to call the hotel on-call doctor and—"

"Jesus Christ, Mom! Last week?" The guilt already buries me, and she hasn't even finished what she was going to say. A few months ago, I decided to move closer to work at my mom's insistence. For five years, I'd been spending almost three hours round trip every day to work at this office. With the move, I shaved off almost an hour a day from my commute, but now, I was further away from her. I asked myself over and over if I was making the right move, and what if something happened . . .

"Now listen here, Gemma Lexie Welch," she says as she pushes herself up. *Yikes.* Even though I changed my name years ago, I know my mom is serious when she breaks out my birth name. "You promised you wouldn't freak out. One more word and I ain't gonna finish telling you what happened."

I swallow the urge to ask every single detail. As she tells me about sporadic dizziness, and the hotel doctor rushing to help when she passed out in the room she was cleaning, I hold back brimming tears. The doctor took her blood pressure, gave her an ice pack, and told her to schedule an appointment. She says she'll do it in the next month, which means she absolutely won't until something else happens.

"Enough of that. I only told you in case I drop dead. You can't blame me for never telling you nothin'," she retorts.

I'm still worrying over my mom's health when the news anchor's sudden shift in tone pulls me back into the room. "Coming up next. A source close to Henry and Mariette Barlowe has announced the engagement of their youngest daughter, Annabelle Barlowe . . ." I leap up to grab the remote. " . . . to Dr. Theodore Astor, son of author and speaker Dr. George K Astor, and—"

Click.

My mom's head snaps to the television. "Did I just hear the name Theodore Astor?" Her eyes turn as cold as the bitterness in her tone.

"Oh, I, ah, maybe, here give me your hand." I pump a few more drops of lotion in my palm and reach for her wrist, but she pulls back.

"A Barlowe is marrying that conniving piece of shit? He doesn't deserve to marry anyone. That man is nothin' but evil."

I avoid her eyes. She's not wrong. If I think I've held a grudge all these years, it doesn't even compare to my mom.

My mom is one of the gentlest people you've ever meet. To a fault. Our family motto is work hard and maintain the peace. You bow your head, you serve, you stay the fuck quiet. But after what happened in Boston, mama-bear mode kicked in and she saw blood. She wrote unanswered letters. She took the bus to the public library and used their computer to send emails. She stormed into the administration office and had to be escorted out by security, screaming about the "dirty fucking Astor family" who destroyed "her baby." For months she tried to get anyone to listen, but people like me and my mom were not worthy of their time. Our words were rendered silent. Finally, with her heart more broken than mine, she gave up.

So, yeah. My mom cannot know that I'm planning Theo's wedding.

But part of me wants to tell her I have much bigger plans for Theo than just his wedding. Plans that I've been sitting on for years, plans that have kept me alive during the darkest days, plans that make up for my humiliation.

And I'm just getting started.

10

Lexie

"This mission is impossible," I say to Sydney as a taxi drives us through Manhattan on a Tuesday afternoon. It's been ten days since Theo and Annabelle showed up at our office unannounced, five days since Sydney and I scoped every available event center we could snag an appointment to, two days since I've gotten more than five hours of sleep, and one day since I doubled my efforts in finding out more about Theo's life since university.

So far, my internet search is yielding minimal results. Scholastic accomplishments and published articles in medical journals is all I can find. Both him and Annabelle's social media is non-existent. But there's something out there that I can use to show Annabelle who Theo really is. Seven years ago, I couldn't prove what he did. Now, I'll go down in flames before I let him get away again.

Sydney drops her cell phone into her purse and looks out

the window. "What's impossible? Making our way through rush hour traffic or the severe lack of available wedding venues?"

Ugh. It's bad enough that we only have an unreasonable six months to plan a wedding, but under no circumstances can I let Sydney find out I'm digging into Theo's past and trying to save Annabelle from a lifetime of married misery. Part of me wonders if it'd just be easier to find nothing, let the wedding happen, and take the promotion and raise I've worked so hard for. That thought tempts me for about three seconds before anger reappears when one of Theo's pretentious emails lands in my inbox or I remember the power plays he's pulled.

Tonight, I'm going to review our cancellation policy. Maybe there's wiggle room to both save Annabelle and keep my promotion.

"Do not lose hope, Lexie. We've pulled some major tricks out of our hat before." Sydney gives me a comforting squeeze on the arm. "Do I need to remind you of the Hendersons' wedding?"

I chuckle. "No, no you don't." That one might go down in history as the most soap-operatic wedding of all time. The best man in love with the bride. The grandpas getting in a very slow, very drawn-out pushing match, the intoxicated groom's mother trying to kiss the priest. Looking back, it'd make for a great rom-com. Although at the time, it felt anything but.

And, as always, Sydney was there, coaching, guiding, and keeping me from spiraling.

When we step into the hotel in the financial district, I breathe a small sigh of relief. The lobby is decent enough, the traffic like any other hotel you'd expect. It doesn't scream Barlowe, but Annabelle herself doesn't even scream Barlowe.

"Would you grab us a few lattes, and I'll check in with the manager?" Sydney says.

"Double caramel, pecan oat milk, or drip with two pumps vanilla?"

She gives me the cocked brow and curved lip look I crave. "How in the world do you know my top three orders?"

This is where I excel. I listen, I read, I study people. We don't often go for coffee, but we've gone enough times over the years that I remember patterns. That's why I know in the deepest part of my gut that something is not right with Theo and Annabelle—the pattern is off. "I used to be a barista. Drink orders are tattooed into my brain." This is not a lie, however. I still have nightmares about screwing up a skinny vanilla latte order.

"You're too smart for your own good," Sydney says, and I have the distinct feeling that if she were twenty years older, she'd pinch my cheeks. "Just grab me the one with the least amount of caffeine. I need to try and sleep tonight."

"Got it." I follow the scented trail of roasted coffee beans down the large lobby, past the small gift shop, and to the corner of the space. In line, I snap pictures of the reception area, the commons, the business center, and the small restaurant to the left.

After I put in our coffee orders, I move to the pick-up line, continuing to scan the space, when the elevator doors across the lobby open. *What in the* . . . My breath hitches. Inside, Theo's arms are linked with a beautiful, legs-as-tall-as-the-sky, twenty-something-year-old, brunette.

Outside of the elevator, they stop and face each other, whispering. Her hand never leaves his. His gaze doesn't break with hers. Maybe it's a colleague, or a relative. But I've never touched a colleague or relative as long, or as intimately, as they are.

I take out my phone, scroll in and record the way her hand grasps his forearm, how she peeks behind him like she's worried about getting caught, the way he pulls her into his fierce, hard chest.

Whatever conversation they're having is intense. She's upset and keeps tugging at his hands, intertwining them with hers. She places her hands on his chest and stares up at him. God, what I'd give to hear what they're saying. Whatever it is, a slow smile appears on her beautiful face. He tucks a piece of hair behind her ear, then kisses her forehead.

That motherfucker. I *knew* it. I absolutely knew that he's a player. The woman cups his face and lifts to her toes like she's going to kiss him, but he takes a step back and glances across the lobby. *Of course* he does. He's getting married. I'm surprised they're doing as much PDA as they are. I dash behind the wall so he can't see me and exhale.

A moment later, they saunter away, chatting as they move through the doors, walk outside, and disappear behind the building. I start to follow, but the barista calls my name and my focus snaps to Sydney waving from outside the manager's office.

As I weave through the travelers, the sweet taste of vindication swirls through me. Theo is the man who could have anyone. Back then. Now. Forever. And he ended up with the golden girl, Annabelle, a beautiful, smart, kind billionaire. And still, she's not enough.

All these years I've hoped for retribution. But now, this nearly decade-long passive desire to see Theo crumble has changed. I need to protect Annabelle from making a life-altering mistake. And if this means I also get my long-awaited revenge, great.

Everything starts now.

11

Lexie

I smooth my hands down my emerald shirt, the one Justin said made the green in my eyes pop, and debate about opening one more button. I add an extra spritz of perfume, fan my chest, and smack my lips together to smooth the gloss.

Today, it all begins. Retribution is no longer a question of if, but when. Talking with Annabelle a few weeks ago, then seeing Theo at the hotel on Tuesday with an unfamiliar woman, crystallized everything. Theo clearly cannot keep his dick in his pants. Maybe this isn't my brightest or most ethical plan, but I'm desperate to show Annabelle who he really is. If he crosses a line with me, then at least I'll have something concrete—something undeniable—to put in front of her.

The plan is simple: earn Theo's trust, lower his guard, and expose the man he truly is. Once I have proof, I'll tell Annabelle *everything*—who he was at the university, who he is now, what he's capable of. I'll destroy him the way he destroyed me. By the time I reach the subway station, I'm so giddy I damn near click my booted heels.

On the subway, I open my calendar and double-check today's schedule that I've reviewed no less than ten times already. Three venue visitations. Two hours apart. Six hours with Annabelle and Theo.

I've got this. I tug my scarf a little snugger and brave the winter air as I make my way to the hotel. When I turn the corner, the nerves hit.

Theo is leaning against the building, casually scrolling through his phone, looking like a model from a New York street fashion site. Sharp dark denim. Black shirt. An open peacoat that looks effortless instead of calculated.

He's infuriatingly good looking.

But what unsettles me isn't how he looks—it's that he's waiting for me alone.

When he looks up and catches sight of me, his eyes do that thing—the subtle, nearly undetectable, head-to-toe graze. My body notices, and it heats. Just because I haven't had a proper fuck since my last boyfriend does not mean that my physiological system has the right to Judas me. I need to stay sharp, and I'm screwed if this happens to me within the first ten seconds of seeing him.

Theo waves. "Hey."

I smile brightly. So brightly, in fact, that my skin stretches and my cheeks warm, because everything starts *now.* "So sorry. Have you been waiting long?" I say, loosening my scarf. "Apparently, I need to up my 'ten minute early arrival' time to fifteen, huh?"

His grin really is quite lovely if you can overlook the ugly personality. White, straight teeth, full, lush lips, dimples that pop underneath that groomed scruff. "I've only been here a few minutes," he says as he shoves his phone into his pocket. "Did you take the train?"

No asshole, I have a driver like you. "Yep," I say. "Where's Annabelle?"

"She's inside. She hates the cold. I kind of love it." He holds the door open to the hotel, and I duck inside, ignoring his heavenly scent as I pass. "Do you live far away from here?"

"About a thirty-minute train ride. Not too bad," I say, searching through the travelers scattered across the lobby until I find Annabelle sitting in a corner chair, scrolling through her phone. When she peeks up at me, her eyes brighten, and she waves at me before indicating she'll be back in a couple of minutes. "What about you and Annabelle?"

"She lives in the Upper West Side, and I have a place in Tribeca."

Wait, what? I shift my gaze from searching for the hotel manager to Theo. "You guys don't live together?"

"No, never have," he says as he removes his coat and drapes it over his forearm. "She's pretty ... traditional ... like that."

There's something in the tone that strikes me, a heaviness that I can't interpret, and I'm desperate to know more. A professional curiosity, or part of my plan I'm not sure, but it's rare to work with couples who don't live together. I didn't get the religious vibe from Annabelle, but I've been known to be wrong. Maybe it's because they both come from money and saving on rent isn't as important to them as the rest of us? I decide to pocket this little nugget of information for later.

Theo tosses a quick glance over his shoulder. "Listen," he says with a hushed tone. "We clearly got off on the wrong foot. I'd like for us to start with a fresh slate. There's . . . a lot of factors at play here, and the last thing we need is more stress with us not getting along."

I go still. He might be looking at me earnestly, but I just *know* that whatever truce he's suggesting is bullshit. But, sure, I'll play along. This might even work to my advantage somehow. "I'd really like that," I say and go to shake the hand he's already extended. Our hands meet and a surprising warmth from his palm shoots through my body. A small gasp escapes my lips, and the corner of his mouth slightly quirks. Then I feel it—the subtle pressure of his thumb brushing against my wrist, slow and deliberate.

My breath catches, and his eyes darken with something unspoken. He wets his lips, and I'm transfixed, the tension between us crackling like a live wire. I don't know who moves first, but suddenly, we're close—too close. Our bodies are nearly touching, his breath ghosts against my temple. He brings his hand up and smooths my scarf that flipped over my shoulder, his fingers grazing the side of my neck. Then, in a low whisper that sends a shiver down my spine, he says, "Oh, we're going to have so much fun."

His words are a bucket of cold ice, and I drop my hand, catching in my periphery Annabelle walking to greet me from the direction of the bathrooms. Oh God, oh God, please tell me she didn't just see whatever the hell that was.

"Hey!" I lean into her hug. She's definitely a hugger, and I hold on a second longer than necessary, praying she didn't notice anything off. "Are you ready for today?"

She nods, but there's a hesitation in her expression, a flatter smile than the last few times I've seen her. Good. The sooner she realizes that Theo is who he is, the better her life will be.

"Sure am," she says. "I'm ready to check this off the list and move on to the next thing."

Wow. Move on to the next thing, huh? Maybe the influx of emails and to-do lists I've sent over the past two weeks are wearing her down. Or maybe it's something else entirely.

I *really* hope it's something else.

"What do you think of the hotel so far?" I ask lightly. "Have either of you been here before?"

"I haven't," Annabelle answers, looping her arm through Theo's. "But Theo might have."

"Maybe once or twice," Theo says, as he guides us through the lobby. "Between work and wedding planning, my life's a blur. Everything else kind of slips my mind."

His hand twitches slightly. Is he nervous?

"When I scouted the place recently," I say casually, "the manager shared all kinds of stories about the hotel.

Spectacular events they've hosted, all the famous guests who've stayed here." I let a beat pass. "She also hinted that it's a popular spot for . . . secret love affairs."

He stills for just a fraction of a second at my last words, then recovers, responding lightly. "I can't say I can compete with the manager's stories. If I was here, I was probably trapped in some painfully dull medical conference. The only illicit affairs that were happening were between doctors and the hotel coffee."

God, he's a good liar. I itch to pull out my phone and show him that he was, in fact, here on Tuesday with a mystery brunette. For now, I'll bide my time and work harder to get the answers I need.

"This place is already surprising me," Annabelle says, "maybe we should add—" Her phone rings and she pulls it from her purse, frowning. "So sorry, I need to take this."

"No problem," I say quickly. "If you two want to take a seat, I'll check us in."

"No. I'm coming with you," Theo says, flatly. The finality in his tone catches me off-guard, like my simple suggestion of checking us in solo offended him.

Theo subtly nods to a man in a black suit standing in the lobby and nudges his head to Annabelle. It takes me just a moment to realize this is probably part of Annabelle's security detail. They didn't have one at our office, but maybe they do in more public spaces? Who knows, maybe Annabelle is surrounded by undercover agents. She is the daughter of a billionaire after all.

After we check in, and return to Annabelle, the same hotel manager walks out from her office to greet me warmly, politely asking about Sydney, while I introduce her to the couple.

The manager probably doesn't know who Theo is, but *everyone* knows the Barlowes. When Sydney arranged the appointment, she used the standard lingo that I'd be visiting with a high-profile client and discretion is top priority.

It's New York. No questions were asked.

"Welcome, welcome," the manager says, smacking her hands once, and talking way too loud. "We are so thrilled to have you here!"

Just as we're about to head off on the tour, Annabelle's phone rings again. "Jesus. I'm sorry. This is going to take a while."

Theo's brows crease. "Everything okay?"

She nods. "Yeah, Nonna stuff. You guys go ahead. I'll meet you as soon as this is done."

No. Wait. I don't want to be alone with Theo—especially not after earlier. "We can absolutely wait for you," I say, panic rising in my chest.

Annabelle asks the person on the phone to hold on, then cups it under her chin. "Please. Go. It's totally fine. I'll be up shortly. Theo, text me where you're at. Security will escort me when I'm ready."

He nods, and when she steps away, the manager leads us deeper into the hotel, waving her hand like we're on the final round on a game show, and she's presenting the grand prize showcase. "This hotel was built in the early nineteen-hundreds, and the development team has gone through extraordinary efforts to maintain the original beauty of the structure. To your left, you'll notice the limestone and brick, which was popular during the Industrial Revolution . . ."

As she fails to take even one single breath, and we step into the elevator, I notice a few things.

One, the elevator is *tiny,* and I pray that I don't have a panic attack. Me and small spaces have never been friends. Living in the city, I've had to rid myself, as much as possible, of the fear of elevators. But this particular one is made of nightmares.

And two, Theo is wearing his distracting scent again, which is exactly what I need right now in this suffocating coffin. I'm not too proud to lean in and suck in a huge breath.

As we pass the third floor, the elevator jerks. I focus on controlling my breathing, counting in for three and out for three, clinging to the rhythm to keep the rising panic at bay. But it's clearly not enough as my hands won't stop shaking. I tap them against my leg, desperate for some kind of release.

Theo's hand rests on top of my own, stilling the movement. He flashes a sharp, questioning gaze my way. "Are you okay?"

I think he might actually mean it. I force a smile, nod quickly as I move my hand away, shifting my body as far as the cramped elevator will allow.

The elevator is painfully slow and the journey up each floor is ricketier than the floor before. By floor five, stars blink in my vision. Theo moves to stand right next to me, separating us by a few inches. Christ he's tall. Imposing. Even in my wedges, he has a good six inches on me. *Jesus Christ*, there's literally no air in this space. I loosen my jacket. It's so hot. My mouth goes dry at the same time as sweat beads pop on the back of my neck.

I close my eyes and try to calm my stomach, when he gives my hand a squeeze. I stiffen. But also, I don't move free. Instead, I latch on to him, accepting the comfort his touch is giving me. Everything about him is so sturdy. He's like an impenetrable wall of strength, and for this moment only, I'm grateful.

Finally, the doors open to the eighteenth floor. I drop Theo's hand and nearly bolt out in search of air.

Less than thirty minutes later, we thank the manager for her time and step away from the front desk just as Annabelle finishes her call nearby.

"So," I say lightly, turning to Theo, "what do you think?" I gesture back toward the lobby. "It can accommodate over a thousand guests, which is why it made the shortlist. But their marketing team really leans into the *turn-of-the-century* charm, which might be less of a draw." What I leave unsaid is that it is *in need of serious upgrades*.

Theo buttons up his coat with an unhurried precision. "That's a hard no," he says, calmly. "I can already picture my future mother-in-law walking in and deciding she's personally insulted."

A slow smile curves his mouth—dark, amused, dangerous.

"Though, honestly, it might almost be worth booking just to see her reaction."

"You sound like someone who enjoys watching people squirm," I say.

The curve of his mouth deepens. "Only when they deserve it."

"Would you say this is the kind of place you'd bring a lover to instead?" His brows knit at the shift, eyes narrowing as he tries to read my angle.

"I wouldn't know," he says, after a measured beat. "Annabelle is the only woman I've brought anywhere like this." He studies me. "What, exactly, are you suggesting?"

Before I can push further, Annabelle's arrival puts a halt to the conversation, and we fill her in on the verdict from the tour. "What a shame, though I'd much rather save us from my mother's commentary. It feels like every moment that passes, this wedding becomes more for our parents and less . . ." she doesn't finish the sentence.

A silence fills the space. Annabelle is avoiding Theo's gaze, avoiding mine, and the heavy words uncomfortably settle.

Theo's phone rings and he pulls it out of his pocket. "Work, sorry, I need to take this."

When he steps out of earshot, I use the time alone to check in on Annabelle to see if she has any clue Theo was here a few days ago with a woman. As much as I despise Theo, my heart aches for her and I don't want to just jump right in and tell her what I saw. Keeping my fingers crossed she knows about his meeting with the woman, I say, "What's Theo's work schedule like?"

"Oh, it's pretty typical for a doctor," she says, tugging her bag up on her shoulder. "Monday through Friday, sometimes he stays late on Thursdays. Works twice a month in urgent care. Why?"

Play it cool, play it cool. "I wonder if we could squeeze in morning or afternoon meetings during the week since we were able to today and that time you all dropped in at the office."

"Sadly no," she says as she shakes her head. "When we popped by, it was because there was a random power outage, and the clinic had to shut down for the day. And today, he took the day off for these meetings. But otherwise, he's pretty glued to the clinic."

He's also glued to a beautiful, nameless brunette. "So, he had the whole week off this week?"

"No. He was in the office all week," she says. "He was only off today."

This is all the confirmation I need that Theo is most certainly hiding something from Annabelle.

"I'm craving a brown sugar espresso," Annabelle says as Theo stuffs his phone in his pocket and makes his way back toward us. "Lexie, do you want a drink?"

I'm momentarily confused by the suggestion but go along with it. "I will *always* take a coffee."

Annabelle places her hand on Theo's forearm. "Would you grab us the drinks from over there?" she says, pointing to a small, open café tucked in the corner of the lobby. "Lexie and I will find a table."

Theo glances at the line that contains at least twenty people and a heavy deflated breath escapes him before he joins the coffee-seekers.

Annabelle smiles and watches Theo as he weaves through a small crowd of hotel visitors towards the café. As soon as he's several feet away, her smile drops, and she turns still. "I think we need to talk."

12

Lexie

Annabelle's words send a ripple of fear through me. Has she been waiting all this time to corner me about what happened between Theo and me in the lobby? I'm not even sure how to name it myself—but whatever it was, it wasn't what I'd planned for today, and it certainly didn't feel innocent.

I guide her to a small table in the center of the floor while actively trying not to pass out. "Is everything okay?"

Once we slink into the chairs, she glances behind her shoulder to where Theo's standing in line and sighs. "I can't stop thinking about our conversation." *Oh, thank God.* "And, well, you signed an NDA, so this is confidential, right?"

"Yes, of course," I say as I prop my elbows on the table and lean forward.

After another deep breath, she says, "In your experience, can you tell when a couple isn't going to make it?"

Oh, shit. She just dove right in and skipped all conversational foreplay. I get the sense she doesn't have a lot of people she can confide in. There's no mom or doting mother-in-law, no maid of honor at her side, no best friend. The best she's got is practically a stranger who's paid to help plan her wedding. I should keep things professional, but the notes of vulnerability in her voice, the way her eyes search mine for reassurance, makes me put aside my biases. She needs a friend right now, not someone holding on to a near decade-long grudge.

"Every couple's situation is different, and it's hard to give you a black and white answer." I steal a glance at Theo from the corner of my eye, measuring how long Annabelle and I have before he returns. Theo will have my head if he finds out we're having this conversation.

As if he could hear my thoughts, he turns towards us and his gaze catches mine. His eyes narrow, clearly not trusting me—I honestly don't blame him—and a sick satisfaction grows knowing I have this power over him. The line moves forward and he shifts back to the counter. A warm hand on my own shakes my attention back to Annabelle.

What am I doing? She doesn't deserve any of this. I need to choose my words carefully and make sure she hears me, because someone like her deserves happiness.

"But I can try to help if you tell me what's going on," I continue. "In my experience working in the industry, I've picked up on certain patterns."

With a shaky finger, she tucks a long, dark lock behind her ear. "When we started talking about getting married, it just . . . made sense. I mean, I've known him my whole life. We've been on and off since we were teenagers." She exhales, thin and unsteady. "It felt like the inevitable next step. And our families—" She shakes her head. "That part's complicated. There are expectations." Her hand twists her ring. "And . . . *shit.*" She glances over her shoulder again. "So, what are the patterns?"

I take a moment, choosing my words carefully. "There's one thing I've noticed over the years," I say softly. "When couples are excited—or even nervous—they usually become *more* themselves."

Her brow furrows, but she doesn't interrupt.

"They have stronger opinions, clearer preferences. More emotional presence," I continue. "Even anxiety has an energy to it. It takes up space." I hesitate, then add, "Excitement does too."

Theo still hasn't moved up the line. I refocus on Annabelle.

"But when you and Theo first came in," I say gently, "what stood out to me wasn't nerves or excitement. It was how . . . careful you seemed."

Her fingers continue twisting the ring.

"Like you were editing yourself," I continue. "Choosing your words. Shrinking your reactions. As if part of you was already adjusting to fit the future instead of imagining it."

She swallows.

"That doesn't mean the relationship is wrong," I say quickly. "But when someone starts to feel smaller—quieter—before the marriage even begins, that's something worth paying attention to." I meet her eyes. "Because marriage shouldn't require you to disappear."

I let the silence stretch, giving her space to sit with it.

I remember feeling like something was off and couldn't pinpoint what it was. But after stewing, it became clear. Brides especially are giddy, ask a ton of questions, and usually take their own notes. When I escort them from our office, they pepper in more and more questions until the elevator pings.

But Annabelle was more indifferent than smiley.

So, yes. I'm just doing my public service duty by pointing this out. But I'm also saving her. No doubt in my mind that she'll be better off without Theo.

Through the hum of travelers rolling bags, phone conversations, and the soft hiss of espresso brewing, she stays silent as her gaze sweeps the hotel lobby.

Theo inches closer to the barista, and my pulse thuds harder. The cheek gnawing and ring spinning increases, but she's silent. Theo's now chatting with the barista and pulling out his wallet. *Come on, Annabelle.* She's so close, but our window for talk time is narrowing by the second.

"And now, you're having cold feet," I say, gently, waiting for a brace in her shoulders, but she only deflates. "You went from not feeling any excitement at all to cold feet. Why do you think that is?"

Well, look at me go. I would've made a good therapist after all had Theo not destroyed those dreams.

She keeps her eyes on her hands. "Honestly, I don't know. I mean, I love Theo. He checks all the boxes. Smart. Good looking. He's a doctor. Gives back to the community." My breath locks. She needs to do this on her own, to have agency in this decision, but she needs to hurry the hell up. I'm just leading her to what she already knows is the truth: she is too goddamn good for him.

"I tend to be, I guess more . . . flexible. And Theo's just very intense sometimes. He likes control. *A lot* of control." She says this with a little chuckle, but heat barrels through me.

"Wait. Does he ever . . ." I don't want to say it. Theo is a lot of things, but . . .

Her head snaps up. "Oh God no. *No.* He's a good man. He would never, ever hurt a woman. Ever."

I can see it in her eyes. She's telling the truth. But he doesn't get a gold star for the bare minimum of not laying a hand on a woman. He still ruins people's lives. He still destroyed mine all those years ago. And if Annabelle stays with him, he'll ruin hers, too.

"I'm just not sure what to do here." Her voice cracks. "I keep thinking about what you said. If someone has cold feet, there's probably a reason why."

And there it is. I'm not trying to exploit her pain, but she *has* to see this. She's kind, generous, the sort of woman who could spend her days sailing on yachts and shopping, yet instead chooses to run a non-profit. We're currently sitting at a four-star hotel—*at best*—and she has not made one snide remark, not even a single scoff, about having her wedding at a place like this.

Run, Annabelle. As fast and as far as you possibly can.

"So, what are you going to do?" I ask.

A long moment passes. Concern flickers across her face. This could all disappear if she just left him. Once she has distance, the fog he's wrapped her in would lift. "I honestly don't know," she says. "My grandmother is having some health issues at the moment. She keeps asking me to come join her in Italy." She worries her lip, visibly conflicted. "But with the wedding and everything," she says, sliding her chair a little closer to the table, "I just don't know if it's feasible for me to leave."

I place a gentle, reassuring hand over hers. "It is absolutely feasible. I can handle the logistics. We can do virtual site visits, daily updates, video calls—whatever you need."

The words tumble out before I can stop them.

And then it hits me. If she goes to Italy, it leaves me alone with him. I don't want that. Not at all.

But I want even less for Annabelle to stay and quietly ruin her own life.

Across the room, Theo is already at the counter, saying something to the barista that leaves her giggling, cheeks flushed enough to be visible from here. Good. Hopefully his flirting will keep him occupied for a few moments longer. Annabelle is on the verge of a breakthrough, and I can't risk him undoing it.

"It can be really hard when family is so far away and you can't be there for them." Time is running out when I see the barista snapping the lids onto the cups, peeking glances at Theo every chance she can. Even though the thought of being alone with Theo—of planning this wedding—makes my chest tighten, I know I have less than two minutes left to give Annabelle the encouragement she needs. "My father passed when I was ten."

Annabelle's eyebrows shoot up. "Oh, I'm so sorry."

"That's okay," I say. The memory still hurts, but I push through knowing that this will help Annabelle find the freedom she deserves. "The cancer took him quickly, which was a blessing in disguise given the pain he was in. For a month, I stayed in bed with him, watching cartoons while he slept." I pause. "Even now, I don't take that time for granted. I'm grateful I didn't hesitate when it mattered."

Theo grabs the drink carrier from the counter and storms towards us. My pulse thuds heavy in my ears as I say, "Sometimes a little distance and time with family can bring you the clarity you need."

Before Annabelle can respond, I glance at Theo and interrupt with a grin, "Oh . . . wow. I can smell those coffee beans from here. Thank you, Theo."

His gaze flicks between us, sharp and assessing. He clocks the way Annabelle's shoulders are drawn in, the tension she hasn't quite masked.

"What did I miss?" Theo asks pleasantly—too pleasantly.

"Just boring girl talk," Annabelle says quickly, forcing a smile. "Nothing you need to worry about."

Theo hums, low in his throat. "Ah. The most dangerous kind." His eyes settle on me, deliberate. "I should've known."

"Relax," I say lightly, despite the growing unease settling in my stomach. "We were talking about family."

"Thank God I arrived in time, then," he jokes. His tone is easy, but his body tells me that he doesn't find the humor in this conversation.

We make small talk while we finish off our drinks and then Theo gets up to toss our empty cups into the trash, gesturing towards the exit. "Shall we?"

As we rise to follow, Annabelle lingers just long enough to catch my hand. Her fingers squeeze tight. "You have no idea how much our chat means to me," she whispers.

Theo turns back at that—just slightly. Not enough for Annabelle to notice. His smile never falters.

But his eyes do.

And that's when the panic hits.

13

Theo

The new espresso machine I own isn't as good as the last one, and I make a note to tell Michael to upgrade. I may have kicked away every inherited toxic trait from my father, but we agree on a few things. Good coffee, good Scotch, and medium-rare steaks. Everything else, he can go fuck himself.

I glance down at a voicemail notification from my mother, and debate for a split-second on playing it. My pulse ticks against my neck until I toss the phone on the desk. This is message number five this last month, and if I don't respond soon, she'll pull some shit like barging into my workplace with a steely smile and loud voice, demanding to see me. But right now, I can't. Especially after seeing Olivia last week.

Every time I encounter a female student my father victimized, rage simmers inside until it nearly explodes. I've met with Olivia at least a dozen times now, and even though she battled through my father's terror, and is braving to go public, she's still shaken to her core.

When she asked to meet me recently at a hotel where my father used to take her, I didn't hesitate. Her therapist thought revisiting the space with someone she trusted might help her reclaim a sense of control. She wanted absolute secrecy, and I honored that. I didn't even tell Anna I'd taken the afternoon off.

But in the hotel elevator, the severity of the situation ransacked her. She clung to me like she was drowning. And I get it—she wanted to feel safe when my father made her feel unsafe. But when she tried to kiss me . . . fuck. She's a fragile, confused woman, broken and shattered by my father, and I had to calmly explain, again, that I'm engaged.

I know I'm doing the right thing. But I'm making these women relive some of the most traumatic parts of their lives. Does the end truly justify the means? Is this really about seeking justice on their behalf, or is it about me, and my need to destroy my father?

My mind shifts to Lexie. I run my hands down my face. Not even five weeks in, and she's making me paranoid as fuck. At the hotel, she kept asking if I'd been there before. So much so that I'd convinced myself that maybe she'd seen me there. But that's impossible. I would've felt her presence a mile off.

Still, Lexie does this—she slips past my logic and invades my otherwise rational thoughts.

I need her out of my head.

My phone knocks against the table as it buzzes. Anna.

Christ. I should be focused on Anna, my future wife for God's sake, and not some venomous, torturous minx.

"You hate me forever, don't you?" Anna says when I answer.

"Why, because you're ditching me for dinner with your girlfriends, and I'll be stuck in New York meeting with hotel managers and learning how to do the foxtrot?"

Anna's sweet giggle comes over the phone. "It's not the *foxtrot*, Theo." And then her giggling stops. "Right? I mean, isn't it the wedding waltz or something?"

"Hell, if I know," I say, stepping to the window to look out on the city below. "You're a woman. Aren't you supposed to know this stuff?"

"You did *not* just play that card," she says. Oh, I love getting a rise out of Anna. It's one of the best parts of my day. "Say something like that again, and I'll force you to do our first dance to Beyoncé."

"Beyoncé?" I say, lifting the mug to my lips. "Did you and Lady Gaga break up?"

"I mean, both are incredible. We have to keep our options open if we choose something besides the waltz," Anna says. "Come to think of it, I've never seen you dance, so maybe—"

"And I'm telling you right the hell now, you never will."

The sound of the phone shuffling comes through the speaker. Anna whispers to someone—probably a house staff—then says, "we'll have to divide and conquer to get this wedding done on time. I'm really sorry that this dinner—*with donors*—came up last minute, but I'll take the next venue tour while you're at work."

I like to give Anna crap that being an art philanthropist basically means that she just sits around with other rich people talking about Van Gogh or some shit while eating delicious meals. But she's genuinely dedicated to the non-profit she co-runs and it often takes up more time than my practice.

I might be pretending otherwise, but I'm not upset she has to miss today's meeting. In fact, when she told me, I thought the timing was perfect. It's been a week since we saw Lexie at the hotel, and I need to see her—alone. Anna has always been the angelic light in my life, grounding me and keeping my inner demons at bay. But Lexie—she knows exactly how to push my buttons, and the way she's been playing me in our interactions has me burning with an urge to strike back.

"You know you won't be learning to dance tonight, right?" Anna says. "We won't start taking lessons until closer to the wedding date."

Fucking dance lessons. The things I do to make others happy. "I'm going to hire a dance double."

"You are insufferable. It's probably why I love you so much," she says. "What time do you have to leave for work today? Since you ditched me for dinner last night, I was going to swing by your apartment and bring you your favorite breakfast sandwich from Jennifer's House."

Dammit. Jennifer's House *does* have the best sandwiches. "Ditched you for dinner? You mean the one with you and your mom where I dodge every invasive, painful question about the most diminutive details about my day?" Anna's snort is loud because she knows it's true.

I cup my hand to block out the mid-morning sun and glance out the window at the surrounding buildings. "But sadly, I'm going to miss the breakfast of champions because I'm already in the office."

"Damn, already? It's not even seven yet."

"I know." The traffic is just starting to pick up below. The slow churn of taxis, buses, and pedestrians fills the street. As the neighborhood springs to life, I scan each face on the sidewalk. "I wanted to get ahead on some paperwork before the clinic opened."

"Jesus Christ, you work too much," she says.

"Honestly, it's not that bad." I lift the mug of subpar coffee to my lips. "You should've seen me during med school."

"I *did* see you. You were an asshole."

I laugh. She's not wrong—medical school hours are brutal. The weight of it nearly broke me. One would think growing up an Astor would've prepared me for that kind of pressure, and in some ways it did. Being the best, *the golden child* as my family painted me, the one my dad paraded in front of his colleagues with a slap on the back and a half-assed remark about following in his footsteps, came with suffocating expectations. The hours I worked back then is what drove my need for control. They were what filled the void after my passion—*my addiction*, the one thing that quieted my mind—was gone.

"Thank you, seriously," Anna says. "You have no idea how much I appreciate this."

What she isn't saying is that the wedding—and all the attention around it—makes her uncomfortable. We've known each other since elementary school. I know her better than anyone. Yes, she's a Barlowe, but out of her entire family, Anna's the one who stays furthest under the radar, skipping public events and donating anonymously. Even as a teenager, she refused to be in family holiday photos. She always joked she was like Sharon and Ozzy's eldest daughter, the one everyone forgets exists. So, her detachment from the wedding planning doesn't shock me.

"Oh! Also, our families reached a guest count," she says. "Can I get a drum roll please . . ."

My back tenses. "I'm scared to ask."

"Six hundred."

"Are you kidding?" I don't know why I'm surprised—our families thrive on adoration. I'm shocked it's not in the thousands. Still, six hundred is absurd. No one has that many friends. The wedding is becoming exactly what Anna and I feared: a semi-formal networking event.

When Lexie described her ideal wedding—just her, the groom, and the lake as their witness—my stomach twisted. Once I pushed past that, it sounded perfect. Intimate. Serene. It wouldn't be a show for six hundred goddamn people like our parents want.

"I know . . ." she says, then pauses. "Are we moving too fast? Maybe we should rethink—"

"We can't." There's too much riding on this wedding—too many interests at stake. But her silence tightens something in my chest. The sigh that follows tells me everything.

Did Lexie say something to her last week at the hotel? They claimed they were just talking about family but what if there was more to it? I haven't forgotten the forced smiles, the way Lexie steered the conversation the moment I returned. I knew I shouldn't have let that woman out of my sight. Because if Lexie planted even a single seed of doubt . . .

Annabelle *cannot* back out of the wedding.

I scratch the back of my neck and push out a burning exhale. "Talk to me. Are you good?"

"Yeah. I just . . . I wish it could be different."

My jaw flexes. "I know. Me too."

And we leave it like that. Fifteen years' of unspoken words, of conversations we refuse to have, of familial pressure we continue to endure. But we know how it is. I'm an Astor and she's a Barlowe and we can't fight the rules we were born into.

"Have you decided about Sunday?" she asks.

"No idea what you're talking about." I roll the chair up to the window and blink against the rising sun beams.

"*Theo.*" Annabelle's voice turns stern, which is honestly kind of cute. She's like a kitten pretending to be a lion, and sometimes that's my favorite version of her. "You need to talk to your mother. If all of . . . *this* . . . is going to work, you need at least one conversation."

Anna doesn't elaborate on what "this" means, but I know.

The wedding. The joining of two families, old-school Godfather-style. The Astor family with the shipping heiress mother and brilliant sociopathic father merging with the Barlowes of hedge fund and investment empires to create one super-family.

Our families have been unusually hands-off so far, which surprises us both—but that restraint won't last. They'll want reassurance soon. Proof that the Astors and the Barlowes will finally be bound in marriage without any further delay.

"Theo," she repeats, with an even sharper edge to her tone. "You can't ignore her forever."

I run my hands along my jaw. "Can't I?"

As far as I'm concerned, my mother's complicit in my father's behavior. She knows. She has to. She's too smart, too powerful not to see what he does—and she lets him do it anyway. The rest of the family follows her lead, pretending he isn't a narcissistic monster, giving him the freedom to carry on untouched.

So, no, I don't need to talk to her.

"Fine, I'll think about it," I finally say to my fiancée, knowing damn well there's no way in hell I will. Besides, I'm meeting with a journalist on Sunday who's agreed to help me with my investigation, and my family can't find out what I'm planning.

Motion outside the window catches my attention and I lean forward, squinting. "Hey, I've got to run. I hear a nurse, and I need to grab him before the patients arrive."

"Okay, sounds good," she says. "I'll call you tonight after

dinner and you can let me know your thoughts on the venue tour with Lexie."

After we hang up, I reach for my camera with its telephoto lens, and a sense of peace settles over me as I spot movement across the street.

The studio apartment is finally mine after three long months of waiting. I moved in last week and I'm already sleeping better than I have in years. This place will become a refuge, a safe haven—far enough removed from everything else to let me focus on what actually matters.

A flicker of guilt surfaces at the thought of Annabelle. I haven't told her about the apartment. But she wouldn't understand this insatiable itch that's corroding my insides or why being here is the only thing that quiets it. I can't tell her how for years Lexie hovered, darkened, *ruined* moments in my life. Lexie, the one I couldn't be with, the one I couldn't fuck, the one who toyed with me like I was her puppet; she was the master puppeteer. I chased her forbidden taste, her smell, those green eyes, and full lips. Sometimes the ache of needing to be close to her, to be *in* her, flooded me to the point where I couldn't breathe, couldn't even fucking think. I'd drown myself in sex and boxing and running because Lexie *was always fucking there.* Unattainable. Untouchable. It was an insatiable thirst that nothing—no woman, no sweating, no academic accomplishments—could quench.

Lexie's poison. She might be the sweetest, most intoxicating kind, but she's still poison. And I need to neutralize that.

I pace the studio, taking in every inch. Scratched hardwood floors. A dark leather couch. A chair that faces the window. A table pulled close beside it. It's perfect.

The neighborhood is decent enough. A small bakery on the corner, a grocery store a block away, a smoke shop. But it's not the neighborhood I'm interested in.

It's the neighbor.

14

Lexie

By the time Saturday rolls around, my head spins with everything that's happened this past week. I sent Sydney in my place to meet Theo at a venue (*he needs to know he's not always in control*). I passed off my assistant duties for my other wedding to a junior coordinator to focus solely on the Astor/Barlowe wedding, Theo and Annabelle locked on the invitation design, and Annabelle left for Italy.

Annabelle left for Italy.

When I started my plan to take down Theo, it wasn't like I had phases in mind. I only had an end goal. But *had* I developed a project plan, one key milestone would've been getting Annabelle physically away from Theo. Less than six weeks after he slithered back into my world, his fiancée leaves for another country.

My fingers and toes are crossed that she gets the clarity she needs to recognize Theo will bring nothing but pain.

My phone pings, my heart skips. I swipe open the Google alert I set on Theo, but it's just an article about him appearing as a guest at another medical conference. My pulse settles.

Still, I know he has secrets. Ever since I saw him at the hotel with that woman and he avoided my probing questions, I've been desperate to find out who she is—and how many more women sit in his contacts. If I were a gambler, I'd put good money on it being a lot.

I slide into slim jeans and a fitted white sweater and zip up my heeled boots. I know I'm playing with fire—but that's the point.

I'm supposed to meet Theo in an hour to tour another venue. Instead, I plan to watch him first. From a distance. Unseen. I want to see how he moves when he thinks he's alone, what slips when his guard drops.

He won't like it when he realizes I'm not where I'm supposed to be. His need for total control will be his downfall.

I can already picture it—him pacing, checking his phone, simmering at my unanswered phone calls, the same way I imagine he did earlier this week when I stood him up. I can't pull that again—not with my job on the line. And yet, I know he won't run to Sydney. I'm certain he enjoys this game between us too much to end it that way.

I might be playing with fire but I'm not reckless. I scoped out the venue days ago. It has potential. I'll show up just in time, armed with a perfectly reasonable "last-minute emergency" that caused my delay.

For now, I'm going to leave my apartment, treat myself to

the city's best strawberry crepes a few blocks away, and savor the knowledge that after years of feeling like a shadow trailing someone else's light, I finally have the upper hand—and I'm not ready to let it go.

By the time I bounce down the four flights of stairs to the sidewalk, I'm giddy with purpose. When I throw open the door, a crisp breeze hits my cheeks and I shiver. I tug my scarf tighter, blink against the fluttering snowflakes, turn the corner, and . . . What. The. Fuck.

Theo.

Leaning against a black SUV, his arms crossed, his eyes narrowed. My breath locks so hard in my throat, I cough.

"Good morning," he says. *Casually.* Like he's not standing outside of *where I fucking live.*

The snow-covered bushes and branches meld together, the street cars distort, ringing thunders in my ears. How the hell does he know my address? "What are you doing here?"

His face. That smug smile. Something hot and reckless flares in me, an urge to wipe it right off him. "Well, the last time we were supposed to meet, imagine my surprise when Sydney showed up saying you could no longer make the appointment. We don't have a lot of time to plan this wedding, after all, and I thought it'd be terrible for you to be . . . held up again." *He knew.* I don't know how, but he fucking knew. "So, I thought it best to collect you myself—just to avoid any further issues."

This motherfucker. He's outside of my *apartment*—my *home*—smiling like he's doing me a favor.

I hate him.

"How did you know where I live?" I ask, but does it really matter? He's here and ruining my entire morning.

"Sydney gave me your address." When I raise my eyebrows, he says, "I told her I'd send a car so you didn't have to take the subway."

I cross my arms and refuse to thank him for the gesture.

"We have places to be, so please, hop in." His lips quirk into the faintest grin. "Unless you're afraid to be alone with me, of course."

"I'm not *afraid* of you."

"Excellent," he says, opening the door. "It'd be rather difficult to maintain a professional relationship if otherwise."

This asshole wants fear. I can see that now. But I refuse to give it to him.

I hold my ground. I'll get into the car eventually—I'm not an idiot. But I won't let him think he's won, even if, for the moment, he has.

"You came all the way to the Bronx from Tribeca to give me a ride?" And now, it's my turn to grin. I glance at the street cars moving behind him and dig a heel into a sidewalk crack. "If I didn't know any better, I'd think you were obsessed with me." I dare him to deny this as he's waiting outside my *fucking home*.

He lowers his chin, boring his gaze into mine. "Trust me, if I were obsessed, you'd know it."

I arch a brow. "Then what would you call showing up outside of my home?"

He eases and a glint of amusement cuts across those demonic eyes. "I'd call it polite."

"Polite?"

A full dimpled smile spreads across his face. "Helpful, even."

Ugh, he's phenomenally irritating. He carries himself with such delusional confidence he could run for office.

"You mentioned in our first meeting that you're an *assistant* and not a lead," he says.

My back stiffens.

"In fact, you were adamant I knew about your lack of experience, and how overwhelmed you'd be managing my account." He casually dusts a few snowflakes from his sleeve and steps closer. "I just want to help."

Everything in me flares. How dare he use my words against me? "I don't need it."

"And yet, you couldn't make our first solo meeting."

"I sent Sydney, *my manager*, in my place," I snap.

"Exactly my point. You sent in your boss to handle your responsibility."

I cross my arms. "If you're seeing a patient and are called away on an emergency, would you not refer them to another doctor, especially one who has more tenure? Or would you just let them sit in pain until you could take their appointment?"

His flexed jaw and narrowed eyes tell me I hit the exact nerve I was aiming for.

And it's delicious. This tension between us shouldn't feel

this good. But like a moth to a flame, I can't help but want to see how far I can push before he finally snaps.

I need to have a serious talk with myself about my body's infuriating habit of betraying me where Theo is concerned.

"I would *never* jeopardize a patient's well-being."

"And I won't jeopardize your wedding." *Doesn't mean I won't find ways to take you down.*

"And yet, you're delayed in your communication or unresponsive. I'm sure since you're still learning you don't realize common client courtesy is informing me ahead of time that you wouldn't make our meeting." His condescending tone ruins any glory I felt from standing him up that day. "That was incredibly unprofessional. Looks like you might need some guidance. Maybe even some handholding as you navigate your career."

No matter how hard I try to not react, my nostrils flare. "You're the client," I say, pushing the words through my gritted teeth. "I don't need *guidance.* Whether or not you like it, I am the one in control. Not you."

He takes another step forward. "In control, huh? I think you must have misunderstood our previous interactions. I am always the one in control. In fact, from here on out, I'll be calling the shots of where we go and who we meet."

"I didn't realize you were so skilled at wedding planning. Is this your first marriage? Have there been others? Or are you planning more in the future?" *Like with that woman from the hotel.* The more his eyes taper, the more my pulse spikes. My mouth twitches into a grin. "I think—"

Theo grabs my shoulders, flips me around and slams me against the SUV with such ferocity that my breath is knocked out of me. "What the—"

An electric bike zooms past where I was *just* standing, so lightning fast the wind swooshes my hair. My body freezes, confined between the car and Theo. Everything around me stills. The traffic, the pedestrians, the city. The only sound is my heartbeat thudding in my ears. Theo's sturdy, firm body crushes me, steals my air, but it's comforting and warm like a weighted blanket. Murder fills his eyes as his gaze flicks at the bike rider but then he looks back at me. *Really* looks at me. When his eyes lock with mine, something shifts. His eyebrows cinch, moving from rage to concern. The air is broken with nothing but rattled breaths and throats swallowing. My heavy pulse thuds in my ear, in my chest, and I swear even through our jackets I can feel his pounding heartbeat against mine. He's so close that his warm breath fogs the air above my head. One second passes. Then another. Time stretches as everything around us mutes. It takes until now to realize that my hands are gripping his waist.

His entire body is flattened against mine. Entire. Body.

Holy shit. His cock hardens and twitches against me and I freeze.

Almost like he realizes what just happened at the same time as me, he drops his hand and takes a wide step back. I immediately feel a cold void.

I shouldn't be disappointed.

"You okay?" he says, scanning me from head to toe.

My insides melt. Theo just saved me, and my mind stutters, trying to reconcile the contradiction. This man I hate, who I'm fairly certain hates me back, who infuriates me, and who I fully intend to destroy, just shielded me.

"Yes." I clear my throat. "Yes, thank you. That guy came out of nowhere, huh?"

This is what I say, because I don't know what else to do. Theo's no longer pressed against me, but a strong, electric current between us remains. It's palpable, heated, and confusing.

And so very fucking wrong.

15

Lexie

After the near accident, Theo and I keep a safe distance from each other as we wrap up the first venue visit much faster than anticipated. His touch lingers on my skin and I feel betrayed by own body—the effect of the man I loathe, the man about to be married, is infuriating.

"We have two hours before the next visit," I say as we step outside. "We can meet back up, or go through more wedding items, or . . ."

"Or we could grab lunch because I'm starving."

Lunch. *Oof.* I'm so not ready to engage in conversation with this man for the next hour. "Sure."

"I know a great spot. You'll love it," he says like he knows me, but he doesn't. He knows nothing, remembers nothing about me. But a guy like him probably assumes everything he likes, every woman will, too. At least he's predictable.

What's next, throwing his jacket over a puddle so I don't get my shoes wet?

And yet, he shielded me with his body. So, who really is Theodore Astor?

His driver brings us to a nearby place. Outside the restaurant, Theo holds open the door. It's such a simple gesture, but it makes me a little weak in the knees. Don't get me wrong, I'm a strong independent woman who doesn't *need* a door held open for her. But my last boyfriend used to slip through first, barely holding it so it didn't slam my face.

I *hate* that it feels nice.

The atmosphere here is lovely. Beautiful cedar tables, large cushy leather seats, wine menus as thick as the bible. I don't even know how we got a table at a place like this so quickly, but I know by now that what Theo wants, he gets.

After the hostess seats us, Theo shrugs out of his jacket. Everything about him screams perfection. Broad shoulders. Defined pecs. The way the fabric of his shirt pulls taut when he leans back in his chair. He rolls up his sleeves, exposing dark tattoos and the subtle ridges and veins nestled below black forearm hair. God, I hope he never finds out what those tattoos do to me. The way his hands could work me, own me, wrap around my neck—

"Lexie?"

Shit.

"What did you say?"

If he caught me looking at him in the most unprofessional way, he doesn't react. *Shake it off.* I'm just experiencing a bout of cognitive dissonance after cheating death earlier. I'll be back to normal in no time.

"I asked if you've ever been here before," he says as he flips open the menu.

"Oh, ah, nope. Excited to try it, though." I scan the menu and exhale through the ridiculous prices while reminding myself that I'm out with a client, so I can expense the meal.

"Hey there, welcome," the server says with a bright smile. "What can I get you two love birds?"

"Oh God no. We are not here, together, like . . . that," I say, quickly. "This is a business lunch."

"Oops." The server grins and poises his pen. "Let me tell you about the lunch specials. Today we have buttered gnocchi . . ."

After we put in our order, I squeeze lemon into the ice water, and glance at Theo across the table. "Sounds like Annabelle arrived in Italy, safely, huh?"

"Yes, she did," he says, his voice, his face, everything, neutral. He should be panicking and distraught that his bride-to-be is across the world and not here to help plan *their* wedding. But he's not—and it's unsettling. "She's been contemplating going there for a few weeks. I think it'll be good for her, even though she's a little worried not everything will get done on time."

The server places a breadbasket in the middle of the table. Theo hands me the basket before he reaches for a roll himself.

"I have no doubt we have things under control," I say.

"Agreed," he says as he cuts a slice of butter. "Looks like we're going to be spending lots of time together, Lexie."

The bread feels lumpy in my throat. I swallow. While I wanted Annabelle away from Theo, I didn't necessarily relish the thought of spending more time with him. "Looks like it," I say, avoiding his eyes.

We settle into an easy, *much* easier than anticipated, conversation about movies, the best pizza in the city, and me nudging him that if these venues today don't work, we have to go to plan B: destination or one of the parents' properties.

He glares when I mention the latter option.

The server breaks the moment to set down our plates. "There's a question I've been meaning to ask you since the first time we met," Theo says, and my heart races at the thought that he finally remembers me. This is it. The recognition, the confrontation, everything spilling into the open—

"Tell me, am I the best client you've worked with?"

I sputter. "Really? *That's* your question?"

He nods, already cutting into his chicken. "See, I have a reputation to uphold. I can't be letting the Astor name down."

I hate that his arrogance makes me grin, and I tamper down the frustration that yet again I never mattered to him. "The jury's still out," I say, schooling my face into a mock-serious expression. "Though Annabelle did warn me I'd have my work cut out."

"Oh, I bet she did. She looks all sweet and innocent, but you can't trust anything she says."

My phone vibrates in my purse, interrupting the moment. Normally when I'm with a client, I'd silence it without a second thought. But after my mom's recent health relapse, I'm abnormally paranoid. I sneak a glance at the screen, relief pouring over me when it's only Justin. I hit decline. "Sorry about that."

"You're a popular woman. I can see why you're hard to pin down," Theo remarks. There's a faint edge to his tone, as if he doesn't *like* the fact I speak to other people. And there's a small part of me that shouldn't like this the way I do.

Before I can respond, my phone lights up on the table and I reach for it—catching Theo sneaking a glance.

I laugh softly at Justin's message, another half-baked attempt to set me up with one of the vendors he's working with on a wedding assignment. Justin is relentless in his search for a perfect mate for me.

"A new date, I presume?" This time Theo's voice is unnervingly still, and a thin line of awareness prickles the back of my neck. With any other client I'd deflect the question. But Theo isn't the type to let things go. He'd keep pushing until he got his answer.

An irrational urge sparks to test the intent behind his curiosity.

"Yes." The lie slips out easily.

Though not a total lie, as maybe tonight I should reinstall the dating apps. I've got too much unchanneled sexual energy, and it needs somewhere to go before I do something stupid.

Theo pins me with a sharp gaze before he bites into the chicken and swallows. "I imagine sitting here, with me, on a Saturday, is killing your social life."

"You're a *client*. It's my job to be here with you."

He sets his fork at the edge of his plate and crosses his arms. "So, I'm just a job?"

What can I possibly say to that? I think if Theo weren't a doctor, he'd make a good lawyer. How can I tell him that he was once my heartbreak? We have history together that he doesn't even remember. Theo has never been just a job. "Aren't I just an employee?"

"You are *not* just an employee."

An unexpected warmth zips through me. "What would you call me then?"

Slowly, his lips tug into a smirk. "Complicated."

The word flutters down like dirty snowflakes. Theo picks back up his fork and knife. When my phone rings with a vendor's name on the screen, he stops mid-cut and holds my gaze. "Do you need to take the call?"

"Probably a good idea." And I can use this excuse to escape whatever we'd just shared a few moments before. How is it that I both know this man and don't? That seven years have passed since I last saw him, and our interactions back then were minimal at best, and yet I *know* him. He wants to know that he's my first choice, that I'll sacrifice for him, that I *want* him. And I refuse to let him live in this delusion. Because no matter how surprisingly civil this day has been, I have not forgotten the woman from the hotel, or what happened in Boston.

I step away from the table, out of earshot, and confirm an appointment with a decorator for early Tuesday. I spend another minute speaking into a dead line, knowing, but really not caring, how fucking twisted it is that I'm fueled by this power trip.

I return to the table and slide my phone into my bag as I sit down. The air between us is different now—thicker, heavier. Theo's posture is relaxed, almost too relaxed, but his eyes are anything but. They track my every move, sharp and unyielding, like a predator sizing up its prey.

"You get your date lined up for tonight?" he asks, his voice low and smooth, but there's a bite beneath the surface.

I freeze at the tone before forcing a casual shrug. "Not sure that's any of your business."

His lips curve into a faint, humorless smile. "Must be nice to have so many . . . interested parties."

This is not a compliment. My stomach tightens, but I refuse to let it show. "What's that supposed to mean?"

He leans back in his chair, his fingers tracing the rim of his glass. "Nothing. Just an observation."

I want to claw his face. A silent standoff ignites as my chest burns and his eyes narrow. The waiter appears at our table, placing the bill between us like a grenade. Theo reaches for it without hesitation, but my hand shoots out, my fingers brushing his as I grab the other side.

"I've got it," I say, firmly.

Theo's grip doesn't falter. "No, you don't."

My eyes snap to his, and his intense gaze sends a shiver down my spine. "I'm not letting you pay for me," I say again, enunciating each word with a knife-sharp edge. I will *never* owe this man. Not even for a meal.

"And I'm not letting you pay for me," he counters, his voice dropping lower, almost a growl.

We're close now, leaning over the table, our faces inches apart, tension palpable. "Do you not like the idea of a woman paying for you?" I say, keeping my voice quiet, but no less cutting.

A muscle in his jaw flexes, his fingers still gripping the tray holding the bill. "No. I don't."

My lips curve into a slow, wicked smile. "Afraid of being in my debt, Theo? What do you think I'd do with that kind of power?"

His eyes darken. "I could think of worse things."

"Fair enough," I say, my voice lowering to a near whisper. "Because you should be." I say this almost to myself, but by the way he stills, I know he caught it. We stay locked in a silent battle of wills. He wants to feel like he won? Sure, I'll let him. But it's all part of the game. The more he lets his guard down, the more I can uncover his secrets.

With deliberate slowness, I release my hold and sit back, my smile never wavering.

"Fine," I say, my tone dripping with mock sweetness. "I'll let you pay. Consider me . . . indebted to you."

His expression doesn't change, but something dark and unreadable flickers in his eyes.

"Careful, Lexie," he says in a soft warning. "Debts have a way of coming due."

I stand, grab my bag, and sling it over my shoulder. "I guess we'll see, won't we?" I quirk up a brow in a silent challenge. "Thanks for lunch."

Without another word, I pivot and bolt away, leaving him at the table, the bill in his hand and a storm brewing in his eyes. God, it feels good. Too good. For years this man held the power. Back in school. With my future. My career. These little wins would make my nineteen-year-old-self proud.

A small, satisfied grin grows as I exit the restaurant and reach outside. Finally, I have the last word. We still have more venues to visit, but I've decided, right now, that I'll go on my own to pre-vet.

I barely reach the end of the block to grab a cab when a firm hand grips my arm. I spin and look into Theo's rage-filled eyes.

"We're not finished," he snaps, his cheeks red, his gaze cutting into me. "No one walks away from me. *No one.* Do you hear me?"

Oh God, he's pissed and I fucking eat it up. And he still has no idea what's in store. "We're done for the day. I think it's best that I visit the rest of the venues myself and send you my thoughts."

"We are finished when I decide we are. The sooner you accept that I'm the one in control, the easier this will be for you," he says, still gripping my arm with enough force to display his dominance, without doing any damage. I hate the way his touch lights me up. "I don't know who you think you are, but you're not nearly as smart as you think."

At his words, a searing pain shoots through my chest. Just like back then, he didn't think I was smart enough, or capable enough, or worthy enough. Nothing has changed. I rip my arm away from his grip.

"Do you even remember me?" I ask, my voice sharp.

He cocks his head. "What?"

A gut-wrenching few seconds pass and heat fills my cheeks. I hate that instead of rage fueling me, my old fear of being insignificant takes hold. "Do you remember me?"

His eyes narrow as his breath fogs. "What are you talking about?"

Stay strong. "You really don't remember me?"

Faint lines crease the corners of his eyes as he squints, like he's racking his brain. But other than that, his face shows absolutely zero recognition. He crosses his arms and his face softens. "Were you a patient of mine?" he asks at last. "I treat a lot of people. If someone isn't a regular patient, it's not always easy to place them."

A patient? My belly sinks. "No." I swallow the stickiness from my throat and shove my hands into my pocket before they do something reckless like slap him. For better or worse, he singlehandedly altered the course of my life and, clearly, I barely register in his. "We, went to the same university."

"You went to St. Benedicts?" he says, still squinting, still studying, still not fucking remembering. "Were you . . . wait . . . were we in the same med school?"

The contents of the Cesar salad roll in my stomach and I absolutely regret ordering extra anchovies. I want to grab him by the collar and scream that he ruined my life. "No, I was in a different program," I say, losing the battle to keep my strength. "And . . . I, um, worked for your father." *And spent a year dreaming of the things your fingers could do to me.* "Back then, my name was Gemma. I go by my middle name now."

If he has a question about the name change, he doesn't ask—which, for anyone else, would be the obvious thing to do. But Theo's never been straightforward. He's calculating, brilliant, and sadistic. If he's not asking, it's for a reason.

Every detail of the moment my university career imploded is burned into my brain. I'd been called into the Dean's office, where Dr. Astor and a few faculty members sat with stern expressions making my twenty-year-old legs tremble. They told me to sit and lamented about my egregious abuse of the trust the Dean had given me. But it was Dr. Astor's look that crushed me the most. After two semesters as his student aide—his *prized* student aide, as he'd often said—the spark in his eyes dimmed, replaced by disappointment.

Even today, I can still remember the panic seeping in when they showed me evidence that I'd somehow stolen the final exam for my course—my university badge was used to log into the Dean's computer, my exam was pre-populated with the correct answers, and my silver heart keychain with my name inscribed (which I'd lost a few weeks before) was sitting on the Dean's desk.

I pleaded. I cried. My voice shook as I insisted it wasn't me. I pushed through my fear, facing people who were so much more powerful, *better*, than me. I knew they saw my working-class neighborhood in the way I carried myself, my second-hand clothes, and the donated backpack slung over the chair.

I couldn't change any of it. But I had to try.

That day, I swallowed my anxiety and said I had a plan to clear my name.

The log-in timestamp on the Dean's computer matched almost exactly with when I'd run into Theo on campus, outside of the Behavioral Science building. I could never forget that moment—after nearly a year of fantasizing all the wicked things he might do to me, and only a week after I'd canceled seeing him to attend the event with Dr. Astor, I finally worked up the nerve to ask him out instead . . . only to be swiftly and brutally rejected.

To clear my name, I had to reopen that wound and do the one thing I'd sworn I never would for Theodore Astor: beg. I asked him to verify my alibi with the university board.

He'd looked at me with unfeeling eyes and said he had absolutely no idea what I was talking about.

Heat flooded my cheeks. "But . . . we talked . . . in the courtyard. I, um, asked you out."

And then he laughed. I'll never forget it—sharp, demeaning. The kind of laugh a star graduate student, cushioned by wealth, pedigree, and privilege, gives an undergrad scholarship girl like me. I wanted to disappear.

I'd spent my entire life playing by the rules, and they were tearing my future away for something I didn't do. Tears streamed down my face as I told him they were going to expel me. He'd shrugged—like I was nothing more than an inconvenience.

But when he turned to walk away, I saw his mouth turning into a smug, private smile.

And I understood. He remembered our interaction that day. More than that—he'd done it. I didn't know how or why, but I *knew* with absolute certainty that he'd played a part in framing me.

Theo clears his throat, snapping me back to present day. "I'm sorry, I don't remember you," he says, dropping his crossed arms and sounding only marginally softer than he did a moment ago. "It's a small world that you worked for my father. Though my father's probably had a hundred interns and aides over the years; it's hard to keep track."

I flash back to my Psych 101 and 201 courses that I loved so much, hours spent studying the physical tells of lying: fidgeting, averted eyes, delayed responses. Theo shows none of it. Just a faint, almost apologetic look.

Maybe he's ruined other lives over the years and I'm just another notch on the destruction belt. Maybe he's done *worse.*

Seven years later, the memory still burns and he doesn't remember a thing.

I'm going to be sick.

"I guess you made more of an impression on me than I ever did on you," I say with a self-deflecting grin. "Honestly, it was so long ago it doesn't even matter."

His tense shoulders drop, and his face relaxes. "I'm sorry." He reaches out, resting a large, warm hand on my shoulder, his bourbon-brown eyes earnest for once. "Med school is like fraternity Rush Week—except it lasts for years. I'm pretty sure by the time I graduated, I barely knew my own name. It's nothing personal."

When he pulls his hand away, the heat of his touch lingers, and it makes me rage. *Fine.* So, he doesn't remember me. I'll swallow the sharp stab to my ego and let his lack of recognition go.

But I promise you, after all of this is done, there's no fucking way he'll ever forget me again.

16

Lexie

Hi Annabelle and Theo,

Lots of new developments—

Backspace.

Hey friends,

I just wanted to—

Backspace.

Hey Guys! Some news—

What's my problem? I slam my laptop shut, press my thumbs against my forehead and push out a long, unsatisfying breath.

Jesus Christ, I need to snap out of this funk. I should be thrilled that earlier this week the mother of all calls came in that Annabelle's parents rented a beautiful, hundred-year-old Victorian mansion three hours outside the city with sprawling grounds that can easily accommodate the guest count.

But even with that win, my thoughts keep drifting back to my last conversation with Theo. It's been over a week since I confronted him and watched for any signs of lying.

He fucking ruined my life, and he doesn't remember me.

I refuse to dwell on this any longer and head to the breakroom to make what I'm certain is my fifth coffee of the morning. At the table, I message a couple guys back who DM'd me on a dating app, and start my daily lunch break routine of scouring social media for anyone connected to Theo. Last week, I contacted the St. Ben's alumni office, convinced them I was the assistant of a large donor who was organizing a university fundraiser, and the school gave me the names of all the students in Theo's graduating class. It's a shot in the dark, but every lunch break, I pull up each of their social media accounts and scroll through all public photos, praying that one contains the woman from the hotel. Even though she looked much younger than Theo, I keep hoping there's a connection to someone he knows.

"Hey, what's up?" Justin says as he tears into a protein bar. "You look frazzled. Even by your standards."

"Such a dick," I say, and throw a straw in his general direction, but, just like everything else this week, it falls two feet short of its intended target. "Ugh. I can't even get that right."

Justin's playful smile drops, and he points at the high-top table. I slug over to it like I'm dragging a cinderblock tied to my ankles and drop my forehead against the cool top. I don't want to do this anymore. Two months in, and Theo's breaking me. Again.

A moment later, a chair squeaks next to me, and a cup of coffee slides into view. "What can I help with?"

I'm not sure Justin can help untangle the chaos rattling around in my head about Theo. Especially not when I can't forget how it felt to have his body pressed against mine.

I pull my head off the table and take a sip of the coffee. "Everything just feels . . . overwhelming right now."

This is one more thing weighing on me. I want this promotion—I need it—but there's so much more to do than there was when I was an assistant. I feel like I'm paddling frantically without getting anywhere.

"I know. But it's got to feel good that the venue piece is done, right?" he says, bringing the mug to his mouth. "I still don't understand why they aren't having it at one of the parents' estates. We're talking about two families with the combined wealth of some entire countries."

"I know, right?" Trust me, the very last thing I wanted to do was see Dr. Astor in his home after he was part of the committee who voted for my expulsion, but my guess is that he probably doesn't remember me. Just like his son. Regardless, the hours spent chasing venues could've been spent on a million other things on the wedding to-do list had they just agreed to their families' estate.

Justin pops a piece of bar in his mouth. "The bride seems pretty cool, but my God, that dude is intense, right?"

I look over my shoulder like Theo might have just walked in. Intense is certainly a way to describe him.

"He's hot as fuck, though," he whispers.

"Oh, I hadn't really noticed," I say, aiming for nonchalance but knowing that I've missed completely.

He laughs. "You are so full of shit. Please, it's insulting that we've worked together this long and you still try to pull that with me." Justin looks like he's going to say more on the subject, then veers in another direction. "You know what might be good for you?" he says. "Going on a date. Getting laid. Getting drunk. Something. You need to let loose."

He's not wrong. But now that Theo's back in my life, it's like my body's tethered to him again, refusing to budge. I'm not sure a hook-up will satisfy anything at this point.

"God, why can't I just find someone like Dylan?" I say, holding the mug between my palms. "I swear your relationship is what greeting cards are made from."

Justin grins. "You're not wrong. I got lucky." He claps off the crumbs from his hands, crumples the wrapper, and gives my hand a squeeze. "You know the right guy's out there waiting for you. Just have to give him a chance."

The last person I tried to give a real chance to is the man whose wedding I'm planning.

"Hey, Lexie," Amanda's voice from the hall cuts through my thought downward spiral. "Sydney wants to see you in her office for an update on the Barlowe wedding."

I give Justin a hug of gratitude, finish my coffee, and make my way down the hall, pushing away untoward thoughts of Theo as I try to do my job.

Sydney's been off-site a lot lately, and with my busy schedule, we haven't had a chance to sync in-person for what feels like weeks. I knock on her open door, and she waves me in. "You wanted to see me?" I ask.

"Yes. I can't find the latest update on your project plan and I don't have time to chase you down for all the details."

Great. All I need is Sydney stressed out, too. "I'm in the middle of updating it now." I'm lying. I hadn't planned on doing that until tomorrow when I had an hour of free time. "I curated a list of caterers who'll work outside of the city, gathered sample menus, and confirmed the county laws for a one-day alcohol permit. We've also narrowed down the colors to three sets and locked on invitations."

"Good," she says with a firm nod. "Did you call the table and chair rental place?"

I swallow. Dammit. Not yet, because there are literally not enough hours in the day. I know I'm ready to be lead, but there's an endless number of details and so little time to get everything sorted. "Oh, um, I'll get on that today."

"Perfect." Sydney nods. "You're doing great, Lexie. It's a huge, high-profile wedding and you're really stepping up. I see your efforts."

I soften. As supportive as Sydney is, she doesn't easily hand out compliments. Her smile drops when she looks at a ping on her phone.

"Is everything okay?" I ask.

It takes her too long to respond.

"Sydney?"

A heavy exhale leaves her ruby red lips. "Let's just say it's *very* good that we've landed a two-million dollar client." The words are so weighty I feel like they're stuck in the air. "I trust you're doing everything possible to ensure the couple is happy—we can't afford for them to back out."

The words spark a flicker of guilt through me. Yes, I'm doing everything I can to make them happy. *For now.* But I'm counting on Annabelle to back out. Once I reviewed the legal contract and saw that the couple is required to pay all fees if they cancel the wedding within thirty days of their wedding date, I finally breathed a sigh of relief. Sydney cannot revoke my promotion if we collect our fees.

Which means, Annabelle can leave Theo for a better life, I still get my promotion, and he will be destroyed.

For the first time today, a genuine smile builds.

I turn to leave the office, then pause. "Hey, from now on, could you maybe not give my home address to clients?"

Sydney thumbs up her dark frames and her eyebrows crease. "What are you talking about?"

Well, this is awkward. I don't love calling out my manager's mistakes to her face. "When you gave my address to Theo so he could pick me up for our meeting. I just . . . I mean . . . the intention was nice, but in the future, please don't."

The ticking on her wall clock, the phones ringing in the

lobby, and street traffic twenty floors below are the only sounds as she studies my face. “Lexie,” she says, after a long moment. “I didn’t give *anyone* your address.”

17

Theo

The stairway to the studio apartment smells like musty concrete and unwashed floors, lit just well enough to avoid a lawsuit. It's dark, dank, and gives off the distinct vibe that someone was once murdered here. I step onto the fifth-floor hallway, passing the neighbors' doors with the sounds of couples arguing, TVs blaring and more. I hate this depressing-as-fuck building. But the second I unlock my door and step inside the studio, everything loosens. My chest relaxes. I can breathe.

I fucking love this studio.

Lexie's been putting me off for two weeks. I told myself there was still a lot to organize and surely she needed me present for something. But the need to see her gnawed at me until I broke my own rules and offered lunch, a drink after work—anything. But she kept responding with the bullshit line "I don't want to waste your time" over email, insisting we handle things offline or over the phone.

I don't want her anywhere but in front of me where I *know* exactly what's she doing. Not because I can't resist her dangerously alluring green eyes or that lying, sinful mouth I can't stop thinking about—but because distance gives her too much freedom.

I keep all the lights off, toss my keys on the countertop, grab a protein shake from the refrigerator, and make my way to the window. I hook a finger around the sheer curtain to look across the way. It's dark, quiet, empty.

The clock shows its ten after six. She should be home any minute now.

I grab my phone and read the latest email from Olivia. She's still on the fence about coming forward, even though I have four other women who will publicly corroborate a similar story, and another five still debating. I exhale sharply. The journalist I'm working with relayed the power of numbers. The more voices, the bigger the story, the larger the take-down. I want to push Olivia, just a little, tell her I'll protect her, but deep down, I understand. I really do. My father holds a ton of social capital, my mother holds financial capital, and it's scary as fuck for those who don't.

Instead of pushing, I respond saying I understand—that she should take her time. I've been investigating for years. Even if it takes a decade, I will find a way to see my father answers for what he's done.

My phone rings. Seeing my mother's name, I click it off. No more than a few moments pass when it rings again, this time with Michael on the other line.

"Yes?" I ask, peeking back out the window. Still no Lexie.

"Sir." There's a hesitation in his voice that I don't like. "Your family would appreciate it if you could check in."

I pinch the bridge of my nose. "So, they've got you playing messenger now? Could you just tell them to fuck off? That'll be my check-in."

An audible sigh. "I know they can be . . . challenging. But avoiding their calls will only delay the inevitable."

My shoulders drop. He's not wrong. "Fine. I'll call them soon." I click off the phone before I take my words back.

I was ten, maybe eleven, the first time I heard a rumor about my dad and a student. At the beginning, there were hushed accusations from my mother and passive dismissal from my father, brushing it off as a *gross exaggeration*. He became more infrequently present in my life, failing to show up to baseball games after promising me he would, convincing me that I'd imagined things even though I'd seen him leave the house dressed up.

Then there were more rumors. I spent a lot of time on campus growing up. My mother loved the attention that came with being married to the *brilliant, gifted* Dr. George K. Astor, parading her *golden boy* to his colleagues whenever she could.

I remember the first time I saw something. The way the student looked at him—idealistic, starry-eyed. The careful, manipulative softness in his voice. How he straightened too quickly, pulled his hand from her back when we entered his office. The defiant look he gave my mother as she greeted the girl with an overly bright, tightly wound *thrilled to meet you*. She knew something was wrong. So did I.

But when I started college, there was no escaping it. I avoided my father when I could—but part of me was trying to catch him, too. I went down an obsessive rabbit hole of tracking his movements and those of his students. I had to know how many innocents he'd manipulated.

Some of his student aides went on to graduate. Some dropped out shortly after their appointments ended. But then there were the deaths. Two girls. Three years apart. Both ruled suicides. I knew, at the deepest part of my soul, that he caused them. He fucks with minds. Preys on the weak. He'd deliberately choose to work with students without financial backing or influential parents. Only ever girls. Scholarship recipients. Young, impressionable, whose voices were easy to silence.

I glance back out the window. *Where is she?* Through studying Lexie over the past eight months, I know she likes the Indian restaurant four blocks away, seen swinging a take-out bag in her hands several times a month. Like clockwork, she picks up prescriptions at the local Walgreens a half a mile away. She's also a runner—but only in the summer.

It's the evenings I pay the closest attention to her, though. Because she's often careless, distracted when she walks home. I've only lived across from her less than a month, but more than once I've watched to confirm no one followed her inside the building, calculating how long it'd take me to race down the stairs and cross the street to reach her if something happened.

Inside her apartment, she flits between reading, watching TV and working on her laptop, sitting cross-legged on her couch in sweatpants and a hoodie. But sometimes, I catch her just staring out into the street through the window. Where does her mind go then? Work? Does she ever think about me?

The light in her apartment flickers on and my pulse stutters. I slide into my usual spot and grab the lens. As predicted, she locks the door, kicks off her shoes onto the mat, and does a full, cat-like, arched-back stretch. I like knowing her routines. It eases the tension of trying to predict what she'll do next. In about ten seconds, she'll step into the corner and return a short time later with leggings or pajamas.

And, yes ... I knew it. Pink pajamas, huh? Those are new. Cute.

Jesus Christ. Cute? I shouldn't care what she's wearing. I don't care. Not at all. I'm just watching to make sure she isn't doing something nefarious. And, to make sure she's safe. She doesn't have protection detail like Anna, and I swear she doesn't understand danger. When that electric bike nearly collided with her, the vision of her hurt, bleeding, helpless ravaged me. My heart didn't stop racing until we finally sat down for lunch.

Fuck. I need to stop letting her have this much power over me.

For half an hour, I watch through the lens as she pops dry

cereal in her mouth, stretches out on the couch, and reads a book.

This is good. She's relaxing. Not scheming or planning. There's no reason to watch her anymore. I've gotten what I need, so I should drop the lens.

Wait . . . where's she going? She makes her way from the couch towards the table tucked against the window. She tucks her t-shirt sleeves to her shoulder and reaches for the lotion, pumping some into her palm and running her delicate hands up those pale, smooth arms. Nothing is rushed. Just long lingering swipes. Is her skin as smooth as it looks? A powdered silkiness maybe, dusted with constellations of freckles? Her thumb digs circles into the top of her shoulder and her eyes flutter close. She's tired. Stressed. And as much as there's a piece of me that eats up her discomfort, there's another piece, a bigger piece, that's wants to swap my hands with hers and bring her some relief.

But she didn't want to see me for two weeks.

The camera dangles from the straps on my neck as I reach for my phone.

> Theo: You can't ignore me forever. We have a wedding to plan.

I lift the camera again, focusing through the lens. She reaches for her phone, her shoulders rising in a dramatic sigh as her eyes roll. Even in annoyance, she radiates. Talk of the wedding should jolt me into making Anna my top priority, but I can't tear my attention away from Lexie.

> Lexie: It's after hours and I'm off the clock. Can it not wait until morning?

I watch as she chews her lips, her thumbs hovering over the screen. She starts typing, then stops, her fingers manically pressing what I assume is the delete button. She takes a long sip of her drink and then types again.

I glance down at my phone.

> Lexie: Or is your highness incapable of waiting?

Her sense of humor is dangerous.

> Theo: Impatient, maybe. Incapable? Never. But I'm starting to think you like making me wait.

She reads the message, and I see the corner of her mouth twitch, a smirk threatening to break free.

> Lexie: Seeing as you've already taken up my time, what can I do for you?

Oh shit. What was I going to say?

Theo: This is an emergency. I need your advice on the color scheme. I'm thinking orange, green, and purple.

I look up into the camera just in time to see horror spread across her face.

Lexie: Okay . . . Can I ask where the inspiration came from?

Theo: Because I like it. Is that a problem?

Lexie: It's a wedding, not a Halloween party.

I can't help but grin.

Theo: So, you're saying it's a no?

Lexie: Unless you want a new wedding planner, then I'm vetoing this idea.

Theo: Fine. We'll go with sage and cream. Boring, but acceptable.

Her shoulders relax as she reads the message and takes another sip of her drink.

> Theo: But just so you know, if you keep bossing me around like this, I might have to find a way to remind you who's really in charge.

Lexie goes still as she reads my message. I watch as she shifts in her seat and brings the glass to her reddening cheek.

My hand grazes my stiffening cock.

> Lexie: Great to have a color scheme locked in. Have you run this by Annabelle? I'd like to send a confirmation email so we can get started on decorations, place settings, etc.

I haven't even asked Anna, yet. *Shit.*

> Theo: Yes. But please don't message until the morning. She's had a lot going on with her grandmother.

The three bubbles pop up and they stop. *Wait, no. What's happening?* The dopamine high I've been riding from our messages drains away. Through the camera I see she's lifted herself up from the couch and is at the door. When her hands unlock the deadbolt, my pulse drums against my chest. Who the hell is coming over at this time of night?

And then . . . *fuck.*

The person behind the door hands her a bouquet of

flowers, bigger than half her body, and a box. She sets them on her desk and pulls open the card. When she reads it, her mouth widens into a smile.

I press the lens as close to the window as I can. She grabs a knife and slices open the box, and, dammit, I need a stronger camera.

Rage starts to boil my blood at some asshole who thinks he can win her over with meaningless gifts. As if she could be bought.

She *is* the gift. The way her silky skin would feel under my hands, the way her lips would part with a gasp if I let myself take what I've wanted for so long. She's not something you throw flowers and chocolates at, begging for scraps of her attention.

She picks her phone back up and her thumbs tap against the screen. *Finally*. In a few seconds my lungs will stop compressing and my veins will shrink. I wait. I stare unblinking at my phone anticipating her reply.

Nothing.

She sets down the phone and sinks onto the couch. My body is burning. She's probably talking with that guy who called her at the restaurant and is now deliberately choosing to ignore me. My jaw tightens. Unbelievable.

I exhale. I'll give her one last chance.

Theo: I'm free this weekend to look at design proposals.

She reads the message. And still . . . nothing. She lays her head back on the couch, rests the phone against her chest, and stares at the ceiling. I can't see her face from here, I can't see what she's thinking, I can't see fucking anything. Why the hell isn't she responding?

My knee bounces as I wait to see if she'll change her mind. I can't pace because I might miss something, but my limbs are firing, screaming for movement, and yet I wait. One minute turns into two then three. I yank my phone off the desk and even though I'm screaming at myself to stop, I can't. My thumbs shoot off a message before I can reason with myself.

> Theo: We can get on a video call with Anna for her sign off if that makes you more comfortable.

Stop. Stop! I don't fucking chase women. She's toying with me. Just like back then. I let her do it to me all those years ago, and I'm letting her do it again. What the fuck is wrong with me? Everything with her is so calculated and she knows exactly what she's doing. I'm falling right into her hands. *Again.*

And so, I stop texting and wait. I wait as she closes her blinds, and I can no longer see into her space. As I settle into bed and my eyes are about to close, my hands reach out to my phone on my bedside table for one last check.

No new messages.

18

Lexie

I've never been inside *Lavendar & Frost.* As one of New York's most coveted high-end bakeries, it was never a place I could justify splurging on. The display cases are filled with the most beautiful items I've ever seen—fruit-shaped confections glazed to a mirror shine, delicate edible roses perched atop gold-crusted macaroons, cupcakes meticulously decorated and stuffed with hazelnut chocolate mousse.

I'm pretty sure this is heaven.

I arrive extra early, giving myself time to prepare for my next encounter with Theo—and to ensure he doesn't get under my skin. When he shows up, punctual as ever, I introduce him to the pastry chef handling today's cake tasting.

For once, Theo keeps his distance, behaving exactly as a client should—listening intently to the introduction, then following along as we're led to a small table tucked into the back of the café. It's perfectly normal.

With him, though, it feels *weird*.

"I've prepared a sampling that pairs well with most things. As you taste, don't just focus on the visual appeal, but really pay attention to the texture. Is it softer than you expected? Lighter? Denser? Does it crumble on your tongue . . ." The chef continues talking about flavor profiles, but I'm barely listening. Because I'm at freaking *Lavendar & Frost*. Besides, I've done enough tastings to know that for amateurs like us, it boils down to one thing: does it taste good or not?

Then the doors swing open and his assistant enters with a tray of impossibly intricate desserts. I have to swallow back a moan at how delicious they look.

Theo eyes the chef. "Did I read that you're self-taught in your craft?"

He nods and clasps his hands in front of himself. "Yes, that's right."

There's a subtle shift in his tone—apprehension, maybe, or the faint tension of someone bracing to defend his credentials. He knows this wedding is for the Barlowe family. No matter how established he is, nerves are inevitable.

"Teaching yourself an art takes a rare kind of discipline and determination. Seeing this—and the care you put into every detail—it's obvious how much heart you pour into your work. I'm impressed."

At Theo's praise, the chef's cheeks redden and he bows in thanks.

As much as I cling to the devil I know Theo is, it's moments like this that are the most lethal—the ones that suggest there might be something human buried inside the monster.

Last week when Theo and I were texting about wedding colors, my heart fluttered more than it should have at the attention he was giving me, and I forced myself to cut off communication. Clearly my heart is sabotaging my better judgment.

I thought no contact would fix this, but it hasn't. I still notice the way he looks today in jeans and a sharp black button-down.

Once the chef steps away, I snap a few photos of the desserts while Theo dives straight in without hesitation—patience is clearly not his virtue. "So many options," he says, scanning the plates. "I don't even know where to start. But I'm glad none of these are vanilla-flavored. I've never been one for just *vanilla*."

I lift the corner of my brow. "That doesn't surprise me."

Oh, God. The look he flashes me would make my knees weak if I was standing up. There's no denying this man radiates danger and sex from every pore—nothing about him suggests he'd ever be satisfied with anything plain.

But, of course, he would infer this from my response and not the fact that he has wealth, a mansion, and private chefs. The way he grew up surrounded by excess, with a palate refined far beyond most people's. Of course vanilla's not enough for him.

As we sample the cakes, silence settles between us except the faint noise of a buzzing phone that sounds from my bag.

Each vibration needles my focus, my agitation building as I resist the urge to check whether it's urgent. Across the table, I can feel something dark radiating off Theo, a coiled displeasure at the interruption, at my attention straying from him.

"For God's sake, just answer your phone." All softness evaporates. "And tell whoever the fuck it is to stop calling."

I don't appreciate the tone, but I step away from the table and take the call, ending it as quickly as I can. When I return and slide back into the chair, I offer a tight smile. "Sorry about that. Vendors just do not take no for an answer sometimes, huh?"

Theo doesn't move. Doesn't smile back. Doesn't even blink.

The air thins. My skin heats under his unyielding stare and I shift in my seat.

"From now on," he says quietly, "when you're with me, you don't answer your phone."

My head snaps up. "*What?*"

"When you're with me," he repeats, slower now, sharper, "you're *with* me. Understood?"

"You can't be serious?" God help me—my body reacts anyway. A traitorous warmth gathers low, my thighs pressing together beneath the table as I wonder what other lines he thinks he gets to cross.

Something is very wrong with me.

"Now," he says, leaning back, crossing his arms, all commanding presence and contained threat, "are you expecting any other calls? Are you working with other clients?"

I shake my head. "You're my only client. Sydney wants all my attention on you."

I want all my attention on you.

Because, eventually, Theo will slip. He has to. And when it happens, I'll be right here collecting every bit of evidence to show Annabelle.

He seems satisfied by my answer and as if the past few minutes didn't happen, he picks up a fork again and resumes eating. "Okay, let's try the raspberry one now," he says.

I bite my tongue and let it slide, reminding myself of the end goal. I pick up my fork, cut a neat corner from the cake, and slip it into my mouth. "Mmmm . . ." Tart raspberry, smooth soft filling, a salted kiss from the almond frosting melts onto my tongue. "This right here, is a ten out of ten." Like the lady I was raised to be, I dive in for one more heaping scoop. "God, that's delicious."

The corner of Theo's eyes crinkle as he laughs. "It must be. I think the whole city heard your moan."

I clap my hand over my mouth. "Stop. That's so embarrassing."

"*Never* be embarrassed to be loud about the things that give you pleasure." Why does he keep saying things like that? "Like delicious raspberry cake," he adds, breaking the spell—thank Christ—and takes another bite.

The words still land, though. Because the men I've been with have always found fault in me—in how loud I am, how much space I take up, how easily I say the wrong thing.

The last guy I dated told me to be quiet while we were

having sex. *Quiet.* Not as part of anything playful or intentional, like recklessly sneaking a quickie in a public place while making sure we don't get caught. We were alone, in the privacy of my own home—*mine*, not even his—and he wanted me to tone myself down.

Maybe someday I'll find someone who'll embrace and celebrate every part of me.

"I've been told I can be . . . too loud . . . sometimes," I say, hesitantly, "so, thank you."

He pauses for a split-second, then resumes eating, reaching over to refill my wine as if nothing's changed. But the seconds stretch, and heat crawls up my spine as mortification settles in. Why did I tell him that? It's wildly unprofessional. Reckless. I've never spoken to a client like this.

And yet, Theo is disarmingly easy to talk to when he's not being a dick. Which makes no sense, given our history.

I down a healthy glug of wine, pretending I'm not painfully aware of how awkward this suddenly feels.

"No one should make you feel small, ever," he says quietly. The leather chair squeaks under his large frame as he reaches over and lays his hand on mine. The touch is charged and electric and the palm cocooning my hand sends ripples roaring through me. *God, those hands.* They could clasp around my neck, limit my air, give me that mouthwatering, intoxicating asphyxiation that I want to experience so fucking bad with someone who knows what they're doing. Someone who understands bodies, and can read me, and my pulse and knows how much pressure is enough, but not too much.

What would they feel like, *everywhere*? My tits, my ass, my pussy? My nipples tighten as I picture those hands landing a hard smack on my ass.

I swallow back the heat in my throat and focus on the cake and wine. These thoughts are intrusive, dangerous and deeply unethical. I would never, ever act on this, but even thinking this way is wrong.

He removes his hand, but not his gaze. "From where I stand," he continues, voice low and deliberate, "there's nothing more beautiful than a woman who has a voice—and isn't afraid to use it."

My face flushes. I force my breathing to stay even while pretending this is a casual conversation and that I'm not feeling something dangerously stir low in my belly.

"That's funny," I say lightly. "Doesn't that go against the whole *I'm the one in control* image you like to project?"

One dark brow arches, amused. "There's a lot of things you don't know about me," he says. "Including how a woman's pleasure is always my number one priority."

"Oh, please."

"You don't believe me?"

I fall silent, realizing too late I've backed myself into a corner and don't know how to get out of it.

"Well, if you were my woman," he says, causing a flare of heat in my chest, "I'd start at your ankles, brushing my hands up the backs of your legs, cupping behind your knees, slowly opening them inch by inch." I clamp my legs together, fighting the temptation to respond to his words. "Then, I'd glide my palms up between your silky thighs, higher and higher, until I meet your beautiful, quivering pussy, your panties doing their best to protect you from me. But they wouldn't stop me. I'd slide them aside and take you in." His voice drops. "Beauty like this must be cherished, not rushed. So, I'd trace the pads of my fingers just outside those sensitive places until your body grows so wet with need it soaks my hand." He pauses, and I barely manage to hold back the moan threatening to break free. "By then, you'd be begging for my touch. And how could I ignore a woman in need?" His smile is pure promise. "I'd move down your body, spreading your legs as I go, breathing you in. My tongue would flutter over you—slow, reverent, worshipping—licking and sucking while you beg me to fuck you." His eyes darken. "But I won't. Instead, I'll slide in one finger, then another, stretching you until your breath hitches and your moans fill the room. Then I'll curl my fingers just right, finding that perfect spot, while my tongue teases your clit . . ."

He smirks before adding in a low whisper, " . . . until you're screaming my name."

Jesus fucking Christ. His words, combined with the stifling air, make the heat feel almost unbearable.

He clears this throat, before following up with, "And then I'd make you pancakes." As if we're just having a normal conversation at the table.

My throat rolls with a hard swallow, and I want to speak, but if I do, my voice will crack and I can't fucking have that. I grab my wine and take another hefty gulp. I hate that he's making me feel this way. I hate that he said what he said, and I hate myself for losing myself in this fantasy.

I set my glass back down and sharpen my gaze. "Wow," I say as flatly and nonchalant as I can muster. "Annabelle's a lucky woman, isn't she?"

19

Theo

What the fuck am I doing? Did I really tell Lexie what I'd do with her beautiful, perfect cunt if she were my woman? My cock stayed hard for so long after I said that, picturing what she sounds and tastes like, that I thought I'd have to dump the ice water in my lap or jerk off in the bathroom.

I need to cut this shit out, immediately. I'm fucking *engaged*, to a woman I love, with what feels like the weight of the world riding on our nuptials. Not only that, Lexie clearly did not give a fuck. Her face conveyed little more than boredom and she immediately brought up Anna. What was I hoping for? That she'd realize what she was missing? That she'd drop to her knees and wrap her lips around my cock?

Fuck.

As we eat our way through the last of the samples, the chef stops by periodically with his assistant to clear plates and check in. I'm only half listening as Lexie chatters on about all the endless wedding details still left to finalize.

" . . . and I got the most gorgeous bouquet of flowers last week, which reminds me that I need to check with Annabelle about what she's thinking for the bouquet."

Now, she has my attention. "You'll have to give her the name of the person who sent them, so she can get their recommendation."

"That's a great idea!" she says, clearly not suspicious about my comment. "Justin has great taste. I'll ask him."

"Justin." So *he's* the guy that stole her attention away from me that night. "Your *friend*."

"Yes." She gives me a faintly puzzled look. How many guys does she have wrapped around her finger? Does she play with all of them like she does with me? "I'm lucky to have him. He just *gets* me. I was having a rough day recently and he sent me the flowers and a gift to cheer me up."

Fuck. How can she always make me lose control? It's like she knows talking about other men is my weakness and I fall into her goddamn trap every time.

I *hate* the way she makes me feel.

"Are you sure it's not Justin's way of trying to get in your pants?" I mumble to myself, but Lexie hears, and she bursts into laughter. My annoyance grows.

"Well, I think Justin's husband wouldn't like that very much. And trust me, neither would Justin."

Relief floods through me. *Christ.* I need to get my head on straight. This is what happens when she gets inside my mind. I stop thinking clearly. I stop sleeping. I teeter on doing some really fucked-up shit. Thank God I didn't have to kill that Justin guy.

"Well, now I've got to know what the gift was."

"Do you, huh?" She lifts a brow and that little smirk of hers is doing something fierce to my insides. "He sent a mug that said, 'I love you so much I'd cut a bitch for you.' I bet twenty bucks Justin picked out the mug and his husband picked the flowers. They've been together since high school, like you and Annabelle."

Everything stills. I love Anna—I do. But every time I'm with Lexie, the rest of the world fades away. It's like being trapped in a cave: dark, wet, sometimes beautiful, sometimes suffocating. I'm sitting here tasting cake for my own wedding and somehow forgetting my bride entirely again. "Yeah," I say at last. "Like me and Anna."

There's so much more tangled up with Anna than Lexie could ever know, and part of me wants to spill it all and see where I'd stand with her. But I can't. Because even as we spend more time together and I begrudgingly enjoy her company, I still don't trust her.

"Are your parents excited about the wedding?" she asks, the subject change throwing me.

My jaw tightens. "I don't really talk to them."

Her head snaps up. "You don't talk to your family?"

"Not if I can help it."

"Even your dad?"

"*Especially* not my dad."

Looking at Lexie now, a part of me wonders, again, if she knew back then what she was getting into. I know it's been seven years, and it's a long fucking time to hold a grudge, but she destroyed me. When she showed up on my father's arm that night . . . my gut tightens.

Now is not the time to relive this. I need to deflect before I do or say something I regret.

Lexie has proven herself a formidable adversary—maybe even the best I've ever had. I know that. And yet, nothing about these last few moments felt like a game. The way she tugs that lip between her teeth, the way she tucks her hair back and slowly turns her wine glass—it doesn't feel like she's teasing.

The chef comes out, asks if we need anything else, and I think we both hold back a groan. After nearly two hours of cake testing, my glucose levels are probably so high they could take out a small army. We decline, and he says we are welcome to stay as long as we need.

Once he leaves, I set the fork on the plate and reach for the coffee. "Thank you for taking one for the team and trying the wine pairings." I drum my fingers on the table, enjoying the softened buzzed look spreading on her freckles.

"You're welcome. Although I'm so full, I'm not sure I can make it up the stairs to my apartment tonight. If you try to contact me later and don't get a response, please call the paramedics and let them know the damage I've done."

I smile. "You know I'm a doctor, right? You can just call me if you need."

She chuckles. Fuck me, she has a beautiful smile. The way her full, pillowy lips highlight those teeth with that same cute, slivered gap she had back when I first met her. Usually, she uses that mouth for evil. She tests me, teases me, *torments* me, but tonight, she's splintered her façade, and I shouldn't fucking like what I see.

But I do.

"Can you do some sort of stomach-resuscitating thing? Is there gut defibrillator where you rub the paddles together, yell 'clear!' and shock some of this sugar out of my system?"

And now it's my turn to laugh. "Sadly, no. Just hydrate, and if you can, move your body."

Why did I say that? I mean, it's sound medical advice. I give the same mindless advice dozens of times a day, but now all I can think about is her, in her home, moving her body, using her hands, writhing . . .

For a split-second, my eyes drop to her lips. And no. I can't do this. *We* can't do this.

But *fuck* I want to.

Buzz. Her goddamn phone shakes against the table, ruining whatever this moment is, and even though it needed to stop, a heat flares through me. "Shut off your pho—"

We both look at the screen at the same time. *My* clinic name is flashing on her screen.

"Why the hell is my clinic calling you?" I ask, and she clearly has the same question. She ignores me and taps it on.

"Hello?" she says and completely stills. "Yes, this is she. Wait, what? What happened? When?"

I know that voice. I work twice a month in the urgent care attached to my clinic and have heard that voice. "Put it on speaker," I say but she's not listening.

"Oh my God, what? Is she okay? Oh God, oh God, where are you located?" She gets up so fast that she bumps into the table and I snatch the wine glass before it smashes into her plate. Her fingers tremble as she grabs her purse and shoves the phone under her chin.

"Lexie, put the phone on speaker," I say again, firm, trying to get her to focus on me but her eyes are frantic, dashing between me, the table, and the entrance. She yanks her jacket off the back of the chair and the chair thuds into the ground.

"I'm coming, I'm coming. Where? Shit, shit, I don't know how far that is from here! Oh God, okay, okay . . . I need a cab and—"

I rip the phone from her ear and put it on speaker. "This is Dr. Astor. Who am I speaking with?"

After the urgent care triage nurse identifies herself, I ask her to tell me what's happening while Lexie stands in front of me, wobbling, and squeezing and shaking her fingers. "We have a patient, Elaina Welch, fifty-five, brought in here after fainting at work and hitting her head—"

"Is she responsive?" I ask, grabbing my jacket and leading Lexi to the entrance.

"Yes. The doctor is doing a concussion evaluation now, we'll be running labs and controlling the bleeding with sutures . . ." Lexie gasps and covers her mouth as the nurse continues to give me this information.

We hang up, I hand Lexie her phone, and she bolts out of the bakery, stuffing her arms into her jacket as she runs to flag a cab. "I have to go. Theo, this is my mom . . . she told me she wasn't feeling good and said she was all lethargic and dizzy, and I should've fucking made her go in . . ."

"Breathe, okay?" I say, grabbing her arm. "I need you to stop right now and take a breath."

"I can't!" she says, her chest rising in quick shallow breaths, and between the wine, sugar, and panic, she's in danger of passing out herself if she doesn't calm down. "Where are the goddamn cabs?"

I cup her face and drag her eyes to mine. "I'll drive you. I have my car." Fuck, *fuck* her skin feels so good underneath my fingertips. I've wondered all these years how soft it would be, but I push away the sensation. Right now, Lexie not hyperventilating is more important than me absorbing the sensation of her skin.

Her eyes frantically flicker between mine. "I . . . no . . . that's not a good idea. I need to go by myself, and . . ."

"You've been drinking. You need someone sober with you in case you need to make any decisions."

It takes a moment, her forehead cutting with worry, when she nods. I grip her by the hand and drag her down the block to the parking garage.

Inside the garage, we run down several flights, with me right at her side as she grips the railing with one hand and me with the other. I open her door to my Audi A8, then hop in the driver's seat and take off.

On the ride, I weave quick and sharp through traffic as she grips her phone to her chest. "They said she fell and hit her head. That's bad, right? It's so bad. Why does she keep falling?"

I pass a car and accelerate.

"What if it's something terrible?" Her voice trembles as she speaks. "Or, or, what if this is it, or if she's really sick and has cancer like my dad and—"

"*Lexie.*" I use my soothing, but firm, doctor tone. "There's no point jumping to conclusions when we don't have all the information. You said this has happened before?"

"Yes, at work. She got dizzy and passed out, and the doctor at the hotel where she works gave her an ice pack and said she might need to get on blood pressure medication." She taps her finger on the back of the cell phone and stares out the window.

"For passing out?" *Jesus Christ.* "Did they check her blood sugar? EKG? Hydration levels?"

"I doubt it," she says, her legs bouncing. "I told her to go in but with her shitty insurance, she knew she'd have to wait for months."

Unreal. I grunt in response.

I roll to a stop at the light and look at her. Lexie looks so small and fragile sitting there that a fierce need to protect her overtakes me. "Tomorrow, call my office, and set up an appointment with me for your mom."

For the first time since she got the call, she snaps from her trance, and her eyes bore into me, questioning. Does she think this is a game? Does she really think that I'd do something to jeopardize someone's health, to what . . . get back at her for what she said to Justin that first day in her office? As far as she knows—which I intend to keep that way—I first met her when Anna and I stepped into her office. I wouldn't exploit her mother's health, or anyone's for that matter, for something like this.

She bites her lip and exhales. "Thank you. But I'm almost positive that her insurance won't cover the costs."

"I don't expect payment. Have her come to my office and I'll take care of her, no charge, okay?" Her eyes turn soft at my words. "Reach out to my nurse Erica. She'll take care of the arrangements."

Tears spring to her eyes, but she quickly blinks them away. I should love this. This is what I want, right? To see little bits of her break?

But dammit. Not like this. A warm, almost tingling sensation swarms in my chest. I clear my throat and focus on the traffic. She's making me feel things again. I'm fucking Theo Astor and I don't *feel* anything for Lexie Welch. And yet, I want to hold her and kiss her forehead and tell her everything's going to be okay. And I shouldn't.

I really, really shouldn't.

20

Lexie

When Theo pulls up to the Urgent Clinic connected to his office, I have my seatbelt off and bolt from the car before he even comes to a complete stop. He tells me he'll park the car, consult with the doctor on duty, and be in as quick as he can, but his words barely register. The next few moments are a blur as I rush to the triage nurse, show ID, and someone escorts me to an exam room.

When I step inside, I inhale a sharp breath. "Mom?" I can see the five or six stitches covering the bright red area of her left temple.

"Nope." My mom flickers open her eyes. "You don't need to fuss. I told them not to call you, but they said they had to because I hit my head. I told them it was no big deal and that maybe it was a gift to knock some sense into me."

She's trying to be strong, but the tiredness in her voice

tells me otherwise. I slide a chair next to the bed and grab her thin, pale hands. "Are you okay?"

"I'm fine, honey. It's these damn dizzy spells. But they're going to fix me up and send me on my way." She pats my hand. "How did you make it here so fast? This is clear across town for you."

I entertain the idea of not telling her. I'll say I was with a client who happens to be a doctor here, and pray when he comes inside, he doesn't identify himself. But my mom's not an idiot. She'll figure it out soon enough.

"My client works here, and we had a meeting nearby. He's going to check you out now, and I'll make a follow-up appointment for you with him. He said he's not going to bill you," I say with a heavy swallow. "It's, ah, Dr. Astor."

Her head snaps at me. "*The professor*?"

I brace myself because the name Theo Astor has haunted us for years. Heat floods my cheeks and I shake my head. "No . . . Dr. *Theo* Astor."

My mom's eyes widen as the reality lands of the person I just mentioned. I'm pretty sure if she had more energy she'd leap from the bed. But instead, she crosses her arms. "Those dirty fucking Astors—"

"Mom, stop." How do I explain this? That I know this man—who we've hated for years—well enough to know that he's surely unfaithful to his fiancée, that he's hiding something, that he ruined my life in Boston, and yet I implicitly trust him enough to care for the most important person to me in the world? "He's a *doctor.* And he promised me that he'd take care of you."

"Absolutely not." Angry red stripes fan her neck. "Take me home right this second. There ain't no way in hell after what he did to you I'll let that man touch me."

A few months ago, I would've agreed. Now everything feels off-balance and it doesn't make any sense. I'm fighting it all the time, but I can't deny the pull I feel towards him. Who in their right mind actively starts to feel something for the engaged man who once ruined their life?

Or at least I *thought* he'd ruined my life.

But the tiniest piece of me wonders if maybe I miscalculated something back then if he doesn't even remember who I am.

"Listen to me," I plead, laying a gentle hand on her arm. "Seven years have passed and I'm not in college anymore. I still don't exactly know how I came to be expelled, but it's a long time ago. And maybe . . . maybe I misunderstood something back then." I hesitate, then say it anyway. "What happened at the school . . . I don't think he did it."

The words land with the weight of a fallen skyscraper, crushing my chest. I'm lying to her because she needs to allow Theo to exam her. But the thought worms its way in anyway. What if there's more to what happened than what I remember? I was so angry back then—frantic, desperate, grasping at anything that might save my scholarship. In that state, I decided Theo had stolen my university badge, hacked into his father's computer, and accessed my student account—all because of a smile. With no clear motive.

Is it possible I got this wrong? Maybe there was a crime ring or something, and I was an easy target to blame because I didn't have the resources to fight back. What if I wrongly accused him, just like *I* was wrongly accused? A gross, tacky sickness weaves through my stomach. And if that's the case, then I have no justification whatsoever to ruin his wedding.

As I hold my mom's hand, I explain that I've been working with Theo for months and how wonderful his bride, Annabelle, is.

My heart sinks with those words.

"And he's going to see me after hours? For free?" she asks, arching her eyebrow.

I swallow a lodged boulder in my throat. "He's . . . a really good client."

"*Gemma*."

The use of my birth name snaps me to attention. Before I can respond, a tap sounds at the door, and a white-coat, stethoscope-slinging Theo comes in, and my heart skips. "Hi Lexie," he says with a perfectly professional nod. But that's the only recognition he gives me as he focuses entirely on my mother.

Please, please be good.

"Hi, Mrs. Welch, I'm Dr. Astor," he says as he takes a seat on the spinning chair.

My mom purses her lips. "I know who you are."

And . . . we're off to an amazing start.

"Excellent, then we can just skip past the introductions," Theo says without even so much as a bristle at the hostile tone. "Would you like your daughter to leave the room so we can talk in private?"

Mom sighs and releases the fierce, rod-like tension in her back. "No, she can stay."

"If you change your mind at any time, we can ask her to leave." Instead of facing the computer, or glancing at notes, he looks only at her. "I spoke to the doctor on duty and got up to speed, but I'd like to know what's been happening these last several months that have led up to this."

She looks at me sideways, and exhales resignedly. Then she dives in about being fatigued, which she attributes to the dreary winter, but became concerned when she'd fall asleep right after dinner and not wake up again until morning. She describes the dizziness, frequency, what time of day. As she continues, I pay attention to what she's saying, of course, but my gaze keeps shifting to Theo. He's attentive, kind, and precise—asking probing questions while never once crossing a professional line.

He removes his stethoscope from his neck. "Is it okay if I listen to your heart?" When she nods, he listens to her heart, then lungs. He asks her to breathe, he checks her eyes, her mouth, feels along her neck. He presses his fingers into her stomach, asking over and over, "Is this tender? Does this hurt?"

I'm invisible. He focuses on her completely—careful, thorough—and my heart lurches, small, unwelcome, at his tenderness. It starts racing when he coaxes a smile out of her, casually bonding over *The Bachelorette* playing in the background, which happens to be my mom's favorite show. My mouth drops when Theo admits he's never missed an episode. All the while he keeps working, seamlessly checking her eyes, skin, performing what I assume is a more in-depth concussion exam, as they commiserate over one particular season, where the Bachelorette apparently chose the wrong winner.

"Who do you think she should've picked?" Mom asks as he guides her to standing and checks her balance.

"Runner-up four," he says with a grin. "Hands down."

"Yes! I thought the same." She gives him a squeeze on the forearm. "The one she ended up with was an asshat. I bet they're divorced by now."

He chuckles, nodding his agreement, and continues his exam.

Tears well in my eyes and I blink them down. He's showing my mom respect. A woman who deserves it more than anyone I know but doesn't always get it. He's not treating her like some hotel housekeeper from Queens with scuffed shoes and a decade-old work uniform.

He's treating her as an equal.

"Lexie," he says, "I've finished here. I'm going to run down to the lab and see if I can pull in a favor to get her tests expedited."

"Okay, I'll stay here and wait."

He shakes his head, a faint frown forming. "No, your mom needs her rest. There's nothing more we can do right now, and she seems to be recovering well."

"Yes, sweetie," my mom adds gently. "Go home. I'm in good hands, thanks to Dr. Astor. I'll be just fine." At her insistence, I nod.

"If you want to say goodbye now, I'll have one of the nurses bring you to my office and you can wait until I'm back. Okay?"

I don't want to leave my mom, but trust that they're both doing what's best for her. After I hug my mom goodbye, I follow the nurse into the adjoining building and in the direction of Theo's office. The wine buzz is long gone, my stomach knotted, and my heart unsteady.

Jesus Christ what a day.

But the relief is tremendous that my mom will be okay.

"Dr. Astor said to make yourself comfortable," the nurse says as she unlocks Theo's office door and holds it open for me. "He's got snacks in the lower right drawer, and bottles of electrolytes in the mini fridge behind his desk." I thank her, step inside and close the door.

Reality hits me hard. This isn't my world. I've *never* belonged in this world. Yes, obviously I know Theo is a doctor. But being here now, seeing how he spends his days, unsettles me. I feel like a kid at the grown-up table, trying not to say or do anything stupid.

I peer around the room. The office is much smaller than I thought it'd be. Only the size of maybe two exam rooms, but it *feels* like him. Cherrywood-framed degrees hang on his wall alongside a framed picture of him and his staff, and a beautiful abstract painting that probably cost as much as my yearly rent. He's only got two chairs, the cushy leather one behind his u-shaped desk and the wooden one in front that's clearly there as a means of punishment. It feels weird, like I'm invading his space, but I sink into the leather one and rest my head on his desk.

A low-grade headache starts to pound against my skull. I need water. Between the sugar and wine, my entire body is probably severely dehydrated. I grab a coconut water from the fridge and slam half down, but I need aspirin. It's a doctor's office . . . he must have some, right?

The nurse said I could help myself, so he can't be too upset if I dig around for aspirin. I open drawer after drawer, finding office supplies, the snacks the nurse mentioned—if gluten free, organic protein bars even count—and a stethoscope. But no aspirin. With my headache pulsing, I yank open the last untouched drawer and rummage through more notebooks and supplies, until my fingers close around a crumpled-up Post-it note. Curiosity gets the best of me.

"Olivia, Feb 13, 1pm, Silver Crescent Hotel, Financial District."

Olivia. The date clicks—it's the same day I saw Theo and that woman at the hotel.

Who is she? My hands scramble, reopening the drawers with new intent, searching for any scrap of buried information. There has to be something else in here.

But at least I have a name now.

It's not much to go by, but it can help narrow down the online search a little more.

My headache already forgotten, I hastily pore through his notebooks, hoping something will reveal itself. I'm so focused on what I'm doing that I barely notice a presence in the room—until they clear their throat. I look up, jumping out of my skin when I see Theo.

He's deathly silent and I can hear my heartbeat pounding in my ears. I offer what I hope is an innocent smile. "Oh, ah, hey," *fuck, fuck, fuck*. "The, um, the nurse said I could grab a snack from your drawers if needed."

My face is on fire. My chest even more so. If I look him in the eye any longer my irises might scorch. "Hope that's okay."

He crosses his arms, and I know he sees through my lie. I'm literally gripping a notebook in my hand with no snack in sight. I clumsily stand up from the chair, and it rolls back on its wheels until it hits the file cabinet.

"And, um, sorry I was sitting in your chair. Is that weird? It just looked so much more comfortable than the other one."

I need to shut up.

Flames have taken over my entire body. His fingertips wrap around the notebook and I release it immediately. "This doesn't look like a snack."

His tone gives nothing away. The room feels suspended, as if time has stalled. He rests the notebook on his desk and takes a step towards me. I back away. He follows. "*Lexie*."

The harsh sound of my name on his tongue sends fear running through me, and my heartbeat thuds louder. I've seen a lot of versions of Theo. Overly charming, considerate, raging, heated, maybe even possessive. But this one is different. This is calm. Stern. Calculated. I step back until my ass meets the file cabinet.

"Lexie," he says again, inching so close to me that I feel the static between us. I plant my palms behind my back to brace myself. I can't run. There's nowhere to go. I can't scream. And I can't fight him off. He's too strong.

A heavy swallow rolls through my throat.

He scoops the hair cascading down my shoulder and lays it behind my back. And leaves his hand. One second, two seconds, three. My heartbeat shoots to my neck. His handprint carries the buzzing vibration of a dirty hymn sung by a church's rejected sinners. I know he's a doctor and touches bodies all day. Maybe he's desensitized.

But I'm not.

"You know what I think?" he says, calmly, his breath warming my ear, his palm pushing into me, and God these terrible, Judas tingles spread across my skin. "I think you were sneaking around my office, touching things you shouldn't."

I shake my head, pressing my ass even further into the cabinet to create more space between us. "No, I wasn't. I told you . . . I was looking for a snack."

God, I sound pathetic. He absolutely knows I'm full of shit.

There's the smallest hint of a grin at the corner of his mouth. He pulls in a breath and slowly releases. His palm is still pressing against my upper back, pushing up my chest, and my breasts brush against him.

"I want to know why you're so curious about me." His voice is steely calm, and I hate, *hate*, that my core tightens with his touch. I want to run and scream and hit him, but unwanted moisture pools between my legs instead. His body is too close. The air turns heated, as his fingertips begin to dig into my flesh. "If you had a question for me, all you had to do was ask."

He puts his mouth back to my ear, the quickest brush of lips meet my earlobe, and my head involuntarily tucks against him. I shiver with the sensation, hating myself, my body, hating him. How dare he? Heat rushes to my core. I can't stop it. My chest is lifting and lowering quickly, my heart is pounding.

His mouth is still right at my ear. "So go ahead, Lexie. Ask me your questions. I'm dying to hear what was so important to you that you'd reduce yourself to a thief."

Fuck him. Like I just plunged into an ice bath, my body screeches to a halt. I push at his chest and he steps back. "I was trying to find a snack, asshole." I yank my jacket and purse from the chair, trying to ignore the imprint of his palm branded into my skin. "Listen, I really appreciate what you did for my mom. But if you *ever* corner me like this again, I'll slam my elbow into your nose, and you'll be the one who needs to go to the ER."

I storm out the door.

But somehow I know that whatever this is, is far from over.

21

Theo

I can't believe I convinced Lexie to still let me take her home after she stormed out of my office.

As I drive us back to her place, I keep stealing glances at her. She's silent, staring straight ahead. I don't feel any remorse about how things went down in my office. She was going through *my things*. Seeing that only confirmed what I already knew: I was right not to trust her. I can't ever let her out of my sight again.

But fuck, the way it felt sweeping her hair back, pressing her body up, watching her chest push high through her shirt. The restraint I needed not to flip her over so she was palms down on the desk, hike up her skirt, and fuck her from behind was more than I've ever known.

What the hell is wrong with me? She's making me break all my commitments, making me do insane, stupid shit in my office. *My work.* My only sacred place. And within minutes, I wanted to dominate her.

I turn at the light, glance at her again, and she's still in that same, angry, cross-armed position. But she's not scared. And I want her fucking scared. Terrified. Shaking. I want her to feel all the fucking things she makes me feel. I want her so tight, so restless, so soaking with a desperate desire that she'll cry, fall to her knees, and beg me to stuff her mouth with my cock. Tears will flood those huge, beautiful eyes. She'll lift her skirt, and show me that glistening cunt, and beg me to fill it. After all these years, I want her to taste the poison of rejection, to have it consume her the way it consumes me. I'll turn her into a feral, primal, savage fiend of need, and she'll know the only cure is me.

And I won't fucking give it to her.

Finally, she'll obsess over me the way she's forced me to obsess over her.

When I pull up to her place, she steps out without a word, slams her door and marches to her apartment.

Fuck.

I peel down the street. If I were playing it safe, I'd park at least a half-mile away. But apparently, I'm not playing it safe, because I find the first parking spot only two blocks away, sprint down the street and up the few flights of stairs to my studio like I'm back in my college track days.

Cake fills my stomach from our tasting. I'm telling myself that's why my gut is fiercely twisting, but I know it's more.

What just happened, what's been happening . . . I can't. *I fucking can't.*

But it doesn't mean I don't want to.

I don't even take off my jacket. I rush to the window, grab my telephoto lens, and hook the sheer curtain to the left a few inches.

I'm only checking that she made it inside. I might be fucking livid at her, at myself for letting what happened happen, but I still can't stomach the thought of her hurt.

She's still leaning against her door. It's been at least a few minutes, and yet there she is, jacket on, purse still attached to her body, her head tilted to the ceiling and her eyes closed. God, I want to know what's going on in her head.

I should text her.

Don't fucking text her.

I should drop the camera. She made it inside. She's clearly digging for something, but she's not actively doing anything that warrants surveillance. She's just . . . thinking. About me? About today?

Drop the camera. It's wrong. Illegal. But something changed. Not only am I watching her because I'm worried that she's sabotaging me, I'm watching because I like watching her.

Fuck.

I can't do this. The way I had to peel myself from her, the way my body screams at me to stomp over there and sink my teeth into her bottom lip is a fierce, magnetic pull, and I'm close to breaking.

More time passes, and finally, she hangs up her coat, kicks

off her shoes, but she forgoes her usual stretch. She disappears behind the wall. Will she change into the pink pajamas or the one with the cherries?

Oh. Tonight, it's a tank and leggings. A tank? Its freezing outside, but with today's events, plus the vast amount of sugar she's digesting, she's probably overheating.

I shrug off my jacket without taking my eyes from the lens as I attempt to get more comfortable.

I watch as she slumps onto her couch and pulls out her phone. Maybe she'll text me.

Or wait . . . she sets the phone on the floor and tilts her head to the ceiling. I'm not close enough to read her expressions, and I want to know what she's thinking.

I know what I'm thinking.

She closes her eyes and flings her arm over her head and freezes. Maybe she got a text from some dickhead. Maybe she's thinking about work. Maybe . . .

I need to drop the camera. It's late. She's going to get up and follow her usual bedtime routine, and the blinds will be closed for the night. I've already clocked this. So, I should just put the camera down and . . .

The slightest swirling of her hips catches my gaze. She drops her hand from her forehead and slides her palm across her chest, trailing fingertips above the tank. Her other hand joins and *Jesus Christ.* My cock immediately hardens against my jeans and I adjust myself. Over her tank, she cups her breasts and massages, her thumbs flicking back and forth, her eyes closed, her mouth parted, and *drop the fucking camera.*

One hand dips lower, under the band of her leggings and a whisper of a smooth pale, belly peeks out. If she lowers her pants, I have to drop the camera. *Have to.* This is not okay. I watch her to make sure she's not fucking with me—not to see her get naked.

But she's so fucking beautiful.

I can't take my eyes off her. I'm too far away to see her freckles, but I want to know how low they trail, if they're sprinkled across her belly, or if it pales . . .

Oh shit.

Her back arches. She tugs down her tank to free her tits, and I'm fucking done. I unzip my jeans and free my constricted cock. Christ they're perfect . . . even this far away my mouth aches to pull them into my mouth. She's squeezing herself, tugging on her nipples, grinding into the couch . . .

Drop the fucking camera.

This is wrong. I've done so much messed-up shit, I can't invade her privacy through the lens like this. But . . . *she's perfect.* My heartbeat climbs, reaching my neck. My cock screams for relief. I shove my hands inside my boxer briefs and fist my cock. I swipe precum across the crown and stroke to the base, imagining what it'd be like if I sunk into her warm, waiting cunt.

She's moving on the couch, bucking against her own hands, her arm gliding up and down, and I need to stop. Right the fuck now. *Stop.* But I'm lost . . . hazed . . . desperate to know what kind of sounds she's making. Her face is so concentrated, her beautiful mouth parted, and I stroke harder, faster. My cock thickens as I watch the way she moves against herself, the way her head tilts up. This is so wrong, so fucking wrong, but I can't stop. Is she thinking about me? Is she picturing what it'd be like if I bent her over that couch and stuffed my cock inside her?

I pump faster. I want to taste her, just fucking once. Drop to my knees and fling her leg over my shoulder and bury my face in that pussy. God, the way she's moving . . . she's getting close. Her eyebrows furrow, her hands are moving quicker, frantic. I keep fucking my palm, watching how hard she tugs her nipples. I want to soothe them with my tongue and suck and pinch and *I know, I know*, I have to walk away, but I can't and—

Bzzzz. "Fuck!" I lower the camera with the sounds of my phone vibrating against the table, drop my fist from my cock, and shut the curtain. A nauseating heat flushes my body.

I stuff myself back inside my pants, yank up my zipper, and look at the phone.

Seeing a message from Anna across the screen makes my stomach drop.

Anna: Call me. It's urgent.

I slump against the couch, wipe my hands off on my jeans, and dial.

22

Lexie

My co-workers are bustling around me, wrapped up in their work, completely oblivious to how my life is spinning out of control. I'm trying so hard to focus on the specs of the Victorian home where the wedding will be held, but everything blurs. Instead of focusing, I keep manically swiping through my phone on my endless search for a woman in New York named Olivia.

I can't stop thinking about that name since I saw it in Theo's office a week ago. I've spent countless hours online chasing every possible lead on this woman. So far, nothing.

But I *will* find out who she is.

The other thing I'll do? Stop obsessing over Theodore Astor, why he hasn't contacted me since he drove me back home, and regain control over my body. It's wrong, sick, and I hate myself for it.

My phone rings and panic flares, a ridiculous flash of fear

that he can read my mind. Relief washes over me when I see the caller ID. *Annabelle.* I paste on a smile I know will carry through my voice and answer. "Hi Annabelle, lovely to hear from you."

"Lexie, we have a major fucking problem."

Shit. That's the sound of a woman with bad news. My stomach knots and my mind races ahead of itself. Theo told her. *Fuck.* He told her everything and now she's calling to fire me. I'm going to lose my raise, my promotion, probably my goddamn job. And the worst part? I wouldn't even blame her. I brought this on myself and she has every right to cut me loose.

"My dress is terrible," she says.

My head stops spinning. "Wait, what?"

"It just arrived for alterations and it's nothing like the pictures online. The fabric will make me break out in hives, alterations cannot fix the monstrosity of the cardboard corset, the tulle . . ." She doesn't take a breath as she lists everything wrong with the dress and how she doesn't have a moment to go dress-shopping because of her grandma.

"I need you to go pick one out for me."

My body convulses into a weird choking laugh until I gain composure. "I can't pick out your dress. This is the most important thing you'll ever wear in your life. You do not want to trust this with a stranger."

"You are not a stranger and I implicitly trust you." Those words shoot a dagger through me. She trusts me. God, I hate myself. Does she know that I've touched myself every night this past week picturing her fiancé's hands on me? I'm sick. I'm so sick. Tonight, I'm looking up confessional times at St. John's and getting rid of this demon.

Annabelle assures me that she's "not picky", and as long as the fabric doesn't feel like shit, it'll be fine. I reluctantly agree, while kindly reminding her that I can't try anything on for her without stating the obvious that my curves, full boobs and ass are totally the opposite of her "reminiscent of a '90s runway model" physique. She sends me her measurements, I call around the city for a shop that has an available appointment, and by four p.m. I'm in a cab on my way to Brooklyn.

I contemplate sending Theo a text and letting him know but decide against it. Distance is the best decision right now.

At the private shop, I buzz the intercom and a sharply dressed gray-haired woman with a tight bun and bright pink lips welcomes me inside the softly lit, plush-carpeted boutique, and introduces herself. "We are so grateful that the bride chose us to find her the perfect dress!"

"Thanks so much for squeezing me in. We are grateful for your help."

"It's no problem at all."

Is it, though? I've been around these places long enough to know that wedding-dress shops rarely care about accommodating bridal emergencies. They're the type of shop that turns people away without a six-month-in-advance appointment. Funny how dropping the Barlowe name along with the required NDA opened the doors.

"I can't say we've ever had a planner try on the bride's

dresses before," the woman says as she escorts me past the main showroom. Inside the private fitting area, floor-length mirrors, plush sofas, and marble tables with elaborate floral arrangements surround us. "But thankfully we have the bride's measurements, though the sizing might be tricky."

Oof. Thank God I love my body, or this little spitfire here might just get a throat punch. "I'm not trying any on. I'm just going to look."

"Okay, then," she says. "Oh, I forgot to let you know that you have someone waiting for you. He's in the back."

Shit. She doesn't need to say who it is—it couldn't be anyone else. I don't need this. Not now. Earlier today, I was terrified his bride would find out about us. Now I'm fighting the stupid flutter in my stomach at the thought of being near him again. *It's so fucking wrong.* He's getting married. I'm planning his wedding. I'm sure I'm not the only one who's developed a crush on a client before, but have they felt *this*?

"Hey!" Theo says, with a wide smile and even wider arms. He pulls me in for a quick, professional hug, and ends it with a pat on the back. Clearly whatever happened last week did not affect him at all.

"Wow, this is a . . . nice surprise," I say, although it's actually a terrible one. "I didn't know you'd be coming here. In fact, you shouldn't be as it's bad luck."

"I figured it'd be a lot of pressure to find the right dress for Anna without a second opinion from the one who knows her best."

I hate when he has a point.

"Let's get started, shall we? Why don't you two have a look at the displays and let me know if you need any help." The woman walks away, leaving me and Theo alone in this too-quiet space.

We fall into quiet concentration, combing through the options as the tension that hit me when I first saw Theo slowly dissipates.

I scoop out a dress to hang on a hook for a better view. "I heard you talked to my mom yesterday." Yes, I'm absolutely prodding for intel because my mom didn't offer much. The morning after her urgent care visit, she mentioned how Theo stopped by the aftercare unit after reviewing her labs. Turns out that she was dehydrated, severely deficient in Vitamin D, and had developed hypothyroidism along with a nasty ear infection. All unpleasant, but thankfully nothing life-threatening. Yesterday was her follow-up appointment. And no matter how many questions I fired at her, she remained tightlipped.

"You know even if I did, I can't tell you," he says. "Patient–doctor confidentiality."

"Seriously?"

"I take my doctor oath *very* seriously," he says, not joking.

I pull out another dress, but I've lost focus. Finally, I let out a shaky breath. "I, um, I didn't properly thank you for last week," I say, glossing over the fact of why I didn't thank him. I catch his eye. "Really. My mom is my everything, and what you did for her . . ."

I feel the beginning of a tremble in my chin and I suck

my lips into my mouth. He inches towards me and lays both hands on my shoulders, dipping his head to catch my gaze. "It's nothing, Lexie. It's the equivalent of what you're doing, right now, as part of your job."

It's so much more, and I think he knows. I've been trying to separate the pieces that make up Theo. He's like a fucked-up divinity triangle. Three separate entities all captured within the same person. Theo—the guy I'm sitting with right now making me blush. Theo—Annabelle's fiancé. Theo—the devil I'm determined to destroy.

A soft grin forms and he gives my shoulders a friendly squeeze before he drops his touch.

"But you'll have to talk to your mom about *The Bachelorette* season six. She is very, very wrong on who she thinks should've been the winner."

I smile and continue swiping through dresses. I soon discover that Theo and I have surprisingly similar tastes. Simple lines, minimal fabric, A-frame. I tug out another dress and stand back, eyeing the cut.

Theo steps behind me. "Since you're on the clock, I want you to try some of these on."

"Ah. No. That's a hard pass."

He lifts a brow. "It wasn't a question."

I feel heat warm my cheeks. "I'm not trying on dresses. Annabelle and I are totally different sizes, it's after five, it'll take hours, and I'd really like you to revisit my first statement that it's a hard fucking pass."

He stays silent.

"Look," I say, gritting my teeth, because really? "I will do a lot of things for you guys. Getting into a wedding dress is not on that list."

He crosses his arms. And stares. "Do I need to let Sydney know you're refusing to help your client?"

"And do I need to remind you that you sound like a little bitch when you threaten to whine to my boss?" I hate that a smile cracks through. "God you're the worst. Truly."

He glances behind me and his lips quirk into a very slow, very diabolic grin. "On that note . . . I think you start with that one."

When he points behind me, I turn and my mouth drops. "You cannot be serious."

He slides back, his grin growing even wider. "Oh, I'm *very* serious." Then he shouts out for the shop assistant's help, explaining that there's been a change of plan.

"Which one do you want to see first?" she asks.

Theo's eyes glint with trouble. "You have such an extraordinary collection, that it's hard to know which to choose. But, I think we start with that one."

The woman's face brightens—no doubt at the dollar signs attached to the dress. "Wonderful choice. Lexie, why don't you get into the dressing room. There's a robe on the hanger, and I'll be right in."

Twenty minutes later, after a lot of tugging, scratches, and a few swear words, I take a long look in the floor-length mirror. *Dear God, it's hideous.* With so much puff, tulle, and fabric, I look like a twelve-tiered wedding cake. When I step out of the room lugging this fifty-pound monstrosity, a very irritating twinkle flashes in Theo's eyes.

"Isn't this stunning?" the assistant says, and tells us all about the Italian designer.

"Yes, it really is," Theo says, digging his phone from his pocket and angling it toward me.

"Do we really need to film this?" I ask, unable to keep the plea out of my voice.

"What a wonderful idea!" the shop assistant chimes in. "That way your fiancée can see all the options for herself."

There's a brief pause before Theo responds. "Ah, yes. Anna will enjoy seeing these." He lifts the phone up slightly. "Lexie, would you mind turning so I can get the full effect."

I push a smile through clenched teeth. "I think that might be a little difficult with the . . . volume of this dress."

The most shit-eating grin crosses his face, and he does a twirl motion with his finger. "What the bride wants, the bride gets. And she will definitely want to see how this dress spins."

Who knew this moody, brooding man could be such a comedian.

"That's right dear," the assistant says as she helps move me in a clunky, uncoordinated circle. "We should never question the client." She moves to my ear. "Especially ones like these."

I mouth *I hate you* to Theo.

The bastard laughs.

One hour passes, then two. Theo takes pictures and videos, I twirl, curtsey, and yawn in between dresses.

Whoever thought trying on dresses is fun is insane. I'm tired and growing crankier by the minute.

I step into the fifth, sixth, maybe hundredth dress at this point, and tug up the strapless gown. With zippers and fabric and satin-ribbon corset binding, this one is the most beautiful, yet most cumbersome, and within two minutes, I'm a complete mess. I call for the assistant.

No response. Cool. I'm in a satin and tulle prison and she's nowhere to be found.

I poke my head out from the velvet curtain at Theo sitting on the sofa. "Hey, can you find the assistant? I can't get this thing on, and my patience is hovering around zero."

He lifts from the couch. "I can help."

Oh God, nope. The zipper on the back isn't even up and I'm very, very aware of the breeze on my lower back and most likely the triangle back panel of my lace thong peeking out. "Can you just grab her? Please. This thing has about a thousand buttons and has to be laced like a corset."

He marches to me. "I said, I'll do it."

Jesus. That tone.

I step outside of the dressing room, towards the mirror, holding my boobs so they don't pop out. He stands behind me and everything stops. The air thins, heats. His breath hitches, my pulse increases. He drags his gaze down my naked back creating the same feather-like sensation as if his fingers were trailing me.

Warmth invades me, rushing down my spine, and reaching my toes. I stand under the soft lights, waiting, breathless, watching in the mirror his every move. He shouldn't touch me. But I want him to. He sweeps my hair to the side. The touch is a whisper. It's nothing and yet tingles fly through me.

He should pull back. Step away. Move from this space because I want more. But instead of dropping his hands, his fingers graze from my shoulder to the top of my arm, I gasp. This is so wrong. So, so wrong, but I ease my eyes closed, drinking in the way his touch makes my skin sing. I shouldn't lean into his touch. I *can't* lean into the touch. But just for a brief moment, I let myself imagine . . .

Moments like this are another little slice of a dream-like, soft-focused fantasy in my grainy world where I get to pretend for a moment that things are different.

I feel his fingers tug at the fabric—zip, then the slow thread of ribbon through each loop. Every movement stretches the moment, the silence thick with an energy I know he feels too. In the mirror, I watch him pull the ribbons taut, his thumbs brushing my bare skin and sending warmth flooding through me.

I can't take this—standing here in this dress, with him so close. My face burns. My body aches, needy, restless, straining not to press back into him. Shame stirs somewhere beneath it all, a shadow waiting to surface—but for now, it's swallowed by the heat.

When he finishes cinching the last binding, he doesn't drop his hands like I need him to. *Please, let go.* I'm not strong enough to fight this.

Our eyes lock in the mirror. Time stalls. Does he feel this, too? Or is this torment mine alone?

My heartbeat thuds against my throat. His hands slide up my back and goosebumps erupt on my skin. I should walk away. Right now. Just one simple step forward and break this moment.

But I don't.

He scoops my hair away from my shoulder to cascade down my back and I hear him sharply inhale. He peeks back at the mirror and when his heated gaze locks on mine again, he expels a soft breath, whispering close to my ear. "You look *beautiful*."

The words land gently, almost tender—and somehow that makes them hurt more, pricking tears behind my eyelids.

I *do* look pretty in this lacy, off-the-shoulder, smooth-silhouette dress. The soft cream color brings out the red in my hair, the green in my eyes, my freckles. But my heart sinks—this dress isn't for me.

"Don't," I utter, but it's half-hearted.

He doesn't respond. Doesn't leave. He doesn't even fucking move. Those eyes are staring at me with so much intensity that my hands tremble. And then, he slides his fingertips down the fabric at my ribcage to my waist.

My eyes flutter closed.

This is all an illusion. This moment, right here, is fake. I'm not really trying on wedding gowns and he's not really picturing what I'll look like walking down the aisle.

I can't breathe.

"Sorry about that," the woman's voice sounds from around the corner.

My entire body stiffens, Theo takes a step back.

"A customer stopped by for a pick-up." Her bracelets bang with a metallic tink as she clasps her hands. "Well, this is absolutely stunning. And fits like a glove, doesn't it? This is definitely a contender, but we've still got more to try on."

I sigh.

The next dress is buttery soft, the strapless feminine sweetheart neckline makes a deep cleavage, and the cinched waist with the gentle, ballgown silhouette makes me feel like a princess. If I ever get married, I'm going with something like this.

If.

Every second I spend trying on dresses for the bride of the man I'm slowly losing my mind over makes those dreams disappear like a feather in a windstorm.

God, help me. Is it the low lighting? This dance we're doing while dress shopping? Or could I actually be *falling* for Theo?

"What do you think?" she asks, turning to Theo who is sitting on the sofa, with a deep frown. "Dr. Astor? Do you like this one?"

He doesn't even respond.

Instead, Theo's gaze drags slowly over me. The dress is beautiful. It fits me perfectly—hugging where the others pinched or sagged. "Do you want to grab a video of this one?" the woman asks.

"No." The word snaps, sharp enough to make me flinch.

I gape at him, stunned. *What in the actual hell*? Who does he think he is, snapping at a woman who's just trying to help, when I'm the one bending over backward so *his* fiancée can find a gown for their goddamn wedding?

He bolts up and storms away. The air tightens instantly, like he's drained the room of everything good and left only misery behind.

Do not cry. Do not cry. I clamp my lip between my teeth and skulk back to the dressing room, my body dragging like it weighs a million pounds.

"Oh no . . ." the assistant says, following me into the fitting area. "I think the groom had enough for today. It's a shame he didn't like this one, but the right dress will come along. Why don't you get undressed and we'll call it an evening."

I nod and slump onto the cushioned bench, the disappointment settling heavy in my chest that tonight wasn't a success and we'll have to try again.

I reach for the zipper when the velvet curtain rustles open.

"Theo?" I gasp, as he steps inside and pulls it shut behind him. "What are you doing? You can't be in here."

"I wanted to talk," he starts. "I shouldn't have stormed off like that. It's a—"

His phone rings, cutting him off. He squeezes his eyes shut in frustration before pulling the phone out, glancing quickly at the screen and angling it away from me.

Not fast enough, though.

Olivia.

"Sorry, I have to take this," he says. And then he's gone.

It feels like a bucket of ice water has been dumped over me. A brutal reminder that I'm just one of many—another woman he draws in, then discards. Shame and embarrassment crash into me all at once. How did I let myself get this blinded again? An unwanted tear slips down my cheek as I curse my own foolishness.

"Lexie," the woman calls softly from outside. "Are you okay in there? You've been a while."

"I'm fine," I answer, my voice unsteady. "I'll be out in just a minute."

I finish getting dressed, leaving the wedding gown behind in the fitting room, and step back out in the lobby. "Theo?" I call out, but there's no answer. The store is silent minus the shuffling sounds of dresses being housed back in their zipped garment-bagged homes. Through the storefront window, I see Theo pacing the sidewalk. He pinches the bridge of his nose, moves his hand like he's trying to calm someone in front of him, and paces some more. He hangs up and takes a deep breath before coming into the store.

"Everything okay?" I ask, and yes, I'm prying.

"Oh yep, fine," he says, softening. "It was just Anna."

Liar! God, I knew it. I *knew* it. Of course, a phone call doesn't prove anything. But everything I've seen, every instinct screaming in my gut, tells me he's hiding something. As cliché as it is, sometimes the simplest conclusion is the right one. And really, who am I to judge, when I've imagined him doing all kinds of sinful things to me? The difference is, I won't act on it.

"You are so full of shit. Do you actually believe the things that come out of your mouth?" I snap. "We both know that wasn't Annabelle." I have no right to ask him who Olivia is, or why he said it was Anna, or literally anything about his life, but my body is boiling with so much rage right now that I can't stop myself.

"What exactly are you saying?" he seethes. "Be really fucking clear in your words so I don't misunderstand."

I shake my head. "It's none of my business."

"Oh no, you don't get to do this. You just made it your fucking business. If you have something to say, now is the time."

"Why would I say anything to you? Nothing I'll say will ever change the type of person you are."

He crosses his arm with an icy glare. "And exactly what type of person do you think I am?"

My eyes narrow, sharp, hot, and very fucking angry. "The type I can't wait to never see again after your account is closed."

A harsh, charged silence stretches when heels click from around the corner. "Ah, I want to thank you both so much for coming in today," the woman says. "Do you want to set up another appointment?"

"No, I'm not sure either one of us could handle another session," Theo says flatly, glaring at me and then dropping the heated look when he turns to the woman. "Truthfully, our wedding planner here has actually disappointed me with her lack of professionalism."

All the color drains from my face before it turns beet red. How *dare* he?

"But I will take the dress before the last one that *the planner* tried on for my beautiful *bride*," he says and the tone stabs me in the heart. "I'm sure my wife-to-be will be stunning in it."

As he pulls out his credit card, my gut tightens, and my heart sinks. I storm out of the store before he can cut me anymore.

23

Theo

Pound, pound, pound.

Sweat builds in my neck, trickles down my back, my heartbeat rages in my chest.

I can't fucking do this anymore.

Pound, pound, pound.

I'm hitting the boxing bag like it's attacking me, landing brutal punches over and over, and the image isn't erasing. Lexie in that dress. Her tits pushed up, her skin begging to be licked. The lush red hair swept to the side exposing the sweet, delicate slope in her neck. Soft lace hugging her mouth-watering curves. It was *exactly* how I'd pictured her. If things were different, if Anna was different, if *I* was different . . .

Beads of sweat run down my forehead. In the dressing room, Lexie's sweet scent assaulted my mind. The sex and sweetness aura she emits is too much and it breaks me. I need to stay fucking focused. When she stood there as I adjusted her dress, I wanted to scoop her in my arms and take her away and pretend, for just a day, that we lived in a different reality. That she was mine, and I was hers, and none of the outside elements existed.

But then, what I said. She attacked, and I hit back. Twice as hard, twice as fast, like I always fucking do.

Fuck.

Red fills me. Why does she do this to me? Every goddamn time. It's been almost two weeks and the wedding dress shop consumes my every waking hour. She's the quintessential forbidden fruit, but I can't stop. My raw desire eats at me, I'm powerless. The feel of her skin under my fingers, the way she looked, how she smelled. Her coconut-scented hair buried into my nose that night. So, like a fucking lunatic, I sniffed bottles of shampoo at a store until I found one that smelled like her and brought it home. She cast a spell on me that I can't break.

Pound, pound, pound.

I need Anna, my anchor and stabilizer, to come home. I need things to go back to normal. The longer she's gone and the more time I spend around Lexie, the further I spiral. Reality feels warped, upside down, while I'm usually razor-sharp. Decisions that once came easily now drag. Sleep barely exists.

When I first decided to use Lexie as the wedding planner, it seemed perfect. After years of her haunting me, I thought being back in her life again, forcing myself to remember exactly why I don't deserve her, would finally exorcise her for good. Instead, I'm ravenous. Nothing extinguishes the blaze. This all started to get her out of my head once and for all—to make sure she couldn't interfere in my investigation and to clear the past so I could settle down and commit to marrying Anna with my whole being.

Pound, pound, pound.

Visions fill me, imagining her on her knees, that luscious mouth wrapped around me, her trailing tongue . . . I slam into the bag. The more brutal I land the punches, the harder I kick, the more strikes I hand out, the worse I feel. *Worse.* Hard and angry breaths expel; my muscles burn from the inside out. But no amount of lifting, running, or hitting the bag is lightening whatever the fuck is happening.

My body verges on breaking. I rest my dripping head against the bag as my lungs seize. What am I doing? Being around Lexie is like watching my heart edge itself outside of my body and dive into rush hour traffic. I want to run, because it's going to fucking hurt when it gets slammed and crushed into the road.

I should take five, but I don't want to. I hit again. And again. I'll keep hitting until I can't breathe, until I sweat her out of my system, until I'm done with this bullshit.

"Hey, Dr. Astor, hitting it hard today, huh?" Lou, one of my patients and the toughest sixty-year-old I've ever met, says as he taps the bag in front of him and starts swinging.

It takes his words to snap me out of it. I drop my arms. "What did I tell you about cardio for men like us?"

Lou grunts through his nose. "Bullshit," he says, his faded navy tattoos stretching against his spotted skin as he hits. "*Men like us.* You look like you just stepped off one of those pretty boy magazines. I've got four teeth left and look like I have one foot in the ground."

I chuckle, thankful for the reprieve. I bite the edge of the Velcro to loosen the gloves and tug them off. "Don't forget to hydrate," I say as I swing the towel around my neck and swipe it down my face.

"Coconut water or some shit, right?" Lou says. "Got it, Doc."

I give him a quick slap on the back and rush to the shower.

When I'm done, I settle into the SUV.

"You doing all right, sir?" Michael says.

I know why he's asking. Because I'm *not* doing fucking all right. I'm hitting the gym two, sometimes three times a day. I'm not sleeping. I'm restless, itchy, and angry. "Yeah, I'm good. Let's go to my place."

He nods, hands me a protein shake, and pulls into traffic.

This man needs a raise.

My phone rings. *Anna.* I exhale a hefty breath and push away all thoughts of Lexie. For now. "Hey, you." I lean back into the seat and watch the city pass by. "Miss me yet?"

"Truthfully?"

"Nope." I grin. "Lie to me and say yes. My heart can't take it that you've left me in New York for an Italian retreat."

"God, you're the most dramatic person I know. And that's saying a lot considering who raised me."

I chuckle. "How's Nonna?"

"Stubborn as hell. She has a perfectly good physical therapist but refuses to do anything unless I'm there, watching." The sound of her slurping what's most likely an iced coffee—even at this hour—sounds through the phone. "But she has some stiffness and today the skin around the incision was inflamed and red—"

I pinch my nose. "Jesus, Anna. You have to call her doctor. It's probably infected—"

"You don't think I've picked up a thing or two by now being in your almighty presence?" She laughs. "Done and done. They already prescribed antibiotics and tomorrow they're going to check if they need to drain it. I don't know how you doctors do it. I almost passed out just from listening to the instructions."

"It's like re-watching the same porn," I say, slamming back the protein shake. "Eventually you get desensitized."

Anna groans so loud I move the phone from my ear. "You did not just compare my grandmother's infected wound to porn, right? Are you trying to kill my sex life for good?"

"Fair," I say, grinning. "Bad analogy."

I ask about her trip, how she's managing her non-profit business remotely, and give her some updates on the wedding planning. I'm focusing as hard as I can, but talk of the wedding makes me think of Lexie again. It's been almost two weeks without her and I can't handle it. Watching her from the window isn't enough.

She manipulates. It's her nature. And she's so skilled at it that I can never tell when she's being sincere.

Maybe I should meet with her again to be sure. Just once and I can move on.

"So . . . it's going to be a few more weeks before I come home," Anna says, and I hate myself right now that I missed whatever she said before this.

My body deflates at the realization that she won't be back anytime soon to save me, so I try to deflect with humor. "No shock. I know you. And unfortunately, I know Nonna too."

"Theodore James Astor. You'll put soap in your mouth for that one," she says with a giggle. "So . . . I don't know if I'll be back in time for dance rehearsals."

Fucking dance rehearsals. "Cool, we can cancel, then."

"You know we can't."

The words weighing down the tip of my tongue could land me in jail, so instead of going off, I take a breath. My future mother-in-law is a conniving, evil, wife of a billionaire who meets and exceeds every stereotype that a wife of a billionaire has. What she did to Anna . . . the heated rage builds in my stomach.

But, thank Christ, so far, she's been more hands-off than anticipated for the actual event. But she insisted on using some former Juilliard prodigy, retired ballet superstar, as our choreographer. I still can't believe I agreed to the arrangement.

"Fine," I say. "But I want the record to show I am seriously taking one for the team on this."

"Filed with the courts and entered into Exhibit A," Anna says. "I should run. I really do miss you. Thank you for everything you're doing back home for the wedding."

I miss her, too. She's been a constant in my life, one of the positive beacons of light, and probably the only reason I'm as grounded as I am. She's always showed me a pure love. One that I never got from my parents, one that I didn't know I needed until she gave it to me. But, as much as I want her home, it's evident that I need a little more time to get Lexie out of my system.

My legs bounce in the back of the SUV. What's Lexie doing tonight? Has she met some asshole? I bet she did. I bet she's laying there, getting railed but not taken care of, by some dumb prick that cums on her ass after they fuck and doesn't even have the decency to clean her off.

Christ, I need to get her out of my mind. Lexie with her wide, beautiful gap-toothed smile. Does she know the effect she has on me? That she must have on everyone? She's a pestilent honey trap, luring people in with those eyes and that wicked mouth, and it works every time.

Lexie shatters my mental dexterity. She shatters everything. My mind, my breath, my clarity. My thoughts and visions.

And if I'm not careful, my future.

24

Lexie

Two and a half weeks.

That's how long it's been since I tried on the dresses. When I got home that night, a piece of me thought that I'd made up what happened in the dressing room. The way the electricity crackled in the air, the way he touched me, the way my skin scorched with need.

I didn't even make it up the stairs that night before I burst into tears. I bolted through the door into the bathroom and threw up. I've never, ever been the other woman. I can't believe I allowed myself to get trapped in his dark, addictive, gravitational pull. I told myself I was only getting close to him to prove he was a cheater. Something I could couple with the video I have of him and Olivia at the hotel to convince Annabelle to leave him. I was doing it for *her.*

But the sheer guilt and shame that consumed me from the way my body responded to his touch showed me I did it for me. When did I become this person? I should demand an immediate reassignment, promotion be dammed. I should turn myself in, turn him in, file some sort of formal complaint, fucking something. Not sit here and drool over the way my core quivered and clenched with a brush of his finger. *A brush.* The lightning-fast heat that zoomed through my body took me off guard, and even though I faked the hell out of it, I didn't recover until I got home and took care of myself.

And God forgive me, I want it again. I want to drop to my knees and run my tongue along his cock and inhale his scent. My body burns with the need to be touched by someone who knows what they're doing. And I bet anything, that person is Theo.

That's all this is. I don't want *Theo* as much as I want someone to make me feel good.

Right?

"And that's when the purple banana crashed into the earth," Justin says and my eyes snap back to him.

"Wait . . . what?"

"Welcome back! I swear you're just like Dylan when the *Real Wives of Salt Lake City* is on," he says as he dips a sushi roll into wasabi. "You're miles away. What's going on?"

Yes, that's right. I'm at work, eating sushi with my best friend, talking about . . . oh yeah, about wedding stuff, and not my wicked urge to blow my client. "God, sorry, I suck. It's nothing." I pop a wonton in my mouth. "I was just thinking about everything I still need to do for the wedding. You know, the bride never fails to surprise me. Just the other day,

I sent Annabelle a list of the top five caterers with sample menus, and she comes back with 'how about a taco truck instead'. She's a *Barlowe*—how can we seriously have a taco truck at the reception?"

Justin shakes his head, rolling his eyes in humor. "People with money have the wildest demands. What did she say after you talked her out of it?"

"Nothing," I say. "Literally, nothing. I followed up with a friendly nudge that we really had to decide soon and . . . crickets. I swear this is the chillest bride I've ever worked with in my life and, ironically, it's still stressful."

"Did you ask the groom then?" he asks.

Don't look at him, don't look at him. Justin will read my face and absolutely see right through me and I can't have this conversation. Theo is not chill. "No, not yet. He's been busy," I say, trying to disguise the fact that I haven't asked Theo hardly anything, since I've been avoiding him at all costs.

"Well, I do have some good news for you," he says as he cracks open a soda. "I booked the string quartet they wanted."

My eyes shoot up. It's the best news I've had this entire week. The quartet was one of Theo's parents' special requests, and even though he clearly didn't give a shit, Annabelle was pretty adamant on it.

"I can't wait to see the groom's face when the bride walks down the aisle to a string rendition of Canon in D," Justin says dreamily.

The image lands like a gut punch. Of course I still believe

this wedding should be called off—Annabelle has no idea who she's really marrying, and she deserves better. And I deserve my revenge for what he did to me back then.

Except doubt has started to creep in. Lately, I've been questioning what I—or what I *thought*—I knew about Boston. A small, irritating voice keeps asking whether I've been clinging to a seven-year grudge for nothing. I refuse to listen. Stubbornness is next to godliness.

I try, however, not to think about the fallout from canceling the wedding. The string quartet. The caterers. Rentals, florists, cake . . . *Stop.* Deposits would be lost, sure, but everyone would still receive a cancellation fee. Annabelle's family are freaking billionaires. With a capital *B.* Money isn't the real cost here.

Theo ruined my life. Annabelle deserves better. And this—this is just money.

"Tell me you got back on the dating apps," Justin says. "You deserve to one day plan your own wedding too."

"You're the best, you know that?" I give him a smile, and after Justin leaves, I reluctantly swipe through the piled-up messages on the dating app that I've been ignoring since reactivating it. *Ugh.* Do mirror selfies of a shirtless guy flexing really do it for other women?

I swipe through the DMs and chuckle at one from a guy I hooked up with about two years back. Decent enough in bed, no spark, but right now, I need some sort of distraction. I shoot him a quick message back that I'm free next Thursday, but then open up a social media app and continue searching for "Olivia, New York." I am going to find out who this woman is if it kills me.

On the walk home after work, dark clouds move in fast and furious, overpowering the sun and quieting the sky into ashy gray. Of course, today would be the day that I not only forget an umbrella, but my coat doesn't have a hood. I speed walk the four blocks from the subway stop to my studio and just as the first crack of lightning hits, I'm racing up to my apartment.

Pellets slash against the windowpane, and dribble down in fat lines. The noise rattles my chest, and I take a moment to breathe. I flip off all the lights in the apartment and gaze out the window. Lightning bolts fissure through the dark sky chased by booming thunder. The window squeaks as I crack it open and inhale the metallic scent of fresh rainwater against brick and pavement. God, I love the rain. The power, the force, the strength it carries makes me momentarily forget everything and just *be*.

Sitting by the window isn't enough. I grab my raincoat and run up to the rooftop.

The bulleting sheets roar and tink off the metal HVAC unit and ventilation system. I tug the hood over my head, but lift my face to the sky, letting the beads wash over me. My face is soaked and chilled, surely covered with streaks of mascara. But my shoulders relax, my chest fills with the sounds of Mother Nature's symphony. Radiant light fills the sky again and thunder roars through my body, shaking me to the bone. The storm is so close it's deafening. I should go back in, but it feels so damn good. I'm not feeling the chill on my skin, or the sharp slivers of rain against my cheeks. I feel freedom. It's powerful and liberating and terrifying. And metaphorical to my life—there's a danger if it gets too close, and I love it.

For tonight, I want to forget. About Theo, and my job, and chasing unreachable dreams. I want to forget about my past. The anger and hurt, the internalized shame of my working-class neighborhood. Instead, I'll latch on to the knowledge that my community made me resilient. Maybe things should've been different. I didn't deserve what happened in Boston, but I still made a life for myself.

A bolt of lightning shreds the sky. The thunder is so powerful, it shakes my ribcage. Why the hell don't I do this more often? Every storm, I need to come up here and breathe. Jesus Christ, it's cathartic. The city below me has slowed. Empty sidewalks. Inching traffic. Bright red brake lights cut through sheets of rain. My gaze drifts to the building across the street, and I squint to see a few other people looking out their windows at the storm. Are they absorbing the power, too? Are the booms and crackles allowing them to forget for a moment? Another hard snap of lightning crosses the sky, illuminating the building across from me like a spotlight and . . . *what the fuck?*

Did I just see what I think I saw? No . . . wait . . . no, I'm seeing things. I'm delusional. The thunder rattles the building as I stare at the shadowed figure standing in a window across the street. Lightning bursts through the sky again, and this can't be right. *No. No . . . no.*

Theo? The body is standing with drapery hooked to the side with their finger. This cannot be him. Theo, the doctor who lives in Tribeca, does not live in the run-down apartments across from mine. Another crack of lightning illuminates the building and my breath hitches. It's him. Holy mother of God, I think it's him. What in the ever-loving fuck is happening? I shake off the accumulating rain from my arms, dig out my phone, and zoom in as close as I can.

With a shaky finger, I tap record, waiting for the lightning to strike again. When it does, my heartbeat pounds so hard in my chest that it almost drowns out the storm. Oh my God, oh my God, oh my fucking God. *That's him.* I might be exhausted, but my eyes don't deceive me.

The buildings and city spin. I grab the metal railing on the edge of the brick to keep from falling. What the hell is happening? Has he always lived here? I'm going to be sick. Spots invade my vision. My neck heats. My heartbeat is thudding so hard into my ears that I think I'm going to pass out.

My shaky feet barely touch the ground as I abandon the storm for the safety of my home. I rush down the stairs and tear into my apartment. Water drips from my jacket and hair into a puddle at my feet. I shake off my drenched coat and kick off my shoes, then bolt to the window to close the blinds. My heartbeat thumps so loud it's the only sound I hear as I lift the phone. I play the video, cropping and scrolling, and even though I can't see completely, I know. *I fucking know.* How long has he been watching me? How have I not noticed?

My God, my God, he can see me. Thunder crashes and I claw at my wet neck. I wrap my arms around myself, my body almost trembling. *Almost.* Why am I not shaking? Why am I not screaming and calling the police? Why am I not disgusted? I should be. This is disgusting. Right?

What the fuck is wrong with me? I flick open the blinds a few inches to peek, then snap them closed and brace myself against the wall. This motherfucker ... But, *why*? If he doesn't remember me from college, it doesn't make sense.

My palms slide down my torso. My gut twists. How often does he watch? Do I always have my shades open? I close them when I get dressed, right? But at night, I love looking at the sky ... Heat rises up my legs.

What kind of sick fucker watches people through a window? Has he seen me touch myself? My breaths quicken and my fingers move to the waistband of my wet clothes. He's sick. I slide my fingers underneath the lace fabric and stroke my clit. *He watches me, wants me* ... my other hand moves to my breasts and I squeeze. I scoop them from my bra and pinch my hardened nipples. *Does he stroke his cock while watching* ... a moan escapes. My pulse thuds in my neck and I rub faster. My pussy turns hot, needing release. *He watches everything I do, the way I move, he wants to be inside me* ... I tug on my nipples until they're tender. My arousal coats my fingers, and I keep rubbing, faster, harder, grinding into myself for friction.

Is he obsessed? *With me*? A burn builds in my core. My needy, traitorous clit swells. This is wrong. This is all so fucking wrong. He's a psychopath. I should be terrified. Urgency builds through me. My body tightens as I keep circling myself. Shaky, uneven breaths leave my wet mouth. Thunder crashes . . . *mmmmm . . . He craves me. He wants to slide his thick cock inside me.* I'm fucking *good* enough . . . Frantic rubs and tugs and hard breaths, and I brace myself against the wall as a shuddering orgasm rips through me. My body convulses and my heartbeat pounds against my chest. Slowly, I retreat my hand and tuck myself back into my bra.

I should feel guilty—angry for my own betrayal, for caving to this reckless need, for releasing at the thought of him when I'm still furious with him. But instead, the knowledge that he's been watching me sends a dark thrill through my veins.

Because this time, I'm not the one being caught off guard.

This time, I'm aware.

And that awareness gives me something I haven't felt in a long time.

Control.

25

Theo

A knock at my office door drags me away from the last of my clinic notes. "Come in," I call out.

"Hey, you're here late," Erica says, stepping inside.

I glance at my watch. Christ, I can't believe it's after six already. The office closed over an hour ago. After volunteering to complete a fellow clinician's scripts when they ducked out early for their kid's choir concert, I still have at least another hour of paperwork. But I always save my heavy paperwork for Thursdays. That's usually when Lexie has social plans or visits her mom. These days, I'm sick of staring at her covered window, of seeing nothing but her silhouette, of counting down the days until we next meet.

I'm heading into week three without seeing her. And I fucking *miss* her.

Not the kind of missing that comes from wanting revenge

or out of anger because she's pissed me off. Not because I need to feed some compulsion.

I miss *her.* The person. And it's eating me alive.

"I could say the same thing to you," I say to Erica. "What's up?"

"I come bearing good news," she says with way too wide a grin after a ten-hour shift, "on the condition that you tell everyone I'm your favorite nurse."

"You strike a hard bargain," I say with a chuckle. "You're lucky I'm in the mood for some good news. Give it to me."

Her smile drops. "Oh, no. Wedding planning getting to you, huh?"

"There's a reason why people elope." This is all I'll say, even if Erica presses. But we won't elope. The wedding plans are my only tether to Lexie, the only excuse I can use to be in her company, the only thing keeping me sane.

Sometimes, I wish Lexie weren't so goddamn efficient and good at her job. Every time I push back, stalling for more time with her, pretending I care about the details when I don't, she returns immediately with a solution before I can blink. I don't like the caterer—she's got four more lined up. The place settings don't look right—she's already switched to my second *and* third choice.

"So true." Erica twists her mouth like she wants to say more but doesn't. "Anyway, I wanted to tell you I secured an appointment for Mr. Lopez at St Augustine's oncology department."

"You did?" My mood immediately lifts, and the first

genuine smile of the day reaches my mouth. I liked Mr. Lopez—a hard-working father of five—the moment I met him, and I'm grateful that Erica could wrangle an appointment with one of the top oncologists in the state.

"Sure did," she says. "I had to use a little bit of Erica magic. A perfect combination of sweetness and threats."

"Like a sugar-laced jalapeño."

She tilts her head. "I like to think of it as a sugar-laced grenade. It just so happens I used to work with the scheduler there, and well, voilà."

Incredible. I lean back on my chair and drum my fingers against the arm rest. "You still have my credit card, right? Will you send her something? A good bottle of wine, Scotch, whatever you think she'll like. Get yourself something, too."

She arches a brow, tugging on her dark ponytail. "You realize those are words men end up regretting, right? Especially when said to a woman with expensive taste."

"I know," I say, rolling my chair back to the desk. "But if you use the card for evil and not good, then I'd have to fire you, and depriving you of my daily presence feels unnecessarily cruel." I wink at her as she rolls her eyes.

"That would be a tragedy." She grins and closes the door behind her.

After I finish sending in scripts, reviewing a last-minute lab result, and entering in the final after-care summary, I can't escape the growing restlessness in my body and I head to the gym. The good mood from Erica's news is short-lived, and by the time I hop on the treadmill, I'm back to raging.

Through lifting, running, and hitting the bag, I beg for my mind to clear. Three fucking weeks and I haven't seen her. Not once. Like I mean nothing. I need the fantasy of me going further, harder, deeper, to leave my hungry mind. *She* was supposed to beg. Not me. And here I am, desperate for her scraps, even after she said she never wanted to see me again after she eventually closes my account.

After an hour, my agitation is still brewing. I shower, head back to the studio, slide open the curtains a few inches, and eat my dinner in my lap.

Jesus Christ this is pathetic. I'm seriously fucked up. For two hours, I've been sitting in the dark, staring at a wall because of her. This is the shit she makes me do. She drives me to the brink of insanity. Just as I stand to do something even more stupid like stream a mindless show, the lights flicker on in her apartment and my breath seizes. *She's home.* I grab my camera and zoom in through the lens.

The shadow of her curves from behind the blinds releases the tension in my shoulders. She's standing close to the window, and several moments pass when she snaps opens the blinds. I exhale. *Finally.*

What's she doing? She's glancing at the road, at the sky, and then . . . *me*? I look away from the lens. No . . . that can't be. I peer again. See, she's making me paranoid. She's looking at the building, at the road, and even if she were looking at my window, she wouldn't see me. If she had a camera and could zoom in, the only thing she'd see is a camera lens.

I really need to knock this shit off. I'm insatiable. When I got this place, I figured I'd be here sporadically. But I sleep here every night. I talk to her daily. I make excuses to see her, drop by her office, request meetings, and it's *not enough*. The closer I get, the more I need. It's never fucking enough.

The phone rings. *Anna*.

Shit. This is the first time Lexie has opened her shades in days and every asshole part of me that I despise wants to send Anna to voicemail. But it's almost three in the morning in Italy, so this can't be good.

"Hey," I say, tapping the phone on speaker and keeping my eye on Lexie who's still gazing at the street. "You okay?"

"Yeah, but I'm in the ER. Long story short, Nonna developed a new infection."

I lower the camera. "Oh shit. How's she doing?"

"Fine. Stubborn. Pissed that she can't drink wine." A tired laugh sounds over the phone. "Even though it's the dead of night, I figured I'd check in on you. I'm sorry, I really thought I'd be back home by now."

I thought she would've been, too. But right now, her absence is exactly what I need to get the Lexie bullshit out of my system for good. Because what's happening to me is not good. Or smart. And I can't stop it. "You know, I'm starting to think Nonna never actually took a spill and you two are conspiring with each other to avoid these wedding details."

"*Oops*. You caught us," she says. "What that woman won't do to help her grandkid."

"Blink twice if you're being held hostage."

"*Theo*," she says in that scolding tone that always makes me grin. "We're not on Facetime, but good try."

Probably a good thing since I'm in an apartment she's never seen, in the pitch black except for the one small green night-light illuminating from the bathroom, and I have a telephoto lens camera hanging round my neck.

"But seriously, how's the planning going?" she asks.

"Nothing new since we last talked," I say. "Except I'll never forgive you for making me learn how to dance the waltz."

She giggles. "You are going to be *sooo cute*."

"Is it too early to ask for a divorce?"

This makes her giggle even more and I don't know if I should be offended or relieved.

"Anyway, I'm going to send you and Lexie an email. My mother changed her mind on the vineyard that's supplying the wine for the event." A moment passes as she exhales. "I really am sorry I'm not more involved in the process."

"It's nothing. Take all the time you need," I say, lifting the camera back to my eyes. Lexie grabs two wine glasses from the shelf and digs out a wine opener from the drawer. *Two*. "The . . . ah . . ." *Why does she need two glasses?* "The planning's going fine. At the end of the day, I know you don't give much of a fuck."

"Oh, harsh words my friend."

My hands grip the edge of the camera. This better fucking be that Justin guy. "But am I wrong?"

"Um . . . I think I hear a code blue or something. Might be Nonna. Better run."

Maybe it's a friend. A girlfriend. I don't see her out with many women, but it's possible. *Shit.* What did Anna just say? "You're so cute when you lie." Across the street, Lexie fills both glasses and swirls the liquid. I need to get off the phone, now. "Tell Nonna I say hi, and that I'm not buying this bullshit infection story."

"Love you! You're the best." When Anna hangs up, I toss the phone like it's burning and shift all my focus into finding out what's going on across the street.

"*Who the fuck is that*?" I mutter, as she talks to someone out of frame. But the second he steps into my view, I size the fucker up. Blonde hair, trimmed beard, the arrogant stance that he's with someone who's way too fucking good for him. My breath locks. I strain to look, wishing to Christ I could lip read. What's he saying that's making her laugh? He keeps talking as she smiles and sips and how is he not kneeling at her feet, worshipping?

She hops up on the mantle next to the window with her back to me, sets the wine to the side, and rests back on her palms. Like a fucking leech, he snakes over and kisses her. *My* Lexie. A burn ravages my gut as his dirty mouth sucks and inhales her lips.

No, no. It's not supposed to be like this. She can't be with anyone else, and yes, I'm a fucking dick, I know it, but she *can't.* She's an angel. A gift. No one knows her inside and out like I do.

When he pulls back, he rakes his fingers in her hair and tugs. My jaw tightens as I clench. Those should be my fucking hands. *Put the goddamn camera down.* I can't do this. I can't watch the way he stands in front of her and opens her knees. The way she wraps her legs around his waist. I can't fucking do this. Is his cock pushing against her, rubbing on her sweet clit, is she squirming and getting wet and moaning? Her head moves and her tongue is in his filthy fucking mouth again. *Stop!* I should call, text, run over there and bang on the door. Anything to get them to stop.

Put the camera down and walk away.

Watching this is killing me. Acid fills my body. Hot and caustic, coiling in my gut and burning my chest. She's *my* fucking Lexie and no one else's.

She doesn't belong with anyone else.

I swallow, hard. I can't think this way, I shouldn't think this way, but it's kicking and screaming and tearing my insides.

There's only *one* person Lexie belongs with.

The fucker's mouth is at her neck and blinding red ravishes my vision. *Stop watching!* Why does he get to know how those lips taste? How smooth her skin is? He hasn't earned the right. He can't possibly know how special she is. How *perfect.* No one can. Not the way I do. My heartbeat slams against my chest.

My knuckles turn white. *Drop the goddamn camera.* His meaty, disgusting hands rub down that smooth, freckled skin and I swear to God I'm going to bolt over there, break down the fucking door, and destroy the man who's in my way.

She reaches behind her like she's going to unzip her dress,

and my cock grows hard. But instead, she drops her hands, slides off the mantle, and turns around. My breath hitches, sharp and loud.

Slowly, she lifts her hands to close the blinds, but before she does, she pauses, and I swear to Christ, she's looking right at me. There's no way she knows I'm here, right? I've been so careful. All these months . . . she can't know. My chaotic mind scrambles. I'm thinking too much and seeing too much and she can't fucking know I'm here.

Jesus Christ. Could she, though?

A smirk crosses her lips. A moment passes, then another, where I'm sure she's looking directly at me. I stop breathing. I wait. I sweat.

And then, she raises her middle finger.

What in the absolute fuck? My heartbeat slams in my chest. I think she knows. She snaps closed the blinds, and everything goes dark. My brain works overtime, conjuring mental images of what he's doing to *my fucking Lexie.*

My cock rages in my jeans and I adjust, trying to relieve the pressure. Is he sucking on those gorgeous tits? *I* want them in my mouth. I want to pinch those hard nipples until she screams and begs for more. I want to suck and squeeze and tug and *fuck, fuck* . . . what is he doing? He probably doesn't know how to touch her. Is he pawing and squeezing like she's a goddam doll? I bet he's not listening to her body, not touching her right.

He doesn't deserve her.

Would he be kneeling in front of her by now? Does he

have that beautiful cunt in his mouth? *Drop the camera.* I can't see anything, but I'm still looking, begging for a visual insight into what's happening. I hate myself for acting so desperate, but *she* does this to me. The power she holds . . . it's too much. It consumes me, drowns me, and she needs to release me.

Please, please walk away. But I can't rip away my gaze. This is too far, but I can't stop.

I fucking *hate* being needy.

I unzip, take out my raging cock, and start stroking. "*Fuck.*"

How dare she do this? I bet she's reaching under her skirt right now and shimming out of her panties. I slide my fist from base to tip. Fabric is probably tossed to the side, she's tugging up her skirt past her hips, maybe planting her palms on the desk. I bet that prick takes one look at her beautiful ass and that waiting pink pussy, and doesn't know what the fuck to do. My pulse thunders through my body. I'm going to punch the fucking window. A white electric raging heat courses through me, jolting acid up from my stomach to my throat.

I'm palming my cock, pulling hard and furious. This is it. I've crossed the line. I need to drop the camera and walk away. Its sick and I don't want to think about *my* Lexie getting fucked by anyone. Is he gripping her hips, and pushing into her? *Goddammit.* Are her tits bouncing, her face stern and concentrated, her body jolting? My cock swells in my hand, the veins harden in my palm. I stroke faster as a sickly heat snakes through me. Is her grip tight on the desk, as she takes his vile, vicious cock? *My* Lexie, *my* fucking pussy. I'm going to tear off his limbs.

I stroke, *faster, faster, faster.* He's pounding into her, over and over, and there's nothing I can do. My balls tighten and I jerk and lurch forward. Hot thick ropes of shameful cum shoot out onto the curtains, a disgusting line that drips onto the floor.

This is what she's done to me. I've lost my goddamn mind.

I refuse to see her with anyone else. I just need to figure out what the fuck I'm going to do about it.

A horrible, traitorous thought comes to mind.

Maybe I should start by being honest.

26

Theo

When Lexie texted me early Friday morning wondering if I wanted to meet for coffee on Saturday to review designs, I couldn't even respond. Visions of her, and whoever she was with, and my wedding, and fucking feelings, trapped in my brain and I couldn't. I read the message twenty, thirty times before finally messaging her back after my last patient of the day that I was busy.

I wasn't.

I spent all of Friday night watching her closed-blinds apartment for hours until I finally drifted off to sleep. Saturday, I did the same goddamn thing.

But now it's Sunday morning, and I've done nothing but stare out the window, praying for a flicker of motion, and the most I've gotten is shadows of movement behind the blinds.

My phone buzzes on my nightstand and my heart leaps. Every fucking time, it skyrockets, and every time I grab it, my heart plummets when it's not her. But this time, it sky-rockets for the wrong reason.

> Dad: Your mother has been trying to reach you. You are a grown man, capable of making your own decisions, and more than capable of reaching out to the woman who gave you life. It appears you are too busy for your own mother. Take a moment and think if she passed tomorrow, how you would settle knowing you refused to return a call.

It's taken me a long time to break my cycle, but I am not responsible for my parents' emotions. Fuck, I can barely keep my own feelings in check. But my father doesn't know why I choose to keep my mother at a safe distance. How I can no longer stomach her enabling his behavior. Neither of them deserves my time.

Instead, the person I want to spend time with, I've somehow pushed her away. Because what? She exercised her free will as an adult woman to have sex? I hate the rage that fills me thinking of what they did. And yet, it's so deeply unjust. I'm getting married. She fucked someone. This is not the same.

The fury grows, and yet the ravenous need to be around her fortifies.

I pick up the phone and text.

Theo: I know its last minute, but wondering if you wanted to grab breakfast then hit up the Chelsea Market to look for guests' gifts?

To my surprise, three dots appear immediately. I stop breathing.

Lexie: there just so happens to be the best crepe place in my neighborhood.

I know the place she's talking about. It is really fucking good.

Theo: Perfect. Will you shoot me the name and address of the restaurant?

Theo: Me and my driver will pick you up at ten.

Two hours later, I'm standing outside of Lexie's building waiting for her to come down. I lean against the building and stuff my hands in my pockets. Wait, this looks like I'm posing. I stand. I pace. I stuff them back in my pockets then remove them again.

Breathe.

I have no idea how she'll act. Will she bring up what happened at the dress shop and want to talk about it? Christ, I hope not. What the hell would I even say? That she's possessed me? That I wanted to tear off the dress and taste her in the dressing room?

And . . . does she actually know I live in the studio across from her? Maybe. No? *Fuck*. I exhale. She can't know. How would she? And yet, her blinds have stayed shut ever since she closed them with that middle finger aimed at the window. That could've meant anything—a fuck you to the universe, even. She *can't* know. Right?

My thoughts keep swirling, when I hear the apartment door swing open.

Goddammit, she takes my breath away. *Always.* Even today, in jeans, sneakers, her crimson hair tugged into a ponytail, she's the most beautiful woman I've ever seen.

"Hey!" she says with a wide smile, a quick wave, and zero torment.

Maybe this isn't awkward for her. Maybe she loves fucking with me. Maybe I'm overreacting for nothing.

"Thanks for picking me up," she says. "I'm so excited to hit the market. I haven't been there in forever."

I open the door, she slides in, and I try hard to not stare at her phenomenal ass. "Are you more excited for the market or crepes? Be honest."

"Crepes, of course. But the market's a close second." She snaps the seatbelt with a grin. "I'm surprised you suggested going to be honest. I thought we were good on the guest gifts."

She's already starting to see through my lie. But I couldn't stand the idea of going one more day without seeing her. "Yeah, I panicked. I think we need more."

She lifts a brow. "Theo Astor panicked? That's a side of you I've never seen. What other pieces of you are you hiding?"

A moment passes when I drop my gaze to her plush, pillowy lips, then lock with her eyes. "More than you can know."

Once we're seated at the restaurant, I order a chicken spinach crepe. Lexie orders one loaded with strawberries, chocolate, and extra whipped cream—while also giving me shit that I need to live a little and get more sugar in my life. I take a sip from my coffee and figure out how best to approach the conversation with her.

"So," I ask casually, "how come I haven't seen you much lately?"

"Oh, you know," she says, "I've been busy." We both know it's a lie. She's not making this easy for me.

"Look, I asked you here today because I wanted to apologize for how I acted in the dress shop. We're planning a wedding together—" I try not to let myself think too much into these words "—and I want us to be on good terms."

She peeks up at me through dark eyelashes. "Yeah, I think that's for the best." She clears her throat. "Thank you. I really do appreciate it."

Relief warms me. I clap once, a little too cheerful. "Great, now that we're friends again, I need to know everything I've missed out on. Not just wedding stuff, but *you*. What's been going on in your life?"

Her eyes narrow at the sudden overfriendliness, but she humors me. "Well, if you insist on knowing, I went on a date."

Yeah, I know. My jaw clenches. *Don't be a dick. Don't be*

a dick. Lexie needs to know that I'm not always an asshole. "How did it go? Did you find 'the one'?"

"Definitely not the one," she says with a chuckle and my body releases. "Actually, it kind of sucked."

The tone perks my ears. "Well, now you have to tell me what happened."

She shakes her head. "Nope. You don't want to hear this."

About a bad date? Yes, the fuck I do. "I'm pretty sure in our contract, subsection B, it states that if Lexie has a bad date, she's required to provide me with full details."

She giggles and my chest swells with pride. "Subsection B, huh? Funny I don't remember that." She chews her lips into her mouth. "God, it's embarrassing."

"Oh good. My specialty."

She looks at me like she doesn't quite believe me, but then the server arrives, setting down our plates. Lexie's eyes go wide at the mountain of whipped cream. Before she can dig in, I stealthily swipe her plate and hold it hostage, "You don't get to eat," I say, grinning, "until you tell me."

"Seriously?" If looks could kill, I'd be dead. "Fine." She exhales. "So, I've gone out with this guy before. A few years ago. Nice enough, but, you know, I didn't text back for a reason. But I didn't remember the reason. Until I did." She pauses and I can already tell I'm not going to like what comes next. "He gets to my place and . . . you know never mind. You're a client. I really need to stop talking about this."

If she calls me a client one more time, I might throw this crepe into the wall. "I'm *not* just a client."

"Yeah, you are," she says, her smile gone. "And you made that abundantly clear in the dress shop."

My face heats. Fuck, I hate myself sometimes. I take a bite and wash it back with coffee. "God, I can be a dick." I pause and carefully choose my words. "There was something about seeing you in that dress that made all of . . . this . . . feel real. I've been letting myself think that the wedding isn't fazing me and I've got everything under control, but the truth is, I don't. I really fucking don't. And I unfairly took it out on you. I'm really sorry."

This might be the most honest and open I've been in long time. And it feels fucking terrible. She studies my face, her brows crease, until a soft smile breaks through. "Thank you for being honest with me. And for the apology."

I nod. "Okay, tell me about the date. The food is getting cold." She hesitates, clearly weighing her options, so I add, more gently. "You can tell me anything."

That seems to do it. Her shoulders relax. "So basically, he comes over and wants . . . you know . . . right away. There's a time and place for hook-ups, but he'd asked me for dinner, so I thought that's what it was." She shrugs. "We start doing some stuff, but then I stop and say, "I thought we were going to dinner?"

They didn't fuck? I shouldn't ask. I don't deserve to ask. But I have to know. "So you didn't . . ."

Well shit. I asked.

"No, we didn't."

Don't smile. Don't fucking smile.

Too late.

"And then he actually laughed when I said we should go for dinner. Told me he thought I knew what he meant—that he never had any intention of taking me out. But he guessed, *after*, we could order take out or something." The blush creeps back in her cheeks and I feel it—there's more. And I will sit here all day until she's comfortable enough to tell me.

Finally, she takes a breath. "I was so insulted, you know? So I kicked him out. And then he just got kind of mean."

I immediately scan her face for any sign of trauma, and I swear to fuck if this guy even thought of laying a hand on her . . .

"He said that the few times we went out back in the day that he knew immediately someone like me wasn't 'wife material'. And it just sort of crushed me, you know? Not that I need to be a wife. Just like, the way he said it made me feel like I wasn't *good* enough to be someone's wife. Then he said I'll never be more than eye candy and the quicker I accept it, the better off I'll be."

I'm going to kill this guy. I'm going to stitch his dirty fucking mouth shut first, hang him by the feet, and crack each one of his ribs with my fists until he dies from internal bleeding.

While I'm mentally plotting this fucker's death, she seizes the moment to steal her plate back. She stabs her fork into the crepe, takes a bite and lets out a dangerously satisfied sound, then flashes me a smug, victorious smile. "Anyway, I should be grateful I dodged a bullet with that guy."

"Lexie." I reach for her hand, my thumb brushing over her skin. Before I can stop myself—before I even realize what I'm saying—the words slip out. "Any man, *any*, would be lucky to have you as their wife."

The moment hangs between us until Lexie breaks it with a soft scoff. "Please, you're just saying that to be nice."

I want to take it back. To laugh it off, pretend it was nothing more than politeness. But I can't—not when the truth is sitting heavy in my chest. "I'm not," I say quietly. "I promise." I squeeze her hand, grounding myself. "You're smart, driven, have a great sense of humor, and beautiful." *So fucking beautiful.* "Not only are you 'wife material', you're what men dream about." *You are what I dream about.* "You will never, ever waste another second thinking about what this guy said to you. Got it?"

The smile that breaks through brightens the entire space. She nods and returns to her crepes.

And I return to wondering what in the absolute fuck I'm doing.

27

Lexie

"Well you look as beautiful as ever," I say to my mom as I walk into her apartment. "Yellow's a great color on you."

"To think I raised you to be a decent human being," my mom says with a scowl. "You're not too old to ground. Just remember that."

I laugh, set a few bags of groceries on her counter and start stacking her fridge. A month after my mom's accident and head injury, the bruising has morphed from a terrible red, to purple, to a now faded yellow. We can joke about it now, but the relief I feel knowing she's not permanently hurt still hits me hard. "Did you have your appointment with Theo yesterday?" I ask, keeping my gaze steady on the fridge rack as I stack yogurts, and not on her eyes.

It's been less than a week since Theo and I had breakfast and wandered through the market together, and if I thought he occupied my thoughts before, I was wrong. I saw a side of him I didn't know existed. Kind. Open. *Human.* Our conversation over crepes seemed to put us both on unfamiliar ground, easing into an easy, almost intimate comfort. So much so that my plans to confront him about being a freakishly obsessed stalker, and demand to know why he rented a place next to mine, evaporated. As we strolled past the different booths, the easy silences felt just as natural as talking. And something in me didn't want to break the spell. It's weird, and creepy, and should be more concerning, and yet, there's a sense of safety knowing he's watching me. It's been a long time since I've felt that way, and it feels . . . nice.

For once, he opened up—about the pressures at work, his strained relationship with his mother after I caught him ignoring one of her calls and I couldn't help myself asking what was up. He even reluctantly admitted, after I forced it out of him, that the approaching wedding was making him *only slightly* nervous.

We've texted every day since. It usually starts wedding talk, but slowly it morphs into swapping movie suggestions, him telling me stories about his patients, me venting to him about vendors, and telling him about former bridezillas, and grooms I wanted to strangle.

My heart is stretching in a way I didn't know it could, and I know any moment it's going to snap. Our budding . . . friendship . . . will end when the job is over. I can't delude myself that when him and Annabelle are married, we'll keep in contact.

And something about that hits *hard*.

"Yes, my appointment with Dr. Astor was great yesterday," my mom says, handing me the rest of the grocery items. "He said I have the body of a healthy seventy-year-old."

I laugh. "You're only fifty-five."

She waves me away. "I'm just kidding. He said the new thyroid meds are working, and the vitamin D levels are inching up, but he wants to see them higher." She hands me the final item, and I close the door. "You know, I sure had that boy pegged wrong."

My heart squeezes so hard in my chest that I grip the countertop. I think I may have misjudged him, too. I've been replaying what happened at the university over and over in my mind and the thought that I might have had this all wrong keeps itching at me.

My mom grabs two sodas and a bag of potato chips, and settles into the couch. "Are you two still spending a lot of time together?"

I nod, and stuff chips in my mouth. She doesn't need to know how much time, even though I want to tell my mom everything. But who in their right mind tells their mom that they're actively falling for an engaged man who once ruined their life? Or at least *thought* they ruined their life.

Maybe I'll never know if he got me expelled. My life is different now. I'm different. He's different. It might be time to finally let this go.

A spotlight shines on the terrible thing I'm doing. Explaining my feelings to my mom, how I ache for him when he's not around, how I've never felt so safe and protected and stimulated, would fall on deaf, judgmental ears. My mom's Catholic. I can already see her reciting the Hail Mary under her breath as her thumb and index finger rub a phantom rosary.

Religious or not, I deserve the wrath.

She must know that I don't want to say much more, because she turns on the TV and we resume our bi-weekly ritual of watching the local news while painting our toenails. Several long moments pass and my mom leans into me.

"My beautiful, sweet girl," she says as she gives me a soft smile. "I love you. And you deserve to be happy. Just make sure you're taking care of yourself too, okay?"

With those words, I return to face the TV and blink back tears.

"Justin, noooo. Don't make me go alone," I plead into the phone, trying to reason with my *former* best friend who just told me that he thinks he has food poisoning and cannot accompany me to an event tonight. "That creepy ass rep, Cody, is going to be there and you know he won't leave me alone."

Tonight, the most connected vendor we work with is hosting a client appreciation night and Sydney said (demanded) that Justin and I attend to represent our company since she's out of town on a wedding. I don't love these events, but they're a necessary evil in this line of work. And now that I'm a lead, my presence is expected. But going alone is going to be miserable.

After Justin apologizes, again, Theo suddenly pops into my head as someone to bring instead, but I immediately shut it down. Inviting a client to a work event would cross every professional boundary, not to mention the fact that he's getting married in ninety days. And I'm still digging into his connection to Olivia, still telling myself I want to take him down—*or at least that I should.* But, my feelings are muddying my judgment. I know I need to focus on the task at hand. I know I need to let him go.

But I can't.

Every moment I spend with Theo, I fall deeper and deeper into his orbit, and it's dangerous. The Barlowe and Astor families are powerful, wealthy, untouchable. If they found out even a fraction of my intentions, my career would be over and I'd be blacklisted from every company in the city.

And yet, I can't shake this feeling that Theo doesn't want this marriage. He rented an apartment next to mine! He seeks me out, talks to me, *sees* me in a way no one else ever has. A man who makes someone feel like this can't want to get married. He just can't.

Maybe he's torn. With Annabelle, he gets the prestige, her kindness and security. And me? I'm not sure. But whatever he sees in me, the way he studies me, wants to know every part of me—it wraps around my heart and makes me feel almost whole.

What I'm doing is wrong. The lines are blurred, and he's a client for Christ's sake. But I made a promise that I'll never act on my feelings, and I won't go back on my word.

I slip on a black dress, my impulsive fingers twitching to open the blinds. I know it's wrong, but the rush of imagining Theo's eyes burning into me is far too tempting. Is he at the apartment tonight? Does he want to watch me get dressed?

I should have confronted him about the apartment when I had the chance. If a friend or my mom or literally any woman told me a man had rented a place nearby just to watch them through the window, I'd call it what it is: sick. Stalking. I'd tell them to buy a gun and go straight to the cops. Every feminist principle etched into my bones is screaming at me now, warning me how deeply problematic this behavior is.

And yet, I can't stop secretly loving it.

Ever since I found out about the apartment, I've gotten myself off every night with the knowledge that he's fixed his attention exclusively on me. Maybe it's awakened something dark and exhibitionistic. Maybe it's the rush of power—knowing that a man like Theo, who has *everything*, wants me badly enough to get an apartment and watch me.

That might be the most dangerous part of it all. Because for the first time in my adult life, I feel safe. Watched. Protected.

And somewhere inside of me, the nineteen-year-old girl who crushed hard on Theodore Astor is giddy at the thought that he might be wanting me back.

Then another thought settles in—he remembers me. He has to. There's no way he rented an apartment opposite to mine after only knowing me a couple of months. Right? Or was he serious that first day when he said he keeps those he doesn't trust closest to him? It's impossible to ignore the fact that even if he wants me, he doesn't fully trust me.

As if he has a sixth sense, my phone rings and my heart skips a beat when I see his name.

"Hey," I say.

"Hey, sorry, I know this is random to call instead of texting," he says quickly. "But I'm heading out to meet some friends and wanted to tell you that I took next Monday off. Can you move our meeting with the florist to then?"

"Sure," I say, and because I can't help myself. "So . . . what are you doing tonight?"

"Heading to an Irish pub in West Village to watch the Mets while I pretend to give a shit when one of the guys pitches me investment opportunities."

I chuckle. "Wow, living the dream. What a coincidence, I'll be a few blocks away at The Cloak and Mirage for a vendor event, pretending to give a shit while a rep pitches 'exciting growth opportunities'."

"That does sound terrible," he says. "My condolences. Remember to hydrate."

"You ever turn doctor mode off?"

A low chuckle hums through the phone. "Careful what you ask for."

Yeah. This man absolutely knows what he's doing.

An hour later, I smack my lipstick, spritz on perfume, and head outside to catch my Uber. I can't help taking one last glance at Theo's place, but the drapes are still drawn.

Just two hours of my life I need to give to this party and then I can call it a night.

I silently beg the universe that even though it's Cody's company hosting the party, he won't be here this year. Last time, he trailed me from conversation to conversation, pretentiously droning on about the accounts he'd landed while I smiled through clenched teeth. The real highlight was when he confidently tried to mansplain my own job to me, apparently under the delusion that I needed his guidance to build connections in an industry I've spent years working in.

As we drive through the city, I casually start scrolling through social media looking for "Olivia, New York" but my heart isn't in it. Maybe I don't want to know who this woman is anymore. I'm no longer interested in destroying Theo. And even if I did find her—what then? It scares me that I no longer know what I'd do next.

Without thinking, I switch to my messages and pull up Theo's name. I shouldn't. He said he's with friends.

Lexie: Did the game start already?

I stare at my screen, waiting for a reply, or at the very least typing bubbles to appear and . . . nothing. He's probably enjoying himself and not thinking about me even once. *Get over yourself, Lexie.*

And then, my phone pings.

Theo: Yes and it already sucks.

Theo: Forgot to mention I bought you something today while out shopping. I'll bring it to you next time we meet.

A picture pops up of a bottle of Catena Zapapta Adrianna Malbec. *Oh my God*. Butterflies flip in my belly. I can't accept this, right? I mean, the wine costs several hundred dollars.

Lexie: I can't accept it.

Theo: You can and will.

Oof . . . that demanding tone. I can just picture him saying this as his dark eyes narrow, as his jaw flexes under that facial hair. I press my thighs together and bite back a grin.

Theo: Besides, I'm learning the stupid wedding dance later this week, so consider this my apology—paid in advance.

I text back a thank you as the Uber pulls over. I shrug my purse over my shoulder and brace myself for what's in store.

28

Lexie

Inside, the dark wood, ambient-lit bar is lively. Some people are sitting in deep-black leather booths, some gathered around high top tables, some hushed in a corner. Wait staff carrying trays of champagne and appetizers weave in between the crowd, and the line at the bar is two-to-three people deep.

I take a breath as a wide-grinned, open-armed, slicked-back hair Cody spies me from the corner and beelines my way.

Kill me now.

"Lexie! I'm so glad you could make it." He pulls me into a hug. One that lasts a beat too long, where his deep musky cologne has now seeped into my clothes, which I'll now need to burn. He steps back, but doesn't drop my hand, and instead twirls me in a circle like I'm a ballerina on top of a music box. "What a dress, huh?" I swear to God if this vendor didn't give us the below-market rates we need, I would've marched my ass away.

As Cody grabs himself a double and hands me a glass of wine, he proceeds to talk at me for the next thirty minutes about deals on specialty items he can "get us", and the big-name clients his firm landed that he's sworn to secrecy about. I almost scoff and tell him that I'm managing a Barlowe account, but I bite my tongue.

Can I leave yet?

"You'll have to excuse me," I say, interrupting his God-awful monologue. "I need to use the restroom."

After weaving through the crowd, I escape into the bathroom and rummage through my purse, looking for my lipstick—any excuse to stall and buy myself more time alone. But my fingers skip past it and curl around my phone instead.

> Lexie: With the way you keep warning me about dancing, I'm starting to think you're underselling it. Are you really *that bad*?

The dots pop up immediately. Like the phone hasn't left his hands since we last messaged, waiting for me.

> Theo: I really am.

> Lexie: I don't buy it. Don't athletes have control over their body?

> Theo: What makes you think I'm an athlete?

Lexie: Call it an educated guess.

I send a gif of a cartoon character flexing its massive biceps with smoke shooting from its arms.

Lexie: Just saying.

Theo: (laughing emoji) I love that this is how you see me. And for the record, I have *excellent* control over my body.

Oh I bet he does. My body heats at the implication.

Lexie: Bold claim from a man who's already admitted he can't dance.

Theo: You know I can't resist a challenge.

I check my watch and realize I've been hiding out in the bathroom far longer than I should have. As much as I'd love to stay hidden, I need to make the rounds. I fire off a quick text to Theo that I have to head back to the party, and re-enter the room, hoping I can avoid Cody.

But the moment I step back into the crowd, he catches my eye. Escape becomes impossible, so I reluctantly make my way over to the bar, where he's deep in an animated conversation with a group of guys.

"There you are," he says, rattling his empty glass at the

bartender. "I was about to send out a search and rescue team."

"Sorry, I had to take a call."

He waves it off. "Come on, we're here to have fun. Network. Not actually work."

"It was personal," I lie, though only really a half-lie, already irritated that I feel the need to justify myself to him of all people.

His smile drops instantly and his eyes start to darken. "Oh, yeah?" he says. "Who's calling at his hour? A boyfriend?" My shoulders tighten at the edge in his voice. "Well, I've got you for the whole evening. So whoever it is, can wait," he adds, punctuating it with a wink.

My stomach twists as something about the way he says those words feels very, very wrong.

Almost two hours have passed, and each second slogs by at the pace of a melting glacier. The group has now moved to a booth and Cody's already downed at least five drinks since. He's so loud, I'm amazed his co-workers' eardrums are still intact. I've tried to make my escape more than once, but somehow he keeps pulling me back—another question fired my way, a small, unwelcome touch to make sure I'm still here.

It's unnerving.

The only thing keeping me sane are the stolen moments when I message Theo. I shouldn't get so excited, but even now I'm hyper-aware of how I'm waiting for the phone in my palm to buzz with his reply to my latest message.

I should be focused on work. Instead, my mind is entirely on Theo, and I can't shake it. Maybe I just need to leave—call it an early night and get out of here before this feeling gets any worse.

As I start to move out of the booth, Cody is suddenly all over me, an arm around me in a way that's far too familiar, his mouth brushing my ear, "Where are you rushing off to?" he murmurs.

He yanks me back, and I fall into him slightly before righting myself. Enough. I might work with this guy. I might know him well enough to fake familiarity. But he has no right to grab me like I belong to him. Powerful vendor or not. Discount or not, I'm done with this shit. My phone starts ringing—the perfect escape—and I answer it immediately.

"Hello," I say, pressing a finger into my free ear.

"Hey, I know you're busy . . ." Theo's voice comes through, slightly muffled, and relief washes over me. He's the only thing I want to hear right now.

"Hold on," I say quickly. "I'm going to step outside so I can hear you better." I tap Cody's arm, already pulling away. "Good to see you again," I add automatically, the words tasting like bile. "I'm heading out now."

This time, I'm not asking.

"The fuck you are."

I freeze in shock. "*Excuse me*?"

"Come on," he says, his mouth twisting into a smile that doesn't reach his eyes. I sense the undertone immediately, and a slick heat crawling up my spine. "Jesus, it's a party.

Drink up, loosen up, and try not to ruin the mood. That's all I'm asking."

"Fuck you," I say, loud enough that a few heads in the booth turn. I'm past caring at this point. My hands shake as I grab my purse and slide out of the booth. I realize I've forgotten all about the call with Theo, and I look down to see it's already ended. I must have hit it by accident. It barely registers, as all that matters now is getting out of this place as fast as I can, collecting my jacket en route.

Outside, the night hits me cold and sharp. Streetlights, car beams, and storefront lights illuminate the sidewalk. I pull my jacket tighter, barely managing to slip my arms into it when a hand clamps around my arm. "Hey, sorry, okay?" Cody slurs. "I didn't know you'd be so sensitive. I was just giving you shit. Come back inside."

"No," I snap. I dash to the edge of the sidewalk and wave down a cab, relief spiking when it slows—only for Cody to yank my arm down hard. The cab speeds off.

What the fuck.

"I just want to talk," he says, irritation creeping into his voice. "Christ. Come on." His apology is all for show; I can see right through it. The tight, panicked knot in my gut tells me he's not letting this go. "I was just fucking around in there. I thought you were one of the cool chicks that could handle hanging with the guys. Guess I was wrong. I'm sorry. Don't be like this."

I barely know this man. He has no right—none to talk to me like this. I open my mouth to tell him to fuck off again, but he grips my elbow, hard, and drags me toward the alley. My feet stumble before my brain can catch up.

"What are you doing?" I gasp.

"I just want to talk," he snaps. "That's all. Seriously—calm the fuck down."

And suddenly, I'm very aware of how dark the alley is—and how alone we are. I try to step around him, but he blocks me. For the first time in my life, I'm truly scared. My mind flashes to the time when Theo cornered me in the office. But it was *nothing* like this. Theo's presence has always been dark, brooding, intense, but never physically threatening. I wrench my arm, but Cody doesn't loosen his grip. If he squeezes any harder, I'm kneeing him in the balls.

"Get your fucking hands off me!"

He doesn't drop them. "You're going to come back inside and stop being a little fucking cunt—"

Hands come out of nowhere, gripping Cody by the back of his collar and yanking him off me, before slamming him into the brick wall. My breath catches, locking painfully in my chest.

A familiar silhouette fills my line of sight.

"What the fuck did you say to her?" Theo barks, his eyes filled with a vicious, murderous rage. His gaze snaps to me, checking me up and down for any injury, then he shoves Cody back against the wall. "You don't get to talk to her like that. Ever."

A stumbling, dazed, red-faced Cody blinks at me through blood-shot eyes and back at Theo. "Who the fuck are you?"

Everything is still for a few, long, sickening seconds as Cody's eyes narrow at Theo.

And then, he lunges.

"No!" I scream, but my voice is snuffed out by shuffling, stumbling bodies, and shouting men. How is Theo here? *Why* is he here? What the hell is happening? "Please, stop!" My words fall completely useless in the chaotic sea of grunts and shoving. There's nothing I can do. I flatten myself against the alley wall. Cody balls his hands into hard fists, and leaps at Theo. *Oh God, oh God* . . . I slam my hands over my mouth. The hard crack of Theo's fist meeting Cody's face echoes in the alley, and acid shoots through my stomach.

A stunned Cody stumbles back from the impact with blood rushing from his nose. Are they done? And holy shit . . . Theo's *here*.

I need to leave but instead, I'm frozen in place.

Cody wipes the blood from his nose and bolts like a bull released from a cage and tries to swing, but Theo's right hook meets Cody's jaw. One hit, two, so lightning fast that I barely register what's happening. Theo grips Cody on the collar and slams him into the concrete with a sickening thud. Theo drops to his knees, his elbows flying up, hitting and punching and raging. "You motherfucker," he's yelling, driving Cody into the pavement. "How dare you touch her . . ." Cody's face is a mess, blood spilling from his nose, his mouth, streaking down his chin. *Oh God.* "You don't get to put your hands on her," he snarls. "Ever. If you so much as speak to her again, I will kill you. I will fucking gut you. Do you hear me?"

The words crash over me, loud and vicious.

"She's mine," Theo growls. *"Mine."*

What the hell is happening? There's too much noise. Too much blood. My brain can't keep up with the violence, the shouting, the fact that Theo claimed me as *his*.

Over and over, Theo lands brutal hits, pure rage driving every blow. The alley fills with the sickening sounds of bones breaking. My stomach churns, bile burning at the back of my throat, yet I still don't move. I don't pull Theo off. I don't scream for help.

I just watch.

I know it's wrong. And still, a dangerous heat coils low inside me, because he's doing this *for me*. Because he didn't hesitate. Because he was willing to burn everything down to protect me.

It's toxic. It's sick.

And it terrifies me how easily that thought takes hold, because the man in front of me doesn't look like Theo anymore. His eyes are black with fury, his movements wild and relentless.

He looks like he's going to actually kill Cody.

"Theo! Stop. *Please.*" When his elbow jerks up, I grab him—both hands locking around his bicep—and wrench him back. Muscle cord hard beneath my grip. Blood slicks his knuckles. Cody's? His? I don't know.

Theo staggers away from Cody's barely conscious and broken body sprawled on the ground. His fists are still clenched, his chest heaving.

Then he looks at me.

His eyes are wild, unfocused—burning with fury—he doesn't really see me yet.

It takes a few seconds for him to come back to himself. But as soon as our eyes lock, time stops. This has to be a dream. A hazed, fevered unreality. None of this could have just happened. The world around us fades, drowned out by the rush of my breath and the thunder of my heart, and for a terrifying moment, I think I might pass out.

Our gaze breaks as Theo glances down at Cody, then back at me. Something shifts in his expression, a split-second hesitation, before he turns and storms towards me. He rakes his bloodied fingers through my hair and crushes his mouth into mine. *Fuck* ... The shock sends me stumbling back a step before instinct takes over and I capture his mouth. The kiss is brutal—rushed, possessive, bruising. His dirty, bloodied hands are everywhere: my jaw, my neck, my ass, leaving streaks of blood in his wake that should make me recoil in fear but only turn me on more. His mouth is intoxicating—soft and devastating all at once—a promise of pain and longing and ruin. I'm already lost to it. He owns my mouth, tugs my hair, bites down just hard enough on my lips to make my breath hitch. My legs tremble. My pulse skids out of control.

I cling to him, pulling him into me, pressing myself closer and closer into his hard body.

"Oh, Lexie," Theo murmurs, low and wrecked. "You taste so good."

The words hit me hard. The velvety tone in how he said "Lexie" . . . Wait. Stop. *What am I doing?*

I yank my head away and shove him back, scrubbing at my mouth like I can erase the last few seconds. "What are we doing?" I manage, my voice breaking.

Oh God, oh God, oh God. We just kissed. I want to spit him out, cry, and do it again all at once. "Get the hell away from me!"

"Wait, no, listen to me." He reaches for me with his bloodied hands, but I put up my arms to stop him.

"Don't say my name. Don't you dare fucking say my name. Oh my God, what the hell have I done?" I push at him, once, twice, then over and over as he stands there and takes my blows. "You're getting *married.* Why . . . why did you just kiss me? Why did you come here?" My stuttered breath locks inside my trembling body. I'm flushed with want and regret and adrenaline, sick from what I did, disgusted that I want more. I finally stop pushing him and step back on my stumbling, shaking feet.

What am I supposed to do now? My body burns. My mouth is raw, scratched from his facial hair. Rage fills me.

He eliminates the distance between us, his gaze boring into mine. "I'm sorry, I shouldn't have done that, but . . . there's more going on than what you know."

"Stop it. Stop talking." My body is on fire, betraying me in the worst way. My galloping heart feels like I ran a marathon, and guilt drowns me. I can't believe he just did that. I can't believe *I* just did that. I need to leave. I'm outside and there's still not enough air. I push Theo away, storm past a groaning Cody to get out of the alley and turn the corner with Theo trailing at my heels.

He grabs my arm and I freeze. "Please listen to me," he says, soft and calm like a fucking lunatic as blood drips down his hands and into his sleeves. "Just calm down for a second and listen."

"Calm down? Calm fucking down? I don't want to hear what you have to say. This is what you do. This . . . goddammit." I hate my aching mouth and simmering body and this craving for him to kiss me again. I want to punch him and fuck him and hug him all at once and I *cannot fucking do this*. "You're messing with my head! This isn't me. I'm not sure what kind of women you're used to, but this isn't me. I can't do this."

"I know, I know, but I promise you there's other things happening that I can't talk about. You just have to trust me—"

"Trust you? Are you kidding me? You're getting married to the nicest woman in the world, you just kissed me, and you want me to *trust* you? You are fucking *poison*."

His nostrils flare as he pulls in a deep breathe. "I know what this looks like, but just . . . shit . . . it's not what you think."

It's not what it looks like? Does he think I'm stupid? I cross my arms. I'm over this. Him, us. Feeling this way and knowing I can't have him. Drowning in guilt from lusting over an engaged man, while wanting to break down in tears knowing no one else has ever made me feel the way he does.

I glare, trying as hard as I can to stop the trembles in my voice, but it's useless. "Then tell me. Right now."

His face drops.

"Tell me why you kissed me like that. Why you make me feel the way I do, and say the things you say, and you rented a fucking studio apartment next to me, when you're getting married?"

His eyes fly wide open. His mouth drops. But he doesn't say anything.

"Why, Theo?" I say, now unable to hold back a choked, trembling sob and I hate that he's seeing me break. "Why did you come here tonight and save me and kiss me like that? Because we're fucking *friends*?"

He stays totally silent, unspoken words flashing across his face, but I need him to speak.

"Why?" I say, half demanding, half pleading, all of me sick to my stomach. "Tell me! Why are you doing this to me?"

He grips my shoulders, his jaw flexing and popping, his gaze so intense that my legs shake. "Because you won't get out of my fucking head!" His voice shatters. "I can't take it . . . I can't take it anymore. You're everywhere. At night, during the day, in my dreams, my fucking nightmares, you are *always fucking there*."

Everything slows. The traffic. The pedestrians. My heartbeat. The sounds of music trailing from whatever bar where we're standing mutes. He steps back and wipes his mouth with his sleeve. "I can't get you out of my head."

And now, he sounds broken.

"It's too much. I think of you *all the goddamn time*," he says more pained than angry. "It's not healthy. It's not even fucking sane. I hate this so much and there's nothing I can do. You've invaded every single part of me. I want to shake you off, I want to be done with you, and I *can't*."

A heavy swallow rolls down my throat and my lips tremble. "Then why are you still with Annabelle?" I say, inching closer. "I don't understand it. I see the way you look at me, I feel the way you feel about me." Silence fills the air, and I feel my heart opening, just a little, dipping itself a little outside of my body. "Why are you with her," I say as my heartbeat rails against my chest, "when I think you want to be with me?"

Theo clasps his hands behind his head, looks at the sky, then back at me. He inhales, then releases a slow, rattled breath. "I'm marrying Anna."

All color drains from my face before my cheeks heat. "Then why did you kiss me?"

He drops his gaze to the pavement, unable—or unwilling—to answer. I'm shaking, a mix of cold and adrenaline still coursing through me. I just opened myself up to him—raw, exposed, painfully vulnerable—and he doesn't have the decency to look me in the eye.

"Fuck you, Theo. I mean that. How dare you? God, you're such a selfish asshole. You know what I think? I think you *love* messing with people's minds. I think you get hard and jerk off to how many people you can hurt. Even after all these years, you're *still* fucking with me, and I fell right into your trap." My voice is raised loud enough that a few passersby give me a side-eye, but I don't care. I'm so done. With all of this. With seven years of hating him, with months of lusting after him, with feeling like that same girl back then who asked him out and he rejected. "This is the type of man you are. I knew it in college, and I know it now. *Nothing* is ever enough. You have a vile need to destroy. What sort of sick fuck are you? Annabelle's not enough, is she? You need her. You need me. You need Olivia."

Whatever quiet, sympathetic, maybe even longing look Theo held disappears. Violent, red-hot flames flare up his face, and he grits his teeth. "What . . . what the fuck did you just say?"

Oh, shit.

He. Is. Furious.

Whoever Olivia is, I just struck a major nerve. And good. I hope I did. My eyes narrow. "*Olivia.* Is she another one, too? Are you obsessed with her as well?" And what the hell is wrong with me that there's this sick, disgusting jealousy terrorizing me that, what . . . I wasn't special enough? The chosen other one? He's *destroyed* me and I hate that he's getting upset over Olivia?

He takes one step closer with black, lethal, rage-filled eyes. "*What in the fuck do you know about Olivia*?"

My breath feels like a knife, stabbing my chest. My lips stammer. "I know enough."

He grips me by the shoulders, digging into me with such force it feels like he might toss me. Veins stretch against his neck, his eyes sear into mine so hard I want to crumble.

"I swear to God, Lexie, if you do something . . ."

His death grip drops from my arms and he steps back. I immediately feel the void, which is so wrong on so many levels. I want to be in his fierce grip. I want to live in his fury. I want him to admit right fucking now the kind of man he is so I can stop dreaming about him.

And then he storms toward me, but I don't back up. *Come get me.* I don't even care anymore. I'm done with his games, and I'm not taking this anymore.

"Fuck!" His jaw flexes and pops. "*Tell me what you know about Olivia.*"

My heart shouldn't be hurting right now, but the confirmation that there's another woman is a punch in the stomach. I thought I was being strong by challenging him, but I'm not. My head swirls with everything that happened tonight, and I'm so close to cracking.

He glares at me with such black, erratic eyes that my mouth turns dry. "Listen to me, Lexie, very fucking carefully. If you do *anything* about Olivia, I will ruin you. Do you fucking hear me? I will *ruin* you. Do not mess this up, do not look into her, do not contact her, do not even fucking think about her."

The words are said with such harsh conviction that tears rush to my eyes. He's said terrible things before, but this is different. This isn't sharp or cutting; it's rusty, jagged, meant to tear something open. My lips tremble. I bite down hard on the inside of my cheek, trying stop it—but a few tears spill out.

"God, I'm so stupid. I thought you'd changed, but you haven't." I swipe my eyes with my hands. "You've ruined me once before. Back in Boston." He doesn't say anything. He doesn't ask questions. He doesn't care. He's worried about Olivia, and not me, and I absolutely hate myself for even caring. "I shouldn't be surprised you want to ruin me again."

I storm away, leaving an unconscious Cody in an alley, and a raging Theo on the sidewalk. By the time I hail a cab, and slide into the back seat, I'm bawling.

29

Theo

What the absolute fuck is wrong with me? I storm into my studio, flip on all the lights because *she fucking knows I live here anyway*, and dig ice out of the freezer.

The second a shattered, crying Lexie stormed off, reality hit, and everything in me broke. What was I thinking threatening to ruin her? Jesus Christ, I *wasn't* thinking. About anything. Ever since I saw her nine months ago in that coffee shop, I don't think, ever. I know why I lashed out. She caught me off-guard with Olivia. I've been protecting that woman for years, building this case against my father, and I panicked.

But it's still not okay.

The second Lexie got in a cab, I jumped into another one to follow her home and called Michael to scrape that stupid prick off the alley and bring him to the ER. Not that I care if he lives or dies. With what he said to Lexie, with how he was trapping her, he can fucking rot. But prison time doesn't sound fun, and I don't want to task Michael with covering up a murder.

And then I called Lexie. Over and over, ten, twenty, thirty times. All calls went to voicemail.

I slump onto the couch, glance to see if by some miracle she opened her blinds (she didn't) and rest the towel-wrapped ice on my knuckles.

And then I call. Again.

She sends me to voicemail. Again.

I flex my hands, confirming full movement, and thank Christ the blood on my fist was his and not mine. By tomorrow, they're going to be bruised and swollen, but nothing's broken thankfully. How the hell would I explain that at the clinic? Tell them there's a reason I'm a doctor and not a carpenter, and I'm never assembling a dresser again? They'd all believe me. No one sees this other side of me, the darkness behind the shiny cloak.

Except now, Lexie.

Fuck.

I'm a doctor, for God's sake. A *doctor.* I heal. I don't hurt.

Do I feel bad for what I did? No. He got exactly what he deserved.

Was it still bad judgment? Yes.

And yet, I soak in the vision of the bloodied, half-conscious prick on the ground, paying for his sins and the vile shit he spewed. When I hit him, it felt good. Really fucking good, and I want to do it again. The intense blinding rage consumed me. In a few months, Lexie will leave my life forever, and I can't even breathe thinking of that world. She's been part of my life for so long, stitched and engraved into my soul, and that guy didn't even fucking care.

But now what? Am I just supposed to walk away? Pretend like it's done? Pretend like the taste of her mouth was enough, that it was the taste I was chasing all these years, and not her? Because now that I've had the taste, I know it's more.

It's always been *her*.

I pace the studio, look out the window, pace some more. Fuck, why did I threaten her like that? My stomach knots, furious and gross, and I try Lexie's number again.

Voicemail.

I still feel the way her body moved against me. How she grinded against my cock, how I wanted to fuck her in the alley and the only thing that stopped me was knowing I had that guy's blood dripping from my hands.

Not the wedding, not Anna, not my commitments. The blood.

It's stupid. It's so fucking stupid, but she has this vise grip on me that won't release.

But that mouth ... now that I've tasted those dangerous lips, I'm obsessed. I need more. I slump onto the couch and push my thumbs into my forehead. The way her lips moved against mine, plush and full and needy. Her velvet tongue. The way she kissed me back, frantic and urgent ... it won't leave me. That beautiful mouth worked me. Her tongue *owned* me.

I grab my phone and send what feels like the hundredth message tonight.

Theo: Can we talk?

My breath locks when I finally see the three bubbles pop up.

Lexie: fuck you

I toss the phone. Not that I expected anything else.

Maybe it's good that she doesn't want to talk, because what the hell would I say? That she's the most beautifully addictive poison, and I need her to stop being who she is so I can breathe again? God, I need this wedding to be over so I can cut her out of my life, completely.

But even thinking that feels like someone kicked me in the chest, and now, I'm back to not breathing. *Fuck.*

How am I supposed to go on without her? This part of me, something that started as a parasite that I wanted to rid myself of, is now etched into the deepest part of my soul. I've known Anna my entire life, but somehow it feels like Lexie knows more of me, the authentic me, *all* of me.

Time is so limited, slipping through my fingers with the speed of a jetliner. So, what the hell am I doing, not soaking up every bit I can? Yes, she doesn't want to speak to me because she doesn't know everything. But I can't tell her, can I? Only Anna knows about the investigation, and even she doesn't know everything. And with the wedding . . . there's so many legalities guaranteeing silence that the details may as well be in a reinforced steel vault.

And when I'm married . . . Lexie would never be the other

woman. Not that I'd ever ask her to. I'd want to be with her, fully. Devoted. Show her the world, treat her to everything she wants. She'd be my pride. My heart. Not someone I keep hidden.

I throw my wet towel aside, flex my burning fingers, and drag myself to the shower. The heated water does nothing to ease the tension. Everything is tight. My shoulders. My chest. My fucking heart.

My *heart*.

I stand under the stream for close to an hour, doing nothing but thinking. I need to fix this. But how? After I step out, I peek one more time across the street but already know her blinds will be closed. I tug the covers over me, but sleep is non-existent as I toss and turn in bed.

My thoughts are swirling, constantly drifting back to how she looked at me before she left. Hurt filled her beautiful eyes. And I should've been happy. I've wanted, *craved*, to see the hurt. Payback for toying with me back in the day. But the way her eyes mirrored my broken insides killed me. Why did her hurt hurt me? This is what I wanted, wasn't it?

I blink at the clock, see not much time has passed. Christ. I'm not going to sleep for the rest of my life. Maybe I don't deserve sleep. Maybe this is my punishment.

After the wedding, there'll be no reason to see Lexie. The thought clamps down on my chest so hard I have to sit up to force air back between my ribs. After the wedding, I have to give up the studio, I'll be moving in with Anna, I have to put Lexie out of my mind.

God, I *hate* this. My insides are torn, my brain is split. Each side is on an infinite fight loop with the other, and at any given moment, I don't know which side is going to win. My love and loyalty to Anna and my promise to her, and my insatiable need to be with Lexie. I press my thumb above the bridge of my nose and exhale.

Everything's spinning out of control. Throughout my entire life, I've prided myself on control. I *live* for control. But Lexie knocks me off alignment, and I can't think clearly when she's around. I was top of my class in medical school, the youngest attendee at my clinic, I've written scholarly articles that have been published in world-renowned medical journals, and yet I can't fucking think when I'm around Lexie.

Finally, at six a.m. I pick up the phone and call the only person who can help me.

Anna.

30

Lexie

My fuzzy white bathrobe normally provides me with some comfort, but today, it's not working. I unravel my dripping hair from the towel, which I toss in the laundry basket, and drag myself to the kitchen. Even though I stood in the shower until my skin nearly shriveled, I still feel dirty from what happened last night.

Cody. Maybe I should be worried. But I'm not. A man like that has probably done—and will continue to do—worse things. Maybe Theo taught him a lesson.

Theo. I want to erase his image, how he made me feel, the way my body burned, but I can't and I'm furious that I can't. But the way he spoke to me, threatening me because of whoever this Olivia woman is, gutted me.

God, *why, why, why* does the idea that this woman is more important to him than me make me want to cry? The man's getting married. I'm planning his goddamn wedding. I shouldn't be getting upset over him.

I need to get my head on straight. Starting now. I'm going to go for a long jog, come back, drink buckets of coffee, read a book by the window, and not think of Theodore Astor for one more second.

A knock on my apartment door makes my head jolt. No one ever comes here. The clock shows it's barely after eight a.m. I tug my robe tighter at the chest, tiptoe to the door, and look through the peephole.

Theo.

What in the hell? How did he even get into my building? Honestly, does it even matter? I don't want to see him, I don't want to talk to him, I don't want to look at his mouth and smell his scent and listen to that voice that makes me melt. How dare he?

I yank open the door, ready to tell him to fuck all the way off, but my breath catches.

Sweatpants. Snug white tank. Messy, unbrushed hair. Firm, rounded shoulders, smooth skin, full sleeve tattoos snaking up his arms. Jesus Christ if I thought this man looked good in a sharp button-down, it is *nothing* compared to how he looks now.

I cross my arms. "What do you want?"

"Can we talk?" he says, his eyes creased, his voice gentle, his palm pressing against the doorframe.

"I'm not in the mood."

He sighs. "I need to speak to you. If . . . if you'll give me a chance to explain, I think you'll want to hear what I have to say. *Please*, Lexie." As I go to slam the door in his face, he puts out his hand. "I'm begging you. Five minutes, okay? That's all I need."

I've seen different sides to Theo during college and over these past few months. Challenging. Haunting. Raging. Laughing. But never have I seen him groveling.

I don't know what possesses me to do it. Maybe I want to see this look on his face a little longer. Or maybe no matter how much I hate him right now, I know deep down that I already miss him. So, I hold the door open. He lowers his head and follows me inside.

It feels weird having Theo here. Part of me wants to ask him if he wants some coffee, part wants to scream about how bad he hurt me, and this other part wants to feel his mouth again on mine, no matter how deeply wrong it is. I'm sick. And disgusting. And I'll never let him kiss me again. But it doesn't mean I don't want to.

I slide into the furthest spot on the couch and tug a blanket over myself.

Theo sits. Then stands. Then sits. Then paces.

Another version I haven't seen of Theo? Nervous.

He walks to the window and clasps his fingers behind his head, and my impatience spikes. I'm so tired of being kept in the dark.

"Are you trying to see your apartment from here?" I ask, not hiding my disdain. "Because you do realize watching me through a window is unhinged, right? Like genuinely disturbing, restraining-order-level, stalker shit."

The words land hard. They're meant to.

And yet—even as I say them—I know the truth I hate admitting: I never once felt afraid of him.

He drops his hands, the tension drains out of him as he exhales. "I have no excuse," he says quietly.

I'm thrown by his immediate defeat, left unsure how to respond.

"Why are you here?" I ask, trying to search his eyes, but he's staring at the floor. Silence builds and I'm annoyed that he begged for five minutes and has barely said a word. "Can we both just be adults and at least acknowledge that there's something supremely fucked up happening here? So deeply wrong, I can barely look at myself in the mirror. Everything that happened last night . . . I'm your *wedding planner.* Whatever this is between us has to stop."

He leans against the wall, crossing his ankles and arms.

"Besides," I say, not withholding the bitterness in my tone, "based on your reaction last night, clearly I'm not the only one who has caught your attention."

This makes his eyes snap to me, but it's not rage filled like last night. He takes a deep breath. "Olivia's not who you think she is."

Oh, please. Not this again.

He starts pacing again. "She's one of my father's victims."

My mouth drops. Did I just hear him right? What does he mean, a victim? "Wait . . . what? Your *father*?"

The pacing slows and he sits on the opposite side of the couch. "I want to tell you everything, but I don't know if it's right for me to do so. These women ... their stories ... it's not for me to share until they're ready. Even saying her name feels like I'm breaking her trust. But, yes, my father did horrible things."

Victims? Dr. Astor, world-renowned professor? My head spins.

A long moment passes. Theo drags his hands down his face, and exhales. "I'm trusting you with this because you deserve the truth. But, Lexie, you have to promise me you won't say anything. There are lives at stake, reputations, years-long investigative work gone into this ..."

Everything in me tightens and somehow softens at the same time. "Of course, I won't say anything," I say quickly. "If it helps, this is all covered under your NDA. Not that I would ever victim blame or shame." The words feel inadequate, but they're all I have. I take a breath, then offer a small olive branch. "Do you want coffee?"

The tiniest uptick happens in his lip, and he nods. "Yes, fucking, please."

After I brew and pour coffee, I return to the couch and wait for him to resume his story.

"I've been investigating my father for over seven years."

Seven years. Since I was his aide.

"It started with a gut feeling I had about him, then I started to hear rumors and ..." And so he talks. And talks. And talks. We drain a pot of coffee, we snack on fruit and dried cereal, we change couch positions, and he keeps talking. He tells me about a freelance journalist who's written articles for the *Times*, *Sun*, and *AP*, who's helping him investigate. But the women are hesitant, understandably so, intimidated by his mother's money and his father's prestige. But he and the journalist believe that if Olivia, and maybe one other person, comes forward, there would finally be enough evidence for the public to listen.

"So, this is why you hate your father," I say.

"Yeah," he answers. "It's part of it. The rest is . . . a pretty fucked-up upbringing."

I have even more questions but I don't pry. If he wants to tell me, he will. "I told you I worked for your father, remember?" I ask. "But I didn't see this. Not for myself." I'm not naïve. I'd heard rumors of his father having affairs with his students. But dorm gossip runs as rampant as a wildfire on dry timber, and I always thought the chatter was just rumors.

Theo doesn't say anything for a long time. "Well, I'm glad. I guess you were one of the lucky ones."

I never thought being unfairly expelled from school was lucky. But maybe . . . he's right. "What's your goal with all of this?"

"For everyone to know what he's done."

I cock my head. "That's your goal? What do you get out of it?"

He stands and moves toward the window. At first I think I've said something to make him mad, but I realize he's just thinking. I wait for a bit, let him process what he's told me, then join him at the window and look at the traffic below.

After a long silence, he says, "It's not about what I get

out of it. Yes, I want to see him buried. He deserves to be destroyed for what he did. Maybe it's a need for justice, I don't know." He crosses his arms and exhales. "But it's less about me and more about the need to give these women back something. Closure. A chance to tell their story. Help them shed something that's been haunting them so they can reclaim their voice. They were left unprotected. And it's my personal mission to make them feel . . . protected."

I hate the way my heart swells at his words. I want to bury myself into his chest and tell him he's a good man. God, I wish he wasn't getting married because all I want is to have him protect me and make me feel safe. I nudge myself a little closer and lean my head against his bare shoulder. He leans down and kisses the top of my head, and *God*, I want to lean into it so fucking bad. But in telling me this, he's lifted a weight I've been carrying around since the day I saw him in the hotel with Olivia, and I'm grateful to finally let it go.

I lift my head and step back, away from his smooth skin and mouth-watering scent. "Thank you for being honest with me. What you're doing for these women, it's really noble. Annabelle is one lucky woman."

A warm smile breaks across his face. *Knowing.* He faces me, lifts his hand to my cheek, and swipes his thumbs across my skin.

Tears spring to my eyes, and I take a wide step back. I'm not strong enough for this. He needs to leave, now. "Please don't do this. Please, Theo . . . my heart can't take it." My lips tremble. "It's too much." He takes another step towards me like I didn't just beg him to stop, and I shake my head. "Please don't."

His dark eyes burn into mine, and there's still this look on his face that I can't describe. Soft, determined, serious. "Are you holding back because you don't want me . . . or because I'm getting married?"

The reason doesn't matter. We can't. If my body and heart would listen to my mind, this would be so much easier. "Because . . ." I pull in a sharp breath, tired of keeping up the act. "Because you're getting married."

I hate admitting it, but it's true.

And then he takes a step closer. And then another, completely closing the gap between us. His body presses against mine and my throat rolls as I swallow. "You have no idea how happy I am to hear that," he says, trailing a finger down my robe, then gripping the belt. "Because the wedding's off."

31

Lexie

Did I hear that right? The wedding is *off*? The thing I wished for since the first day he stepped into our office—what began as a desire for revenge and slowly transformed into something deeper, something that made me want *him*—had just come out of his beautiful, smiling mouth.

I'm dreaming. This isn't real. But when he cups my face with both hands, I feel the warmth from his palms spread across my cheeks, down my chest, and lower . . .

"Sorry—what?" I blink. "The wedding's *off*?"

His smile widens into a slow, unapologetic smirk, clearly enjoying my confusion. "Wow," he says. "I knew I had an effect on you, but I didn't think I'd render you temporarily unable to process complete sentences."

I ignore his remark, still struggling to understand. "So . . . you and Annabelle aren't getting married?" I ask needing to hear it again to believe it.

"Nope." He swoops my hair to the side and presses his mouth so close to my ear that his breath tickles my skin. "You are looking at a very single man."

And then his lips softly brush a tender spot right behind my ear. My eyes flutter shut. I press a hand on his chest, in an attempt to stop him, but every part of me protests. "Is she okay?" I manage, my voice betraying me and I open my eyes to read his expression.

He bites his lip clearly trying—and failing—to look casual. "She's good."

His mouth drifts lower, unhurried, pressing a warm kiss along the side of my neck. I swallow hard as his hand slides to the back of my head, tilting me just enough to give him more access. "And, um," I ask, breathless. "How . . . are you?"

Heat ripples through me as he nips lightly at my skin, then soothes the sting with his lips.

"Relieved," he murmurs.

The word settles between us—heavy, intimate—and my grip on his chest tightens. I push my hips forward, just a little, drink in how his fingertips graze my jaw, how his thumb gently tugs on my lower lip.

"Wait." I step out of reach with heavy breaths. "We should probably talk about this. What happened between you and Annabelle?"

He licks his lower lip and God I want to taste, lick, suck on those lips.

His fingers rake through my hair, gripping it with enough

pressure to force my chin up. Heat fans through my body, spreading fast, lighting up every nerve in its path.

"For fuck's sake," he mutters, exasperated. "If I promise to tell you *everything* later . . . can we please stop talking now?"

That does it.

The fight in me sparks to life. I let my gaze linger—on his mouth, then lower to those infuriatingly perfect gray sweatpants, up the hard lines of his torso beneath the tight white tank, to his mouth, and finally back to his eyes.

"If we stop talking," I murmur, my voice rough on purpose, "what exactly do you think we're going to do?"

His eyes flare at the challenge and his mouth crashes into mine in a brutal kiss. He sucks on my lips, plunges his tongue against mine, grips my head, my waist, my neck. Nothing is gentle. It's frantic. Urgent. Desperate. Heat rushes through my body and settles between my legs, and my mind races. Is this actually real? His mouth is so firm, demanding, owning. God, he tastes so good.

My body turns feverish. I grind my greedy pussy into him, seeking friction, and . . . oh . . . his hard beautiful cock presses against me. I feel how much he wants me.

This is no longer a game. This is guttural.

I need to feel him. In my hands, in my mouth, on me, in me. I snake a leg around his, and pull him closer, as close as he can get. One hand grips my hair, exposing my neck, and his lips drag across the skin, biting, nipping, sucking, and pleasure zaps through me. The other hand drops to my ass outside of the robe, and squeezes. Tight, rough, hard. He's leaving fingerprints, and I want it. I want the rage and the fire. The bruises and the pain.

I want *everything.*

He pulls me tighter, his mouth never leaving mine. I can't breathe. His hungry, ravenous, fierce kisses steal all my air. My mouth is already swollen and I can't get enough. *Feed me.* I want more. I need more. My hands grip his back, his arms, anything I can grasp to hold myself up because I'm so fucking dizzy. I'm feverish and ravenous and want him right fucking now.

My thong is soaked. I grind against him, nearly collapsing with how hard he is. I need more. My hands drop to his sweatpants and my desperate, shaking fingers fumble to untie. The sound of heavy breaths and fabric being tugged down makes me salivate. I reach inside his boxer briefs, and *oh . . . oh Christ*, his cock is perfect. I need it, now, filling my mouth. I need to taste and lick and suck . . . I break the kiss and drop to my knees. The cold hardwood floor is a stark contrast to the heat in my legs. I'm so hungry for him that I dive in, taking his cock into my mouth as far as I can in one motion.

"*Fuuuuuck*," he hisses and holds the back of my head. One of his hands slaps against the wall, holding himself up, while the other remains protecting my head. I pull back, swirl my tongue over his crown, and moan at the masculine salty precum and smell of soap. He tastes *so fucking good.* I glaze my lips with him, lick down the silken skin and back up, savoring every part. His cock. His skin. His moans.

I'm making a man like Theo crumble. He can't hold himself up without support because of *me*, because of what *I'm* doing to him. I'm high on power. He feels so good in my mouth. My palm grips him at the base. I wrap my lips tighter and slide up and down his thick shaft along with my hand, taking him in as deep as I can. I gag and choke. I can't breathe. Hot tears run down my face.

And I still want *more.*

He's swelling inside my mouth, his ragged breaths increase, and I want to feel him lose control. I want every fucking drop of him to fill my mouth and slide down my throat. I shove my free hand under my robe and rub my aching clit, moving, more, faster, harder . . .

He lifts me to my feet, tugs up his sweatpants, and grips the back of my head so tight that my breath hitches. "Didn't I tell you that a woman's pleasure is *always* priority?"

He crushes his mouth back into mine, claiming my breath. My knees buckle with the impact, my heartbeat pounds so loud, so heavy, in my chest, it throws me off balance. But I already know to the deepest part of me, Theo will never let me fall.

In any sense.

I'm clutching the muscles in his arms, his back, his incredible ass, desperate to get closer. My breaths turn ragged and choppy as I paw and tug at his tank top. He grips it from behind his neck and tugs it off and *is he fucking kidding*? In the alley, I felt his chest and torso, but it was rushed and frantic and I didn't really know. God . . . the mouthwatering ridges, the deeply defined pecs, the hard stomach . . . I flatten my hand and run it down his body, feeling each solid line.

My robe slips, exposing my shoulder, and Theo sinks his mouth onto it, biting and licking, sending shivers through me. I'm melting. My body, my mind . . . wherever he's taking me, I'll go. He lifts me on to my desk, grabs the front of my robe and yanks it down.

"Jesus Christ, you're so fucking beautiful."

His hunger-filled look makes everything sizzle. My exposed nipples harden in the cool air, and I tug him into me, pleading for his mouth. When he tilts his head, cups my tits, and latches on, I moan. "Oh God, so good, Theo, so good . . ." He sucks and licks. Slurping, wet, hungry noises fill the room as he works my other breast with his hand, squeezing and pinching and making me squirm. I lean back on my palms, pushing my chest up for easier access and wrap my legs around his waist.

"God, these gorgeous fucking tits." He sucks so hard, so good, that I'm trembling again. Fingers pinch my nipples with such delicious strength that I nearly scream, pushing me right to the edge of searing pleasure. When the sensation tiptoes on pain, he moves to the other and heat rushes to my core. "Do you have any idea how much I've dreamt about putting them in my mouth?"

A heated pleasure tears through me and pools at my center. He knows *exactly* what he's doing. I'm grinding my clit into his delicious hard cock so much I nearly fall off the desk. I slide off, dragging myself down until my lips meet his, and slip my tongue against his.

His hand leaves my jaw, slides to my neck, and squeezes. I gasp with the limited air and it feels *so fucking good*. My knees tremble. I close my hazed eyes and let the incredible feeling of someone else being totally in control overtake me.

"Do you like this?" he asks.

I give a short, furious nod.

"Good."

He leaves his large hand against my neck for a few more moments as his finger presses into my clit and a sharp shock of pleasure bursts through me. "Do you want this as bad as I do?" he asks, forcing my head back to look at his smoldering eyes. "I want to hear if you want this, too."

My body quivers as I nod.

"I didn't say nod," he says in a deep, guttural tone. "I need to know how bad you want this.

Oh God, I need this now. Please. I'm panting and breathless. "*Yes. Yes* . . ."

"Say it," he growls. "I want to fucking hear it."

My ache consumes me. I'm in peril, fighting for relief, and I need to release. My skin is on fire, sweat beads at my neck, and my lust-soaked moans fill the air. I need Theo's touch. His body. *Him*. He's protecting me in the way that I wasn't protected before. He will save me from falling too hard. He will cushion the blow.

I'm ready.

I need Theo to fuck away my past.

"Please fuck me," I whisper.

His hands tug at the rope belt, my body shakes, we're frantic, breathless, rushed until the robe falls to my feet. I kick it away, standing only in my white lace thong. He steps back, his eyes trailing every single part of me, as the air hits my skin and I shudder. "Christ . . ." he says, dragging his hand down his mouth. "You're so fucking perfect."

When my bare chest meets his, the heat of his skin and the soft dusting of his trimmed chest hair make my knees go weak. His mouth never leaves me, moving with intent from my lips to my throat, lingering just long enough to make me ache. Then he stops, his hand closing at the nape of my neck. "What did you say to me at your office?"

I swallow, thrown by the question. "I don't know what you're talking about."

A slow, dangerous smile curves his mouth. "That's disappointing." He leans in, voice dropping. "Guess I'll have to remind you."

Before I can react, he turns me, guiding me forward until my palms rest on the table and I'm bent just enough to feel the shift in power. He sweeps my hair aside and says softly, "Looks like I can get you to bend for me after all."

Oh shit.

His hands trails down my back, inch by agonizing inch, until they settle at my ass, giving it a firm squeeze. "And now, here you are bending so beautifully for me."

I want to protest, say something defiant, but he drops to his knees, and I'm rendered totally speechless.

"You have no idea how long I've wanted to do this," he says, as he hooks his fingers at the band of my panties and drags them down, past my thighs, then my knees. He lifts one foot up and slips it off the ankle, then the other, then shoves them in his pocket.

Dirty, dirty boy.

"Mmmm . . ." he moans as he grips my hips and tilts up my ass. He buries his nose into my pussy and takes a breath like I'm pure spring air after a long, excruciating winter. "Fuck, I want to live in this cunt." Facial hair prickles against my sensitive skin. His fingertips glide against my glazed skin, back and forth, teasing the outside of my cunt, near my clit, along the crease of my thighs, and I swear to God, if he doesn't put something on me or in me, I'm going to scream. My legs tremble, my skin sensitive, my breaths heavy, and oh . . . oh fuck, *finally.* He dips a finger inside me and my body melts. He flutters his tongue from my clit to my cunt and back again, and my body quivers. All I hear are moans and sighs as the pads of his fingers press into my clit, circling, spreading my moisture on me. I feel like a goddess. Worshiped, cherished, desired. "Jesus Christ, you taste incredible."

My heartbeat is thudding so fast I feel like I'm going to tip over. I glance behind me. Theo on his knees, his head buried into my ass, his hazy eyes lost in a daze. His mouth devours me, owns me, makes me feel beautiful. *Worthy.* His tongue pushes inside me, his thumb and fingers work me, and *oh . . . fuck . . . it's so good.* I'm shamelessly soaked. My body quivers and trembles as urgency builds in my core.

"Yes, yes, there, oh God, this feels so good." *I'm close, I'm so close* . . . his mouth keeps working me, possessive and angry, his tongue slides and circles with the most acute perfection, *and yes . . . right fucking there* . . . I reach behind me and pull his head deeper into me as an orgasm tears through my body. He coaxes it from me, sucking my clit and pressing his fingertip into that glorious sensitive spot. I sink into the desk, shaking, breathless. He grips my hips and steadies me, until my quivers stop.

Once the aftershocks wear off, Theo lifts himself. When I turn to face him, his eyes are closed and he's sucking my orgasm from his fingers. When he blinks open, the look of raw, unfiltered longing in his eyes makes my pulse spike. I swear to God this man could ask me to do anything, and I'd say yes.

He lifts me up, cradling my naked ass. I wrap my legs around his waist, kissing him, tasting myself, tasting him, breathing in his air. He walks me over to my bed, and with how ravenous, hungry, possessive he was just a moment ago, he now lays me down gently. He climbs on top, one leg between mine, and drags his lips across my neck.

Is this actually happening? Is the very man I once loathed really sliding his hand down my body, firm yet gentle, owning, yet exploring? This touch, this moment, is surreal. I feel like I'm going to blink, and he'll be gone.

I climb on top, straddling him, and rock my naked pussy into his gloriously hard cock under his sweatpants.

Urgency builds again in my core. I grind into him, rushed,

hungry, desperate. *So fucking desperate.* "I'm tested and clean," I say breathlessly between kisses.

"Me too," he says as he dips his head and licks a nipple.

My head flings back and I dig my nails into his neck. "I'm on the pill."

"Good," he says among the beautifully dirty slurping sounds.

I need him. Right now. All of him. I've needed him this whole time, since I met him seven years ago, since I reunited with him. Everything I've held back these last few months has peaked, and my body screams to be filled. I grab his jaw and force his head up.

"Are you gonna fuck me yet?"

The smoldering, fiery look he gives me shoots straight through me. I lift my hips but don't climb off, terrified if he gets up, he might leave. He can't leave. My desperation to have him inside of me, to have him claim me, is all-encompassing. He slides his sweatpants down past his hips. I climb back on top, and palm his huge, beautiful cock. He's so much bigger than I've ever had, and it's going to hurt like a bitch going in, but I want the pain. I *need* the pain. His breath is heavy and rough as I hover my wet flesh over him.

God, I want him. *So, fucking bad.* But I want to see him hurt first.

Time to make this motherfucker beg.

When I don't put it in, his expectant, furious, lust-filled eyes glare at me. "You want me to fuck you, don't you?" I say huskily into his ear, dragging my tongue up his deliciously salty neck as I circle the tip of his cock against my shamelessly wet cunt. He lifts his hips, and I sit up, not giving him access until I get what I need to hear.

His fingers dig into my hips so hard they're going to be bruised tomorrow and I'm hungry for him to mark me. Power surges through me, and now I know exactly how he felt earlier when he made me beg.

"I want to hear you ask for it." The deliciously torturous words fuel me. I lower myself, just a bit, brushing my silky wetness against his crown. "Tell me how bad you want me to ride your thick, beautiful cock. I want to hear how much you want to fuck me."

He swallows, heavy, hard, his chest springing frustrated beads of sweat. "*Please*," he says through gritted teeth, and *oh* if it doesn't make me melt. For years, I've waited to hear it, and I want to absorb it.

"Again," I say as my heart gallops in my chest. Feral, primal, desperate eyes pierce into mine. I lick his mouth, pull him in for a hard kiss, and release.

"Please," he growls again, and I can't hold back anymore.

A burn ravages me as I sink into his cock, not even adjusting to the size. "Oh . . . God . . . oh shit . . . oh God . . ." The sharp, stretching pain is heaven. It hurts so fucking good, and I want more. I want him to stretch me and break me and heal me. My tits bounce as I fuck him, as I slide up and down, bucking against him, building momentum.

"You're so beautiful, so fucking beautiful . . ." he groans. The sounds of my thighs slapping his lap, of wet kisses, of my nails scratching, joins the screams and moans. His hands are at my hips, guiding me, lifting me up and down. His mouth meets my neck, my jaw, my tits, back to my neck. Firm hands grip me tight. He bucks his hips to my rhythm, slamming into me, going impossibly deep. Its dirty, messy, totally unhinged, and I've never been more sheltered, protected, *alive.*

He's holding me so tight. All I want is him. It's so good, and I don't want to come yet, but my walls clench around his cock, and waves tear through me, shaking me to my core. He holds me and lets me ride it out, lets me use him for my needs. His movements stop as I collapse against his shoulder, as my breaths shatter, and my heartbeat pounds. My limbs are gummy and boneless. He's still hard inside me, but he stays unmoving, waiting for me to calm down.

When I do, he scoops me up and lifts me from the bed, then lays me down on my back. He kicks off the rest of his clothes, then climbs on, grinning at my wide eyes. "You think we're done?" he says with a smirk. "Oh, beautiful girl . . . we're just getting started."

He then lowers himself, positioning himself between my legs. He kisses my lips, my neck, my jawline. His fingers lightly stroke my nipples, my thighs, my breasts, until my body turns warm again. When I do, he gives me a look. And when I nod, he thrusts into me so hard, my back lurches and my breath seizes. *Holy shit.* His body owns me. His cock fills and stretches me again, and the pleasured pain is so savagely good that I'm moaning and panting and screaming into the room. He hooks my legs over his shoulders and slams into me so deep, so hard, I blink away stars. I feel like I'm going to break, but it's the sweetest, most delicious pain I've ever felt.

He keeps pushing into me, breaking and healing me with each thrust. My body builds again, and he slams, so fast that the bed springs screech for mercy. His body tightens, crushes me, and I can't fucking breathe but I don't care if I ever breathe again.

"Right there, yes, Jesus fucking Christ, Lexie, you feel so good." And when I quiver and shake and scream, he shoots into me. His cum overflows and drips out, and I want to stuff it back in. I want to lick it and swallow it and keep every part of him in me.

When he catches his breath and slides out, I'm prepared for him to run. To leave me. To say it was a mistake, and it should never happen again. That this was a rebound, and he's heartbroken over Annabelle, and I was a temporary means to a painful end. I hold my breath, wait for the crushing rejection to hit my heart, and prepare to camouflage the pain of absence.

But that doesn't happen.

Instead, he scoops me into him, guides me to his chest, kisses the top of my head, and falls asleep.

32

Lexie

After Theo gave me the most mind-blowing sex of my life this morning, he fell asleep like he'd been chasing it his whole life. For the first twenty minutes, I lay there, as still as I could, but trembles ransacked me. After destroying my body in the best way possible, I was sticky, sore, and sweaty. I convinced myself that if I moved, he'd wake up, apologize, and leave.

But he didn't. He lay there, cocooning me against his chest like he was scared I'd escape. Then I fell asleep, too, into one of those daytime naps where your entire body sinks into the mattress and you completely lose track of time. A few minutes ago, when the late afternoon sun woke me to a naked Theo intertwined with my body, it took several long moments for my disorientation to dissipate.

The air smells like sex and sweat, and I inhale, filling my lungs. I cannot believe that happened. I have so many questions. Him and Annabelle. My job. The wedding.

And what the fuck happens next?

Theo's body stirs and I hold my breath. What if he wakes up and says this shouldn't have happened? What if he slips out of here with a half-assed apology and look of regret? I slowly exhale, trying to elongate this moment as much as possible, when his lips meet the top of my head.

"Good morning, beautiful," he says in a groggy, tone.

I lift my head to his warm eyes, relaxed face, and soft smile. "I hate to inform you that it's actually late afternoon, and we're going to have the worst case of self-induced jet-lag tomorrow."

He slides his index and middle finger under my chin to tip up my head and places a gentle kiss on my mouth. "Totally worth it."

This is exactly what I need to hear.

He lifts himself, bunches the sheets to his waist, and grabs my hand. "Come on."

"Um . . . where are we going?"

"Shower. Then hydrate. Then take-out. And then we're fucking doing that again."

My smile grows. I follow him into my tiny shower. He guides me to stay under the heated stream and only dips himself under the water to quickly wash himself. Soft moans escape as he lathers soap in a warm rag and cleans himself off me with languid gentle strokes across my boneless body. My scalp tingles as his magical fingers massage shampoo through my hair, as his lips meet mine.

No one has ever done this to me before. I thought

aftercare was a myth, or part of a BDSM lifestyle. I had no idea it'd be so *heavenly.*

He steps out of the shower first, wraps a towel around his waist, then holds out his hand to help me out. As if I haven't gotten out of the shower by myself since I was a kid. He holds out the towel, wraps me up, then holds me, tight. My cheek presses against his warm chest and I sigh into his skin.

"Are you good?" he asks, still not letting me go. Maybe he was worried, too, that when he woke up the spell would be broken. "Are . . . we good?"

This is the most confident man I've ever met in my life. And the flicker of vulnerability in his voice nearly brings me to my knees. "We are *so* good."

He kisses my head again, then steps back. "I'm starving. Let's get some food."

An hour later, after Theo made me come on the couch with his fingers, a delivery driver drops off enough sushi to feed my entire complex.

"So," I say, tucking my legs under me on the couch, and dipping a sashimi in soy sauce. "You owe me an explanation."

He swallows his tuna roll and reaches for a napkin. "Where do you want to start?"

"You got a fucking apartment next to me?"

The most sheepish grin crosses his face, and he reaches for another roll. "Yes." He takes a swig of water, and holds it out for me. This man is obsessed with hydration. "What's the next question?"

I groan at his deflection but decide it's the lesser of two

evils to let this one go. Theo does a lot of things that I'll probably never understand.

This one, maybe, I don't need to.

"I want to know everything that happened with Annabelle." I reach for another sashimi. "Yesterday, you were marrying her. Today, you aren't. What changed?"

He exhales. "You want the long version or the short version?"

I arch a brow.

"Fine. Shit. Where do I even start?" He dunks another roll in soy sauce, and chews. "Anna and I have been friends forever. I love her."

Heat fills my face, and he reaches over and gives my leg a comforting squeeze.

"But I don't love her the way you think. She's my best friend. Has been since we were little. And we tried dating, off and on. She's comfortable. *We're* comfortable. But, it never felt right." He takes a breath. "We haven't slept together for years. Not since college, actually."

"*What*?" The chopstick nearly slides from my fingers. They haven't had sex for nearly a decade? Why? I have so many invasive questions burning on the tip of my tongue and it takes everything in me to not pepper him with them all.

"Yeah," he says. "And when we did back then, it was always just sort of a . . . I don't know . . . a release, I guess?"

"Wow . . . Okay." I'm lost for words.

"Growing up, we used to take bets on which family was more fucked. Mine or her controlling family, with their archaic ideas on marriage and deep-set paranoia about anyone they deemed an 'outsider'."

As he polishes off the food, he talks about the few times that Annabelle dated—her family ran multiple background checks, hired private investigators to tail the men, and had their security intimidate the men until they were scared off. "I don't think she had a boyfriend that lasted longer than a month."

Wow.

"So, about ten years ago, maybe more, her parents started pressuring us to get married. I was vetted. My family was vetted. Anna and I honestly thought it was a joke at first, so I brushed it off. But the pressure intensified, and eventually my parents joined in too." He takes a sip of his drink before telling me about the forced holidays, joint vacations, and constant badgering. "I told my parents to fuck off, but I couldn't stand watching the stress Anna's parents were putting her under. It killed me. The more she pushed back, the harder they came down on her. And then last year, they gave her an ultimatum: marry me by the time she turned thirty, or she'd lose her trust fund."

Holy shit. My stomach knots. "Her birthday is July fifteenth, isn't it? The uncompromising wedding date."

"Sure is," he says. "We pushed the wedding out to the very last day in case they'd change their mind."

Jesus Christ. I can't even imagine having that much pressure. "So now what? The wedding's just off? What about her trust fund?"

"Anna and I have been talking for months, trying to figure out a way out of this. We thought we'd eventually find a loophole or get an annulment after a year, something. But the more impossible it started to feel, the more we resigned ourselves to eventually living separate lives as a married-in-name-only couple and we'd each hopefully meet someone who understood the situation."

God, this is a lot to take in. "Why didn't you tell me this earlier?"

"I couldn't. If her parents had any idea that we were planning a way out of this wedding, they would've stripped her trust fund immediately," he says, then fans his fingers on my knee. "I'm sorry. I just . . . I didn't know if I could trust you."

Even though it stings, I understand. "No, I get it. I was still a stranger to you, so it makes sense you didn't trust me."

He avoids my eyes at my words. Maybe I'm pushing for too much—but I need the truth. My conscience will not rest until I know, without a doubt, that Annabelle is happy.

"And she's okay with ... this ..." I point between me and Theo.

A diabolic grin spreads and his hands slide up my thigh. "Elaborate on *this*."

"Theo." I glare, ignoring how my body immediately heats, and remove his hands. "I'm serious."

"Not only is she okay, she's thrilled. Who do you think I've been talking to about you? When I told her I was going to come over and tell you everything, I think her exact words were 'Thank God, now you can shut the fuck up about her.'"

He laughs. "She said it in a loving way, of course. Once she filled me in on her plan to get us out of the wedding, she told me to come over here immediately."

"She did?"

He nods and glances at his hands. "And she said something about being vulnerable for once."

"Whoa." My heart skips a beat. "Do you know what that word means?"

"Nope."

Everything in me wants to climb in his lap and show him just how much I appreciate him opening up, but I'm also desperate for more details. "So now what? How will she both get her trust fund and cancel the wedding?"

"For now, we have to play it cool," he says, regret edging his voice. "She's still working out the details. Her Nonna is a feisty fuck and apparently they've come up with a plan. But Anna's paranoid and didn't want to share too much over the phone, which I respect. I wouldn't put anything past her parents."

My brain tries to process all the information. "What does 'playing it cool' mean?"

"It means, to the outside world, we're still getting married."

My heart sinks.

"Not for very long." He grabs my hand and kisses my wrist. "Just a few more weeks while she's working everything out. But Lexie, you can't tell anyone. *No one.* Not your boss, not Justin, not your mom, no one. I am totally trusting you with this, okay? This is not about me, or my life. It's about Anna's life and safety."

He's right, of course. And I get it. Still, the thought of keeping this from the people who matter most to me—especially my boss, whose company is planning their special day—makes my stomach tighten. "Of course, I won't say anything," I say, taking a breath. "So, we keep planning the wedding?"

"Yes. I'm still working with your firm, we'll still take the usual meetings, and—"

"Ah. Wait." A smile grows, pushing back the nagging feeling of keeping this hidden. "Does this mean you still have to learn how to dance?"

He laughs and pulls me into his lap. I giggle at the sudden movement and moan at the way his hands slide up my body.

"Fucking dance lessons . . ."

33

Theo

"Welcome, welcome, Theo, amazing to meet you!" The dance instructor, Nikolai, says, his Russian accent thick, his smile bright, his slim body radiating with more energy than a uranium fuel rod.

In Nikolai's private, way too bright mirror-laden dance studio about twenty minutes away from my parents' home, I shake his hand while trying to push out of my mind that I'm going to be dancing for the next six hours.

Dancing. This is what my life has come to.

But, my life has also become so much more. *Lexie.* Ever since I showed up at her place two weeks ago, I haven't left. I mean I've *technically* left every morning to get dressed at my studio, but other than that, I haven't left her side except for work. Every second of the day, I want to bury myself inside her, watch her smile, and sleep with her on my chest.

This is all new. But at the same time, part of me has been

in love with her since I was barely legal enough to drink. She's branded into me, carved into my soul. We laugh. We fuck. We sleep. Jesus Christ, the sleeping. I've been chasing rest my whole life and finally found it.

I don't know why this pure angel is with me, but she is. She sees past the monsters, past the worst parts of me, and accepts me exactly as I am. I know I don't deserve her—someone like me, carrying this much darkness, doesn't deserve her light. And yet, she gives it to me anyway.

Nikolai has me sit on the studio floor as he talks about posture, breathing and a bunch of other bullshit that I don't want to listen to, because I'm going to be stuck in this room without Lexie for six hours. The second this is over, I'm rushing out of here and crashing the wedding in downtown Boston she's working for Justin when his bout of what he thought was food poisoning was actually appendicitis. Of course, it sucked for him, but the logistics of me and Lexie being in Boston at the same time could not be more perfect.

You'd think I'd have had enough, but I haven't. I'm completely insatiable. On the five-hour ride here from New York, I raised the privacy window and we christened every seat in the SUV. Everyone, Michael included, thinks me and Anna are still getting married. But he's paid for loyalty and discretion, not opinions.

He never even batted an eye.

The dance lessons go better than I expected, and even though I won't need them now, canceling would raise major red flags with our families. I hate that I have to keep Lexie hidden. Anna keeps reassuring me that she's close to finalizing the paperwork, and I know these things take time, but the second it's done, I'm telling everyone who'll listen that Lexie's mine.

Lexie. Is. Mine.

I hate the flicker of hesitation that comes with this thought. Lexie's too good for me. I already know this. But I'm going to do whatever I can to be the man she deserves.

A few hours later, I roll up to the venue where Lexie's working with my sharp dark gray suit, a generous bottle of wine as a gift for the couple I don't even know, and stroll into the reception area. I scan the long white tables, the groups of people chatting and drinking, the silver tray carrying wait staff weaving in between tables when I finally see her in the corner in a dress, light sweater, and heels, and I stop breathing.

She's the most beautiful woman I've ever seen.

When her eyes meet mine, they grow wide and a grin crosses her face. She whispers something to a staff and then makes her way to me. "Theo," she says in a hushed tone. "You can't be in here."

"And yet, here I am," I say, drinking in the way she's beaming at me. "Relax. No one will ever know I'm not a guest. You're about to witness a master at work."

She shakes her head, laughing. "Your confidence truly knows no bounds." Something catches her eye and she sighs. "I have to help someone. Behave," she adds pointedly. "I mean it."

"I always behave." Like now, when every part of me wants to smack that juicy ass of hers, but I refrain. As she walks away, I start making my rounds. I grab a glass of champagne, chat with a few guests, tell some of them I'm a second cousin of the bride, tell others that I'm a friend of the groom. For an hour, I follow Lexie's movements, earning amused glances, eye rolls, and the occasional head shake—each one feeling like a small, well-earned victory.

When the DJ calls for guests to join the couple on the dance floor, I beeline for her. "Care to witness my new moves?" I ask. "Nikolai has turned me into a pro."

"No," she says, her brows creasing. "People will see us."

"Do you think I care what these people think?" I grab her hand and lead her out to the dancefloor.

She glances across the room, at me, back at the room, and then sighs. "Fine. But I'm not going to make this easy on you." She smiles. Bright. Warm. *Teasing.*

My beautifully sinister Lexie is going to make this hard as hell on me.

I can't fucking wait.

The moment our bodies touch, everything in me feels right. We're on a crowded dancefloor, but within moments, everyone around us fades away. She relaxes, shielded by the dancing guests, and sways effortlessly in my arms.

It's clear she's danced like this before, and I have to rein in the flicker of jealousy at the thought of another man touching her the way I am now.

Her sweater slips, exposing her shoulders. Underneath the

thin strap of her dress is that creamy, pale skin of hers which is begging for my teeth to sink into it. I haven't even touched her yet and I'm aching for my hands to be up that skirt, dragging my fingertips across her skin until she trembles.

Jesus Christ. Focus.

The ballroom light streaming into the room highlights the sparkle in her spring-green eyes, reminding me of the first day I met her all those years ago. Those eyes had sucked me in and refused to let go. Seven years later, they have the same hold.

Ever since I told her everything about my dad, the investigation, and Anna, we talk about everything. But there's one crucial piece that I still haven't confessed.

And I never fucking will.

She will never know that I remember her from Boston.

I've let this lie go on for too long and I can't take it back now.

My hand rests at the curve of her waist as her small, impossibly soft palm slides effortlessly against mine and the other rests on my shoulder. There's a sliver of space between us, but the heat radiating from her feels like velvet needles against my skin. *I will not break. I will not break.* I draw in a careful breath and pray she doesn't notice.

The song ends and another begins, but I don't release her. The curves of her body, the smooth skin of her arms, the freckles dusting her nose and cheeks and her scent alone are weapons. She licks her lips, slow and deliberate to grab my attention, and it works because my mouth goes dry. I know exactly what she's doing. She *loves* games.

I hate that it's working.

My grip tightens at her waist—just a fraction. A challenge. I pull her closer, testing, and feel the answering heat of her palm move down my bicep and up like a warning shot.

The air around us becomes suffocating. Her breath stutters. Color blooms across her cheeks. Her thumb strokes lazily on my shoulder. She looks up at me through thick dark lashes and nibbles her lip. It's subtle enough that no one would notice, but I fucking do. *Games.* She's dancing along the edge, seeing how long she can hold before she burns.

Fine. If she wants to play, I'll play right back.

But the way she's dismantled me these past weeks, like her body was handmade for me, leaves me dangerously close to losing. Her tits brush against my chest and my heart pounds. Before I can stop myself, I tug her in, hard, and she exhales softly.

Her body melts into mine and the way she moves, the way she breathes . . . *fuck.* A subtle tug lifts my shirt, just enough to bare skin and I wait for her fingers to find their target. But she only smooths it back down into place and my skin is burning with the need for her touch. Anyone watching should probably look away because I'm about two seconds away from slamming her against the nearest wall and reminding her who's in charge.

I grip tighter. So does she. My fingers trace slow, deliberate patterns down her back. She presses against my cock. That single move nearly undoes me.

"There's a private staff room down the hall," she whispers. "If you're ready to admit defeat."

Then she's gone, leaving me on the dancefloor, horny and frustrated, watching her hips sway with just a little too much intention.

A wolfish smile curls across my mouth as I follow her into the small, dimly lit break room. Besides the table in the center of the room and a few chairs, the room is empty. She locks the door, leans back against the wall, and looks at me with a dirty, smoldering gaze.

"Well, well," she says, voice sugar-laced and sharp. "Look who couldn't help himself."

I don't care that I've lost.

Two strides put me in front of her. My palms hit the wall on either side of her head, caging her in. Her lips twitch into a devilish grin—unafraid. "I'm not going to break, no matter what you do."

She peers up at me with feigned innocence. "I have no idea what you mean."

I lean in just enough for the words to land where she'll feel them. "You know *exactly* what I mean." I slam my leg between hers, and the soft whimper that leaves her luscious mouth drives me insane. She grips my hips, tugs me in tighter. "You and your fucking games," I husk and glare down into those wide eyes, biting back a grin. "You feed off this, don't you?"

She lifts her chest, rocks her pussy against my thigh, and my focus is gone.

This is what she does. And God, I fucking love it. A pounding grows in my head, in my ears, my vision blackens. I grab one of her wrists and pin it to her side. I need her to stop moving against me, stop looking at me. She peeks at my cock and that fucking smirk of hers . . . I yank the other one and pin it to her other side.

Her smirk grows, and then she lifts herself onto her tiptoes and drags her tongue across my lips.

I have no self-control. I drop my hands and grip her hair at the nape of her neck, forcing her head up. My hand seizes the fleshy part of her inner thigh, my defiant cock screams for release. "Is this what you want?"

If she's going to play, then I'll make her pay for it. She'll want this as badly as I do, she'll *need* this as much as I do. She'll ache for it, crave it, be driven half-mad needing this fix the same way I am.

Her skin feels so goddamn good beneath my grip. Lexie possesses me, melts my resolve.

She doesn't just distract me.

She fucking *owns* me.

Her breaths turn ragged, pink blossoms under those freckles and she whispers, "*More.*"

Fuck.

I slide my hands all the way up that sensitive, smooth, tight skin at her inner thigh. She whimpers when I reach her center, and the side of my hand touches her naked pussy. My jaw clamps. "You're not wearing any panties?" This beautiful naked cunt was right there, waiting. I grind my palm into that damp silken flesh, and her breath hitches. God, I want to slide inside her, drop to my knees, taste her, but I want to see hot, frustrated tears stream down her cheeks first.

Her body writhes against me, searching, but I'm holding back. For so long, she's made me beg. It's her fucking turn.

"You love this, don't you?" she says with a ragged breath. "You love feeling me like this and knowing I was right there, open, *waiting* . . ." Wetness seeps into my hand and I want to lick it off. I yank her hair again, exposing her neck, and her eyes flutter. She's so vulnerable in this position. The whimpers, the way she's digging her fingers into my arms and pushing into me . . . the struggle feeds me. She's trying to be strong, but she's failing. I love watching my goddess fail.

Her hips buck against me, desperate, searching for friction and release, but she's not getting it. I'm going to hold her here as my cock grows painfully hard until she breaks.

She has to break first.

Her hands slide over my pants, feeling the outside of my cock and her face flushes with a satisfied smile that I'm going to destroy later. Her green eyes turn dark. "You liked watching me this morning, didn't you?" *Stop fucking talking. I can't* . . . "Did you like the way my tongue played with you? The way I licked your skin and choked on your cock and controlled you?"

Stop talking. I can't concentrate. Lava surges through my veins. My head pounds with my frantic pulse. She drops her hands, and in a hard, swift tug, she yanks down her dress and bra and her tits spring free. *Fuuuuck.* The rose-colored nipples begging to be sucked, but I can't . . .

"Stick out your tongue," she demands. How does she control me like this? *I'm* the one who's supposed to be in control, *I'm* the one who's supposed to make her beg. But I do it. I stick out my tongue as my heartbeat rails against my chest. She cups her tits and drags them across my tongue and when she moans, I grab her and suck. I pinch and suck and flick my tongue against her nipples, moving back and forth, desperate for more. Her fingernails grip into my neck with so much force she might break my skin and I suck harder.

And then she pulls them away, and I chase them back in my mouth. My body is hot, my face red, my cock so hard it hurts. She's a drug, and I want more.

She lifts her skirt and *fuck me.* Beautiful, pinked from my grip, glistening with heat, and my logic, my breath, my mind is gone. I need my mouth on it. I need her taste, her smell, her skin.

"I can feel how hard you are," she says, her voice raspy and taunting. "You want this pussy, you want me, and it's killing you that I'm making you shatter your control." She lowers her skirt and presses her mouth to my ear. "And I fucking *love* watching you squirm when you don't get what you want."

Flames shoot through my chest. "Did you say I can't have it? Oh baby girl . . . I *always* get what I want." My hand grazes her neck and slides to her chest. Under my palm, her rapid heartbeat betrays her confidence. Now, it's her turn to struggle. My thumb brushes over a nipple and I pinch. Hard. The gasp this elicits fuels me. "Not so fucking confident anymore, are you?"

Sharp, rapid breaths follow. I push my palm against her pussy and she wiggles, seeking. I want to see her break. *On* me. I want wet heated desire to coat my hand. My fingers spread and trace over her soaked entrance and she immediately widens her legs. *Dirty girl* . . . "You're so fucking wet, Lexie. I think you're the one who wants this, aren't you?"

Slickness runs along my fingertips. I glide back and forth on the smooth, perfect skin, devouring her hushed moans and the soft yeses. The need to taste her consumes me, waters my mouth, acutes my senses. Legs quiver against my thigh. Fingers dig into me. Nails scratch my skin. But I'm still not going to give it to her.

Her hands move from me, and she cups her breasts. She squeezes and pinches, and I can't hold back. I drop my hand from between her legs, yank away her hands, and put her tits in my mouth. I'm frantic. Feverish. Sucking and licking. Red grip marks flush her pale chest. I wipe her arousal on her tits and lick it off and . . . *oh, fuck* . . . she tastes so good. I want my mouth on her chest, on her pussy, on her ass, and there's not enough time.

Hands grip the back of my neck, pulling me into her. "*More . . . harder . . .*"

I suck harder, lick faster, I grip her ass and press my hand back on her sweet cunt. "God, you're perfect," I moan, pushing my fingers against the slick skin.

Agony fills her face, and her heavy-lidded eyes plead with mine. "Please . . . please . . . I can't take it . . ."

"Please. What?" I demand, loving the way her body crumbles, the way that if I wasn't steadying her, she'd collapse.

My fingers stay right at her entrance and she's trying to push herself on them, but I won't let her. Her chest heaves against mine. My heartbeat thunders. I want to touch her so fucking bad, but I want to hear her say it. "Please, *what*?"

A stuttering breath releases from her sweet mouth. "Please . . . make me come."

The hushed, weighted, lust-filled confession is exactly what I need. I slide in a finger, and her head drops to my chest. "God, you feel so good." The silken walls of her perfect, tight cunt hug my finger. I glide in, out, eating up the sounds she's making, licking my way from her nipples to her neck, and back again.

Another finger slides in and my moans match hers. My cock rages in my pants. I press my thumb to her clit, circling, absorbing the way she moves, the way her breath hitches, the way she digs into me.

I need more.

I drop to my knees. She lifts her skirt and *oh Christ* . . . the bare, soft pink pussy, her slick arousal spread across her skin, her thighs trembling . . . I press my face against her and pull in a deep inhale. "You smell like heaven . . ." I hook a leg over my shoulder. My tongue travels along the delicate skin on her inner thighs, the sides of her velvety flesh, the outside of her clit. The feminine smell, the taste of salty skin is everything, *fucking everything.*

Fingers run though my hair, hips move against me. She's a goddess. A queen. I'm her servant, licking and worshiping the way she demands, the way she deserves. Oh, the luscious moans. The sounds trigger a ravenous craving. This right here, is not enough.

When I stop and stand, the cry that leaves her mouth leaves me breathless. In a flash, I pick her up, grip her naked beautiful ass, and lay her on the table. Her hazed eyes widen as I hike up her dress to her hips and open her knees and *Oh, Jesus Christ . . .*

This angle is one of my favorites. She's so fucking beautiful. My hands trace her creamy pale thighs, and I'm trying to slow down, to savor, but I can't. The sight of her wet exquisite cunt is too much. My cock screams to thrust in her, but my mouth wants her just as much.

"Please . . ." She squirms against the table, reaching for me.

I push her knees back and trail one finger against her silky slit. "Tell me how much you want my mouth on you."

Ragged, sharp breaths release as her chest moves up and down. "Theo . . . *please.*"

"*Tell. Me.*" I growl the words, drunk on power and desire and needing to hear it as much as I need to taste her. She's powerless. *Begging.*

My hands brush, slide, inch to where she needs me. She seizes my wrist, dragging me to her, but I hold back.

"Please, *please*, put your mouth on me. I need this." Red fills her face and she swallows. "I need . . . *you.*"

The words impale me, an arrow to my soul, and my eyes close.

And then . . . I devour.

My tongue and fingers work her over, coat in her essence, her scent, her taste. I swirl my tongue and suck on that plump beautiful clit as she moans and squirms and clenches her thighs. The moves and sounds turn me feral. I want her to scream, and I don't care who hears. I suck and release her clit with a pop, and she yelps and grips at my head. One finger joins my mouth, then two. I slide in and out of her as I keep licking and kissing her flesh, as I drown myself in her taste. My cock is so fucking hard that when her legs start trembling, I almost come.

Her moans are a symphony, radiating in the room. "I'm close . . . I think I'm going to . . ."

"Come for me." I sink my tongue into her warm, waiting cunt, sucking on the dripping sweet tang. Her body trembles underneath my touch, her arousal coats my chin. "That's right, beautiful girl. Let me see you shake. Show me how pretty you look when you quiver against my mouth."

She's pawing, gripping, nails dig into the back of my head as her breaths grow faster, louder, frantic. "Right there, don't stop, don't stop . . . ah, fuck!" Her body curls and her walls clench around my fingers, squeezing, and pulsating. I coax the orgasm ripping through her as she shakes and holds me tight against her. The sensations push me to the edge as I gently lick her glazed skin. When she collapses back on to the table, I lick off my fingers, needing one final taste. No matter how many times I've done this to her these last few weeks, her dazed eyes watch me with that same wide-eyed fascination as if she doesn't know how good she tastes, as if she can't fathom how I'd keep my head buried in her cunt for eternity if I could.

When she reaches for me, for my cock, I put a firm hand on her wrist. "Oh, no you don't," I say with a grin even though everything in me wants me to unzip and stuff my painfully throbbing cock in her mouth to release. "I want to hear the words."

"Don't make me say it," she says with an exhausted, satiated groan.

I grab a paper towel from the sink and soak it with warm water. I press the towel across her body, with slow, easy strokes, taking time to clean her, giving her a moment to settle.

Pale, exhausted, trembling legs. Flushed cheeks and ragged breaths.

I've never seen anything more beautiful.

When I'm done cleaning her, I gently tug her dress back down as she fixes her hair. "Say it," I demand.

"Ugh." She narrows her eyes, but she can't hide her growing smile. "Fine. You won."

34

Lexie

Oh, God. I know I should be more bothered about how wildly unprofessional it was to leave the wedding unattended like I did, but the way Theo played with me today—on the dancefloor, in the break room—was too delicious to regret. Completely worth it.

The images replay on a relentless loop as we make our way to Theo's parents' home. When I first suggested this visit earlier in the week, he was adamant about not going. But we needed to stay in Boston anyway because of the wedding and I'm desperate to know more about him, all of him, including the home where he grew up. When he checked with Michael and learned his parents would be away for the weekend, he *very* reluctantly conceded.

Sometimes I feel like what Theo and I have isn't real at all—more mirage than substance. We're living in denial, acting as though broken hearts and irrevocably altered lives aren't waiting just beyond the horizon. I've tried to tell myself that I'm just being paranoid, that Annabelle and Theo are working hard to cancel the wedding, that this is simply how things work when families have obscene amounts of money and an army of lawyers.

And yet, the doubt lingers, quiet and insistent, refusing to be dismissed.

I sit upright suddenly, holding my breath, as Michael rounds the vehicle into the Astor property. My gaze sweeps past the circular cobblestone driveway, the pristine manicured hedges, the pillars nestled on top of marble steps leading to a stone archway and massive double doors. It looks like a hotel. I've seen homes like this—in the movies and real estate ads—but never in person.

When I glance back at Theo, his face is not reflecting any of the wonderment of mine. He's stiff, unsmiling, and scratching at the back of his neck.

I place my hand on his thigh. "Are you okay?"

He exhales sharply through his nose. "Yeah, I just don't like being here."

A long moment passes, when I press my hand to his leg. "Thank you for sharing this with me. It means a lot that you'd let me see this part of you."

We step out and Theo places a hand on my lower back as we walk up the stairs. Before we reach the cathedral-sized double doors, a smiling woman in a housekeeping outfit opens them and waves us in. "Dr. Astor, welcome home. Please come in."

The door opens to an expansive mahogany and gold-accented open space, a grand double staircase, and twelve-feet-tall Italian paintings. It's beautiful, but in the way a cold museum is beautiful. My mom's studio apartment feels homier than this place.

Theo nods at the housekeeper, offering her a small smile, but otherwise stays silent. I take another step inside and hold back a low whistle. "I can't believe you grew up here," I say. "How the hell did you not get lost as a kid?"

"You get used to it, I guess," he says as he escorts me further into the home. "There's a family wing where we mostly stayed. A lot of the house is for entertaining and guests. I wasn't even allowed into some of the areas until I was older."

Although he says this matter-of-factly—and maybe this is normal for people in this socioeconomic class—my heart dips. Never once did my mother make me feel unwelcome in our own home.

With every step, his face grows sterner, his eyes darken, his body tightens. Normally, I'd reach for a joke, a touch, anything to ease the weight settling between us. But tonight, I can't.

By the time we reach the top of the stairs, his jaw is clenched, and he hasn't said a single word.

I ask him where the bathroom is. He jerks his chin down the hall, offering nothing more than a grunt. When I come back out, he's gone.

I try to find him, peering into a den-like space, sitting rooms, and then landing on a cozy reading room. "Theo?" I call.

It's quiet. Too quiet. *What the hell?* My heartbeat ticks higher as I pass a bedroom, an indoor theater outfitted with a dozen leather recliners and a screen that rivals an Imax, then another bedroom. But still no sign of him.

It's not like he just disappeared.

Did he duck into one of the kitchens?

"Theo?" I repeat and again I'm met with silence. The house might be well lit, but it's still eerie as fuck, and a shiver runs through my body.

I turn another corner when hands seize me. A scream claws up my throat, only to be smothered by a palm wrapped tightly around my mouth. My brain barely registers what's happening as I'm picked up, dragged into a dark, poorly lit room, the door slamming shut behind us.

"Let me go!" The words come out panicked, but thankfully the hands are gone. I stumble back, clutching my chest, my heart hammering violently as I put as much distance between me and this person as I can. The room spins. My lungs burn.

Then my eyes adjust and relief crashes through me.

Theo.

"Theo! What the fuck are you doing?" I breathe, still wired.

His head moves, as if assessing me like a predator and I'm his prey, and then stalks towards me with measured intent, like he knows exactly how cornered I am—and exactly how much I don't want him to stop.

"I'm kidnapping you," he says calmly. "Obviously."

A shiver runs through me. My body reacts before my brain can catch up—heat blooming, pulse stuttering. The way he looks at me, like I'm something he's claimed, makes my knees buckle.

I glance past him, taking in the room for the first time. I can just about make out a wooden-framed canopy bed, trophies lining a shelf, a long black desk. "Holy shit . . . is this your bedroom?"

He's behind me before I can ask another question. A hand tangles in my hair, the other possessively cupping my breast. I gasp at the sharp, jarring movement, and the way his mouth feels at my ear, his voice low and measured. "Rules of captivity," he says, pausing long enough to let the words settle. "You do exactly what I say."

My breath catches.

"Now," he murmurs, closer still, "lift up your dress."

I lean back into him and push my ass into his rock-hard, waiting cock. "Are you . . . sure . . ." I swallow. "We're in your parents' house . . ." His fingers slide across my nipple, and he pinches so hard that a bolt of heat jolts through me like lightning.

"I was very clear about the rules."

My shaky fingers lift the fabric, so it skims just above the crease of my butt cheeks.

"That's right, my dirty, beautiful girl. You know you want this." He reaches under my dress and inside my panties and I whimper. His touch is rough and demanding and so fucking good. "Tell me who this belongs to."

Mmmm . . . My legs quiver. This is wrong . . . so, so wrong. We're in his bedroom at his *parents'* house. There are staff and people . . . and . . . *ohhhh* . . . his grip tightens on my pussy and my breath locks in my throat.

"Tell me who owns this beautiful fucking cunt," he says with a rasped, throaty breath as his palm grinds into me. "Say it."

Need and heat ripples through me. I reach behind me to grip his legs and push him harder into me, shamelessly grinding into his length. My thong is already wet, filled with my unabashed arousal. My body begs to be filled, but we shouldn't . . . His hand slides up to my neck and he squeezes. "*Fucking tell me.*"

Hot, erotic fear tears through me. His hold on my throat tightens enough where I can feel my pulse thud against his palm. "You . . ." I stammer, breathless from restricted air and dizzy with desire. "It belongs to you."

"That's my good fucking girl." He drops his hands and swings me to face him. Even in the dim light, I can see his eyes darken with a look that sends me stumbling back until I hit the bed. "Lift up your dress and show me your perfect tight pussy."

A hard swallow rolls through my tender throat. I bunch the fabric in my palm, until I expose my white lace fabric.

A wolfish grin forms, and he licks his lips. "Mmm . . . so beautiful . . ." he growls. "Sit on the bed, spread your legs, and show me what's mine."

Like I'm possessed, my body shivers as I slide back on the

bed, dangle my legs off the mattress and tug my panties to the side.

"*Wider.*"

I spread my legs farther and tug. I hear him move towards me before I feel him pulling me onto my feet and flipping me over. I brace my palms on the mattress as air rips from my lungs. A belt buckle unclasping and zipper being pulled is the only sound before he yanks my panties down to my knees and slams into me so hard I'm lifted onto my tiptoes. The impact crushes my insides, but the pain is so good, so deep, and I want more. He pulls completely out and does it again. The single, brutal thrust is raw and possessive. He's claiming me. *Marking* me. And God, I want to be marked and scarred and branded. I want to keep him with me, etched into my soul, feel him from the inside forever. One more time, all the way out, and he crashes back into me with such ruthless force my body lurches forward.

"Oh God, yes . . . more . . ."

And then, he moves. Fast, hard, carnal. "That's right, fuck . . . take this cock. This beautiful fucking cunt is mine. Do you hear me? It belongs to *me*." His words are as harsh as his movements and my ass slaps against him. "Stick your ass out more. *Higher.* That's right, baby . . . Oh . . . right there, right fucking there. You know exactly how to take me, don't you? Good girl. Such a good fucking girl." He fucks me with a frenzied possessiveness. With a raw savageness. Like a man possessed. Over and over, he pounds. My head wildly jars with each thrust. His fingers dig into my hips. Guttural moans and screams echo in the room. Dizzying stars fill my vision. My breath seizes and locks as he keeps going, furious and unrestrained. I grip the bed, the comforter, anything in reach, but I'm losing balance, losing air, and it's *so fucking good.*

"Give it to me, give it all to me," I demand with a thick, husky breath. "Show me what you can do. I want you to prove that you fucking own me."

He perches my ass and rails into me. Frenzied. Frantic. Unhinged. My heartbeat thunders against my chest. Choked cries rush from my mouth. He pushes into me, pumping more and more until my body, my entire being, trembles as urgency builds. I want him to keep going, to never stop, to brand me and bruise me and own me. I want the pain, the break, the way he'll rebuild me. "Fuck, yes, right there . . ." I scream and everything in me clenches and shakes, ravaging me with a rattled sob. His cock throbs inside of me and he collapses against my back as the pulses continue, as his warm cum fills my insides and slides down my thighs. He stays there, holding me, pulsing, his heart beating so fast I can feel it on my back.

When his cock stops throbbing, he pulls out but pushes me onto the bed and puts his thumb inside me. "Keep it in you. *Absorb* me," he says against my ear as his thumb stays in me. "And know that you will *always* belong to me."

35

Lexie

"So, do I owe you my left or right kidney for covering me at that Boston wedding?" Justin asks as he steps next to me in the breakroom.

"Ah, welcome back!" I hop up from the table. It's been two weeks since I've seen him and I give him the gentlest hug I can muster after his appendicitis surgery. "I missed you."

"Same," he says, easing gingerly into the chair. Even though we've texted almost every day, he didn't want any visitors while recovering. I notice he's a little thinner, a little paler—but his golden smile is still there. "All right," he adds, grinning. "Catch me up. What did I miss?"

If he only knew.

I wish I could tell Justin everything. My God would my best friend grab a bowl of popcorn and eat this up like he was watching one of his reality shows. I hate lying to him.

Hate. It. But instead, I weave as much truth as I can into my story and pray that lying by omission counts as a forgivable best friend sin.

Over the past two nights, Theo and I have talked at length about when the details will finally be settled—when we won't have to hide anymore. It's not that I need some sort of grand, public declaration that he's mine. I just want to have an ordinary relationship, one where I can hold his hand on the sidewalk or kiss him at dinner in public without feeling like we're living in shame.

I'm trying—really trying—not to be paranoid and clingy, but I can't quiet the worry. I have no control over the timeline, but what I do realize is that the longer the wedding charade continues, the more believable it looks as last-minute cold feet and doesn't raise suspicion. It also doesn't hurt that extending the withdrawal date means our company retains more of its fees.

And if I'm being honest, part of me is banking on Sydney seeing the sheer amount of work I've poured into making this wedding perfect—and it might be enough for her to still consider my promotion.

But still . . . my gut knots.

"Lexie?" Justin says, waving a hand in front of me, trying to grab my attention. "The wedding?"

"Oh sorry, my mind was elsewhere. Ah . . . It was good," I say avoiding his eyes. I can't tell him that I took a client to the wedding, even if he did show up unannounced. I definitely can't tell him I crossed every professional line imaginable and snuck away to have mind-blowing sex with the very client whose wedding I'm in charge of.

A piece of me still feels like I'm living in a dream that's set to end in seven weeks. I know the crash is looming—there's a high chance my world will implode and leave me broken. For once in my life, I'm trying to ignore that and simply enjoy being wanted and worshipped.

I don't come from a billionaire family like Annabelle, so when Theo tells me the logistics around cancelling the wedding are taking longer than expected, I want to believe him. But in the quiet moments, the doubt creeps in, reminding me of how much I stand to lose if I'm wrong.

God, I need to focus. "Enough about work! What about you? How's recovery been? Please tell me the pain was worth it because you had a hot nurse by your side?" I grin.

Justin lifts his brow, and I know he can read right through my pink cheeks and shifty eyes. But he lets me off the hook and tells me all about his recovery time and sadly not any eye candy, much to his spouse's relief.

The rest of the day flows like any other day. I return calls to vendors. I double check with Annabelle and Theo about guests' allergies for the caterers. I pore over the seating arrangement—again—following the endless instructions from Annabelle and Theo's parents about who must sit together, and who absolutely cannot.

And somewhere in the middle of it all, I find myself smiling at the dichotomy that is Theo. The possessive, commanding man who will challenge me at every opportunity.

And the thoughtful, attentive one—the caregiver who rubs my feet and brings me incredible food and *always* makes sure I'm taken care of first.

At my desk, I drain the last of my coffee, knowing I should finish my tasks for the day. Instead, I feel the familiar pull to check in on Theo—to make sure he's still there, still *with* me. I'm reaching for my phone when a throat clears. I jump, startled, to find Sydney standing by my desk.

Guilt floods me. My shoulders tense, panic flaring that I've somehow exposed my secret relationship with Theo. Lying to Justin is one thing; lying to my boss is far riskier. And for some time now, I haven't been able to shake the sense that Sydney hasn't been her usual self with me.

"Hey, lady," she says, sliding into Justin's vacant chair and nudging it closer. "How are you holding up with everything?"

Her tone eases me slightly, though I still swallow hard, praying my cheeks don't give me away. *Better than you could possibly imagine* is not the right answer. "Great," I say instead. "We're ahead of schedule. Now that Justin's back at work, I handed his account back and I'm free to help wherever I'm needed."

She waves a hand dismissively. "No, I want all your focus on the Barlowe/Astor wedding," she says, and the guilt resurfaces. "Everyone's eyes will be on this day. I don't want you distracted by smaller events. If you're caught up, you should treat yourself to a few days off."

Um, what's happening here? Sydney is many things. Smart. Driven. An empathetic leader. But encouraging time off in the name of work-life balance has never been one of them. I take in the new dark circles under her eyes, the deep lines etched into her forehead.

Something is definitely off.

"I really appreciate all the extra effort you've been putting in," she says. "The overtime, meeting after work to accommodate Theo's schedule . . ."

I'm dying here. Don't look at her in the face.

"Yes, of course."

Her arms are still folded and her stern look makes me shift in my seat. I'm close to telling her that I have work to do, when she says, "By the way, I haven't seen any expense reports for all the food and travel tied to the Barlowe/Astor account. I'm finalizing the quarterly financials now, so I'll need those submitted for reimbursement."

I hesitate. "Oh, um, there won't be any. Theo pays for everything."

She raises an eyebrow. "What?"

"Yeah, ah, he says that's the least he and Annabelle could do. A sort of thank you for going above and beyond."

She cocks her head, studying me in silence for a long moment. If I've ever felt like I was being hauled to the principal's office, this is it. She thumbs her frames back up her face and nods. "Well, that's awfully generous of them." A weak smile appears. "Must be nice to be a billionaire."

Her comment has alarm bells sounding. If she knows about me and Theo, I wish she'd just say something. The waiting and second-guessing is terrible.

"Is everything okay?"

She straightens at my question, her smile widening, though I can tell it's fake. "Yes. All good."

This conversation is starting to feel unbearable, the paranoia creeping in fast and unwelcome. Whether Sydney knows the truth or not, I can't stand the uncertainty anymore. "I know you said you want me focused exclusively on the Barlowe/Astor account," I say evenly, "but is there any issue that I should be aware of?"

"Oh no, not at all! Just, keep up all the great work. The Barlowe wedding is *exactly* what we need. I'm so proud of you for managing it so well."

The sincerity in her voice reassures me that maybe she doesn't know about us. Still, I can't ignore the tension in her posture, the sense she's holding something back. She's my boss, after all, and it doesn't feel like my place to pry.

For the rest of the day, I can't shake the ickiness. *I'm not doing anything wrong. I'm not doing anything wrong.* But I'm lying to everyone, and my patience is wearing thin.

Theo makes me feel things I've never felt before. When I first saw him after all those years, it was pure, gut-wrenching rage. When I started to realize he might not have been the reason I was expelled from college, it turned into an ache—to go back, to reclaim the years I spent hating him. And now . . . my heart actually hurts when he isn't with me.

I need to stop fretting over the what ifs and just enjoy each moment as it comes. Things like this have a way of working themselves out.

I hope.

After I get home, I catch myself peeking out the window, hoping for some glimpse of him, but all I see is a drawn curtain. I've developed a severe case of co-dependency of late. Even knowing Theo has a seven p.m. work call he planned to take in his studio, I hate being apart.

I try to distract myself by running a bath and doomscrolling, but by eight p.m., I'm restless and keyed up.

Eventually, I give in and message him.

> Lexie: you still on your work call?
>
> Theo: yes, sorry. It's going to be at least another hour.

Ugh. I understand they didn't want to interrupt clinic hours and had to coordinate a time between their west coast clinic partners, but *still.*

I slide into bed and snap a selfie of a sad face, and he gives it a heart. A heart? Nope. I need more. Am I needy? Obsessed? I blame Theo for the person I've become.

I roll over and slip my hands inside my shorts, picturing the ravenous way Theo looks at me, the way my body responds to him, the way he makes everything flush with heat. I trail my fingertips over my clit, but I want Theo's hands here, not my own.

I take a photo of my partly obscured hand and lower belly and hit send.

My phone buzzes immediately.

Theo: Wait for me.

A grin spreads and I type back.

Lexie: No promises.

He sends back the hot, sweating emoji and I eat up his frustration. God, he's so sexy when I'm pushing his buttons. I let a few minutes pass before I lift my tank, exposing the underside of my breast and the tiniest peek of my peaked nipple, and hit send.

Theo: You're killing me.

Lexie: Good.

If his call was about a patient or procedure, I wouldn't dare. But he already warned me it's just a dreaded quarterly budget meeting, which is mandatory since he bought into the practice. So naturally, I need to remind him what he's missing out on. I flip on to my stomach, slip my shorts below my ass, and snap. The perfect photo takes more shots than it should, and a Pilates-inspired flex move. But when I finally capture the right one, I grin. Theo will die when he sees it. My man is a certified ass man.

Holy shit. My man. Is he? I think he is. We haven't had

"the talk" which seems premature since he's fake engaged to someone else. But, the idea of him not being in my life nearly guts me.

A moment after I hit "send", I get the exact response I'm hoping for.

> Theo: Babygirl, you are playing with fire. You better prepare yourself because when I get to your place, you will pay for this.

Oh God, I fucking hope so. Thirty minutes later, a loud pound on the door jolts me upright in the bed. I look down at myself, my cotton shorts, my tank with no bra, and grin. Through the peephole, Theo stands in the hall, his face serious and determined, and my heart skyrockets.

I tilt up my head, and open the door. He chooses to ignore my teasing stance, storming in past me and slamming the door. "I warned you."

That's all he says, and my body quivers as I back into the corner. He spins me to face away from him. My chest slams against the wall, and I yelp. The air has shot out of my lungs and it's fucking *heaven*. I look over my shoulder and the devil stares back. Dark, primal, savage need faces me, and I'm so dazed I might collapse.

He grips my jaw, hard, and punishes my mouth with his lips. When he releases, I press my chest into the cool wall and push out my ass. He reaches around, slides into my shorts, and grips my pussy with so much dominance I nearly choke.

"You're already wet. Were you up here tonight, touching yourself because you love distracting me?" He grunts into my ear with a throaty taunt. "I told you I was working and you didn't fucking listen, did you?"

God, I love pushing him. Slickness spreads, wetting my inner thigh, knowing that I can make him break. "That's what you get for ignoring me." I need him to touch me, now, but I restrain. "You need to learn you're not always in control."

Oh fuck, he does not like that. Which makes me *love* it.

"You think you are so fucking tough, but I feel you shaking," he husks against the shell of my ear as his tattooed arm around me tightens. "You want this so bad you're trembling."

He's right. My control is slipping and the more I try to grasp it, the more I lose. He drags the length of his cock against me through fabric but the tease isn't enough.

I need all of him.

A hand slides up my stomach, rips down my tank, and my tits bounce free. As the knuckles in one hand graze my slit and his other tugs on my tight nipple, a wild heat invades me. My knees buckle, but his powerful arms hold me steady.

"You're soaked," he says with a low rumble as he keeps tracing my clit, my cunt, my skin. "You greedy fucking girl, look at the way you're coating my fingers."

He grips my jaw again, dragging it to the side and kisses me, hard. An unsteady, shaky breath leaves my mouth. I reach behind me to grip his cock outside of his jeans, but he tilts away. "You don't get to touch what I don't tell you to fucking touch."

His words nip at my skin like a flogger. This is my punishment for defying him. "Don't you want me to touch you?" I say, breathless.

He doesn't answer, but a finger slips inside me, and I moan. He moves to the side of me, and grips my jaw, forcing me to look at him. "Keep your fucking eyes on me when I'm touching you," he says and slips in a second finger. "I'm in control now, do you understand? You will do exactly as I say."

Oh God, oh God . . . I can't stand upright. Pleasure soars through me as he's knuckles deep in my cunt. Stars fill my vision, my breath turns choppy and ragged. The wall and his arms are the only thing keeping me upright, and *oh . . . oh fuck* . . . he pinches my swollen, throbbing clit and heat surges through me.

"Did you honestly think I was going to let your behavior slide?"

I swallow at the harsh tone and moan as he shoves his hands in my shorts and drags his fingers across the collection of nerves. "I . . . love playing with you," I stammer without any of the confidence I'm trying to portray.

He stiffens, yanks my shorts down to my knees and lands one, then two, then three hard, sharp smacks on my ass. My breath seizes. Hot, blinding tears spring to my eyes, and I moan into the wall. "That's what you get for making me so fucking crazy today I couldn't concentrate."

And then he's on his knees. The flat of his tongue runs over the stinging pink flesh on my cheeks and he smooths it out with his palm. He lifts each ankle to slide off my shorts and tosses them to the side.

And then he spends the night deliciously making sure I pay for what I did.

36

Lexie

Denial is a lovely state of being and I'm happily living in it. The wedding is six weeks away. *Six weeks.* Even though I'm stressing at the timeline and pretending I'm not worried that they were supposed to call it off over a month ago, even though I try not to cry when I'm alone anticipating the worst, the sense of what's coming sits heavy in my bones.

Annabelle gets back from Italy next week. While it seems like we're all on the same page about the wedding, she's still a silent invisible entity that generates a little fear. When she returns, I'm sure things will be different. Right now, Theo's at my place every night, or I'm at his. We're together as much as humanly possible. But when Annabelle comes home, he'll want to see her. Of course he will. What if being around her makes him wonder if he made a mistake? What if Annabelle looks at him and decides she doesn't want to cancel the wedding after all? And then . . .

I cut the thought off before it can sink its teeth in, just as Michael pulls up outside Theo's place in Tribeca.

The elevator takes me up to the penthouse, but when I let myself in, he's not there. *Weird*. He should be home by now. I dig my phone from my purse and type a message.

Lexie: Are you almost home?

I decide to grab a protein shake from his refrigerator. I drink it in front of the beautiful skyline.

And I wait a little more.

Theo: No

The brisk response jars me. Maybe he's with a patient and just tapped his smartwatch. I can't keep dissecting every message, every pause, every imagined slight—or I'll drive myself crazy.

I take a shower, slip into pajamas even though it's not even seven p.m., and watch some TV on the couch, when I finally hear the click of the lock opening. I toss my phone and go to greet him, but the second he walks through the door, my chest sinks.

His eyes are dark—not the sexy kind, not the ravenous kind. Just dark. His mouth is a flat line, nostrils flaring slightly. It throws me, because since we got together, every time he sees me, it's like I'm his favorite thing in the world and he can't believe his luck.

He throws his phone on the counter, followed by his keys, and dumps his backpack onto a chair, storming past me to grab a water from the fridge.

I hesitate, unsure what to do. Is he mad at me? Did I do something? "Are you okay?" I ask, pressing my palm against his forearm. He's strong—*he's so fucking strong*—but tonight, the veins popping from under his skin are tighter than I've ever felt. When he doesn't answer, I drop my hand. "Do you want to go grab a drink? I can get dressed."

The muscle in his jaw stretches. "No."

No matter how much I want to straighten my back and lift my chin to show him that his bad mood doesn't affect me, I can't. My shoulders slump. "Did I do something wrong?" I hate the slight insecurity in my voice, but it's too late to take it back.

His eyes soften. "No . . . you didn't do anything."

The sliver of relief is not enough to counteract the internal raging storm. "Do you want dinner?"

"No."

A long silence passes as he keeps his arms crossed. Like he wants to keep his distance from me.

"What's wrong?" I ask, searching his eyes, but they're filled with so much anger that I step back.

"I don't want to talk about it."

Okay . . . We've never really had a fight. Sure, technically we fought a lot in the beginning, and we still have the occasional heated debate over who gets control of the remote (me) or whether I'm allowed to wear a certain dress without becoming an accessory to whatever crime he commits to every man who sees me in it (him). But nothing like this.

"Okay," I say, calmly, ignoring the way my stomach feels like someone's squeezing the insides. "Well, you need to eat something. Maybe we could just order takeout and watch a movie or something."

He ignores me, and anxiety starts to turn into anger. What the hell? Between our four p.m. text saying he couldn't wait to rush home to see me and his behavior now, something has happened.

"Theo?"

"No." He grabs his backpack from the chair and swipes his keys from the counter. "I can't be here. I need to go."

What? Where the hell does he need to go? Fuck him. I can't even imagine what he'd say to me if I pulled this on him and *I'm* not the one walking around fake-engaged. I fold my arms tight against my chest, the movement a barrier of protection. "What the hell did I do?"

"It's not you. It's . . . fuck . . ." He rubs a hand down his chin. "I just . . . I need to . . . I can't be around you right now."

"You can't be around me? Are you serious?" Theo has never made me feel anything but a queen. But right now, he's making me feel worthless. I stare at him, trying to read his eyes, but they're scattered and angry and I'm over it. "Fine. Then don't."

I storm down the hall toward the guest bedroom, never more thankful in my life that he has two rooms. I'd stomp all the way to my apartment if I could, but Michael's off for the night and I do not feel like getting an Uber in my pajamas.

Even though he's barely acknowledged me since he got home, I still find myself listening for the front door—waiting for him to leave. Instead, he exhales loudly before I hear his footsteps following me.

"Wait," he says.

I swing open the guest bedroom door. "No. You don't get to do this. You don't get to fucking ignore me, then tell me you have somewhere to go and can't be around me and then ask me to wait. I'm sleeping in here tonight, and do not for a second think of waking me up from wherever you magically have to be." I want to hurt him the way he's hurting me. It's small, maybe event petty—sleeping in the guest bedroom is nothing. His room is right next door, the wall between us paper-thin. But we've never not gone a night without sharing a bed, and he needs to feel that absence.

"But—"

I slam the door before he says another word, climb into bed, and try hard not to cry.

But before I reach the pillow to muffle, I break into sobs.

37

Theo

Fuck.

My fists hit the bag, over and over and over, pummeling against it until the demon inside me releases. The murderous rage blistering my insides has elevated so high, that for the second time in my life, I feel like I might kill someone. The first time was when I saw that Cody fucker lay his hands on Lexie.

The second time was three hours ago, when I got a call from Olivia.

Sweat pours down my forehead and I rage against the boxing bag in my condo's gym. The people around me have headphones on, paying no attention to me thank Christ, because if anyone came up to me, I don't know what I would do.

When Olivia sent me a message this afternoon saying she needed to talk, I set my patient notes aside and spent the next hour on the phone with her. The hysterical crying was the first sign something was wrong. Then she proceeded to tell me that she'd found an envelope in her mailbox with the note saying: *Choose your words carefully, Olivia. There are ears everywhere.*

I said it could have been from anyone, but we both knew that this note could only be from my dad. My father is a sadistic bastard, and this is exactly something he'd do.

But if Olivia pulls out, the others will almost certainly follow. She's the strongest link I have to taking my father down—not just because she has the receipts and evidence, but because she also has the means to protect herself when this goes public. Ironically, when she was a student, she had none of that. No power, no visibility—my father's perfect target. That changed later. Her father, a local union organizer who made noise about unfair labor practices and is now running for state senate, gave her a level of protection she never had before. With Olivia attached in the exposé, the other women believed their stories would be taken seriously. That someone would finally listen.

But what am I supposed to do? Force her to tell the journalist everything? She was a mess on the phone, terrified that if she came forward, she'd jeopardize both her dad's campaign and her new job. And I couldn't do a fucking thing.

I pound into the bag. *Fuck. Fuck!* Of course, I understand. My father is powerful and cruel, and he already took something from her once back in school. And now her voice has so much fucking power, whether she realizes it or not. But if

I made her feel like shit, or coerced her into coming forward, I'd be no better than him.

But the investigation has to continue. My father needs to be held accountable. These women deserve their restitution. And I'm failing. I'm fucking failing them, Lexie, Anna . . .

Everything is spiraling. Anna's been quieter with me lately—acting vague and evasive. She's always been someone who tells me everything, which is how I know she's holding something back. I keep reassuring Lexie that everything will be fine, that Anna's just waiting on final details from the lawyer. But the truth is, I'm stalling. It shouldn't be taking this long. Every time we think we're at the finish line, another delay crops up, stretching my patience thinner.

I'm terrified that if it doesn't happen soon, Lexie will leave. The idea of her no longer being in my life guts me so badly that sometimes it feels hard to breathe. I know what that fear means—that she matters more to me than anyone ever has, that my feelings run deeper than I'm ready to fully confront.

I've done too much fucked-up shit in my life to pretend I deserve her. I know that.

But I'm a selfish man. And I can't seem to let her go.

The gym bag sways against every hit, and my pulse is pounding so hard in my chest that if I don't take a break soon, I'm going to collapse. I'm a doctor. I know the signs of over exertion, but I don't fucking care.

Lexie. *Fuck, fuck, fuck.* Why did I treat her like that when I got home? Nothing about today had anything to do with her.

What the hell is wrong with me? I feel the way I did when I first hired her as the coordinator—anxious, off-balance, out of control. Terrified of what I couldn't fix: my future, not saving Anna from her parents, the women who might walk away from telling the truth about my father. Instead of sitting with that fear, I lashed out. God, I'm such a piece of shit. I took it out on Lexie. And she didn't run. She had every right to storm out of my condo and tell me to go fuck myself. I would've deserved it. But she didn't. She stayed—and the condo's door alert confirms she stayed. She's waiting for me—someone unworthy of her love, her devotion, fucking unworthy of her.

So, what the hell am I doing in the gym instead of burying myself inside of her, begging for her forgiveness and reminding her how much she means to me? I bite the glove with my teeth to rip it off, grab a towel, and bolt to the elevator.

When I arrive at my condo, sweat still drips down my forehead, my breaths are labored, but I'm desperate. I enter my place, kick off my shoes at the door, and head straight to the guest bedroom. I slow once I reach the door, unsure whether she'll let me in. I lift my hand to knock—

The door swing opens.

Lexie stands there, defiant and devastatingly beautiful, like she's been waiting for me to finally knock some sense into myself.

I capture her mouth with mine. She doesn't hesitate—doesn't pull back, doesn't ask where I've been or why I'm here now, doesn't even wrinkle her nose at the sweat still clinging to me. Instead, she jumps, wrapping her legs around my waist, and I carry her to the bed.

Euphoria rushes through me with the feel of her body against mine. Her plush lips are hungry and frantic. Her heartbeat thunders where our chests meet, breaths tangling, fingertips raking through my hair and holding tight.

I kiss her with desperate urgency, like touching her is the only way to convince myself she's real and still mine. *Please don't ever leave me.* My lips move to her neck, burying myself in her taste and smell. *She's here, she's here.* When I lay her on the bed, the longing in those beautiful eyes nearly takes me out. I crawl on top and her legs seamlessly wrap around me, waiting. My mouth glides across her dewy skin, kiss below her ear, my hands slide down those impossibly smooth arms.

I don't want to think of anything but her. I don't want to imagine a world she's not part of. I want to be here now, in this moment, savoring the way her nipples harden when my thumb grazes her, drinking in the way she shivers under me, soaking in the moans leaving her mouth.

"I'm so sorry, baby. I'm so fucking sorry . . ." I whisper as I dance my lips across hers.

Her lip trembles. "You left me . . ."

The shattered words make me want to choke. I will *never* leave Lexie. She's part of me. My world doesn't exist if she's not in it. "I will never leave you again."

I lower the strap of her camisole and kiss her collarbone, the freckles on her shoulder, the delicate skin on her neck. My tongue traces the line of her jaw before brushing her lips, memorizing her. I want to take my time—let her taste, her scent, the sounds she makes brand themselves into me until there's no part of me left untouched by her.

Silently, she lifts my shirt up and over my head, and I remove hers, and guide her back down. I drag my tongue against a nipple and pull it into my mouth, sucking and licking as she moans against me. Oh . . . those moans. I want those to be the last sounds I hear before I die.

My cock is hard inside of my gym shorts, eager to get out, but I force myself to slow down. I need this to last. If I can somehow stretch the moment—maybe the world outside will stop spinning, time will hold its breath, and we can stay suspended here, like this, forever.

I slip my hands inside her pajama shorts, and the moment I reach bare, moist skin, my breath hitches.

Sometimes I try so hard to keep everything between us raw and feral and emotionless, but I'm fighting a losing battle. This time, it's more than that. This is me sliding down her shorts like she's the most precious thing on earth. This is me dragging my tongue up from her ankle to her knees to the inside of her thigh like she's the goddess I live to serve.

Hands grip the back of my sweaty head as I kiss her center, run my tongue across the soft skin, soak in the taste of her arousal. Silky heat fills my mouth, and I'm already craving more. I brush my fingers against her entrance and when she quivers, I slide in a fingertip.

"Mmmm . . . that feels good," she says, lifting her hips to meet me.

I slide in further and God . . . the way she feels against my fingers makes me disintegrate. The feel of her slung legs over my shoulders now pressing into me, growing with urgency, fuels me. I want to breathe, fall asleep, live inside her.

"I could live off your pussy forever . . ." I hum against her skin. My tongue swirls her plump clit. I give it a quick suck and release and devour the sounds she makes. Nails dig into my back, and every scratch, every moan, every word about how good I make her feel, how much she wants me, fuels me.

I'm obsessed with this woman.

I lift myself and flip her on her stomach, taking my time to slide my palms down her smooth back, over that beautiful round ass, and in-between her thighs. I plant kisses on her cheeks, I slide my thumb back up to her entrance and press inside, and I moan at the same time she does. She's exquisite. An immaculate, flawless angel, and she's mine. I don't fucking deserve her. She chose me. I don't know what I did to make this happen.

But she's fucking mine.

"Please . . . I'm so ready for you . . ." she says, gripping the sheets.

I'm ready for her, too. From here until eternity, I will always be ready for her. But, I need just a little bit more time with my mouth on her body. I grip her hips and pull her ass up until she's on her knees and her cheek is resting on the pillow and *fuck me* . . . I love her in this angle, seeing her glistening pink flesh, how open and ready she is for me.

A throaty moan releases from my mouth as I slide the flat of my tongue from her clit to her entrance and melt in her taste.

"Please . . . please . . . I need you, now," she whimpers.

Those words gut me, because I need her, too. Now, forever. I turn her back over so I can see her heated, hooded eyes, so I can take in the swollen lips, the hard nipples, the pinked flushed face.

I remove the rest of my clothes, climb back onto the bed, and finally, I push into her, sinking into her warm, silken world. And I stay. I don't move, I don't thrust, I just hold. I'm taking in the way her plush walls hug my cock, the way my heartbeat races in my chest, the way this moment is more intense but less frantic than all the other times.

She grips my face and brings me to her, but she doesn't kiss me. She *reads* me. "I'm right here, Theo, okay?" she says like she knows what I need to hear. "I'm not running."

Those eyes . . . they destroy me. I cup her face back and press my forehead into hers. Slowly I start rocking. Long, slow, intentional strokes. My eyes don't break contact with hers. I've never had a moment like this. Weightless yet heavy. Euphoric yet sobering.

Lexie makes me forget everything. She's my healer and my savior.

And to the deepest part of me, I'm terrified she'll be my heartbreak.

38

Lexie

I pick up my phone and stare at the empty screen. I flip it over, put it down, pick it up. I—

"Lexie, you're driving me fucking nuts," Justin says, holding his hand out. "Give me your phone. For your own good. Seriously."

"Sorry, sorry. I know." I force a smile and drop it into my purse. He's right. For the past five days, Theo and I have barely spoken—just a handful of texts and one rushed phone call. I feel like a starved caged animal, restless and on edge, and I hate it. Annabelle came back last week, and just like I feared, Theo pulled away immediately. He warned me he'd go dark while they worked through the final "break-up" details. He just didn't warn me he'd go pitch fucking black.

I glance at my computer screen, but I can't absorb a single thing—my mind is too scattered. How could it not be, when I'm supposed to be fine-tuning the final details of a fake wedding that's three weeks away and I'm falling in love with the groom.

"Is this about the new guy?" Justin asks as he leans back on his chair. "Need me to pull the best friend card and have a conversation with him about how to treat a lady?"

"No. Not yet." I take a sip of coffee and it slides to my sour stomach. "Let's try not to scare him off before you get the chance to know him. First impressions and all."

Or, in this case, fifth impressions. I say a silent prayer that once everything is out in the open, Justin will understand why I've kept the details from him and only mentioned I started seeing someone "special".

"This one's pretty serious, huh?"

Serious doesn't even begin to explain my feelings.

And it terrifies the shit out of me.

"Yeah, I hope so. And I hate that I'm in so deep now that I start freaking out when he pulls back, even though I understand why. It's just . . . hard."

"I really feel that. I don't think it ever gets any easier—even when you're married," Justin says gently. "But if something doesn't feel right, it's better to be honest with him about it so you know where you stand."

I sigh. He's probably right.

"If what you have is worth fighting for, then maybe it's time to fight."

I mouth that I love him—even when he's being insufferably right about knowing what's best—and go back to reading phantom emails.

But the days continue to pass, and I hardly hear from Theo. With a knotted stomach, I reread the text message I sent last night, which he still hasn't responded to.

Lexie: I miss you. When can I see you?

I start writing another message to check if everything's okay, when, by some miracle, typing bubbles appear. I freeze, holding my breath.

Theo: sorry, missed this text. I'll figure something out.

Bullshit. I'm not playing this game where Theo thinks he can walk all over me. Been, there done that, got the trophy. But no more. So I don't reply.

Days crawl by, and my simmering anger starts to boil; out of stubborn principle, I don't reach out to him. He doesn't contact me either.

When I check my phone for the millionth time that day at work, and see no new message, I storm down the hall to take a breather, away from my desk and the annoying wedding reminders popping up on my computer. As I pass Sydney's office, I stop in my tracks when I hear sniffling coming from inside. I hesitate. I'm not sure if it's my place to check in on her or not. But the knowledge that Sydney never cries, not at work anyway, and that she prides herself on being the consummate professional spur me on to tentatively knock on her office door.

I hear a weak "Come in" and see Sydney trying to quickly wipe away her tears with a tissue. "Oh, hey Lexie. Come in and shut the door." Not even her chunky glasses could conceal the bloodshot eyes.

I shut the door and lower myself into the chair. "Is everything okay?" I ask, when *clearly* everything is not okay.

Sydney takes a sip of water and fans her face. "Yes. Um, how are you? You looked upset earlier."

It strikes me that even in her misery, she's still looking out for me. I push my own concerns aside; right now, this is about Sydney. "What's going on?"

Her mouth parts like she wants to say something, but then closes it. I've never seen her break like this.

"Sydney, please. Tell me what's going on." I place my hand on her desk. "You've been there for me all these years. Let me be here for you now."

A long moment passes as she studies my face, warring with her own indecision. Finally, she takes a deep breath. "If I tell you, it doesn't leave this room. Understood?" I nod. "I just got off the phone with the company's investors. Even though I saw it coming, it still hit me hard." Her voice shakes as she speaks. "I have to lay off five staff members."

What!? "Five?" My mind swirls like I was just spit out from a tornado and landed on my ass. We only have *ten* employees. What the hell could've happened that would constitute laying off fifty percent of our staff?

Panic sets in.

Am I one of them? I can't leave. This is my home, for

better or worse. I'm endlessly grateful to Sydney for taking a chance on a young girl recently kicked out of college and I don't know if any other company would've done the same. The wedding industry is cutthroat and unforgiving, built on reputation and prestige. Black spots fill my vision, and I blink through the murky, thin air.

"As of now, you are safe," she says and I let out the biggest breath of my life. "But I need to look at which team members I can bear to see let go." Her lips tremble. "I don't tell you all often enough, but this here is my family. You all mean the world to me."

My heart swells and I want to hug her. "Is there anything I can do?"

"No . . . not right now. You have to keep this confidential while I figure out the next steps." She props her elbows on the table and rests her head in her hands. When she pulls back, she gives me a soft smile. "Actually, there is something you can do."

I straighten my back. "Anything."

"Make this Barlowe/Astor wedding the most spectacular event of the season. Do whatever you need to make them happy. We need our names in every paper, gossip site, we need every guest to know who we are." Heat fills my face. I choke down the nauseating burn of acid in my throat. "God forbid, if this wedding doesn't go through, our company will close its doors for good."

The shock of what Sydney told me an hour ago still hasn't worn off. I've called Theo twice, sent a text, had no reply, and my anxiety is through the roof. Having to work in the office for the rest of the day has been torture. I can't stop myself from peering around at my co-workers wondering who'll be cut. The twin receptionists, Amanda and Megan? Seeing their smiling faces greeting me every morning is something I've taken for granted. Someone else? It feels like I'm watching the living dead, people moving through their day without any idea of what's coming.

God, please let it not be Justin.

Right now, the wedding that I'm so desperate to have canceled—*which is somehow still going ahead*—carries the very real possibility of shutting down my workplace and leaving me without a job. It's not just my life on the line, but everyone else's in this company. What sort of fuckery-laced hand did the universe deal me? And what kind of selfish, vile person am I that I still want the wedding called off?

But, since Theo and Annabelle are still officially engaged to be married in two weeks, between the three of us, it hopefully buys us enough time to come up with a solution. If only I could just talk to Theo.

I grab my purse and phone and head for the door, fixated on tracking him down and forcing this conversation. He's had enough time to reunite with Annabelle and talk it out with her. Now I need answers.

Less than an hour later, I'm in the elevator heading up to his apartment. It's only four p.m. and I know he won't be home for a few hours, but I'll sit and wait all goddamn day if that's what it takes to make him talk to me.

When I let myself into his condo, I'm prepared to meet a silent, open room, instead—"Theo?" It takes a moment for me to confirm my eyes aren't deceiving me. A pale, unshaved, messy-haired Theo, wearing a wrinkled t-shirt and sweatpants, staring out his floor-to-ceiling window with dark purple halos under his eyes. Is he sick? Has he been ill these last ten days and that's why he's disappeared?

He makes no movement. He doesn't even look surprised that I'm here. He looks *defeated*.

My heart sinks to my stomach.

"What are you doing here?" he asks, but it's not accusatory. The voice is resigned, almost timid, pushed through a throaty, exhausted voice.

I want to scream at him for blocking me out and that I deserve so much more than this. I want to ask him if I did something wrong, tell him how shitty my day has been and Sydney's news, how scared I am of everything crumbling around me. But instead, I slip off my purse, set it on the counter, and take a few, hesitant steps. "What's wrong?"

He sinks into a lounge chair, pushes his elbows into his knees, and presses his thumbs into his forehead. When he glances up at me with regret-filled, red-brimmed eyes, I already know what he's going to say. My body weighs a million pounds. The air in the room is so heavy it turns into a noose. I drag myself to sit across from him, each step feeling like I'm a prisoner taking my last walk before the darkness closes in.

"I'm so sorry," he says as he keeps staring at his hands.

Three words that carry so much weight. He doesn't need

to elaborate. I know what he's trying to tell me. "Please don't say this." My voice cracks. "I don't want to hear this. I can't fucking hear this."

He barely catches my gaze and says, "We tried everything."

No. No, no, no, this can't be happening. His voice sounds as drained as his face looks, and my world shatters along with my heart. It's done? We're over, just like that? "There's nothing else you can do?" I ask, too softly.

"Anna tried, she really did," he says, focusing on the ground. "She hired lawyers, worked with her grandmother's team, brought in international consultants, we—"

I stand up and move to the door. I don't need to hear a single other word. Whatever he has to say it doesn't matter because he's getting married, and this is over, and my heart feels like a razor blade is slicing at the muscle.

"Lexie, wait."

"You promised me, Theo," I say as my trembling hands strap my purse across my shoulder. "You *promised* me that everything was fine and all I had to do was be patient and not fucking worry. How many times did you tell me not to worry?"

"I know, I know. We thought we could find it. Anna's lawyers—they found a loophole, money was transferred, they . . . I just . . . she thought everything was set. We thought we'd already have broken off the engagement by now. I've . . . we've . . . spent the last week doing everything we can to find an alternative."

I can't hear this. I don't want to hear that he's given up,

that they tried, but still have to get married. My stomach hurts. My chest hurts. I swipe dripping tears and march to the door.

He leaps from the chair. "Maybe . . . I don't know, maybe you and I can figure something out. Anna already knows about us and is cool with everything. We couldn't tell anyone that we're together, though." Now his voice elevates and I've never wanted to slap anyone so hard in my life. "We could keep doing what we're doing—it's been working for us, hasn't it? Annabelle and I would handle the stuff we need to do with the families and appearances, but you and I can still be together. I could come over to your place, and you could come here, and we could even leave the country for a while or something—"

"Stop!" I release a fiery choked sob. "Don't you dare do this to me. Do not ask me to be your fucking side piece, Theo."

"No, no, I'm not asking that, I'm just—"

"That's exactly what you're asking. You want all of me, but you're only willing to give me a portion of yourself? Fuck you. How dare you ask that of me? How dare you assume I'm not worth more?"

He drags his hands down his face in anguish. I turn and walk out the door, but he's right at my heels. "We can figure something out. I'm just asking for you to wait."

"For how long? For what?" Even though there's a piece of me that feels like I'd wait for a lifetime for him, I know I can't.

I press the elevator button, and step inside.

He follows, gripping my shoulders until I'm forced to look at him.

"Maybe we can put something in the paperwork. A five-year contingency or something, where Anna gets part of her trust fund for every year we stay married."

I scoff. "Five years? Five fucking years?" My voice echoes in the confines of the elevator. "Stop, just stop. There's no way I want to hide a relationship with you for five years."

I can't believe this is happening. My paranoia, my worry, was justified. Deep down I knew something would go wrong, and I ignored all the warning bells in my gut. I let myself get caught up in Theo. What the hell was I thinking getting involved with him in the first place?

I need to get out of here. I drag the back of my hands across my face to wipe off the tears and suck in a breath, refusing to break down in front of him anymore. When the elevator doors open to the expansive lobby, I push him off and take a few steps out, Theo close on my heels.

And then, I freeze.

So does Theo.

I wonder if I'm hallucinating, because standing in front of us in khaki slacks, a tweed coat, his gray hair swept in a manicured cut, stands Dr. George K. Astor.

39

Lexie

"Dad," Theo says the word with a sharp, acidic bite, as he steps in front of me. "What the fuck are you doing here?"

When Theo said he hated his father, he wasn't kidding. You could cut the tension between them with a knife.

"Your mother and I've been trying to reach you for some time," Dr. Astor says, flatly. "Since you failed to respond, I was worried about your safety. I figured an in-home visit was the best way to gauge your well-being."

Theo still stands between us, and I swear he widens his stance, blocking my view of his father even more.

I couldn't think my day could get any worse, but now I'm standing in a lobby with Dr. Astor, one of the last men I want to see, praying to Christ that he doesn't remember me.

"*Gemma.*"

The voice drags me back to being a naïve and impressionable young student, desperate to make him proud. But now

I know better. I still shrink into myself a little and raise my hand in a half-hearted wave. "Oh, hi, Dr. Astor."

"We're leaving," Theo says, and takes one step toward the door when Dr. Astor moves closer.

"No, no, please stay," Dr. Astor says, setting his hands in his jacket pocket. "I've traveled all this way to see you."

"That's your fucking problem, not mine."

Jesus Christ.

The man is not backing down. Maybe Theo was just a bratty, angry teenager. Maybe this is simply how his family talks to one another. Or maybe Dr. Astor really is as arrogant and narcissistic as Theo said and feeds off this kind of energy.

Even so, confrontation has always made me uncomfortable. "*Theo, stop,*" I whisper under my breath, and the moment the words leave me, I know it's a mistake.

Dr. Astor's smile changes. Something a tad darker, more sinister, more knowing. He can smell it on me. Did his home security alert him to our visit that one time? Did he watch the footage of me screaming and moaning as his son's cock ravaged me in his childhood bedroom? My cheeks feel like they've turned the color of my hair.

"Gemma, my goodness, it's been so many years since I've seen you." He pauses. "I hope you're doing well?"

"Don't." Theo pushes these words through a clenched jaw.

"Don't what, Theo?" Dr. Astor turns his gaze towards Theo. "Don't ask how one of my former student's is doing?" He shifts his gaze back to me, and I feel like I'm going to choke. "I must apologize for my son's behavior, Gemma.

Looks like those sleepless nights are finally catching up to him."

"It's, ah, fine." I need to get the hell out of here. I haven't even processed what happened upstairs in Theo's apartment, and I can only dissociate so much. "Planning a wedding is stressful. It's totally understandable to be . . . on edge."

Dr. Astor's quiet chuckle fills me with dread. "Well, I'm so glad you were able to reconnect with your friend, Theo. You must have been thrilled to see Gemma after all these years and to have her help plan the wedding."

Friend? Theo has never once said he remembers me. Maybe Dr. Astor is mistaken. Maybe he's testing me. "Oh, ah, no, I mean, working with your son has been . . . lovely," I say, silently begging him not to read my face. "Yes, we were at school together, but Theo and I didn't really know each other then. You don't always remember everyone you might have crossed paths with, and I don't blame Theo for not recognizing me."

Dr. Astor cocks his head and the corner of his lip twitches in the faintest of smiles. "Didn't remember you? I find that extremely hard to believe." I glance at Theo, who seems nearly frozen in place. "Funny how I saw more of Theo during the semesters you worked for me than I did throughout his entire schooling. In fact, if memory serves, you spoke quite a bit about Gemma after the unfortunate incident."

My gut coils into a hard rock at those words. No . . . this doesn't make sense . . . I don't understand. Theo was interested in me? At school?

"I do believe my boy was quite smitten back then, not that he'd ever admit it," Dr. Astor says, with a sliver of a twinkle in his eyes. "But a father always knows."

"What are you doing?" Theo snaps at his father, then tugs on my arm. "Let's go."

Dr. Astor's gaze locks on the motion, and he inches closer. "Oh, please indulge me for at least a few more minutes. I traveled all this way to check in on my son, but what a surprise my former student is here, with him, at his *home*."

"Dad." The words hold a sharp, heated warning.

The lobby is too hot. I grip my purse and debate about how quickly I can get out of this place. Whatever bullshit is happening between the two men, I want absolutely no part of it.

"You know, Gemma," Dr. Astor says, "I thought about you so much over the years, and wondered if you ever sought help—"

"*Dad.*"

"I felt terrible after everything happened," Dr. Astor continues. "You had *such* a bright future ahead of you."

"Dad, *stop.*"

"I remember the way you talked about graduating early, moving on to graduate school and your dreams of opening your own practice . . . and now, it appears you plan weddings?"

"Enough!" Theo barks, but I barely register it over the thunder of my own heartbeat.

I'm not where I originally thought I'd be in my career, but goddammit I still made it. I pulled myself out of the deepest despair and became a steady, good, reliable worker. I was trusted with a high-profile wedding, and considered an essential enough employee that they want to keep me at the company during layoffs. I stand a little straighter, rage simmering under my skin at the judgmental tone in Dr. Astor's voice.

"Here I am, a psychologist that lectures all over the world, and yet I failed to recognize the classic signs of self-sabotage in my favorite student."

No . . . no that's not true. I didn't do anything.

"Shut the fuck up." Theo's voice booms into the space. He grabs my hand and pulls. I want to shake him off, but my body's immobile. "Lexie. We're leaving. Now."

Dr. Astor takes another step forward and focuses a hard gaze on Theo's hand against mine. "I have to wonder if some of those unfortunate tendencies are still haunting you today."

Theo drags me outside, and Dr. Astor casually follows a few steps behind like he's on a Sunday stroll. On the sidewalk, Theo's dark, fiery gaze burns into his father. "What the fuck is wrong with you?" Theo snarls, then turns his gaze to me. "Do not listen to him, okay? This is what he does. He's a sick bastard who loves to torture people. You block it out, you hear me?"

I shake my head as my brain flickers, fuzzy and hazed. Dr. Astor's holding my shame up to the light, and he's not wrong. Do I sabotage myself? Am I the reason to blame for everything that's happened—now and then? Maybe I didn't steal the tests at school, but did I somehow invite it anyway?

"Don't do this, Lexie," Theo begs, his frantic gaze searching my face. "Do not let him get inside your head."

Dr. Astor crosses his arms, his face still so passive it makes me uneasy. "I see that years-long flame you carried for Gemma still burns bright, doesn't it, son?"

None of this makes sense. Theo has never acknowledged our past, not once, not even when I confronted him about it. After everything we've shared, he's always seen me as Lexie, never *Gemma.* His father is just saying shit to mess with my head, and it's working. Is he really this sadistic a bastard, though? "No . . . that's not true . . ." is all I can force out because my unfocused brain can't grasp onto any other words.

"It's truly unfortunate," Dr. Astor continues, looking like he's holding back a grin as his gaze flicks between me and Theo. "It seems you never learned how to rein in your impulsive tendencies after you stole those scores—"

"Fucking *stop.*"

"—and got expelled—"

"Dad, enough!"

"—if you've allowed yourself to get wrapped up with a man who will be married in a few short weeks."

"Gemma didn't fucking do it!" Theo yells so loud that it feels like the traffic stopped.

I see black spots. Did he just say I didn't do it? Does he know? And . . . did Theo just call me *Gemma*? No . . . no, I'm dizzy. I could not have heard that right.

"How could you possibly know if she didn't do it?" Dr.

Astor says. "All the evidence pointed to her. The committee performed an investigation—"

"Because *I* fucking did it, okay?" Theo yells and reaches for me, but I pull away.

Oh my God . . . oh my God. I was right! Back then, Theo did this. The man that I've given my body, my *soul*, these last few months, has lied to me the entire time. This can't be happening. Someone—anyone—please shake me awake from this nightmare and tell me it isn't real. My breaths turn shallow, tightening in my throat, and my feet go unsteady beneath me, and I lean on the wall for support.

Dr. Astor just stands there, saying nothing in response. One sick moment passes, then another, before Theo breaks the silence. "Oh my God . . . you *knew.*" Theo's voice is barely above a whisper. I'm stunned silent, but my legs tremble. "You fucking knew I framed her, and you did *nothing*? You didn't even fight for her? How could you just let her walk away?"

My hand clasps over my mouth.

A sick, satisfied grin spreads across Dr. Astor's face. "As a father, sometimes we need to make difficult decisions for our children. It's important that they learn lessons. And my son, you needed to learn a lesson. With Gemma. *And* Olivia."

Theo inhales a sharp venomous breath.

Time seems to still as he shifts his gaze from Theo, to me, then back to Theo. "And the lesson is that even you, Theodore James Astor, do not always get to have everything you want."

I decide I've heard enough and bolt down the sidewalk.

40

Theo

Outside of my condo building, my knuckles turn white with the blazing desire to hit my father for what he just said. For Lexie. For Olivia. Does he know about the other women? Has he known all along? I'm torn between my need to finally have this out with my father and my need to go after Lexie.

The latter wins, and I turn my back on my father and sprint after Lexie before she disappears at the end of the block. I manage to grab her arm, but she yanks it away and glares at me with red-hot fire in her eyes.

"Don't you *dare* fucking touch me," she barks, and marches down the sidewalk. "Don't ever touch me again."

Fuck, fuck, fuck, it's not supposed to be like this. She just needs to listen. "Wait, please, just give me one second to explain things."

The blinding sun scorches my face as I fall in step behind

her, Lexie marching through the crosswalk. My brain fires on all cylinders, thoughts colliding and choking me. Don't let her get away. She has to understand. I did this for her. And my father—he fucking knew? That sadistic, evil bastard did this to punish me. He saw the way I wanted Lexie back then, couldn't stand the attention not being on him, and he let her dreams get crushed just to hurt me.

She storms to the end of the block, then looks out at the neighborhood. Her eyes are frantically flicking back and forth. We're on a side street, no taxis, blocks away from a subway station, and I'm not letting her fucking leave until she talks to me.

"Just, wait, please, let me explain," I beg.

She faces me with such raw anger in her eyes that I step back. "I *asked* you, Theo. I asked you if you knew me, and you said you didn't. You fucking looked me straight in the eyes and said you didn't." Her lips are trembling, and everything in me wants to take those away. "You've lied to me this entire time!"

She's going to leave. Please, please, don't leave. "I know, I know, but there's so much more—"

"You ruined my fucking life! Do you know that? I was going to be a psychologist. A *doctor.* I don't come from money like you do. When I got expelled, they stripped my scholarship, and I couldn't go to school."

Oh God, no, I mean, yes, but that's not . . . *shit, shit.* "Wait, no, I mean, you got kicked out from *this* school, but you could've gone to a different one. I just thought you'd go to

NYU or something. Why didn't you transfer? With your grades and—"

"How fucking obtuse are you? Seriously. Do you have any idea of how the real world works?" Her words snap like a spiked whip, ripping into my flesh. "You don't get to bring a scholarship from school to school like a fucking Black Amex. You get expelled, that money disappears. And when I applied for new ones the following year, they all got rejected because of the expulsion."

Beads of sweat pop against my back. That was not what I meant to do. She had to get away from my father, she had to get away from me, but I thought she could just use it . . .

"I worked my ass off my entire life. Do you have any idea how much shit I had to wade through to actually make it out of my neighborhood and into a prestigious private university? I gave up friends, my childhood, for this dream, and *you* destroyed it." Tears flow, and she swipes at them with angry hands. "Why would you do this? Is this because you knew how much I liked you and devised some sort of sick fucking twisted game of getting rid of me?"

The words hit me with such force that I feel my body sway. *What? What the hell is she talking about?* "No, no, that's not true. You were with my father. He was pulling you in. You wanted *him*."

"What in the absolute fuck are you talking about? I was never interested in your father. I was only ever interested in *you*. I used to wait for you to stop by at the coffee shop I worked at. Every time you came to your dad's office, I'd get flustered, hoping you'd talk to me even though I knew I wasn't good enough for you and . . . fuck you. Seriously, fuck you." She spits out the frantic, flustered words with harsh fury. "Even so, how *dare* you strip me of my entire future? You're fucking sick, Theo. *Sick*."

The way she's looking at me, the pain, the anger, the betrayal, twists my stomach tight with the realization that I'm losing her.

But . . . this isn't true. She's confusing reality. I saw her everywhere because I *looked* for her. I went into his stupid office all the time just to catch a glimpse. I talked to her at the coffee shop, and she gave me the same polite smile she gave everyone else—nothing more. The one time I asked her out, she ditched me for my father.

I'm going to choke, my veins are tight cords strangling the air from my chest. She doesn't understand—but she has to. I had to get her away from him.

I pull her into me, desperate to keep her from leaving. She slaps at me, but I keep my hold. If she can feel me—feel my presence—she'll understand. She'll know I'm sincere, that everything I did, I did for her.

"Why did you do this?" she asks, pushing me, scratching me, flailing against me, and I take it. I'll absorb the hits and claws ripping at my chest, the frustration and the tears, as long as she'll listen to me. "Why?" she pulls back, breathless and wiping her tears. "Why did you do this to me?"

"I was *saving* you."

"Saving me? Are you actually serious right now?" She

pulls in a ragged breath. "You're so fucking delusional. You *ruined* me, Theo. You didn't save me."

No, she doesn't understand. There were the girls that killed themselves, and the ones that dropped out, and the ones that got into drugs, and the ones he ruined, and she doesn't understand . . . "You didn't know what you were getting in to. You couldn't have known." I inhale hard to slow my chaotic thoughts. "My father ruined so many lives. You didn't understand what he was capable of. You don't know who he is. He would've damaged you beyond repair."

The tear-filled eyes have swapped with white-hot anger. "I never asked to be saved. I didn't *need* to be saved."

She can be mad, that's fine. It means she still cares. She can yell at me, hit me, scream at me as much as she wants, as long as she stays. "My father is a vindictive man. I told you about Oliva and the others. He takes what he wants, when he wants. He's a predator. I saw him like that with you, and I had to stop it. You understand that, right? He manipulates and lies and deceives everyone."

An ice-cold look passes her face, crystalizing her spring-green eyes into a sharp, dark emerald. "So, you're telling me you are just like your father?"

I freeze like she slapped me. My molars grind. "I am *nothing* like my father."

"You are *exactly* like your father." She pulls her head high. "You lie. You manipulate and destroy. You use people for your own pathetic selfish gain, and for what? Did the world really not hand you enough? I cannot believe I thought any of this was real."

Terror rips through me. "No . . . no, it is real. This is real." Christ . . . my inarticulate words are falling flat. Right here, right now, she needs to hear me, whatever it takes. "This is the most fucking real I've ever been."

She pulls her quivering lips into her mouth and exhales sharply through her nose. "Listen to yourself. You are getting *married* in two weeks. You destroyed my life and had every chance to tell me the truth—and you didn't. You lied to me for months. You fucked me, kissed me, and held me all while pretending our past didn't exist. *None* of this is real. You see that, right? This," she gestures between us, "is not reality."

My gut burns so tight and hot I don't think it will ever settle. *Don't leave me.* "Please Lexie, just hear me out." Desperation drives me. I will stay here, get down on my knees and beg if I have to. "Five minutes, Lexie. Come on. *Please.*"

"I can't, Theo. Fuck . . . fuck . . ." A choked sob breaks free, and she clamps a hand over her mouth. "I've . . . always just been a game to you."

"No, no that's not true. This isn't a—"

"Stop! Just stop." The raw, exhausted pain in her voice guts me to my core.

"Lexie, *please.*"

The gut-wrenching sob impales my soul.

She's completely broken.

I broke her.

She swipes at her tears like she's angry at herself for breaking and I'm so desperate to hold her I think I might collapse. She pulls in a sharp, shaky breath. "You're responsible for the two most shameful periods of my life. Do not talk to me after this. Do not call, do not text, do not come over." The words cut me like a blade. "I'll finish planning the wedding. Not because I'm a professional or a better person. But because you left me no fucking choice. You stole that from me. *You.* Not your father." Her eyes narrow with unfathomable darkness. "I never, ever want to see you again. You've done nothing but bring me misery."

She rushes over to the edge of the sidewalk and waves down a cab. Even though I don't want to let her go—though I know I could scoop her up, carry her back to my apartment and force her to stay by my side forever—though everything inside me has shattered and bled out onto the pavement, I step back.

She doesn't even look at me when she gets into the taxi. The door slams shut, and they take off.

I drag my hands down my face. "Fuck!" I scream.

I stand there, praying she'll come back.

She doesn't.

41

Theo

I can't shake the image of Lexie's devastated eyes. I'll give her space—for now—but this isn't over. I refuse to let her erase me that easily.

Rage consumes me when I think about the other problem I have to deal with. *He* did this. My father has built his legacy on destruction and pain. On fucking with people. With women. With my mother. With me.

It's the one thing he's ever been good at.

And I'm done letting him get away with it.

I head back to my condo, where he's leaning against the building, watching traffic like this is nothing, like my whole world didn't just collapse. I'm going to fucking kill him. My fists curl into a fierce, tight ball. "How *could* you?"

My dad simply crosses his arms with a sick, twisted satisfied smile.

His gaze swipes at my hands, the smile never leaving. "Are you planning on assaulting me?"

"Fuck you." My father is a sixty-year-old man who I outweigh by at least forty pounds. No matter how bad I want to hit him, he knows I won't. "What sort of sick sociopath are you? What do you gain from this?"

"From pushing you to look at your own behavior?" His voice is maddeningly calm. "I would be failing my duty as a parent and one of the leading psychologists in the field if I didn't teach my own son that choices always have consequences."

I try to push past the sickening suggestion that he's a caring father, a mentor.

"It may not feel like it now, but this is for the best," he continues. "Annabelle is about to become your wife. She must be your priority, and I'm simply helping you to understand that. I do this because I love you—and because I want to protect your future."

White-hot heat fills every piece of my body at the mention of Anna's name on his lips. I see through the lie. This has never been about protecting me. It's about protecting the family name—about what the Barlowe association will add to his already greedy sense of prestige. It's the same patronizing lecture he's given me my entire life. The same justification used when he locked me away for twenty-four hours at a time to "test my mental dexterity" or deleted my coursework so I'd be forced to redo it—pain masquerading as discipline, cruelty rebranded as character building.

"You don't love me." My gaze hardens, sharp as glass. "You never have, you sick fucking bastard. The only person you've ever loved is yourself."

My words don't faze him. I didn't expect them to. His mind, his prestige, his reputation, are the only things he values.

"We are done. You and me," I say with finality. "Stay away from Anna and me." I want to also add Lexie's name, but I won't give him the satisfaction of exploiting my weakness even further. "You are not allowed to contact us ever again. That includes the wedding."

This finally gets a reaction from him. Not because he cares about my wedding, but because people will talk, and my father cannot stand losing control of the narrative.

The displeasure he's trying to hide only fuels me further. "I want you to listen to me very fucking carefully. You may have scared Olivia away. But you forget one thing." I don't blink. Don't breathe. "I'm your son. And the worst monsters are forged by the ones who teach them." I watch my threat land and hit its mark. The faintest twitch in his eye gives him away. A slip in the mask. "So, I won't stop," I continue quietly. "Not until I expose you for exactly who you are. I will take you down piece by piece. I won't stop when you beg. I won't stop when you deny it. I won't even stop when you're dead." My words are sharp and humorless. "Your precious legacy will rot. People will learn your name only to curse it."

For the first time in my life, I see fear cross his face. "You don't mean that."

I take a step towards him. "You've studied people your whole life. You've built your entire career on it. So do it now. Look me in the eye. *Read* me. Do you think I'm bluffing?"

Another first in my life happens—my father is rendered silent. I step back and walk away from him for good.

I've called Lexie twenty, fifty, maybe a hundred times by now, and it keeps going to voicemail. I said I would give her space but I'm a selfish prick. The worst. I know this. I always have been. But Lexie has taken an axe to my dark, demonic shell and somehow cracked it open. Flickers of light seep through because of her. She's angelic. Pure. And so many things I've done in my life are fucked up and wrong, but with her, everything felt right.

I have no right to ask her not to leave. The end is coming, the wedding is happening, but still . . . she has to stay. She fucking *has* to. My life cannot be without her. Not ever. And fuck, fuck, she deserves more than watching me belong to someone else, more than the moments I can spare when I'm not playing the part of Anna's husband, but I swear we could figure something out. Acid floods my gut thinking of my life without her. All of this started as a way to keep an eye on her while I investigated my father—to make sure she didn't interfere, didn't ruin anything. I needed to maintain some illusion of control while everything spiraled. But deep down, in my vile, rotten soul, I know the truth. It wasn't because of the investigation. It's *always* been for me. *Fuck*, I hate myself. I can't believe I touched her with hands this dirty. And it's wrong, it's so fucking wrong, but I still need to keep her here. Just a little longer.

Even if it means trapping her in my hell with me.

I can't be in my place anymore. She wasn't here that often, yet every corner feels empty without her. I decide to go for a run around my neighborhood instead. Am I running to her? Am I running away from what I've done?

I need her to understand. Maybe she's had time to calm down. Maybe she's realized that what I did back then was for her.

Fuck. It wasn't.

It was for me.

How could I have done this? I honestly didn't think that she wouldn't be able to transfer school after the expulsion, but does that even matter? Or is that just another excuse I'm feeding myself? What the fuck is wrong with me?

And still . . . I had to save her. Those girls . . . what happened to them . . . if that had happened to Lexie, I would've died. *Fucking died.*

But she *has* to talk to me. Doesn't she see this? We'll talk, we'll make up, we'll fuck, we'll spend the night intertwined, she'll sleep on my chest, we'll be okay. All she has to do is talk to me.

I keep running, my lungs on fire, sweat dripping down my face. Maybe I should confess to her how much she's haunted me all these years. That from the moment on the quad, as she stood with her wide, beautiful green eyes, haloed like a sun fire in the golden afternoon, she seeped into my hallowed soul and altered me. For better or worse, she's etched herself permanently into my heart.

I'm finally forced to slow, and as I walk, her broken sobs replay in my head. For the first time in my life, I turn to an unknown entity to take away her pain. Even if she never speaks to me again, even if I can never touch that porcelain skin, or kiss those plush lips, or hold her, I pray for her to stop hurting.

I walk without direction in the city, street after street, carried forward by nothing but a foreign, inexplicable helplessness. And I think—about how different my life looks now than it did a few months ago, how different it will look in two weeks. I once believed happiness was a myth, an emotion people pretended to understand.

Until her.

Pain—what remains when the happiness you once tasted is gone. I didn't know it until now.

A crimson-haired angel infiltrated the devil's lair and showed me a slice of heaven that I never earned. I will never forget her. And as I walk until my legs give out, until the streets are unfamiliar, until exhaustion claims me, I keep praying.

42

Lexie

For hours, I cry on the floor of my apartment, feeling the shattered pieces of my soul skirt outside my body. Everything hurts.

I need to get out of here. There are too many memories of him in my room, and I can't process, or think, or heal, or do anything but cry. I pack a small bag and take the subway to the one place that will help give me the comfort I need.

When I reach my mom's apartment building, I drag myself up the stairs and rap on the door. She opens it with surprised eyes. I collapse into her arms and sob.

"Oh, my sweet girl . . ."

I crawl onto the couch that was my bed for so many years and bury my face into the pillow. Even in the July heat, she grabs my tattered childhood blanket, drapes it over my body, and runs her fingers through my hair until I fall asleep.

When I pry my crusty eyes open into the familiar, warm

space, my mom's left a note on the coffee table that she didn't want to wake me, but there's coffee in the pot and bread in the fridge. I glance at my phone to check the time. I'm late for work, I've missed dozens of calls from Theo, Justin, Sydney, and the receptionist, Megan.

But I don't care.

The sun beams inside my mom's tiny studio, but everything is dark. I can hardly drag myself to the bathroom, much less force down food and water. I pick up my phone to call Sydney to tell her I won't be in today. But I can't. My limbs are tree trunks, my fingers numb, my head weighs a thousand pounds.

I go back to sleep.

When I wake again, the afternoon sun is setting. I finally lift myself and fill a plastic cup with water from the tap, take a bite of bread, and glance at even more missed messages.

I return to the couch, drag the blanket over myself, and go back to sleep.

The door closes with a soft click, and I peek out at my mother removing her shoes at the mat. "How you doing? Did you eat?"

I shake my head. She spends the evening bringing me soup and tea, brushing my hair, and finally tucks me back under my blanket. My eyes flutter closed.

When the sun wakes me up again, there's another note from my mother, two full glasses of water on the coffee table, accompanied by a box of saltine crackers, and another nearly twenty missed calls. My head is pounding. But it's mild compared to the pain ravaging my insides. I finally reach for the phone, delete all the ones from Theo without reading, but send a group message to Justin and Sydney that I came down with something horrible and will be back to work when I feel better.

Even the effort of letting people know I'm alive makes me feel like I've run a marathon. I turn my phone off completely and go back to sleep. Maybe if I stay here, at my mom's, under this blanket, I can pretend that none of this is happening. That Theo didn't lie to me for months and kill my dreams all those years ago.

Choppy, dark, fevered dreams scatter my mind, and I blink open to my mom gently shaking my shoulders. "Come on," she says, holding out her hands. I shake my head. "It's been three days. You need a shower, food, and to get up off this couch."

I pull the blanket over my face.

She snaps the blanket off me and points to the bathroom. "*Now*, Gemma." The sharp tone is one I haven't heard since I was a kid, and it makes me straighten. I stumble into the shower like anchors are attached to my legs. Under the hot shower, I cry some more, swear, lean my head against the wall, but finally, *finally*, something in me releases.

I spend the rest of the evening eating one of Mom's classic ham sandwiches with mustard, that for some reason tastes delicious, eating a half of a package of saltines with peanut butter, and guzzling back what feels like gallons of water. My mom drags my feet into her lap and polishes my toenails pink. This simple act of normalcy makes me crack, and I tell her *everything.*

She doesn't judge, doesn't rage, doesn't even say that she's going to kill Theo for what he did to me in college. She just listens, fans my toes with her hands, and brings me more water. Before I settle back into the couch, she picks up my empty plate and wrappers, and glances sideways at me. "He didn't go about it in the right way, but sounds like Theo may have saved my baby girl back then." She scrapes the cracker crumbs from the table on to the plate, then dusts off her hands. "Now, it's time for you to get back to work. I didn't raise no quitter. You're my daughter. Strong and fierce. Time to act like it."

The next day, I finally leave my mother's house (I think much to her relief), go back to my studio, and force myself not to open the blinds to check if Theo's light is on across the street. I sleep in my own bed, I change into something other than the pajamas I've been wearing for days and make my way to work.

When I arrive, I make up a terrible excuse to Amanda and Megan about having the worst fever and flu of my life. At my desk, I skirt Justin's eyes, who's watching my every movement as I set down my backpack and reach for my laptop.

"Feeling better?" he asks.

"Yep," I say, and it's not a lie. I'm not over Theo. I don't think I'll ever be over Theo. But I've at least stopped crying like I'm being held hostage and tears are a condition of my release. "That was . . . um, an intense week."

Justin's silent. Too silent. I plug in my laptop, sure that when I look up, I'll see his "no bullshit side eye". Instead, a frown curves his mouth and my heart pinches.

"Want to talk about it?"

My chin quivers and I shake my head.

"Okay. I'm here whenever you need me."

Not *if*, but *when.*

I love my friend.

My fellow co-workers move around me like nothing has changed. Soft chatter. A few laughs here and there. The steady click of keyboards. Clearly, Sydney is still deciding who she's cutting, and I'm still clinging on to the hope of a Hail Mary—some miracle that lets us all keep our jobs.

The thought that half of these people will be gone in the next month makes my stomach turn. Against all odds, this place became my home away from home, and I'm not ready to watch the doors close.

I go back to check my schedule for today and freeze when I spot a particular meeting in my calendar. "Actually, I need your help." I turn to Justin. "Annabelle and Theo are coming in soon for their appointment. Will you take it?" When his eyes narrow, I quickly add, "Who knows if I'm still contagious. I'd hate to get either one of them sick before the wedding."

I think he knows I'm lying. But he nods anyway.

When they arrive, Justin leaps up to greet them and I run to hide in the breakroom. But I can't stop myself from looking back. Annabelle's arm is looped through Theo's, her body pressed into his side. He leans toward her, solid and steady. The sight steals the breath from my lungs.

Before the tears can spill, I shut the door.

Inside, I pretend to focus—scrolling through emails on my phone and double checking my project plan, until the soft click of the door breaks the quiet.

I turn and Theo stands there.

"Can we please talk?" he says, taking one step towards me then stopping.

I cross my arms. "We have absolutely nothing to talk about."

His jaw goes tight before he exhales a breath. "I am so fucking sorry for everything."

I want to break down, to cry, to collapse into his arms, but I don't. "Your words are worthless. You lied to me for months. *Months.* You had every opportunity to tell the truth and you chose not to."

"That's not fair."

"Fair? *Fair?* You want to talk about fucking fair?" I snap with a harsh, hushed tone. "You told me you never met me, you told me you weren't going to get married, and you made me feel . . . this . . ." my chin trembles but I force it to stop.

"I'm so sorry, but you need to understand why I didn't tell you."

"Fucking stop, Theo. Seriously just stop." I swallow back a cry that's inching its way up my throat, refusing to let him see me break again. "Just leave, okay. Go be the man that Annabelle needs you to be. Forget about me. Forget about us." I swallow and push through the next words as steely as I can. "Because I sure as fuck am going to."

Yes, I want to hurt him, and yes, I get a small sense of satisfaction at seeing the softness in his eyes tighten and morph into anger. His flushed neck, the way he looks like he wants to say something, the way the muscle in his jaw pops. And then, just like that, he's gone, slamming the door shut.

Goddammit. Hot tears spring to my tired eyes. A moment later, Justin's face falls when he steps into the room. He holds out his arms and I take the hug. I let my friend hold me when I'm so sick and tired of holding myself. God, I'm such a mess and I don't even know how to not be one. What did I expect to happen? Did I really think getting involved with Theodore Astor would end with fucking rainbows and hearts? I shouldn't be surprised. And yet . . . the loss cuts so deep, I don't think I'll ever stop bleeding.

Justin pulls back and his sincere blue eyes bore into mine. "Can you tell me what's going on?"

Part of me doesn't want to say anything. The shame of lying to Justin for months gnaws at my insides. But I need to purge these last few months, these last few years, from my soul. I need to tell him about the embers that started when I was nineteen that grew into an all-consuming wildfire that ravaged me and left me scorched and charred.

And so, I take a deep breath.

After I tell him everything, he reaches over and gives my

hand a squeeze with nothing but kindness and love in his eyes. And I continue. "When I first started working with Theo, I was so focused on showing Annabelle the monster I thought Theo was, while getting my revenge. It was like a two-for-one special—ruin Theo, save Annabelle."

Justin's quiet look and soft eyes hit me hard. "So . . . similar to what Theo did to you at school. He convinced himself that what he did was to save you. Just like you thought this was for Annabelle."

My breath stutters and catches in my throat, forcing me to drag in a sharp, uneven lungful of air. Like the metal teeth on a zipper cinching together, everything locks into place. This is the same conclusion my mom came to. And even though I know her loyalty will always be to me, I told myself she'd forgiven him simply because she had grown to like Theo after he'd treated and cared for her.

Did I start doing to Annabelle what Theo did to me? Is it the same thing? Under the guise of protecting her, I almost hurt her. And if that's true, is there a part of me that understands why Theo did what he did back then?

My elbows dig into my thighs, and I drop my head into my hands. *I don't know . . . I don't know . . .* I had already made as much peace as I could with what Theo did all those years ago. But he *lied.* For months. In a week, he's going to marry Annabelle. His love for her has never wavered. So, I can forgive him, sure, and maybe that would help me move on.

But what's going to heal my heart?

The next morning, I wake in a clearer headspace—until

the anger sets in again. It simmers as I replay my conversation with Dr. Astor: the snobbish judgment in his tone, the way he looked at me like I was beneath him.

No matter how fucked up Theo's actions were, I don't believe for a second Dr. Astor is innocent. I saw the sincerity when Theo told me about his dad, the genuine panic and fear that he thought I might be hurt. And after hearing about Olivia and the other girls, I know it's all true.

And looking back now, replaying the moments Dr. Astor and I were alone together, I see everything in a new light. Back then, his father touched me. *A lot.* A hand lingering on my back, my arms, a brush of his fingers. He asked about my dating life, if I had a boyfriend who would be upset about the number of extra hours I'd be working. He offered to tutor me after hours, when campus was "quieter" and he could give me the "attention I deserved".

And Theo was there, constantly dropping by his father's office, interrupting the moments when I was alone with his dad. Even though he barely acknowledged me, maybe that was the point. Maybe those drop-ins were meant to deny his father the opportunity to hurt me. I'd like to think that I would've smelled a predator a mile away. But I'm realizing now it's never that simple.

But Theo still took away my right to choose. He stole my future. Maybe that wasn't his intention, but it's reality. And he lied.

So, then, why do I miss him so fucking much? Why haven't I been able to force myself to wash his pillow that carries his faint, lingering scent? Why do I keep thinking about being wrapped in his arms, the way he made my body burn alive, the way he pressed his lips into that little crook behind my ear that made me melt into him? Why do I crave the questions he'd asked me like he was a scholar and me, his fascinating subject?

In the shower, my lip starts trembling. My skin aches for his touch. My heart is breaking with the knowledge that what we had, as short-lived as it might have been, I'll never feel again. Since I was nineteen, he's penetrated my world and impaled by heart, he's invaded and assaulted my soul, he's brought me unimaginable, unbearable pain. Twice. But being without him hurts the most.

I miss him. But I fucking hate him.

All those years ago, he stripped away my future. I knew it then, and I deluded myself when we were together that he was telling the truth when he said he didn't remember me. As someone who relies so heavily on gut and intuition, I pushed away my suspicions to be with him. I made a deal with the devil, and the devil won.

So fine, I have to live with the consequences.

But there's one thing I *can* do. Maybe it's a way to reclaim something taken from me. Maybe it's something I should've done the moment Theo told me about Olivia, and the other women, and the investigation. Fueled with the rush of a purpose, I open a new tab on my browser, take a deep breath, and type in the name of my old dorm mate.

43

Lexie

The morning of the wedding is beautiful, showing hopeful signs it will continue to be a bright, sunny day with a light breeze. The rain contingency plan I built won't be needed. On any other day, I'd be breathing a massive sigh of relief. But not today. In the passenger seat of our rental car, Sydney talks a mile-a-minute, either unaware of or indifferent to my silence and the sympathetic glances Justin keeps sending my way. She barrels on, oblivious to the heaviness filling the car and the two-word answers I've been mustering all my energy to provide.

Getting dressed this morning in my A-line midi emerald-green dress and pinning back the sides of my hair took a herculean effort.

The wedding day is actually here.

Last night in the hotel, I reread every message Theo and I exchanged these last six months. I paced the room, I stared at the wall, I took a bath and buried myself under an avalanche of thoughts and what-if scenarios. Yes, Theo lied. And it will take a long, long time to move past that. But what if he'd confessed from the start? Would these last few months have played out the way they did? Probably not. And if that is the case, even with how much I'm hurting, would I give up the time we shared? The way he made me feel? Probably not either. Justin's words roll through me like tumbleweeds in a windstorm. Is it fair to have that conversation with Theo and ruin his day? Is it fair to stay silent and let it ruin my life? What does fair even mean anymore? None of this is fucking fair. Not for me, not for him, not for Annabelle.

The words "*this is the most real I've ever been*" played in a loop in my head until I fell asleep last night. If this is the most real he's ever been, then why didn't he try harder to find another way out? Or maybe he doesn't want to be "real". Maybe "real" is as terrifying for him as it is for me.

Ugh. By the time the rental car pulls into the driveway, beads of sweat prickle at my neck. I take a deep breath and put on a game face. As much as humanly possible, I need to pull off a wedding that I'm desperate to *not* pull off.

Come on, come on. Just move your feet. The wedding doesn't start until five—eight hours away. Pictures start at noon. Guests arrive at three.

It's showtime.

As of right now, my only two jobs are coordinating the shit out of this day and avoiding Theo—unless I decide to speak to him.

And . . . back to the swirling.

The next two hours fly by quicker than expected. After Sydney informs security, again, that Theo's parents are not allowed on the premises, she stands in the circular drive playing the role of an air traffic controller with the catering, florists, photographer, and videographer teams, while Justin and I manage the courtyard activities. Yesterday, the decorators did a phenomenal job. Six hundred crisp white chairs, perfectly aligned on the sides of an ivory runner, lead to a sheer fabric and white-light draped, Greek-inspired archway. The venue hums urgency—caterers assembling standing bars and food stations, crews loading tables and chairs, florists weaving beautiful sage and cream bouquets along the aisle-facing chairs with seamless precision. Justin and I move in sync, checking the officiant's acoustics, verifying table settings, and directing crew members as needed.

I step underneath one of the huge maple trees to take a breath and watch as the courtyard comes alive in a wedding-day wonderland.

Six hours to go.

Six hours to determine the fate of the rest of my life.

Justin finds me beneath the shade of the trees and hands me a bottle of water. "God, this is giving me some serious flashbacks to when Dylan and I got married," he says, twisting the cap off his own. "I mean, minus the harpist flown in from the UK, the Michelin-level menu, the actual champagne from France . . . other than that, it's basically the same."

I chuckle and gulp back the water. "Practically a mirror-image."

Our attention snags on one of the bartenders polishing glasses. When one slips and shatters, we both politely look away, pretending nothing happened.

"My wedding day was the happiest day of my life," Justin says. "And it wasn't just the day itself. Not Dylan in his tux, nor being surrounded by our friends and family." He pauses. "It was knowing that from that day forward, I was going to spend the rest of my life with my person."

He nudges my arm and points to a bench a few feet away. We crunch through the perfectly trimmed grass to make our way to the resting spot. *Oof*, it feels good to sit down. On wedding days, I'm normally running around like a mad-woman. And today is no different. I've literally not stopped for a second. If I stop, I think. And I'm not sure I can survive my thoughts right now.

"I was *so* terrified to ask Dylan out. The man was larger than life. Still is," he says. "I'm so glad I did. I thank God every night that I took a chance, even though I was scared."

I slide my sandals off and dig my toes into the lush grass. I know what Justin's doing. And I love him for it. But . . . was he *this* scared? Asking someone out and begging someone on their wedding day to not go through with it are two totally different things.

I don't even know what I want.

"What should I do?" I ask, quietly.

"I don't know," he says, softly. "I love you, Lex. You

deserve happiness, whatever that looks like. But what I do know is that you don't want to live with regrets. If there's something that needs to be said, now's the time to say it. And then, you'll know. Knowing and having it not be what you want to hear is better than not knowing at all."

The words settle heavily.

"I've done a lot of thinking about your situation," he says, sliding closer. "And who knows what the future looks like? It's terrifying—I get that. But all I know is that, all those years ago, I'm incredibly grateful I took a chance on something. And . . . I think you deserve to take a chance on yourself."

I lean my head on his shoulder. "I love you," I whisper. "Thank you for being the best friend a girl could ask for."

"I love you, too." A long moment passes as I take in his words. He gives my knee a pat and lifts himself from the bench. "Now . . . I better go find Sydney before she starts terrorizing the wait staff. Take some time if you need. We got this. You take care of you."

As he walks away, I stare at my trembling hands and slowly stand. I really should check on the bride. I told her assistant I was here if she needed anything but otherwise would stay away. I said I was doing this for Annabelle. But really, it's for me. I don't know if I can look her in the eye. I'm jealous and hurt. *Broken.* I think she'll take one look at me and see everything, and I have no right to make this day any worse for her.

However, duty calls. The photography team is scheduled

to start shooting within the next two hours, and I need to confirm hair and make-up is on track.

I drag myself through the kitchen and make my way into a guest bedroom doubled as bride's prep room.

One of the assistants opens the door with a frantic look, with no sign of the bride in the chair.

"Where is she?" I ask.

The frazzled assistant shrugs. "Annabelle said she needed air about an hour ago; she's not been seen since."

Panic starts to set in. "Are you telling me what I think you're telling me?"

"Yes," she says with a heavy sigh. "The bride is gone."

44

Lexie

I stare at Annabelle's assistant. I force out a sharp breath, fighting the surge of panic. If we have to delay the wedding, that's fine, we'll use the excuse of her hair and make-up overrunning. But I need to find her and make sure she's okay.

I call her. It goes straight to voicemail. I send a text. No response. I'm about to call Sydney, who's no doubt rushing around the courtyard trying to tick off all her jobs for today, when my phone pings with a message.

> Annabelle: Can you meet me in the gazebo in the east-side property?
>
> Annabelle: Please come alone

I bolt from the room, down the stairs, and make my way outside where the gazebo comes into view.

Annabelle sits alone on a bench, wrapped in a white robe, her hair twisted into large curlers. Her posture is still, her expression solemn—nothing like a typical bride on her wedding day.

I approach carefully. "Hey you," I say, forcing a smile I don't feel. "Congratulations on your big day." It's the first time we've spoken in person since she left for Italy.

Her smile is as forced at mine. "Not sure if congratulations is the right term." She peeks under heavy, fake eyelashes with kind, gentle eyes. "How are you?"

Even now, when she should be putting herself first, she still cares enough to ask about me. It says everything about who Annabelle is. I sit next to her and stare at the stone waterfall in front of us. "Probably as good as you are."

A long moment passes and she sighs. "This sucks."

It sure does. She doesn't want to marry Theo. Theo doesn't want to marry her. I don't know what I want, but it's not this. And yet, here we are, each of us ending up with the person we're not meant to be with, or alone.

This is totally uncharted territory for me. Brides are either freaking out and yelling at everyone who dares step in their path, calm and cool, or so giddy that I worry they dipped into the champagne early.

But Annabelle is straight-faced and dejected.

She tugs at the robe fabric by her knee and takes a sharp breath. "I just want to thank you for everything you did while I was in Italy. You took on so much, and I really, really appreciate it."

My stomach turns into a knot.

She slides back on the black iron bench and stares at the waterfall. “Did Theo ever tell you how we first met?”

I dig my toe into the ground and sigh. “No.”

“It was kindergarten. He stole my favorite strawberry-scented pencil, and I punched him in the stomach. We’ve been inseparable ever since.”

Despite myself, a small grin forms. “Ouch.”

“Well, it was a good pencil, and he needed to be taught a lesson,” she says with a grin. “We found out later our parents had the school put us in the same classrooms for years. They were really close friends, as much as . . . sociopathic-leaning people . . . can have friends. Since we were kids, they’d have dinner parties and constantly joked that someday Theo and I were going to get married.”

“That’s a lot of pressure, huh?”

“*So* much pressure,” she says. “But it was fine, I guess, when we were younger. But after a while, it was no longer a joke. It was an expectation.”

My stomach knots tighter. Theo told me this, in his own way, but hearing it from a woman who sounds trapped, hits hard.

“Theo has this . . . thing. A savior complex, maybe? An obsessive need to protect. I think it’s partly why he chose to be a doctor.” She pauses for a moment. “As kids, he saw so many similarities between his father and mine, and he latched onto it. The more time Theo and I spent together, the easier my father was on me, and it became this almost sick, twisted cycle. I'm no psychologist, but I think Theo felt helpless with his own dad, and protecting me from mine gave him back some power? I don't know . . ."

Everything about this makes sense. Now that I know Theo and understand more about him and his father's relationship, and witnessing his obvious love for Annabelle, it's a textbook example of how under-protected people turn into overprotective ones. I push my feet into the ground to give our bench a gentle swing.

"While I was in Italy, I had so much time to myself," she says, taking a breath. "I took long walks, I meditated, I painted, I *breathed*. Growing up the way that we did, I never felt like I could breathe, you know? Yes, I was there for Nonna, but I stayed so much longer than needed because I wasn't ready to return to reality."

I keep swaying the bench, waiting for her to continue.

"Some families have parents who do everything for their kids," she says. "And some families curate a life and expectation for their kids and use any means necessary to see it through. And that's the life my parents built for me."

She adjusts herself on the bench and sighs.

"I love Theo. I've loved Theo since I was six. I can't imagine my life without him."

My heart sinks. Maybe this isn't going the way I thought . . .

"Theo's loyal to a fault," she says. "Honestly, sometimes it's to his own detriment. Once he zeros in on someone, he'll protect them no matter the cost." She pauses—long enough that I glance at her, wondering if she's finished.

Then she adds, "I think you should know how loyal Theo can be."

Over the steady gurgle of the stone waterfall and the muted sounds of crew members moving behind the hedges, she tells me more—about Theo, about her family, about the cage they built around her. "When they threatened to cut me off, I was scared of course, but I was also prepared for it. Because I didn't *want* to marry Theo. I was going to tell them no." She swallows. "And then Theo talked me out of it. He said he couldn't stand by and watch me throw my life away." Her gaze drops to her hands.

"I think he was angry with himself for not having another solution. For not being able to save me like he promised he would. So, he agreed to marry me. To protect me. He sacrificed everything out of loyalty, and I let him. That was the most cowardly thing I've ever done, but it's why I stayed in Italy so long. Watching him destroy himself for me was killing me."

Tears spring to my eyes, but I blink them back.

"Do you love him?" she asks.

My chest seizes with the question. No. No . . . right? I don't *love* Theo. I hate him. For years, I've hated him. It's essentially been my baseline emotion as an adult.

Whatever this is, it's just the fallout. The aftershock of the best sex of my life being ripped away from me, my body scrambling for meaning where there is none. I'm misreading the signals. That's all this is.

But even as my mind fills with these thoughts, my heart

aches, and I know I'm not being true to myself. "I . . . don't know."

"It's a scary emotion. The vulnerability, the way it leaves you exposed. Honestly? Sometimes I think love is worse than fear." She takes a breath. "Well, it's obvious to me that he loves you."

Does he? He's never uttered those words to me before. But even if he thinks he loves me, I'm not sure he knows what love is. He hurt me. He lied to me. That's not love.

Annabelle puts her hand on my arm. "Lexie . . . it's *always* been you. Theo's been in love with you since the day he met you. If I weren't in the picture, I swear he would've claimed you the moment you crossed paths in the quad."

My heart absolutely stops beating. The quad? What? When? "What are you talking about?"

"God, he used to never shut up about you," she says with a laugh. "But, things were complicated with us, with his dad . . . it was all so messy. And, I had no idea what happened back then with you in college and the expulsion until last week. Christ, that man makes some terrible decisions. But, I really do think what he did back then, he did for you."

Everything is spinning. I rest my head in my hands.

"When he brought up the idea of using your company to plan the wedding, he begged me to pretend like I didn't know anything about you. And I figured that was the least I could do since, you know, he was marrying me and all."

Oh God, oh God. Okay . . .

"He never chose me over you. Please don't ever think

that." She starts moving her hand up and down on my arm in a comforting gesture. "I need you to really hear me on this, Lexie, okay? *He never chose me over you*. He chose *my* happiness over *his*." She pauses, letting it settle. "He made the greater sacrifice in letting you go and keeping his promise to me. Does that make sense?" Her voice softens. "You were always his first choice from the moment he saw you."

My fragile, broken heart starts to stitch and balloon so quickly that I feel dizzy. I sit upright, staring at the trickling waterfall, and try to retain all the words. *Theo chose me the first day he met me.*

"Let me ask you again. Do you love him?"

I think I know. But it all hurts so much that I'm terrified if I say yes, it's going to hurt worse than it does now. "Would it matter if I did?"

Annabelle turns all the way to face me and grabs my hand. "I think you need to find Theo and get clarity. Once you talk to him, maybe you'll know what to do."

With this, she rises from the bench, gives me a squeeze on the arm, and leaves me to think.

Right now, I'm faced with the proverbial sliding door moment. And I must decide if I step through it or not.

45

Lexie

My whole body feels numb, but I lift myself from the bench and move towards the courtyard, unsure of where to go next. This is all too real.

My heart pulls me one way and my brain another, and yet my body makes an independent decision to drag me into the house and up the stairs. I need clarity and closure and I'm not going to get either if I don't do something. With every step, my brain flips between what I should do. By the time I reach the top, I'm still lost.

All I know is that I need one more moment with Theo.

Standing outside his bedroom, my heart thuds so loudly it climbs into my ears. I press my knuckles against the wooden door, but my body refuses to let me knock. *Come on, come on. Just do this.* I exhale a shaky, hard breath, then tap.

No answer.

I rap my knuckles again.

Still no answer.

Is this a good or bad thing? Maybe he's looking for me. Maybe he's searching for his bride. Maybe he's at one of the bars, drowning his sorrows. My stomach knots. I crack open the door and step inside the empty bedroom.

My gaze immediately sweeps to the bed that loosely resembles Theo's bedroom, and I think of how he claimed me, marked me, convinced me I was his. Those fleeting moments were the last time I felt whole.

Whole.

Goddammit. I don't want to be broken. I don't want to keep wondering what could've been. I brush my hand against the silky goose-down comforter. I close my eyes and picture his mouth, his smile, the way he looked at me these last few months. The way he *saw* me more than anyone has ever seen me. I picture his fingers brushing my skin, his lips moving against me, his scent. I'm lost in my own world when I hear the soft click of a door behind me.

"*Lexie.*"

When I turn around, my breath catches at a clean-shaven Theo, standing in mirror-shined shoes, a white button-down shirt with a black tie, a sharp black tuxedo vest, and black pants. He looks every bit the dashing groom, and my aching heart leaps into my throat.

"Hi." My voice is barely above a whisper, and from where he's standing at the corner of the room, I'm not even sure he can hear me.

"Hi." He shoves his hands in his pockets and takes a long,

sweeping gaze over me. But the heat-laced look that he usually gives me is gone, replaced by one that is more grief-stricken than lust-filled.

He's not happy. Anyone can see it. Regret fills his whiskey-brown eyes. Is it for me? For what he's about to do? I'm hanging on to a delicate thread of hope and wondering how much weight it can take before it snaps.

I swallow back all the nerves. Am I going to do this? Am I *really* going to do this? I don't know if I can. I *want* to. If I don't tell him how I feel, I'll regret it for the rest of my life. But, my insides are trembling so bad, I'm not sure I can push out the words. "I can't believe your wedding day is finally here."

His eyes don't sparkle. But they're not sharp, or narrowed, or angry. They're more . . . soft . . . and I struggle to interpret the meaning. "Yeah. Same."

My mouth is bone dry. Fuck, this is *terrible.* I should run. Just turn right around and run right out of this room. After a long pause, I sigh. "Feels like the end of an era, huh?"

The tiniest bit of his lips curve, but it's not a smile. "It really does."

Everything with Theo feels like it has come full circle. From college, to seeking revenge, to being together, to heartbreak. And now, after today, the Theo I once held onto, who seesawed between saturating my dreams, then nightmares, then dreams again, will be gone.

"I . . . uh . . . I think I can help with your investigation," I say and his eyebrows crease in confusion. "What you said about your dad, it didn't sit right with me. I kept thinking how strange it was for my dorm roommate to drop out of school like that, so I tracked her down. I told her how I'd taken over her student aide position with your dad, and if she was doing okay, and apologized for not reaching out to her at the time. She didn't say much at first, but the more we spoke, the more she opened up about her experience at St. Benedicts."

I twirl the rings on my finger, fully aware that I'm hiding behind the investigation to postpone the conversation I really need to have with him. But Theo deserves to know there might be a way to get justice for these women. "After she dropped out, she ended up going to Penn State," I say. "She's a doctor now."

A sliver of hope flickers through his eyes. "A doctor?"

I nod. "A pediatrician in Pennsylvania."

We both know what this means. As much as it shouldn't matter what position a woman holds, or the socioeconomic class she belongs to, our twisted society pays closer attention to these women than others. A doctor willing to corroborate the stories of his father will lend weight to the rest. It would force people to listen.

"We're going to meet next week when she's in the city," I say, still hardly able to look at him. "I think she'll come forward, especially if it'll help the other women."

His throat rolls with a swallow. "This is incredible, Lexie. Thank you."

I nod and finally drop my hands. "I can share your contact

information with her. And if it'll help, I'll vouch for you."

"You'd do that?" he says.

"Of course. You're fighting for these women. I hope you don't stop."

So many moments stretch between us. I wonder if he's thinking the same thing as me. The surreality of the day settles in the last few months, the last nearly eight years. How we each found love, then lost it. How today could be the day we finally go our separate ways.

We found love.

I found love.

Annabelle's voice is in my head, encouraging me to tell Theo everything, but fear still controls me. "Are you nervous?"

He nods.

"That's perfectly normal." I need to leave. My heart hurts, everything fucking hurts. I want him to hold me and tell me that he's choosing me. *Please, please choose me.* "I'm nervous, too."

I inch forward with all the ache and longing, with all the nerves and vulnerability, with a swelling heart that's expanding so quickly that soon it's going to push against all my organs until my air is gone. When I'm close enough to the cedar scent, to the sharp, angled jawline and chiseled chest that my cheeks rested on so many nights, I take a long moment to fix his already perfect tie. Tears fill my tired eyes. My insides verge on exploding, my heart is pounding so hard that I'm getting dizzy, but the sliding door moment has arrived. I need to step through and pray that I'll not only land upright, but he'll step through with me.

His hands stay stuffed inside his pockets, but he's letting me touch the tie, letting my fingers brush against the buttons, letting me take all the moments I need.

I can't wait any longer. Even though the nerves are killing me, and the tingling in my chest has upgraded to a stabbing, I need to tell him. "You don't have to go through with it." The words are barely above a whisper. I clear my throat and look at his regret-filled eyes. "Please don't go through with it."

He can see the pleading in my eyes, he can hear the broken notes in my voice. This is the part where he's supposed to scoop me into him, tell me that he loves me, and that he won't go through with the wedding. I hold my breath, waiting for him to do something, to say anything.

But he doesn't.

Instead, the sternness in his face shatters, and he removes my hands from his tie. "Lexie . . ."

No. Please, no. I can't hear my name whispered with remorse and regret. "Please," I say, and this time I reach for his hands. I've never felt more raw or vulnerable in my life. I want to run away and hide from this moment, but I stay, holding his hands, begging him to see me.

"Don't marry Annabelle. Be with *me*. Tell me what we have is real, that I didn't make this up." Dangerous, dangerous hope fills my voice, as my gaze dashes between his eyes. "Tell me that everything I'm feeling, you're feeling, too. Tell me you're hurting the way I'm hurting, that you want to be with me the same way that I want to be with you."

His silence is excruciating. I've climbed to the top of a skyscraper without a safety harness, I'm dangling my toes off the edge and wondering if he's going to catch me, jump with me, or let me fall.

Deep lines cut his forehead, and yet, he stays silent.

My chin trembles and I pull in an uneven breath. "Tell me you love me." My words are a shaky, hopeful whisper. "Tell me you love me . . . the way I love you."

My voice cracks on the words, and I can barely lift my head. My heart's bare, standing unprotected in a battlefield, bracing for the spray of bullets, while praying for air support.

For a brief moment, gentleness breaks through the torment in his eyes. Then it's gone. "What are you doing?"

The sharpness in his tone makes me recoil. *What am I doing*? I'm standing here, taking a reckless leap of faith, hoping he'll choose me.

"Don't do this," he snaps, stepping away from me. "You don't know what you're saying."

My chin trembles. "Wh . . . what?"

His cheeks flush. "Tell me right now that you forgive me for lying to you. I want to hear you say it."

My searching gaze flicks between his fiery eyes, and I feel my stomach knot. "We, ah . . . there's a lot to talk about. But, we, I mean, we can talk—"

"Stop. Just fucking stop," he barks and my breath locks.

"You're never going to forgive me. I can see it all over your face—and how could you? I don't even blame you for feeling that way." He shakes his head. "So what's the point of telling me you love me? You came to see me on my wedding day just to get payback? To fuck with my head?"

Unshed tears glisten in my eyes. "No . . . I'm trying to tell you how I feel." I start to reach for him, when he steps back even farther. "I said, *I love you.*"

His eyebrows creasing is the only indication that he even heard me. He drops his crossed arms and storms to the door. "Get out."

"You don't mean that."

"Get the fuck out!" he barks with such venom that I lose the battle to hold back my tears. "We don't need to see each other again. Ever."

My heart shatters.

With all the strength left in me, I move to the door. Behind me, I swear I hear a whispered, "*Lexie . . .*" but it's swallowed against the empty hallway, and through the house, and into the breeze as I make my way down the courtyard. It's swallowed by the photographer setting up the cameras, by the florists adding their final touches, by the quartet unloading from the van. It's swallowed by the guests arriving.

It's swallowed by my broken, shattered heart.

I keep walking. Past the courtyard, past the front steps, past the cobblestone path leading to the driveway. To the edge of the yard, past the fountains, behind the valets. I hear my name called, but it's not Theo's voice. I turn to see Justin, rushing to catch up to me. When I swipe my tears and shake my head, he puts a hand to his heart, and I keep walking.

And yet, there's part of me filled with a wistful, naïve hopefulness, that allows me to turn around, just one last time, to see if Theo's following. To see if maybe he had a change of heart.

But he's not there. I walk to the side of the property where Sydney is standing. "Hey, Lexie, good, you're here. The photographers are ready to start taking photos of the bridal party. So let's check in with Annabelle's team . . . oh. Oh, no. What's wrong?"

Tears stream down my face. "I'm so sorry. I . . . can't do this."

Her body softens. "Of course you can. I know it's a lot of pressure, but you did it, Lexie." She waves her hand to the pristinely decorated estate. "*You* did this. Look at this! In six months? You've done the impossible, and I'm so damn proud of you."

The tears flow even harder now, and I shake my head. "There's so much to tell you, but . . . I can't. I just . . . *fuck*." I swipe my thumb under my eye. "I'm in love with the groom."

I cannot believe I just said this to my boss, but I genuinely don't care anymore. Everything is broken. My heart, my soul, probably even a piece of my sanity. Tears trickle down, rolling under my chin, and I wipe them.

Sydney's eyes go wide and she stands open-mouthed, looking like she's stopped breathing. She looks behind me, behind herself, then finally exhales. "Oh ... my ... wow." She tugs the clipboard to her chest. "Is he in love with you?"

I thought so. But I was wrong.

I glance at an unmoving Sydney and shrug. "I don't know."

She sets down the clipboard on a stone garden table and puts her hands on her waist. A long moment passes as she scans the decorated tables, the gathering family members, then back at me. "I've given up a lot for my career. Family, a social life, love. I wish I could say that I know how you feel, but I can't. I *don't* know what you must be going through, but, it must hurt like hell to be here today."

I swallow and nod.

"You've done everything you could to get us ready for today. It'd be cruel to make you stay."

The relief flooding my body is the first ray of sunshine I've had in weeks. "*Really*?"

"Yes," she says with a sympathetic smile. "Go. You've set everything up perfectly, you deserve a break. I want what's best for you, Lexie, and watching the person you love get married ... that might not be something you'll ever get over."

And then Sydney does something so un-Sydney-like that my brain takes a moment to reconcile the action with the person. She reaches over and pulls me in for a full, warm, engulfing hug. "Take the rental car. Justin and I will figure out how to get back to the city."

I thank her profusely, quickly gather my items resting

on our prep table, and race to the car. The relief I feel from leaving is quickly overshadowed by grief. Before I reach the end of the block, I break into sobs.

Today, I experienced true heartbreak. The kind that reaches inside of you, squeezing you so tight you're sure you'll never be able to properly breathe again.

Theo and I are done.

For better or worse, this chapter of my life is officially closed.

And my world crumbles.

46

Theo

I haven't moved. I don't know how long ago Lexie left. Two minutes, five, fifty? My feet are rooted to the hardwood floor, and I stay there, locked in forced immobility, for as long as it takes. Because if I move, I'll chase her. I'll run out of this house, drag her into me, and never let her leave.

But I can't.

The way Lexie looked at me. *Fuck*. Regret and pain tear at my skin like I'm submerged into an acid lake. The willpower and restraint I'm using right now to not fall at my knees, makes my legs shake.

But I had to push her away. Because I'm not strong enough to let her go.

The pain is unbearable. It's as raw as my flesh being ripped from my bones, as sharp as a machete through the heart. It feels as though my insides are being burned alive. I can't breathe. I don't think I ever can again. For the rest of my life, the image of hope, love, and heartache that swirled in those emerald eyes will haunt me. Watching the glimmer of hope fade will be the last look I see before I go to bed, it will be the stagnant ache that will never heal.

This is the punishment I deserve. The torment of choosing one type of love over the other. Of deciding between loyalty and heart. Of knowing an angelic light flickered in the blackness of my soul before going dark again.

I'll live in this punishment for eternity, if it will remove her hurt. If my self-flagellation can be her balm, I'll do it. I'll take this and a million more. I'll walk barefoot on broken glass, I'll inhale the poison, I'll stand in the fire. For Lexie, I will do almost anything. *Almost.* Except what she wants.

I finally move. I'm sniffing the air like a dog, hoping for a hint of vanilla-scented skin, but it's gone. God, I have to get used to this.

I'm not a good man. I don't deserve either of these women. But everything has come to a head and I'm running out of solutions. I can't walk away from Anna. But I can't be with Lexie either. I need to protect her from me, from who I really am, from the sick, broken part of me. Even though my insides burn at the thought of her being with another man, maybe letting her go is the only way she'll find someone more worthy.

A twisted, unhinged piece of me welcomes this torment. Maybe pain is atonement. Maybe through my suffering, it will set Lexie back on the life she deserves.

I drag myself to the window and watch the wedding

preparations in full swing, but feel none of the excitement a groom should on his wedding day.

My phone sits heavy in my pocket. I know what I need to do. I'm going to be married in a few hours, and I can't hold on to this past any longer. My fingers hover over Lexie's photos I have saved on my phone. From the sexy selfies she sent me, to one of me kissing her cheek, to the snaps I took of her when she was sleeping. I need to let her go. I don't deserve to hang on to her like this. Even though it's going to fucking kill me, I pull in a full breath, hit delete, and push on through the pain.

She's gone. In every sense of the word, Lexie is gone from my life, and everything in me breaks.

A knock on the door jars me from where I'm standing, and I hate that for a fleeting moment, I wonder if she returned. But when I open it to see Lexie's friend Justin standing there with a stern look, I'm both relieved and disappointed.

A silent standoff ensues between us. He clearly loves her, and even though I'm raging that he gets to be with her for the rest of his life, I'm also grateful she has someone who won't abandon her like I did. I brace myself for whatever he's going to give me. I'll take it. I *deserve* it. Will he tell me I'm a piece of shit who ruined her life? That I deserve nothing but misery? Is he going to hit me—because right now, wedding day or not, I'd let him.

Instead, he says, "Can I get you anything to eat or drink?" When I shake my head, he checks his watch. "Photos start in thirty minutes."

When he turns to leave, I take a step forward. "Is she gone?"

His shoulders brace, and he slowly turns to face me. "Yeah."

I exhale through my nose. I already knew this, but hoped that maybe, as fucked up as it is, she'd stay for my wedding. "Is she coming back?"

His jaw flexes and the words that must be on the tip of his tongue—because how can they *not* be, how can anyone who loves her not want to defend, protect, and honor her in every regard—he swallows back. A long moment passes when he straightens his back. "No."

And then he closes the door.

The hollow ache in my gut spreads and totally consumes me.

My wedding day.

The loneliest day of my life.

47

Theo

After Justin leaves, I pace the room, thoughts ricocheting between Lexie and the courtyard where I'll soon take vows that were never intended for Anna and me. I don't stop until a knock breaks the silence. It's probably Justin, returning to finally throw the punch I know he's been itching to release. But when I open the door, I sigh.

Anna.

She's in one of the dresses that Lexie tried on, her long dark hair pinned back, her make-up heavier than normal. She looks incredible.

But no amount of make-up can hide the look that's mirrored on my own face—despair.

"You look beautiful." A lump grows in my throat. I want to be strong for her, tell her that everything will be okay, but I'm too broken.

And clearly, so is she.

She tugs on my hand and guides me to the bed. After she smooths her dress underneath her and sits down, she pats the mattress, and I take a seat. "You know what I was thinking about today?"

I focus on the way she's spinning her engagement ring, and sigh. "What's that?"

"Do you remember the time when we were like, fourteen, maybe fifteen, and we stole that bottle of Scotch from my parents?"

Despite my mood, a chuckle escapes. "How could I forget? I'm not sure what made me sicker that night—your father screaming at me, or my inexperience with booze." Even with how much I drank that night, I remember most of the evening pretty clearly. It was one of the million movie nights Anna and I enjoyed together as kids, but we were bored and restless and thought getting drunk for the first time sounded like a good idea. "I remember thinking, your dad's a billionaire. Why's he so mad? He can just buy another bottle."

"Right? Like how were we supposed to know it was a gift from a Prime Minister?" She grins. "But I specifically remember you taking the heat and telling my dad it was your idea to ransack his whiskey room, even though we both knew damn well I forced you into it."

And I'd do it again in a heartbeat. "What made you think of that night?"

She shrugs. "I just keep going over all the moments in my life where you've been there for me. From elementary school, when you tore into my bullies, to junior high, when you sat with me at lunch after those girls turned on me, to letting me snot cry on your shoulder over that stupid crush on an older boy . . . God, what was his name?"

"Nathan. And he was a dick."

A soft smile spreads on her pale face. "Interesting how that guy ended up with a black eye the day after he told everyone we had sex even though we didn't."

"See my earlier comment," I say.

She loops her arm in mine and drags her fingertips across my hand. "I'm really glad my first time was with you."

My heart caves in as I kiss the top of her head. "Same."

Another long silence fills the room. She leans her head against my shoulder, not caring if she messes up her hair. "And well, here we are getting married," she says. "Because you're doing what you do. Protecting me, as usual."

I don't know what to say. Of course, it's true. I love Anna. I've loved her since I was six years old. For almost my entire life, I thought my sole purpose was to protect her. Somedays, knowing Anna was safe was the only thing that kept me going.

"When I was in Italy, Nonna and I talked about so many things," she says. "She used to be a dancer, can you believe it?"

I chuckle. "No chance. She's as graceful as a baby goat."

"You're such an asshole." She digs her elbow into my ribs. "But my grandfather didn't want her to dance, so she stopped. And to this day, she regrets it. She gave up *everything* for him." She lifts her head from my shoulder and sighs.

"God, the pressures our families put on us, huh? Your dad. My dad. My mom. We've compromised everything to make them happy. And for what? Money? Approval? Out of fear?"

My chest turns tight. Anna's not wrong. As much as I despise my father, I still molded myself into the man he wanted me to be.

She picks at the fabric of her dress, a tell I know too well. She's nervous, about to say something I'm not going to like. "I can't do it anymore."

Her words send a wave of dread through me. "Anna . . . no . . ."

She lifts herself off the bed and stands in front of me. I have the urge to wrap my arms around my best friend and rest my head on her stomach. I want her to tell me everything will be okay, that whatever we have to face, we have each other—and that's all that matters.

Hands rest on my face, and she lifts my head to meet her eyes. "I love you, Theo. I have *always* loved you. I cannot imagine my life without you. You are my person. You will *always* be my person." She tugs on my tie as the blue in her eyes shimmers with unshed tears. "And, I love you so fucking hard for what you've done for me. But . . . I can't do this to you. I cannot let you go through with this wedding."

No, no. She doesn't know what she's saying. She's panicking, second-guessing everything—and that's okay. But she absolutely cannot back out. I jump to my feet. "Don't do this," I say, gripping her arms, holding her gaze as fiercely as

I can. "Listen to me. I'm not letting you do this. You'd . . . you'd be giving up everything."

"I could say the same thing about you." She clasps her hands over mine. "All I have to lose is money, Theo. *Just money.* Being in Italy, getting away from the madness of my family, made me realize I'd rather live poor than live under their restraints. But if you go through with this . . ." Her voice breaks. "You're giving up *love*." The tears she's been holding back finally break free and roll down her cheeks. "I'll recover. You forget I'm a Barlowe—I have connections. But you . . . you've been in love with someone else all these years. *Years.* And you stayed away because you thought you had to protect me, which you don't, and because you convinced yourself you weren't good enough." Her hands move back to my face, and they tighten. "But you are. I'm telling you right now, *you are enough*."

I can't take in the words. I hear them, but the steel wall I've built around myself refuses to allow Anna's words to penetrate. She doesn't know everything. If she did, she wouldn't think this way. "I'm not a good person. The stuff I've done . . . "

She shakes her head. "What's the phrase about glass stones? Everyone's done bad shit. But think of all the good you do. With your patients, with the women your dad hurt, with me. You've sacrificed everything for me." She smiles weakly through watery tears, determination bright in her eyes. "And I'm not letting you do it one second longer. It's my turn to protect you. Even if it means protecting you from yourself."

My pulse thuds inside my chest. "Anna, you *can't*."

"I can. And I will. No matter what you say, I'm leaving this room and telling my mom the wedding is off. I should probably let Lexie's boss know too. Then I'm taking two bottles of the champagne, locking myself in the honeymoon suite we booked, eating greasy pizza and watching trashy movies, and *I will be okay*."

Is she really doing this? I'm searching her eyes, and deep down, I know there's nothing I can say or do to change her mind.

"Go, be brave and tell Lexie everything," she says. "And know that she deserves you as much as you deserve her."

Everything in me balloons and fortifies—my love for Anna, my love for Lexie, the desperate need to reconcile my past with my future. "Do you think it's too late?"

She gives me a sad smile and drops her hands from my face. "Honestly, I don't know. But there's only one way to find out."

I pull Anna into my chest, my pulse racing. Is there still time? Will Anna be okay? Is Lexie gone forever? "Are you going to be okay?"

"I will be *fine*," she says, her eyes rolling fondly at my overprotectiveness. "I feel like I've finally released myself from the golden restraints that have trapped me my entire life. I can finally breathe, fully, on my own."

Are we actually doing this? I look at her one more time, search those Caribbean-blue eyes for any hesitation or fear or regret, but there's nothing but relief. "God, I love you. Are you sure?"

"I'm sure. More than I've ever been." Her smile fills her entire, sweet face. She lifts to her toes and kisses me on the cheek. "I love you, too."

We stop and take in the moment. What will happen when we step out on the courtyard and tell her parents the wedding's off? The fall-out, the threats, the clenched, controlled anger of a family who's more worried about public persona than anything else.

But I'll face this with Anna, by her side, for as long as it takes.

As far as Lexie is concerned . . . I have no fucking idea what I'm going to do.

For now, I glance back at my best friend, grab her hand, and kiss it. "You ready to do this?"

She nods, her smile brighter than I think I've ever seen. "Let's do this."

48

Lexie

Before I reach the first hour of my drive back to New York City, the burn in my eyes has reached a fever pitch. The tears dried up a long time ago, leaving everything raw and exhausted, desperate for relief. But I have a sinking feeling I won't find this any time soon. By the second hour, I can't take it anymore. I pull the rental car up to a gas station, splash cold water on my face in the bathroom, hoping it might help.

It's useless. My cheeks are red and streaked with ruined mascara, my dress stained with the salty remnants of the tears that slipped past my chin, the pins in my hair are hanging by a literal strand. I pluck them out and toss them into the metal garbage can. I'm a mess. But I don't want to go home. There's only one place I want to be.

I book myself a room at a bed and breakfast, and an hour later, the car crunches over gravel as I pull into the Lake Welch public parking lot and kill the engine. I take a moment to breathe. It's over. This here—the quiet, the hollowness—is my new normal. It's reminiscent of when I was expelled from school. The pain is different, sharper, more acute. It's a death of a dream. Back then, the stages of denial skipped immediately to rage. I was riddled with anger and the fierce injustice of being accused of and punished for something I didn't do. But this is a sadness that cuts me so deep, it's hard to know if I'll ever heal from it.

I leave the car to walk through the parking lot, past animated people carrying supplies for the beach. Laughter and splashing water fade into the background as I push through dense birch and oak, twigs snapping beneath my sandaled feet. I continue on until I find a perfect fallen log resting on the edge of the serene water and take a seat.

If my calculations are correct, Theo and Annabelle should be walking down the aisle any minute now. I shoot Justin a quick message telling him where I am, that I'm safe, and that I'm going off-grid for a few days to reset. I grab a few rocks to plop in the water and try to push away the image of them standing in front of the officiant, exchanging rings and promising to love and cherish each other forever.

I need to stop torturing myself.

Maybe if I stay here forever, reality won't sink in. I hurl rock after rock until my shoulder burns. The physical pain is a welcome distraction.

"Now what?" I whisper into the water, wanting it so badly to provide me with the clarity I'm seeking. But really, now what? I clinch the promotion that I was promised while losing five colleagues, and wrestle with the sickening guilt of getting a raise while they're being let go.

The sound of twigs crunching behind me grows louder. If this is a bear, I'm out. Seriously, I'm officially fucking out. I shift on the log and look over my shoulder, my breath hitching. For one ridiculous second, I imagine Theo appearing in a tux, begging for forgiveness for what happened in his room, telling me he's not marrying Annabelle, that we're running away together to live some sort of impossible fantasy life.

But it's not him. It's a bunny.

It looks at me, cocks its head, then disappears back into the forest. I let out a shaky sigh. What am I thinking?

I stay at Lake Welch for hours, as time becomes arbitrary and meaningless. When my butt turns numb from sitting on the log, my belly growls, and my arms ache from tossing rocks into the water, I tuck my feet back into my sandals and slowly start making my way to the car.

I don't have any more clarity than when I got here, but I do know that Theo is gone. He's never coming back. And the sooner I accept this, the quicker I can try to move on.

49

Lexie

I'm sure I haven't slept. The sky is a dark amethyst blue, highlighted by a full moon. I should try to go back to sleep, get rid of this pounding headache, but I know that my attempts for rest will fail. I squeeze my eyes shut, but five minutes later, I force myself to get out of bed.

Last night the owner of the bed and breakfast mentioned that a hiking group would be heading out at six a.m., and I was welcome to join. I'd originally declined—six a.m. is a god-awful hour—but since I'm up anyway, I may as well go.

On the hike, I try to make small talk with the group, but mostly I just walk and watch as a sliver of magenta sun peeks through the trees. Lake Welch holds a cathartic power and I need to absorb it as much as I can while I'm here.

The lake is quiet at this hour. Only a handful of people dot the beach, while a couple wade into the water and push off in a canoe. I walk with the group through the forest, breathing in the water's mineral scent. It's so peaceful here. Maybe as part of this whole self-discovery thing, I need to come here once a month.

Hour two melts into hour three. We stop to snack and hydrate, then set off again. I catch myself smiling at the grandma beside me, who somehow has more stamina than the rest of the group combined. By noon, we make our way back to the bed and breakfast, and I consider extending my stay for another night.

The owner of the place is wiping her flour-dusted hands on her apron as I walk up to the front porch area. "Excuse me, Miss Welch, there's someone waiting for you in the back. By the creek."

I'm not expecting anyone, and my stomach tightens at the thought that I worried Justin enough to come looking for me.

"He's been here for hours. I asked him if he needed anything, but he said no."

After I thank the owner, I follow the walking path from the back of the residence that leads to the creek and my mouth drops.

Theo.

Tuxedo pants, untucked tuxedo shirt. Sitting on top of the picnic table, staring at the water, his back to me.

I'm delusional. Any moment now, I'll wake up. There's no way Theo is here. He got married yesterday. He should be in his honeymoon suite planning the rest of his life with his *wife*. Not sitting here in another city—where I am.

As if he senses my presence, he turns to me, meeting my gaze with tired eyes and an anguished smile. "Hey."

Even if I wanted to, I can't move. My body is frozen in shock.

"Care to join me?" he casually pats the space next to him, as if he didn't just leave his wife to come find me on a rough, splintered, wooden picnic table.

I feel torn. I bite back the urge to tell him to fuck off from how he treated me yesterday, but the fact that he's driven the three hours to get here probably means I should at least hear him out. "I drove by the lake," he says, resting his elbows on his knees. "You're right. It's beautiful."

Theo. Is here. With me. "How . . . how did you know where I was?"

A hint of a dimple appears on his beautifully chiseled face, his expression sheepish. "I forced Justin to tell me."

I shake my head in disbelief. "Aren't you supposed to be waking up in the honeymoon suite right now?"

His gaze sweeps mine and his plush lips lift into the slightest grin. "I had somewhere more important I needed to be."

"You did?"

He nods. "I did."

A moment passes as I study is eyes. "What does this mean?"

"It means the wedding is off."

His declaration leaves me numb. A part of me would love nothing more than to say this is the best news ever and jump into his lap, but I can't. My heart is too fragile, like a bird with a broken wing, perched at the edge of a branch, knowing it can't fly.

We sit in silence. The faint murmurs of visitors chatting in the background and the breeze rustling leaves are the only sounds around us.

I can't believe he's here.

He's barely looking at me. I want to ask him so many questions. How did the parents deal with the news? Has the wedding been postponed or canceled for good? But self-preservation kicks in and stops me from asking anything more.

"I'm so sorry, Lexie. For everything." He runs his hands down his face. "The way I spoke to you yesterday is unforgivable. I . . . I needed to push you away, to make you hate me. I wanted to save you from me." He takes another long pause and stares back at the creek. "I'm so fucking sorry."

I respond with a nod. I don't doubt that he's sorry. For what happened in Boston, for lying, for breaking my heart. But still, I don't know what him being here, now, means.

"If you don't mind," he says, "Annabelle would really like to talk to you."

I nod. He taps his phone, hands it to me, then stands up and steps away to give us some privacy.

"Hey, Lexie," Annabelle says after only a few rings. Her voice is a little hoarse, still groggy, but warmer—lighter—than the last time we spoke. "I'm so glad Theo found you, and that you at least let him let me talk to you. I'm sure your head is spinning right now."

Understatement of the year.

"When we spoke yesterday and I encouraged you to go find Theo, I truly thought he'd come to his senses and tell me the wedding was off. I'm so sorry I put you through that. You must've been heartbroken."

Another understatement.

I glance at Theo who's staring at the ground, no doubt trying to eavesdrop.

"You don't owe Theo anything," she says gently. "I completely understand if you're hesitant. I'm sure you're angry, hurt, and probably terrified of giving him another chance. After some . . . let's call them challenging conversations last night, he got stuck in his own head and decided he wasn't going after you. Not because he doesn't want to be with you. The man has wanted you since the moment he met you." She takes a breath and continues. "I think he felt like he didn't deserve you, that you'd be better off without him. But I see the good in him, flaws and all. And I know you do, too. So, I told him to come find you. That he deserves happiness, just like you and I do. All I'm asking is that you listen to what he has to say. Okay?" She pauses before cheekily adding, "Besides, you can't say no to the bride."

I finally exhale the breath I've been holding, a small, strained laugh catching in my chest. A moment passes, then another, when I say, "Okay."

I hand the phone back to Theo, and his fingers graze mine before I pull away. I'm not ready to touch him yet. Not until I know where we stand.

"Do you want to tell me what happened?" I ask Theo.

A hopeful expression appears on his face. "Do you really want to hear this?"

Honestly, I don't know.

But I give him a small nod.

"After we decided to call things off, Anna went to find Sydney while I tracked down Justin first and gave him the news, though I asked him not to call you. I needed time to think about what to do next, to do this on my terms, as much as I could."

A slow, heavy thud starts in my chest. I'm sure Sydney immediately agreed without hesitation, but the reality of me leaving my boss to deal with this mess makes my stomach knot.

"How did Sydney take it?" I ask, even though I know the answer. Sydney is the epitome of professional. If a client—especially someone like a Barlowe—asked her to handle something, she'd do it without question.

"Like a champ." A short chuckle leaves his mouth. "Maybe it wasn't the best plan in the world . . . but . . . it worked. Sydney said she'd handle the announcement and manage the fallout. But Anna and I were very clear that you were to be kept completely out of this and to make up for the trouble, we offered her a bonus."

"A bonus? What does that mean?"

"Ten percent of our original fee."

My eyebrows shoot to the cloudless sky. "You gave my boss *two hundred thousand dollars* so she wouldn't call me?"

He shrugs. "I protect what's mine."

My eyes narrow at his words, but my mind swirls. *Two hundred thousand dollars?* I've barely registered that I'm sitting on a picnic table with an unmarried, half-tux wearing Theo, much less that he gave my boss enough money to keep the business afloat for a few more months. "But . . . but . . . Annabelle won't have any money after this. She told me she's giving up everything, her trust fund, her inheritance and—"

"Okay, not to sound like a dick, but you do remember that I'm the son of one of the largest shipping heirs in the world, right?" I roll my eyes at his remark, though I hate to admit it that I did, kind of, forget. I'm always so focused on the Barlowe name and influence that I forgot the Astor name comes with its own wealth. "We will be *fine*. I wouldn't do something if I didn't think it would be worth it."

A slow ripple of warmth stirs in my chest and flutters through me. How is this even real?

"Can I tell you about the first time I ever saw you?" he asks.

My lips curve into a soft smile. "Sure."

"It was September seventh, the third day of classes, almost eight years ago. I even remember how brutally hot it was. High nineties, suffocating humidity. That's how deeply the day has been burned into my brain." He kicks at a rock, staring down at his folded hands. "And I was pissed, too. Shocking, I know." I grin at this and wait for him to continue. "I'd just found out a professor was giving me preferential treatment because I was George Astor's son. Not because I was a good student who he wanted to help." He exhales. "That same day, my dad called me into his office. We got into an argument, and I couldn't stay there another second. I was still completely in my head when you stopped me on the quad."

My head snaps up. "I did?"

His beautiful dimples deepen. "Yeah. You handed me my dropped headphones and asked for directions. I wasn't in the mood to deal with people, so I tried to get rid of you as quickly as possible. But then I looked up, and fuck, Lexie . . ." he drags his hands down his face. "You had on these pink Converse, cut-off shorts, and a St. Ben's t-shirt. Your hair was in this long braid all the way down to your waist. And I swear—the way the sun hit you, like some kind of firestorm, the way it pulled out the green flecks in your eyes, the way that your freckles were darker from the summer—it stopped me. Everything just . . . fucking stopped. I didn't care about being late to class, or my dad, or even the heat. I couldn't see anything but you. And I swear to Christ, Lexie, I honestly thought I was going to pass out. You were so goddamn beautiful. But it was more than that. You had this pure, angelic innocence to you and . . . I knew that was it. I fell so fucking hard."

I can't believe he remembers all this, when all I remember from that time was how worried I was that I'd get lost on campus.

Theo shifts to face me. He still looks hesitant to touch me, like he's scared that if he moves too quickly, I'll run.

But I know in this moment, I will never run. I want to stay locked inside his orbit forever. Nothing has felt more whole or complete than when I'm with him. Sitting on a picnic table, wrapped in his arms in my tiny apartment, or feeling him inside me, he is the glue that adheres my broken, jagged pieces together.

"Anna told you everything, didn't she?"

I nod.

His beautiful soft brown eyes bore into mine. "You have to understand—there was so much at stake. It felt like there were no good options left."

I fan my fingers across his tattooed arm, a quiet reassurance to him that I'm here—that I understand. It's the first time I've touched him since he showed up, and his skin is warm, heavenly, under my fingers. "I *love* your loyalty to Annabelle. You've been the one constant in her life, and I'd never ask you to give that up. I know how much you mean to each other."

He tightens his grip on my hand. "I need you to know that since the beginning, it's always been you. I've done so many fucked-up things in my life, made difficult choices because of it, but I keep coming back to the same truth—you are mine, and I am yours."

The tears that were clinging for dear life under my eyelids, release and roll down my cheeks, and I swipe them away, my emotions a mess.

"I am . . . " He hesitates, pain flickering across his face. "Sorry. For lying to you for so long. I should've told you right away about what I did at school. But I was terrified you'd leave and after all these years, I'd just gotten you back. It was selfish and so fucking wrong. But I swear, with everything in me, I will never, *ever* lie to you again."

Theo isn't someone who apologizes lightly. I know that when he says it, he means it—and warmth spreads through me.

"When you told me yesterday, at the house, that you love me, it . . . it broke me," he says as he tucks a loose strand of hair behind my ear. "No one has *ever* made me feel that exposed. I've never let them. I wanted to say so much back to you. I just . . . couldn't."

Gentle fingers brush away the tears streaming down my cheeks, and I lean into the warmth of his touch. Something like hope starts to nestle in my heart as years of uncertainty, months of love and pain, feelings of being inadequate, vanish with each passing moment. "What did you want to say to me?" my voice cracks.

He shifts and kneels in front of me until our faces are close. So many unfamiliar emotions move through his creased eyes. Hope tangled with uncertainty. Fear threaded through love. Apologies wrapped up in quiet promises. My chin trembles. Somewhere deep in my soul, I feel everything he's trying to say.

"I fucking love you, Lexie. I *love* you." He cups my face and leans closer. "My world has always revolved around you. I thought I could let you go. Back then, now, for years, I thought I could leave, but I never could. You are both my biggest weakness and my greatest strength." My tears come freely now, traveling down my face and onto his hands. "You have no idea how much I regret everything—getting you expelled, the way I acted, letting you go. I was a fucking idiot, and I wasted seven years of our lives apart." His gaze sharpens, pleading but steady. "If you'll let me, I swear to God I'll spend the rest of my life fighting for you, proving to you that you belong with me, that we . . . belong together. I'll show you every day how sorry I am."

A beat passes as I hold my breath.

"If . . . you'll have me."

And I cave. A choking sob breaks loose as I wrap my arms around him, pressing my face into his shoulder. My heart feels like it's been revived. It was nearly destroyed, but it didn't stop. It's still beating, still fighting, still clinging on with everything it has to the belief that I am enough.

I'm broken. But Theo will heal me.

I will heal me.

His shirt absorbs my tears. His strong arms hold me as tight as a corset, his heart pounds against my chest, his shaky breaths intertwine with mine. So much time passes where I just let him hold me, until my brain, my body, my heart, accept that he is here with me and refuses to let go. He's stroking my hair, he's whispering in my ear, he's supporting me when I feel like I'm going to collapse. Finally, after the sobs quiet, and my breaths even, I pull back and dash my gaze against his eyes. "What would you have done if I wasn't here?"

His thumbs swipe off the rest of my tears, and he presses his forehead into mine. "I would've burned down the world to find you."

My heart soars like it's gotten its wings. I cup my fingers against his cheeks, the stubble tickling my fingertips, and sigh. "I love you, too."

He pulls me in for a kiss. It's nothing like the possessive, urgent kisses from before. This one is unhurried—intentional, deliberate. His lips move against mine like I'm the air he needs, the lifeline he's been waiting for. He kisses me as though he's releasing himself of the past and welcoming me into his future. I kiss him back with forgiveness, with the promise of tomorrow, with the quiet certainty that I am here, now, with him in this moment, where we're meant to be.

Somewhere along the blurred lines of history, revenge, and ownership, of hope, sorrow, and love, our worlds collided. What I thought was a game turned into reality. What I thought was a trap became the truth.

Our love. It's messy and impracticable and deeply imperfect.

But it's ours.

And it's worth fighting for.

EPILOGUE

Lexie

12 MONTHS LATER

The entry door closes with a soft click, and my heartbeat immediately rises. I tiptoe across the room as quietly as possible—which is not easy to do in these monstrous heels—and lean against the master suite bathroom door to wait. Keys and a phone tossed onto a counter, shoes being removed, and a jacket getting hung up are the only faint sounds that travel into the room.

"Lexie? I'm home," my husband calls out, and I bite back a smile.

My husband. I will never, ever get sick of saying that. We might be approaching our one-year anniversary, but I use the word "husband" as much as humanly possible.

Our engagement was the quickest in history. Or at least in *Shades of White* history. Once Theo professed everything that day at the bed and breakfast, he proposed the next day. Literally, the next day. I actually thought it was a joke. I woke up the next morning to find hundreds and hundreds of flowers (I still don't know how I slept through that) and Theo kneeling beside the bed. Instead of proposing with a ring, he used one of my hair ties—no one can ever accuse him of not being romantic—and we spent the rest of the week shopping for rings.

After the shock wore off, I pointed out that literally less than forty-eight hours earlier, he was supposed to marry someone else. Wasn't this a little fast, I'd asked. But he said he'd waited almost eight years to marry me and didn't want to wait another second.

A month later, our wedding at Lake Welch was everything I could have wanted. Justin was my best man, and Annabelle Theo's maid of honor (*yeah, I know, it's backwards*). My mom and Dylan acted as witnesses, and Sydney was the officiant. Everything was simple and tailored to *us*. I decided to forgo shoes because of the sand; Theo wore a casual linen shirt and slacks. We had a fabulous dinner on a bar patio with more wine than should be legal. The only extravagant thing about the day was my dress. Theo and I went back to the store where I'd tried on dresses for Annabelle and he bought the one he loved on me the most.

Oh, the look the saleswoman gave me when Theo referred to me as his fiancée when we'd asked for the dress . . .

I wasn't sure if things would change once the exposé on Theo's father finally got published in the *Times*. Six months ago, Theo was tense, agitated, and fearful for the women leading up to the article. And I thought he'd remain that way. But once the story dropped, it was like a decade-long weight had been lifted. His father's fall-out was swift. The school opened an investigation. More women stepped forward. His literary agent and publisher dropped him, speeches that he was supposed to give at various corporations and colleges were canceled. Theo's mother remains steadfastly by his side, however, not to Theo's surprise. But when Dr. Astor was finally removed from his tenured position at the university last month—which apparently is near impossible to do—Theo and I took a quiet, weekend-long trip to Nantucket Island to let it all sink in.

Marriage to Theo has been much easier than I thought. I used to secretly carry this fear that what we built was born out of infatuation and revenge, twisted into something obsessive—that it might fade once real life settled in. But it hasn't. If anything, I can't get enough of my husband, and he very clearly can't get enough of me.

Do we fight? Of course we do. Mostly about my packed schedule and Theo's constant worry that I'm overexerting myself. That, and he really, *really* doesn't like other men touching me. His jealousy simmers just beneath the surface, and I know exactly how much to push before he'll exact punishment by spanking me red and angry fucking me just the way I like.

But, just as easily, he reads me like a manual. He knows when I need to be held instead of challenged and when I need quiet reassurance, whispered reminders of how much he loves me.

"Where are you?" Theo calls from the lower level. I hear the impatience in his voice at not having met him right away.

We've only lived in this place for a few months, and I'm still getting used to having stairs *inside* our home. Inside! Do Theo and I really need to live in a four thousand square foot apartment overlooking the most beautiful lower Manhattan skyline? No. It's over the top, totally gluttonous, and completely impractical.

And also, really fucking amazing.

The place is a little closer to my mom, too, who flat-out refused our offer to buy her a new place. She said her home holds too many memories, and she loves her community. She did, however, agree to let us upgrade all her home furnishings and appliances, and didn't need convincing to take us up on our offer to support her so she could finally retire.

Now, if I could only reclaim my title as her favorite child, that'd be great. I blame *The Bachelorette* for being my mom's weakness and the one advantage Theo has over me, which they insist on watching together every week.

Whatever.

"Lex?" Theo calls again, more urgently.

"I'm upstairs," I call back, biting back a smile.

"Working or studying?"

"Working," I lie.

It's a fair question. Ever since I enrolled in business school in the fall, my evenings have been split between work or studying. I'm only taking a few credits this semester, but once we hire more staff at *Shades of White*, I plan to increase my course load to part-time. Even though I don't technically *need* to work, as Theo has reminded me more than once, the thought of not going to the office anymore broke my heart. And now, with my promotion to lead coordinator, I'm happier at work than I've ever been.

And . . . insanely busy.

Last year, the Barlowe/Astor wedding fiasco exploded across New York gossip sites, spreading like wildfire through blogs, articles, endless reels. Once word got out about how brilliantly the owner of the wedding planning company handled the fallout, Sydney was flooded with dozens of interview requests. Within the next week, it seemed like everyone, and anyone, wanted to work with her. *Shades of White* no longer needed to close its doors, but instead was able to double its staff to keep with the surge in business.

Which was the best news for everyone . . . except my deeply neglected husband.

The sounds of Theo jogging up the stairs and walking down the hall sends an excited thrill through me. I lick my lips in anticipation, barely breathing as our bedroom door creaks open. When Theo steps inside, he freezes. His heated, hungry gaze slides down me, inch by glorious inch. "*Fuck, baby . . .*" he says under his breath.

A blush springs to my cheeks. "You like?"

His hooded eyes darken as he takes in the way I'm leaning into the bathroom door in nothing but my thigh-high shiny leather boots, his stethoscope slung over my neck, and his white doctor jacket. I've stuffed my hands in the pockets to bring the fabric together, covering his favorite part of me *just enough*.

"I fucking *love*."

He storms over, but I step back, feeling the stiff fabric of the jacket lapels graze my nipples as I do. "Not so fast," I say and his stormy, dark eyes narrow. "What do you say?"

The muscle in his jaw tenses. "Please."

Christ, that one word fills my core with so much heat, I don't know how long I'll be able to hold out. "Again."

He drags a hand over his mouth and exhales a rattled breath. "*Please*."

Tingles spread through me from his look alone, and the dull ache in my pussy intensifies. I curl my finger to motion him forward. Even though he looks like a caged cheetah ready to pounce, my very obedient husband stops when I put up my hand.

My mouth waters as I take in the outline of his cock hardening in his jeans, the way his chest strains against his shirt, the crimson deepening in his neck veins. "First," I say as I lick my lips. "I'd like to know what you intend to do to me."

A devious grin shadows his face. "Oh, baby girl," he says with a low, raspy growl. "Are you sure you can handle what I have in mind?" He grips the jacket lapel. My breath catches and I stumble forward a few inches. He slowly drags his hands down, *excruciatingly* slowly, as his knuckles brush my nipples. A warmth rushes through me. My nipples tighten, anticipating his mouth. He lifts the stethoscope to my ears and presses in the earpiece. "I want you to listen to how my touch makes you feel."

When he presses the cool scope diaphragm to my warm chest, a shiver runs through me. *Da dum. Da dum. Da dum.* His fingertips brush my hair over my shoulder, and he presses his lips against my neck.

"Now, listen to how it beats when I do this," he says as he trails kisses on my jaw, right below my ear, and along my collarbone.

Da dum. Da dum. Da dum. My eyes flutter closed. "Mmmmm . . ."

"Now," he says with his warm mouth still skimming my neck, "what does it sound like when I reach that beautiful ass of yours?" His hand slides down the outside of the jacket until he reaches bare skin.

The single graze makes my pulse increase, and a thudding floods my eardrums.

"What about when I do this?" He grabs a solid chunk of my ass, and the rough, possessive grip makes my heartbeat thunder. "Or this . . ." He reaches in between my warm, tingling thighs. When his fingertips slide over my slickness, the thudding coming through the stethoscope grows feverish. "That's my beautiful wife . . . do you have any idea how much I love to feel how you're ready for me?"

My hands twitch to pull him into me, but I stay firm, swallowing back my desire and forcing myself to not touch him to elongate the game. He tugs one of my hands from my pocket and guides me to hold the diaphragm against my chest myself. When I take over holding it, he drops his hand, and yanks open the jacket in a swift tug. The cool air hits my exposed tits, and he tugs on my nipple. "Oh . . . yes . . . mmmmm . . ." I say, breathlessly.

He turns me, pushes his hard cock against my ass, and I moan at the sensation. "Is your heartbeat loud in your ears?" he asks, reaching around and teasing his fingertips across my clit. "Is it going faster?"

"Yes," I whisper, rotating my hips, needing either his cock or a firmer touch, but he's refusing. The *da dum, da dum, da dum*, in my ears sounds like I'm underwater. A dull, yet loud thudding that's moving impossibly fast. I want to stay strong, to tease him and make him ache, but my body is screaming to be filled. He slips in a single fingertip, and I drop my body, searching for more.

"Do you hear the way your heartbeat strains when I do this?" When I nod, he removes his finger and a whimper leaves me. He pulls me into him, hard, and presses his mouth to my ear. "Tell me, my beautiful, dirty wife. Which one do you want more right now? My tongue on that gorgeous pussy, or my cock inside you?"

Oh God, oh God, I'm going to lose this game. I'm desperate to stay strong, but the ache overwhelms me. "Both."

He cups my tits and slides his tongue up my neck. "My greedy girl." He pinches and tugs on my nipples, alternating between soft and hard, sending a rippling heated wave through me. "What if I said you had to choose one?"

My arousal leaks onto my thighs, and I swallow. "Don't make me choose."

His hand slides up and grips my neck and I swear, I'm done. He knows all my weak spots and will exploit everything to win. "Are you going to do what I say?"

"*Yes . . . yes . . .*" I say through my urgent haze.

"Good." His voice is dangerously gruff. "You know I don't like these games."

He's lying. My husband fucking loves these games.

And in a snap, he turns me to face him, and *oh . . . oh shit . . .* he gives me the look, the one that shoots fear-laced shivers through my entire body. Dark, demonic, dominant. He rips off the stethoscope and throws it on the dresser, grips my jacket and yanks it down in such a quick, sharp moment that I almost trip in my heeled boots. But since he came back into my life, I know he will never, ever let me fall. The fabric bites into my skin, and I moan at the sharp sting. He traps my arms behind me, handcuffing my wrists in his palm, and dips his head. He latches on to me, sucking and licking on my nipple as he pinches and plays with the other.

"Harder," I moan and he sucks deeper, harder, leaving searing red marks on my flesh and *oh God . . .* it feels so good.

I wiggle an arm free from his grip, grab his jaw, and drag him off my chest to face me. I slam my lips against his, claim him, push my tongue against his, and bite his lower lip because he's fucking mine. He grips my ass under the coat, and he tugs me into him. "Looks like my baby wants to be in control today, huh?"

"I *am* in control," I say, challenging him.

The sardonic grin that flashes on his face leaves a trail of heat down my spine. "What if I want to be in control?"

Without breaking my gaze, I shag out of the white coat, let it drop to the floor, and stand before him with nothing but my thigh high boots. His eyes travel me with such raw hunger that my belly quivers. *That's right, my love . . .* I feed off this look, the sensation that if I snapped my fingers, he'd attack with such savage aggressiveness that I might never recover.

Fuck, I love him.

I bring his hand to my mouth and drag my tongue along his index finger that carries a hint of my taste and devour the way his eyes grow hungry. I suck on it, then guide the moistened fingertip down my neck, my chest, my belly button, as Theo's gaze travels along with it. When I press his fingertips into my wet, impatient, heated flesh, his breath turns ragged. "How bad do you want this pussy?"

His eyes turn feral. "Give it to me. Now."

Oh, God, I love teasing him. Feeling so wanted that my deeply controlled husband verges on breaking makes me salivate. "How bad?"

The muscle in his jaw tightens. "*So fucking bad.*"

A satisfied grin forms. "Good. Then you'll do exactly as I say. Get on the bed." Theo immediately starts to take off his shirt, and trust me, I *love* my husband naked. But tonight, I want it different. "Keep your clothes on," I demand. "On the bed, on your back."

He gives me a suspicious look, but does as I say, lying fully clothed on his back. His chest rises and falls in quick, shallow breaths, as he watches me saunter to the bed. The ravenous look he's giving me sends jolts through me, and I don't know if I can hold out.

When I stand at the side of the bed, his hand instantly comes up to rub my ass. Clearly asserting his dominance, he gives my cheek one sharp slap, and I moan. Shit that feels good, and I might just change this entire scene and switch spots with him.

Stay strong.

He smooths out the sting, and even though I'm desperate for another spank, I grab his wrists. "And now, you don't get to touch me."

"Lex . . ."

"You know the rules," I snap, trying to keep the desire out of my tone. "Hands at your side."

Through a low growl, he does as he's told. God, he's so mouthwateringly sexy. His eyes are wide, dilatated. *Hungry.* I take my sweet ass time sliding his shirt up each firm, shuddering stomach muscle until I reach his chest. A moment passes, then another, as I feel his heartbeat thud under my palm. I plant a kiss on his skin, then scrape my nails down his rippled torso.

"*Fuck . . .*" he hisses. When I bend over to kiss away the burn, my tits dangle in front of him, and he tries to lick me. But I move out of his reach, saturating myself in his frustrated groans, and sliding my tongue along the red claw marks.

When I get to his jeans, I slide my palm over his cock that's pushing so hard against his pants it must hurt, and the sadistic side of me relishes in his frustrated pain. My lips press against his stomach, trailing kisses against his tight, ridged torso, and my fingers hover above his jeans button. I go slow, savoring the way my breath increases as I unbutton his jeans, the way his muscles flex, the way the metal zipper sounds as I tug it down.

When I slide my hands inside his boxers and palm his beautiful cock, I can barely hold myself back. I tug down his jeans until his cock releases. *Mmmm . . .* God, the glistening sheen, the silken skin, the hardening veins . . . he's so fucking beautiful. My mouth waters, but I hold back, instead spreading the precum around his crown with my thumb, and grazing my hand up and down, polishing him like a trophy.

"Oh, baby, that feels so good," he says with a rattled breath. "Put it in your mouth. I want to feel your lips wrapped around my cock."

Even though I'm supposed to call the shots, my mouth needs him. I drag my tongue on the side of his skin, all the way to the tip, and back down again, losing myself in his moans. "God your mouth is heaven." He reaches for me. I immediately stop and lift a brow. "*Fuck . . .*" he says with an exasperated groan and grips the comforter.

"Good boy." His cock twitches in my hand. He'll never admit it, but my husband has developed a bit of a praise kink over the last year. I resume my slow torturous licks, taking in the salty skin and masculine scent that drives a possessive, raw hunger deep in my core. I relax my throat, taking him as far as I can through the chokes and gags, through the tears streaming down my cheeks.

"*Oh yes, baby, God, so good, so good.*"

There's something deeply animalistic about Theo being clothed. My pussy is feverish and throbbing. I start rubbing my clit, but it's not enough. I need him. His legs jerk when I give him one hard suck and release.

"Have you been good today?" I ask as I climb on to the bed, and swing a leather booted leg over him to straddle.

"Yes," he says with a throaty rasp.

"Are you ready to get fucked by your wife?"

His chest jerks. He *loves* when I say this. "Yes, baby. Please."

Such a good husband. I didn't even need to remind him to use his manners this time. Behind me, I palm his cock and hover my soaked cunt over the tip. I swirl against him, power surging through me as I watch his fists turn white from gripping the sheets. I linger, one moment, two, three, and then slide him into me.

"Oh, fuck yes, Lexie, it's so good, it's so fucking good."

A hot shock runs through me as I fist his shirt and bury him in me. Moans and sighs and heavy breaths leave me. My ass slaps against his lap when I bounce to meet his harsh thrusts. "You feel so good inside me. I love how you fill me like this."

"Let me touch you." The pleading in his voice nearly

pushes me over the edge, but I want to feed off his agony a little longer. "Please, baby, let me touch you."

I love the desperation in his voice. I love it even more when I feel my insides hug his cock. Giving up control, in any aspect, drives him insane. I slide myself up and down a few more times with heavy, labored breaths. A thin sheen of sweat glistens on my chest. I feel him expand inside me, growing impossibly hard. I keep bouncing, faster, harder, taking him as deep as my body can handle. I lean into him, press my tits on his chest, and pull him in for a deep kiss. "You want to take care of me?" I ask.

"Always."

Yes, right now, we're talking about sex. But we both know it's so much more. His personal mission is to right any past wrongs and to take care of me in every way. I don't have to work. For the rest of my life, I wouldn't have to work. Even before we were married, he put me on all his accounts and gave me access to everything. It's more than the chest tattoo he got of a raven-haired angel holding a gem with Lexie scripted underneath. It's more than letting me pick out our home or supporting my mother. It's more than helping me apply to schools, cooking dinner for me, and supporting me with my promotion even though it takes time away from him.

This man has given me his life. His soul.

He loves me and protects me.

And, *my God*, does he fuck me. "You can take care of me now," I whisper.

The light in his eyes flicker. In one swoop, he lifts himself, rips off his shirt, grips my ass, and slams me on my back. "Oh, shit . . ." My breath locks in my chest. His mouth destroys me. His lips are on my mouth, my neck, my tits. He's sucking on any available skin, squeezing everything he can grip. It feels like he's been starving and this is the best meal he's ever had.

He kicks off his jeans so quickly I barely register what's happening, then scoops my legs. In a flash, he's kneeling in front of me. Tingles spread through me as he licks my skin, starting right above the boots, then going higher and higher, until his tongue meets my pussy.

Sometimes Theo takes his time. He teases. Makes me work for it.

And sometimes he devours.

Today, he devours.

His tongue swirls and licks at my swollen clit and *fuck, fuck,* it feels *so good*. He sucks on my quivering skin and slides a finger inside me. "Mmmm . . . God, I love you so much . . ." his murmurs vibrate against my skin.

My body heats at the way my fingers look raking through his dark hair, the way his broad shoulders push open my pale, trembling thighs, the way the shiny leather boots look pressed against his muscular back.

He lifts himself, slides his tongue up my stomach, leaving a trail of goosebumps, and sinks his mouth on to mine. I taste myself on him, my wet desire, my love for him. I lick and suck on his tongue, I kiss him, I pull him into me.

When he pushes into me, a warm shiver runs through

me. "Oh . . ." I moan into his mouth as he stretches and fills me. As he thrusts and owns me. As he shows me over and over that I'm his. Every kiss, every touch, every moment, he proves I will always be his. I want to eat his moans for eternity. I want to sink into him completely, to be held there. To be marked, branded and joined together for life.

As he keeps pumping, feeding my starving body, whispering how much he loves me, he holds me, breaks me, and rebuilds me. Against all odds, Theo and I weathered our storm and found each other. With all my broken parts and all his, we continue to rebuild.

From now, until I die, I will love, honor, and beg for my husband.

And he will do the same.

This, I vow.

Acknowledgements

First, I have to thank Melanie Hayes at Simon & Schuster for being a dream partner on this project. From our calls to our emails to the many revisions and restructuring we did, I knew that your heart was fully invested in this story. Thank you for believing in me and bringing these characters to life! And my agent, Jenna Satterthwaite. I bow to you my queen (*too much?*). Seriously, having you by my side and knowing you have my back has given me the confidence I need to dive into various projects. You are the captain of this intense journey and there's no one else in the world I'd rather steer this ship. Thank you for everything. Jennifer. Your guidance, feedback, and friendship is unwavering. Thank you for everything. Shelby. My person. In writing, in life. Thank you, always. Erica. Thank you for being an early reader! I trust your judgment implicitly and am so grateful for you. Megs. What would I do without you? Claire and Ashley. Thank you for celebrating with me. Thank you to Gabriella Nemeth and the rest of the team at Simon & Schuster UK for all of your work. And my family. I love you!

About the Author

Kiera Fallon is a hopeless romantic and spends her time dreaming up what fictional boyfriend she can fall in love with next. With a taste for the forbidden and darker side of romance, she writes stories for those readers who like their characters flawed, fierce and impossible to forget. Whether she's writing outside under the trees in summer or curled up in a coffee shop with a large mocha in winter, chances are she's also usually rewatching '90s movies and snuggling with her animals. Kiera Fallon also writes under the name of Natasha K. Lauren.